A.D. AFTER DEATH

written by Scott Snyder
illustrated by Jeff Lemire
lettered by Steve Wands
copyedited by Brendan Wright
with special thanks to Jeanine Schaefer

A.D.: After Death created by Scott Snyder & Jeff Lemire

A.D.: AFTER DEATH HC. First printing. June 2017.
REGULAR EDITION ISBN: 978-1-63215-868-0 / BARNES & NOBLE EDITION ISBN: 978-1-5343-0367-6 / DCBS EXCLUSIVE EDITION ISBN: 978-1-5343-0390-4 /
NEWBURY COMICS EDITION ISBN: 978-1-5343-0391-1 / FORBIDDEN PLANET/BIG BANG COMICS EDITION ISBN: 978-1-5343-0392-8 / CONVENTION EXCLUSIVE EDITION ISBN: 978-1-5343-0393-5

IMAGE COMICS, INC. / Robert Kirkman–Chief Operating Officer / Erik Larsen–Chief Financial Officer / Todd McFarlane–President / Marc Silvestri–Chief Executive Officer / Jim Valentino–Vice-President / Eric Stephenson–Publisher / Corey Murphy–Director of Sales / Jeff Boison–Director of Publishing Planning & Book Trade Sales / Chris Ross–Director of Digital Sales / Jeff Stang–Director of Specialty Sales / Kat Salazar–Director of PR & Marketing / Branwyn Bigglestone–Controller / Sue Korpela–Accounts Manager / Drew Gill–Art Director / Brett Warnock–Production Manager / Meredith Wallace–Print Manager / Tricia Ramos–Traffic Manager / Briah Skelly–Publicist / Aly Hoffman–Events & Conventions Coordinator / Sasha Head–Sales & Marketing Production Designer / David Brothers–Branding Manager / Melissa Gifford–Content Manager / Drew Fitzgerald–Publicity Assistant / Vincent Kukua–Production Artist / Erika Schnatz–Production Artist / Ryan Brewer–Production Artist / Shanna Matuszak–Production Artist / Carey Hall–Production Artist / Esther Kim–Direct Market Sales Representative / Emilio Bautista–Digital Sales Representative / Leanna Caunter–Accounting Assistant / Chloe Ramos-Peterson–Library Market Sales Representative / Marla Eizik–Administrative Assistant / IMAGECOMICS.COM

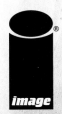

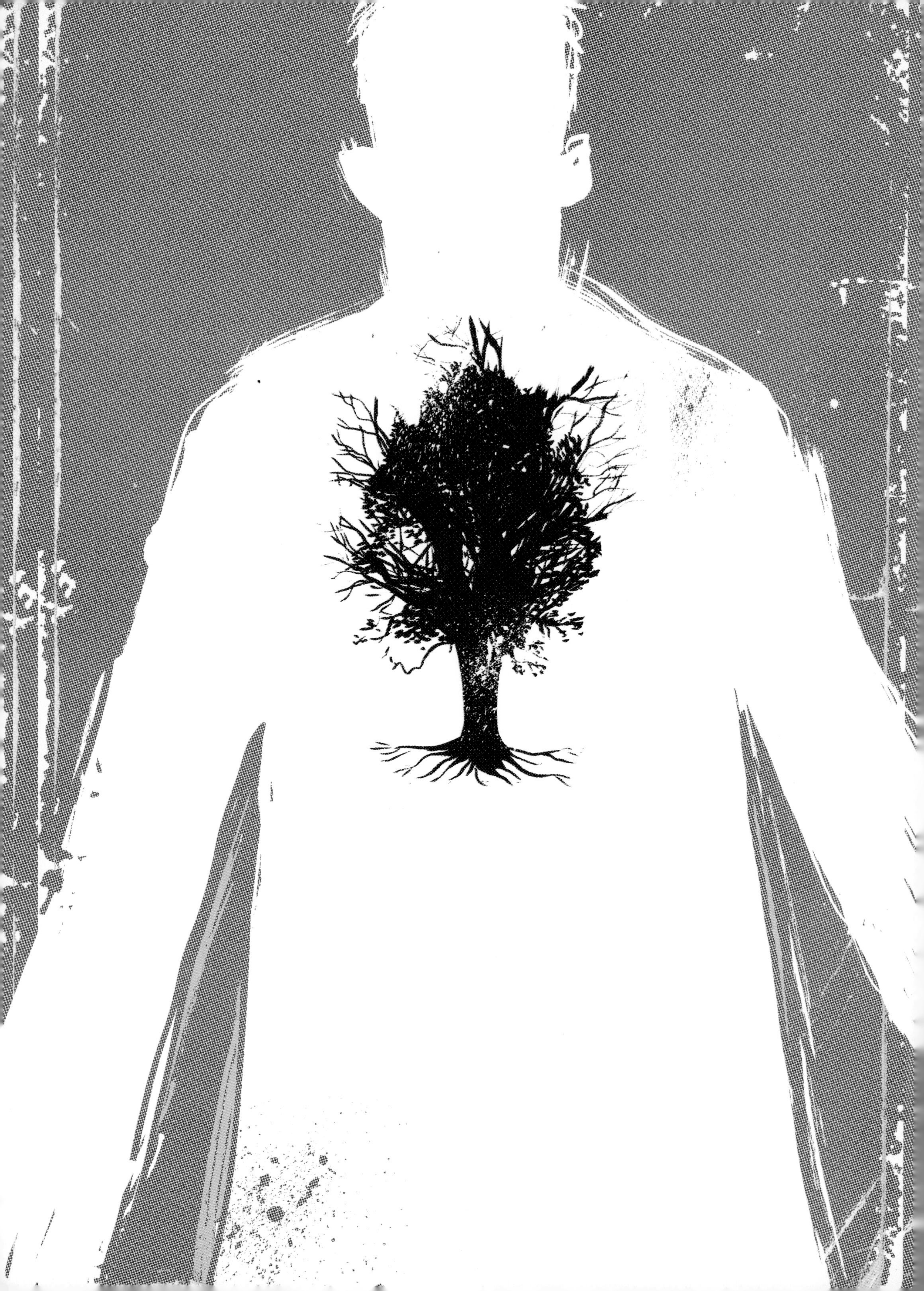

Someone once told me that all the clues to your
life lie in your first memory.

Your fears, your strengths. What you'll struggle with...

...This is mine.

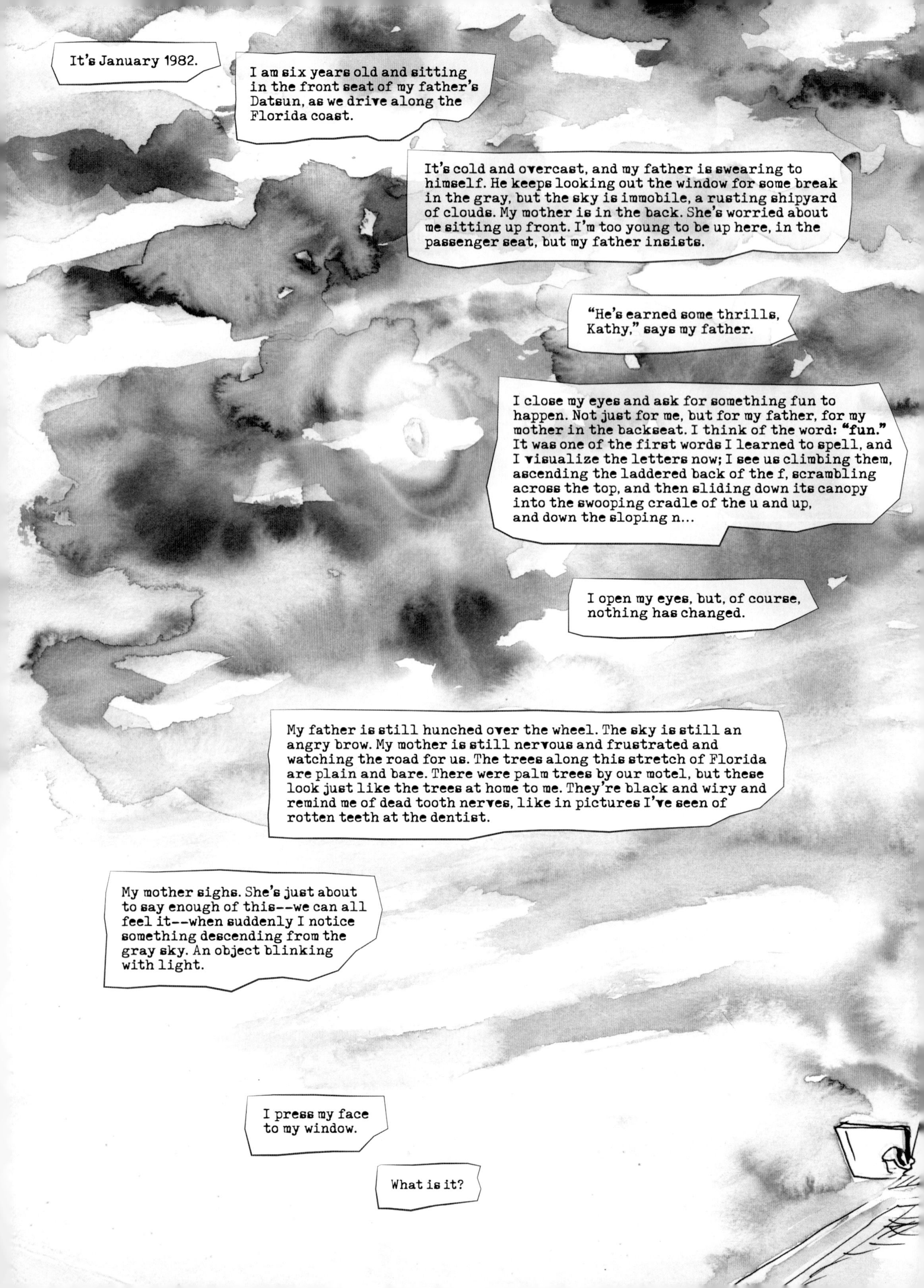
It's January 1982.
I am six years old and sitting in the front seat of my father's Datsun, as we drive along the Florida coast.
It's cold and overcast, and my father is swearing to himself. He keeps looking out the window for some break in the gray, but the sky is immobile, a rusting shipyard of clouds. My mother is in the back. She's worried about me sitting up front. I'm too young to be up here, in the passenger seat, but my father insists.
"He's earned some thrills, Kathy," says my father.
I close my eyes and ask for something fun to happen. Not just for me, but for my father, for my mother in the backseat. I think of the word: **"fun."** It was one of the first words I learned to spell, and I visualize the letters now; I see us climbing them, ascending the laddered back of the f, scrambling across the top, and then sliding down its canopy into the swooping cradle of the u and up, and down the sloping n...
I open my eyes, but, of course, nothing has changed.
My father is still hunched over the wheel. The sky is still an angry brow. My mother is still nervous and frustrated and watching the road for us. The trees along this stretch of Florida are plain and bare. There were palm trees by our motel, but these look just like the trees at home to me. They're black and wiry and remind me of dead tooth nerves, like in pictures I've seen of rotten teeth at the dentist.
My mother sighs. She's just about to say enough of this--we can all feel it--when suddenly I notice something descending from the gray sky. An object blinking with light.
I press my face to my window.
What is it?

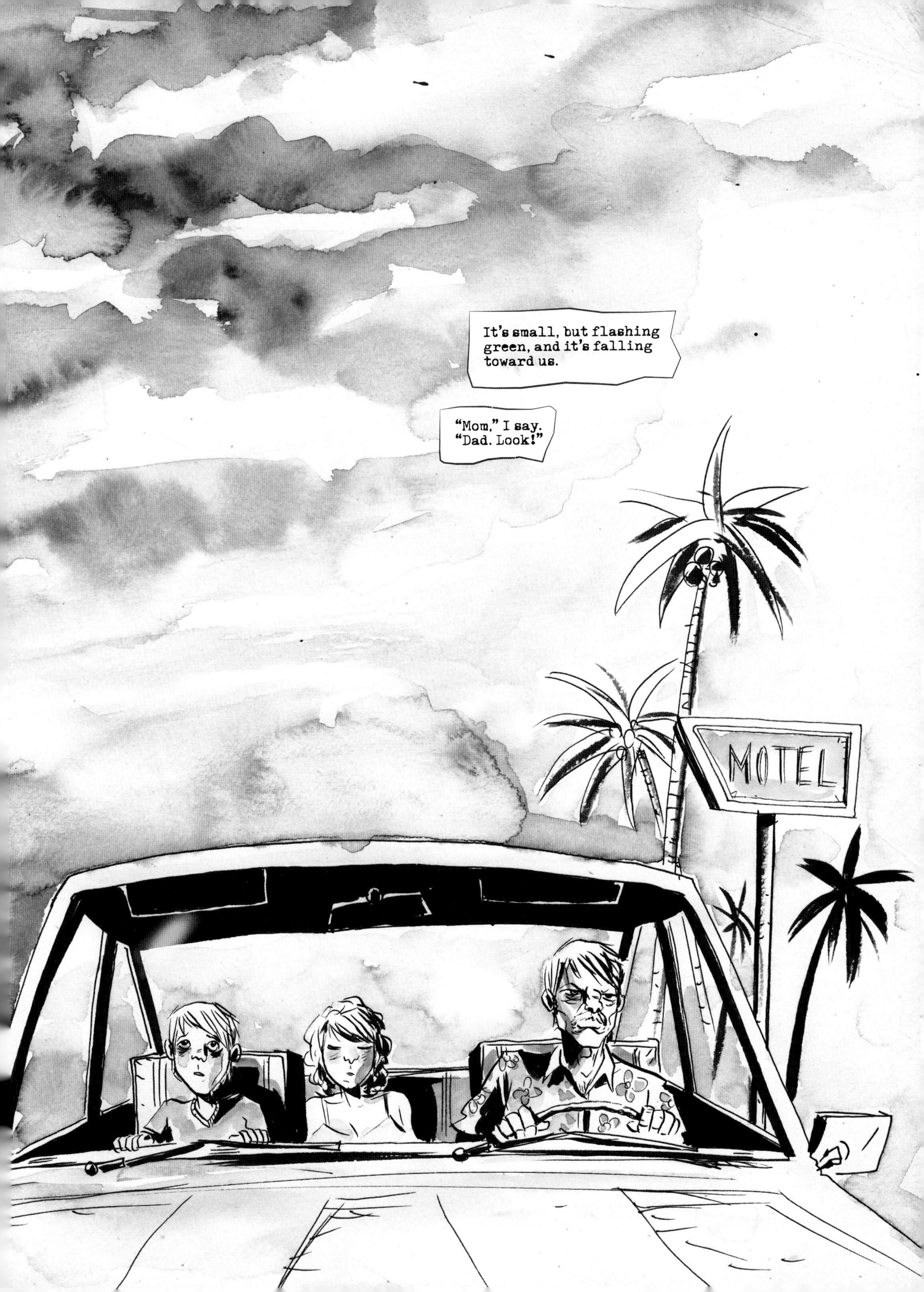
It's small, but flashing green, and it's falling toward us.
"Mom," I say. "Dad. Look!"
MOTEL

My father took us to Florida on a whim. He literally came home from teaching on a Friday afternoon, appeared in my bedroom doorway, and told me to pack.

"We're taking a vacation," he said. "I mean now. Like, today."

We all needed a break, he said. And he was right--we did. It had been a tough year. The school where my father worked had its budget slashed, and he'd been worried about his job for months. He was an activist; he taught high school physics, but his passion was his elective class series about twentieth-century political protest. Lately, there seemed less and less a place for anything he loved.

My mother was an optometrist and had a small shop in a strip mall near our house. Sometimes I'd stay with her there after school, and we'd have what she called "eyeball fashion shows," during which she'd try on different-colored contact lenses. Colored contacts were still a novelty then, and she'd come out from the back with her eyes closed, and then open them and--surprise--her eyes were purple, or gray, or even yellow, and we'd make up stories about who she was that day. There was a cartoon on TV around that time called Cryos, about a moment in the distant future when every-one who'd opted to be cryogenically frozen throughout history was simultaneously woken up, only to find themselves in a world devoid of humans, but filled with dinosaurs and aliens and all sorts of dangers. My mother loved the show as much as I did, the strange sense of adventure to it, and our eyeball fashion shows spoke to this affection. Open your eyes and be reborn!

But her shop was always empty.

On top of this, my parents had been trying to have more children and had suffered a series of miscarriages. Of course, I knew none of this, but I understood it in the way that children do, seeing the color if not the shape of things.

So Florida.

But then it hadn't worked out. The weather was unseasonably frigid, and we spent most of the vacation in the motel room, watching television and playing cards. There was a little patio behind our room where I passed time burying my action figures in the mud, hiding and digging them up with a plastic spoon. I remember one figure coming out with a worm wrapped around her waist.

On the second to last morning, my father couldn't take it anymore, the disappointment of Florida, of all of it, and so we packed up for home. But, before getting on the highway north, he insisted we take a final spin around the area, in case we missed some last, fun thing.

The object in the sky is closer now.

I call to my father again. Tell him to look. Look there!

Finally, he looks.

"Kath. Eye exam?" he says. It's an old family joke. Anytime we see something that isn't to be believed, we say this to my mother, the optometrist.

"Huh. Twenty-twenty," she says, meaning: yes, what you're seeing is there.

As the thing descends, we all see that it's a balloon--but a balloon with some sort of blinking light inside of it. A ribbon dangles from it with a card attached--a small, white sign with red writing on it. We can't read what it says from the expressway, but it's clearly all big letters and exclamation points--something urgent--and we're all fascinated by this.

In no time, the balloon becomes the game we've been waiting to play together all weekend--it's JUST the thing--and we follow its descent from the car as it spins and twirls downward.

"Can you read it, Jonah?" my father says to me, turning the wheel hand over hand. "Cooke family! Eyes on it!"

"I can't read it yet, but it's close! Engage, Daniel, engage!" my mother says, laughing, her face pressed to her window. Her eyes are bright and full of light. I think of our eyeball fashion shows: "And...blue. And...white."

The balloon is right there now! "Get closer!" I say. "Come on, Dad!"

My father actually turns off the expressway and gets onto the interstate so we can follow this balloon.

It's dropping more quickly now, swinging this way and that, updrafts poking at it, pushing it into erratic arcs, and we start estimating where it's going to land. Behind the laundromat! Nonono, it's swinging the other way...it's going to land behind the army navy!

Finally, it vanishes behind a daycare center--my mother and I screaming and pointing--and my father swerves across four empty lanes of traffic to chase it.

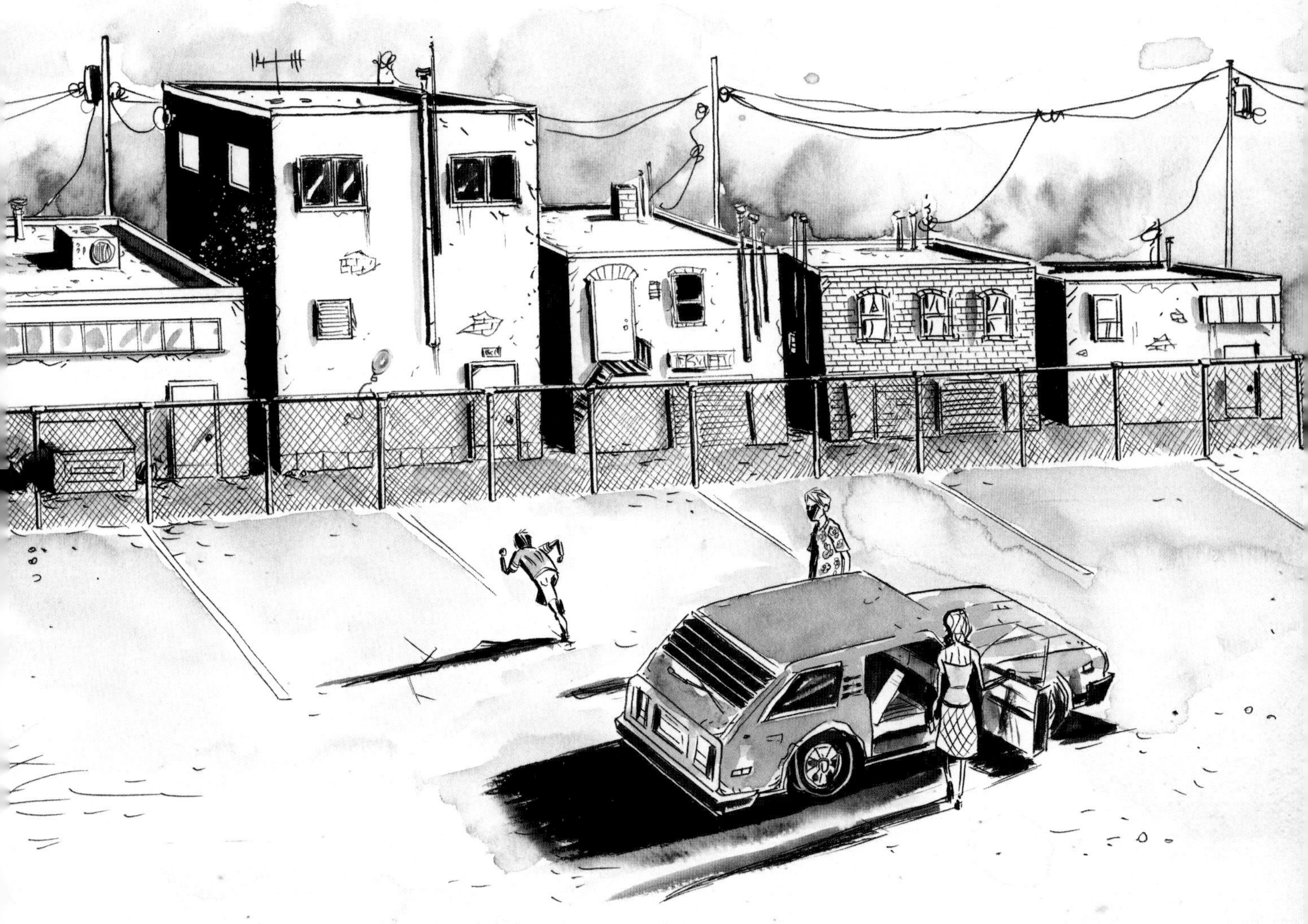

It takes us a minute, but we find the balloon in an empty lot across from the daycare. It's caught in a chain-link fence, whipping about in the breeze, and we exit the car and rush over to it without even closing the car doors, like it's a pet we need to free from a thicket.

My father gets it loose and holds the sign so we can see.

If you find this balloon, call the number below and you will win a prize!

Below the message is a phone number.

We look at each other. This is even better than we'd expected, and we are ecstatic. A prize. My mother hugs me--and you spotted it, Jonah!

Miraculously, there is a half payphone in the lot, and my father hurries over. All of this feels right, like this is the reward for the chilling weekend, for Florida, for everything over the last year. Everything.

My father calls the number.

As he waits for the pickup, he combs his hair with his hand, like this is a job interview.
Then he looks at my mother and me and winks.

Eventually, someone picks up and my father, full of enthusiasm, explains that we've found the prize balloon, that our family has it here, with us--he looks around--somewhere off Route 4. In his hand, the balloon pulses erratically, like a dotted message from some faraway land.

A plastic bag blows by. I hear my father repeat himself, slower and louder. The next few minutes are confusing, and less clear to me looking back, but what soon becomes apparent is that the balloon was part of a contest put on by an elementary school in New York. A bunch of students let balloons go from the campus, with this same placard attached--the school number--and the goal was to see whose balloon flew the farthest.
A woman from the school is telling my father this.

My father laughs, looking at the balloon, the ribbon in his fist. "Well, clearly this balloon won," he says. "It must be a thousand-mile trip. Hard to believe such a thing is even possible."
Hell, he teaches science and he can't believe it. It defies physics.

"Can you believe it, Cooke family?" he says, covering the receiver for no reason.

My mother and I are laughing. No, we can't believe it.

I am thinking about the prize. I hope it's money, Not for me, but for my father. For my mother.
I don't understand money all the way yet, but I know it makes things lighter.
That's the word that keeps coming to me. The word I've pictured all year. "Lighter."

Then my father's face begins to change.

"What is it, Daniel?" my mother says.

Moments from now, what we'll learn is that, yes, our balloon's flight sounds incredible, but the thing is, the contest was over weeks ago. The winning balloon made it to New Jersey.
Trenton, to be specific. Farther than any balloon before it.

"Trenton," my father says. "We're in Florida."

The woman explains that she understands this, but that the contest is over.
The prize--a personal video game system--was already given away.

I can see my father tense, the muscles of his back bunching.
"But we're in Florida," he says.

She tells him something like she's sorry, but--

"We're in Florida," he says.

She starts to say something again, but he cuts her off, yelling now.

"We came to fucking Florida."

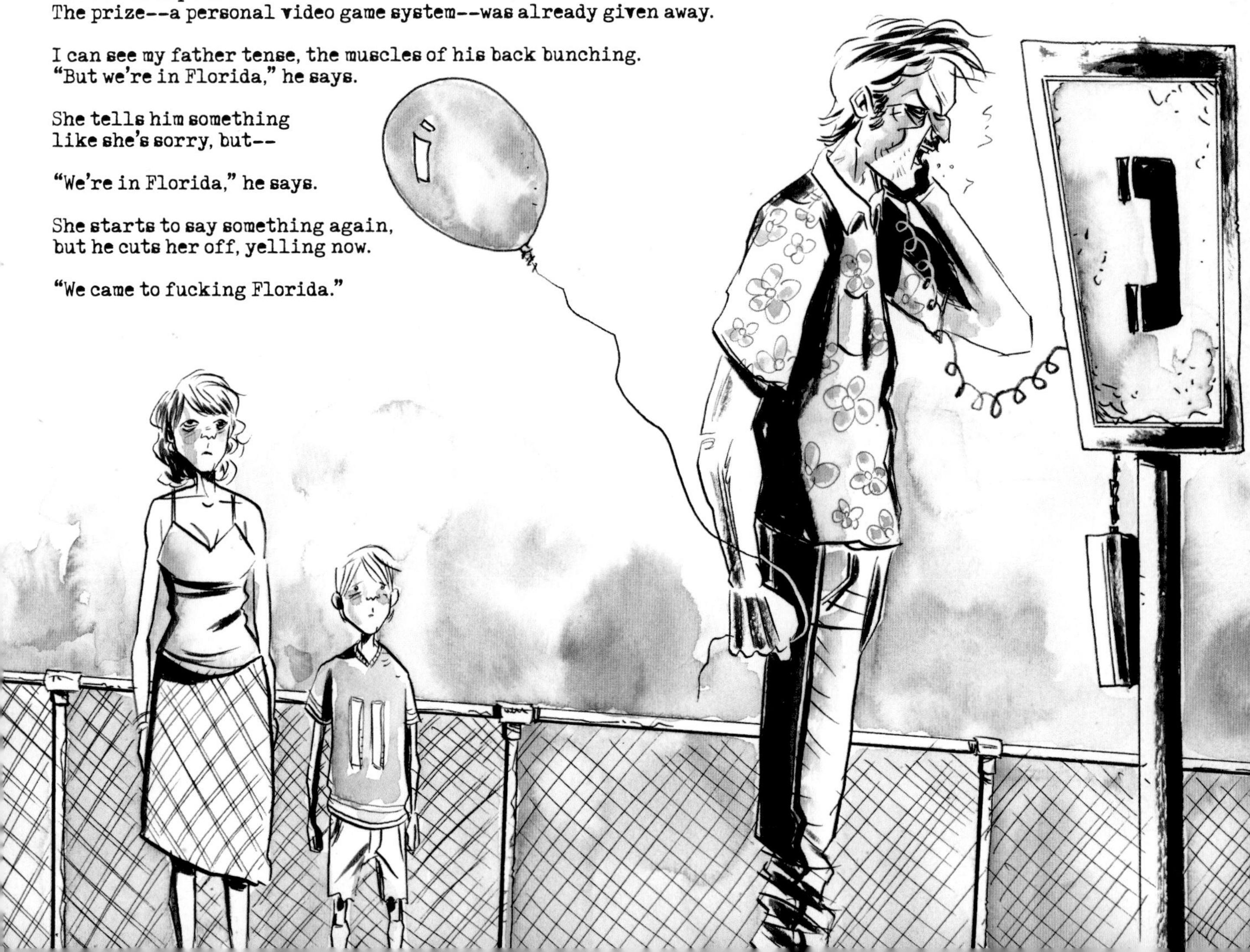

And she's talking to him, trying to explain, and he's screaming, cursing about how that game system is ours. About how he'll drive up to New Jersey and prove it, how we deserve that goddam system, and that's when my mother begins to shake.

She falls to the ground like something shut off, no hands out to break the fall, no sound, just goes limp. Falls. Her head hits first.

I yell to my father, but he doesn't hear. He's screaming into the phone. In his hand is a balloon that has traveled a thousand miles--its journey a mystery, something that exists outside and above us all. It pulses green.

My mother begins to shake, her head thudding against the concrete. I am screaming and my father is screaming.

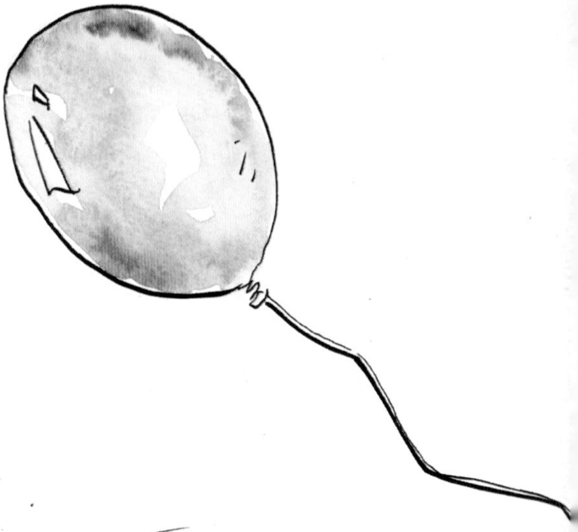

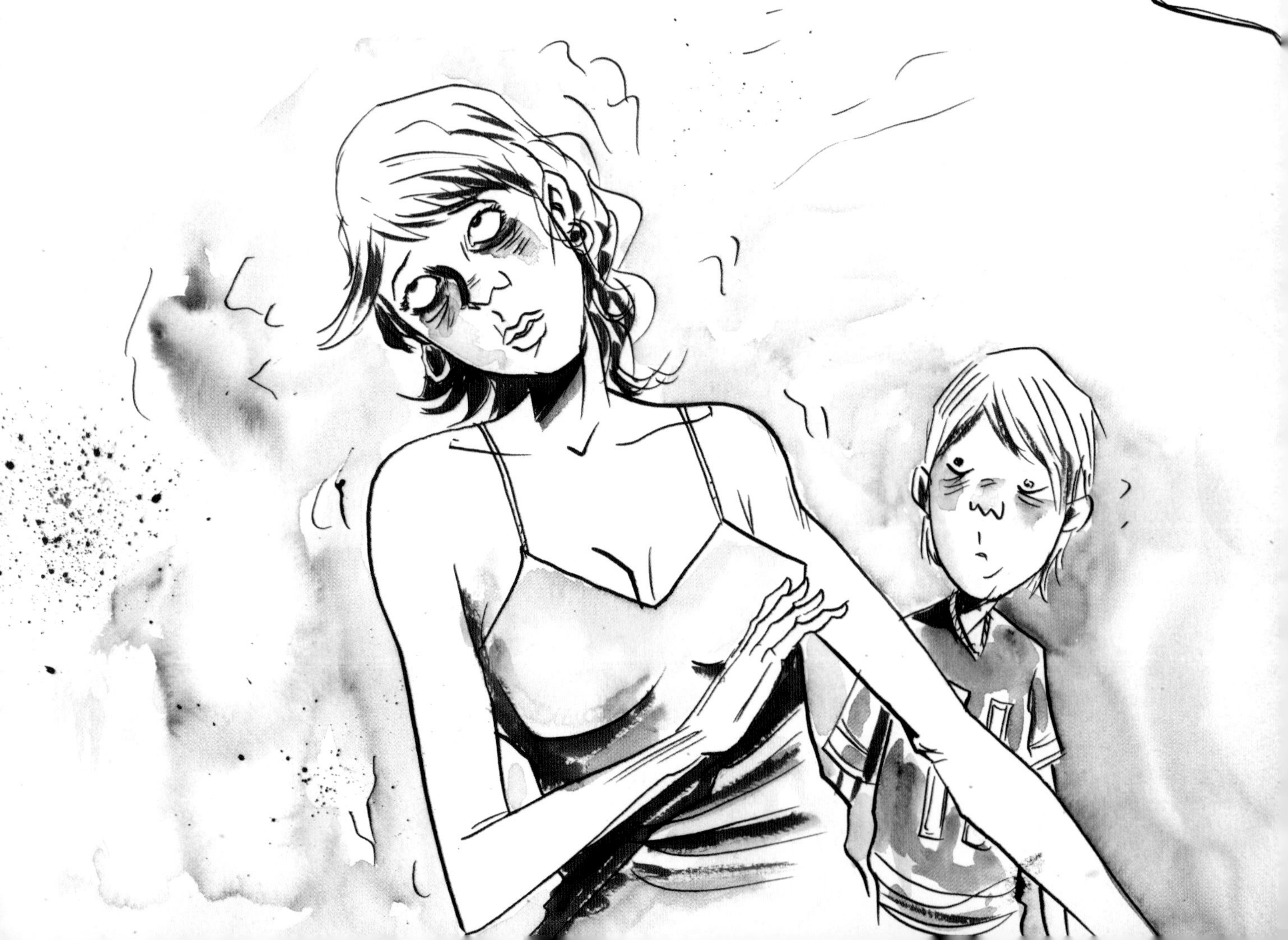

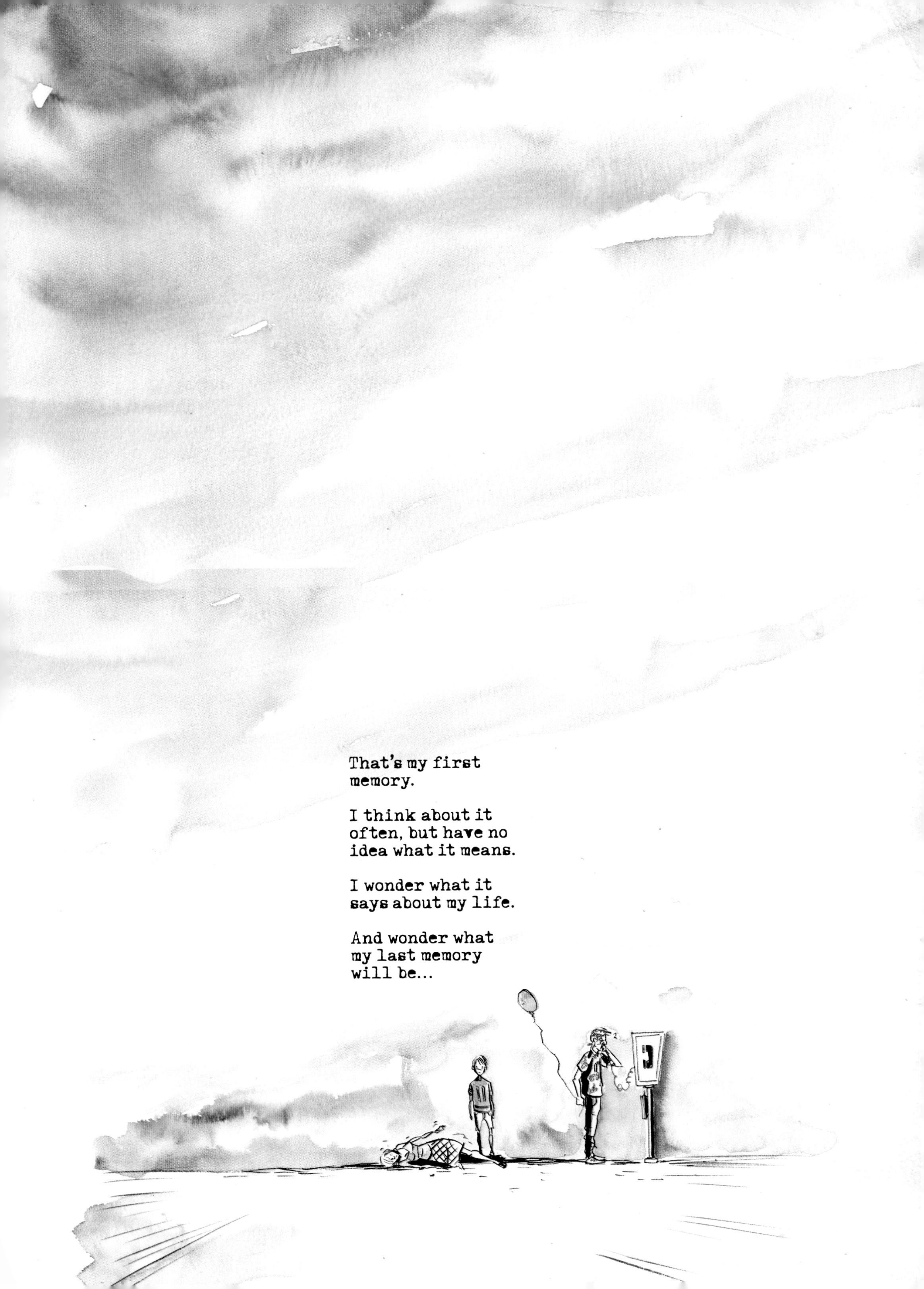
That's my first memory.
I think about it often, but have no idea what it means.
I wonder what it says about my life.
And wonder what my last memory will be...

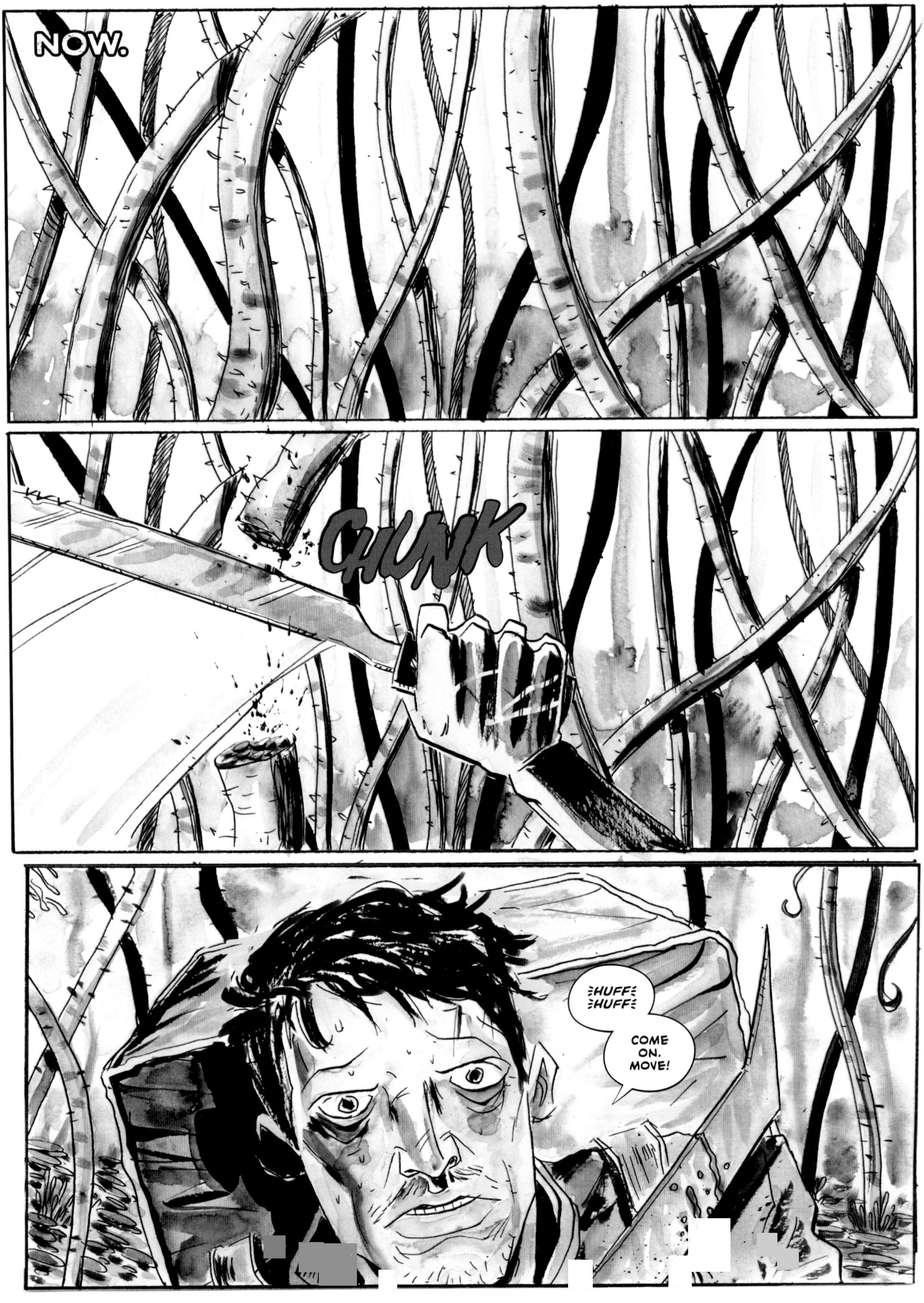
NOW.
CHUNK
HUFF HUFF
COME ON. MOVE!

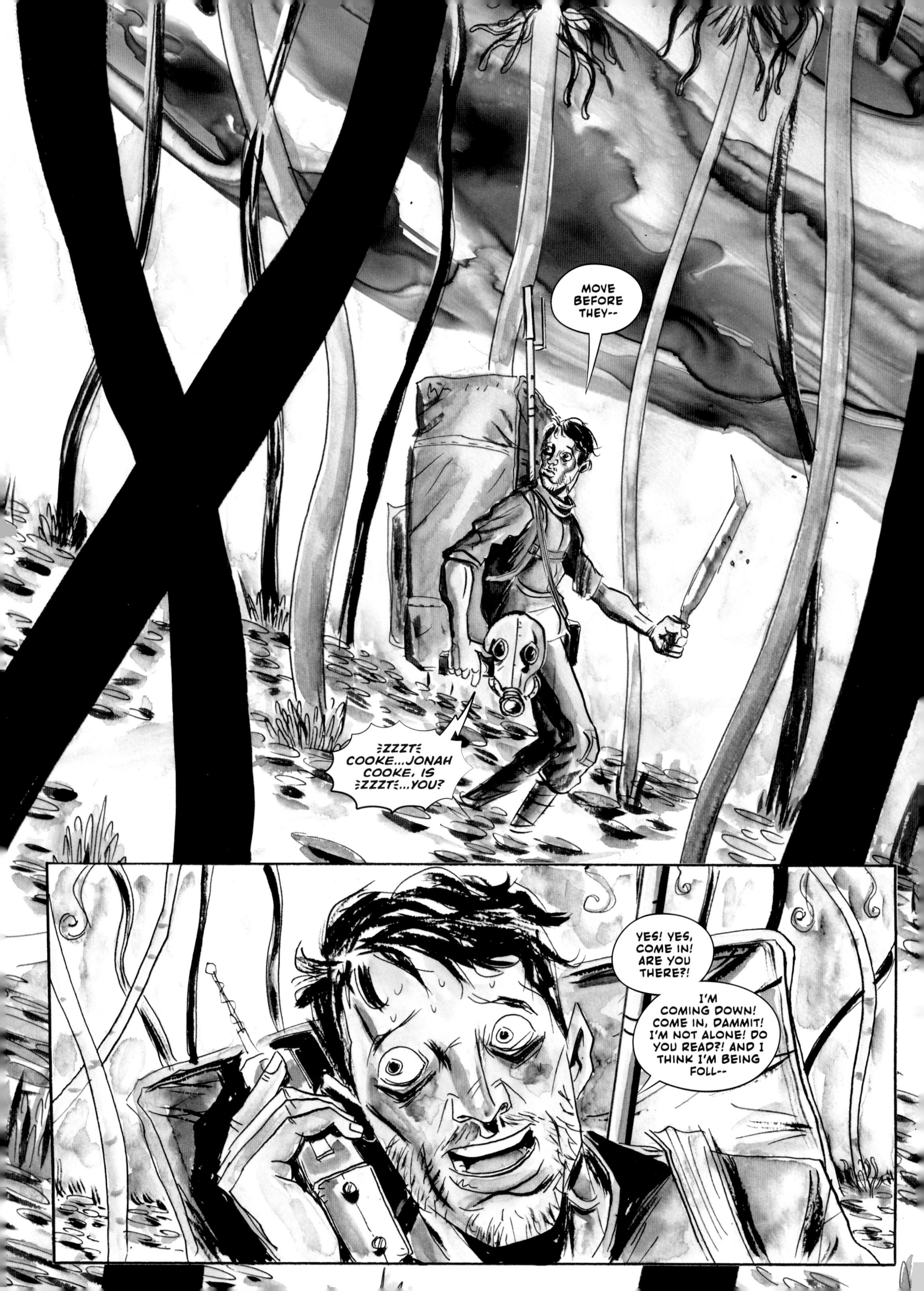
MOVE BEFORE THEY--
ZZZT COOKE...JONAH COOKE, IS ZZZT...YOU?
YES! YES, COME IN! ARE YOU THERE?!
I'M COMING DOWN! COME IN, DAMMIT! I'M NOT ALONE! DO YOU READ?! AND I THINK I'M BEING FOLL--

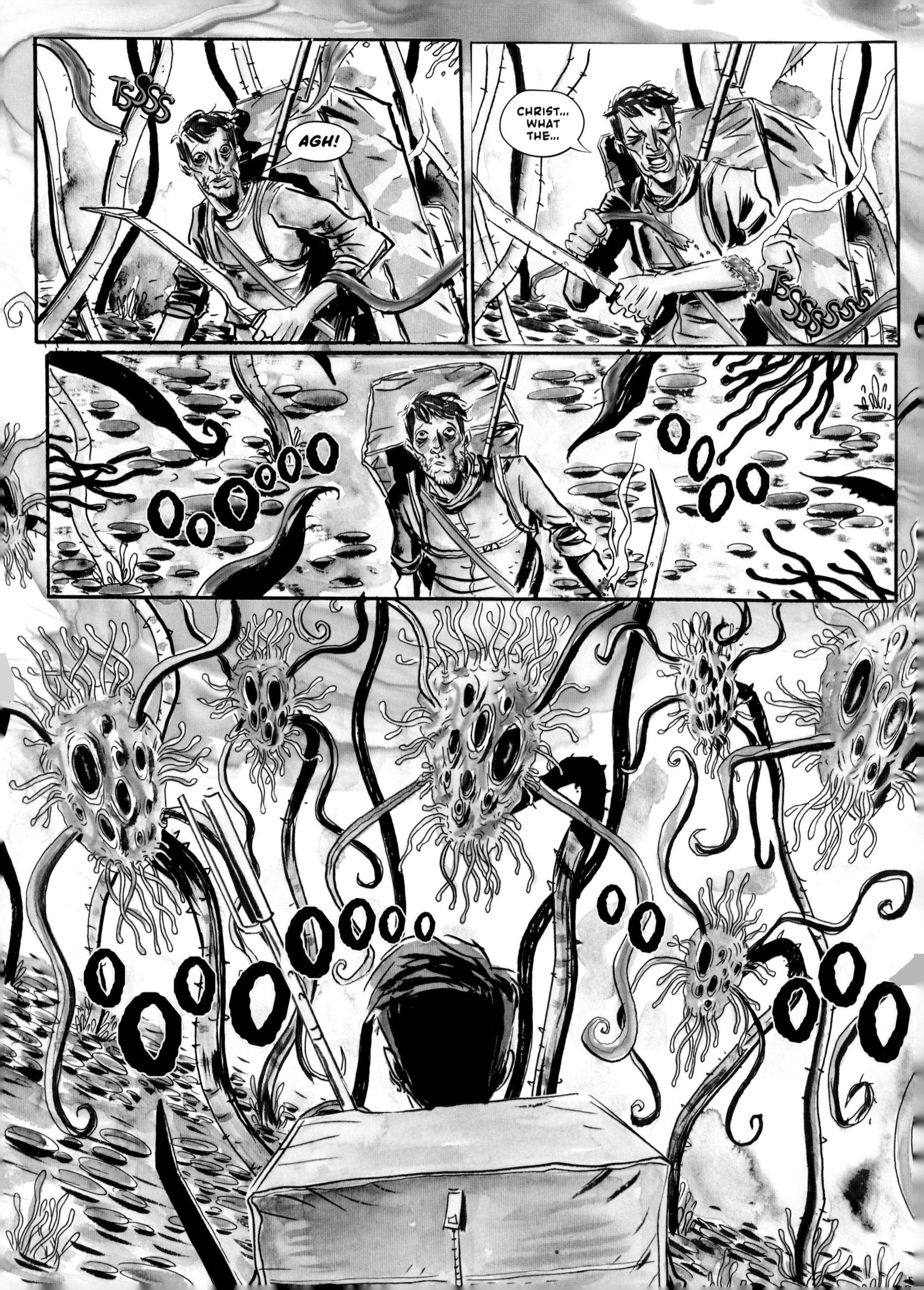
TSSS
AGH!
CHRIST... WHAT THE...
TSSSSSSS

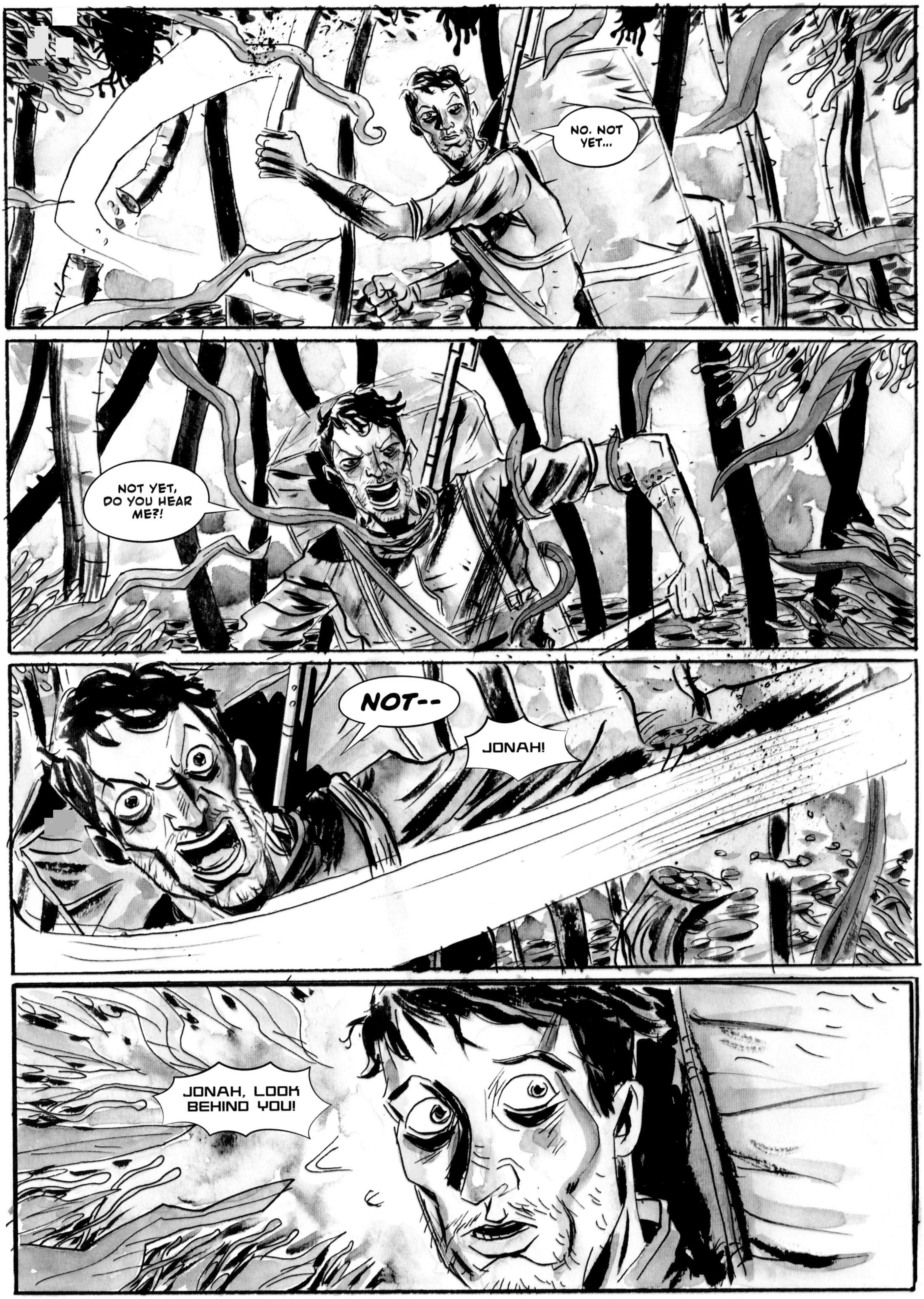
NO. NOT YET...
NOT YET, DO YOU HEAR ME?!
NOT--
JONAH!
JONAH, LOOK BEHIND YOU!

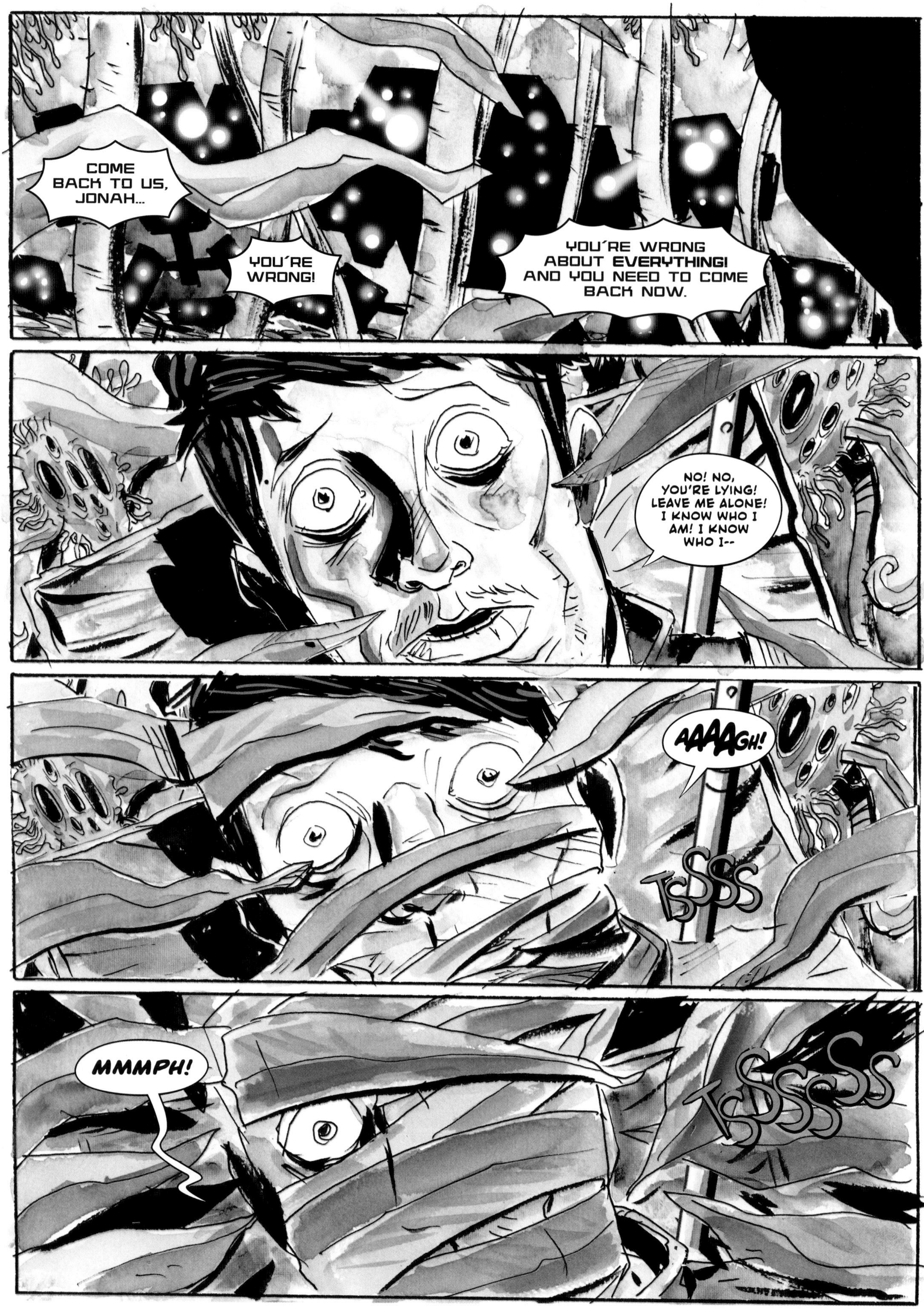
COME BACK TO US, JONAH...
YOU´RE WRONG!
YOU´RE WRONG ABOUT EVERYTHING! AND YOU NEED TO COME BACK NOW.
NO! NO, YOU'RE LYING! LEAVE ME ALONE! I KNOW WHO I AM! I KNOW WHO I--
AAAAGH!
TSSSS
MMMPH!
TSSSSSS

PART ONE
THE LAND OF MILK AND HONEY

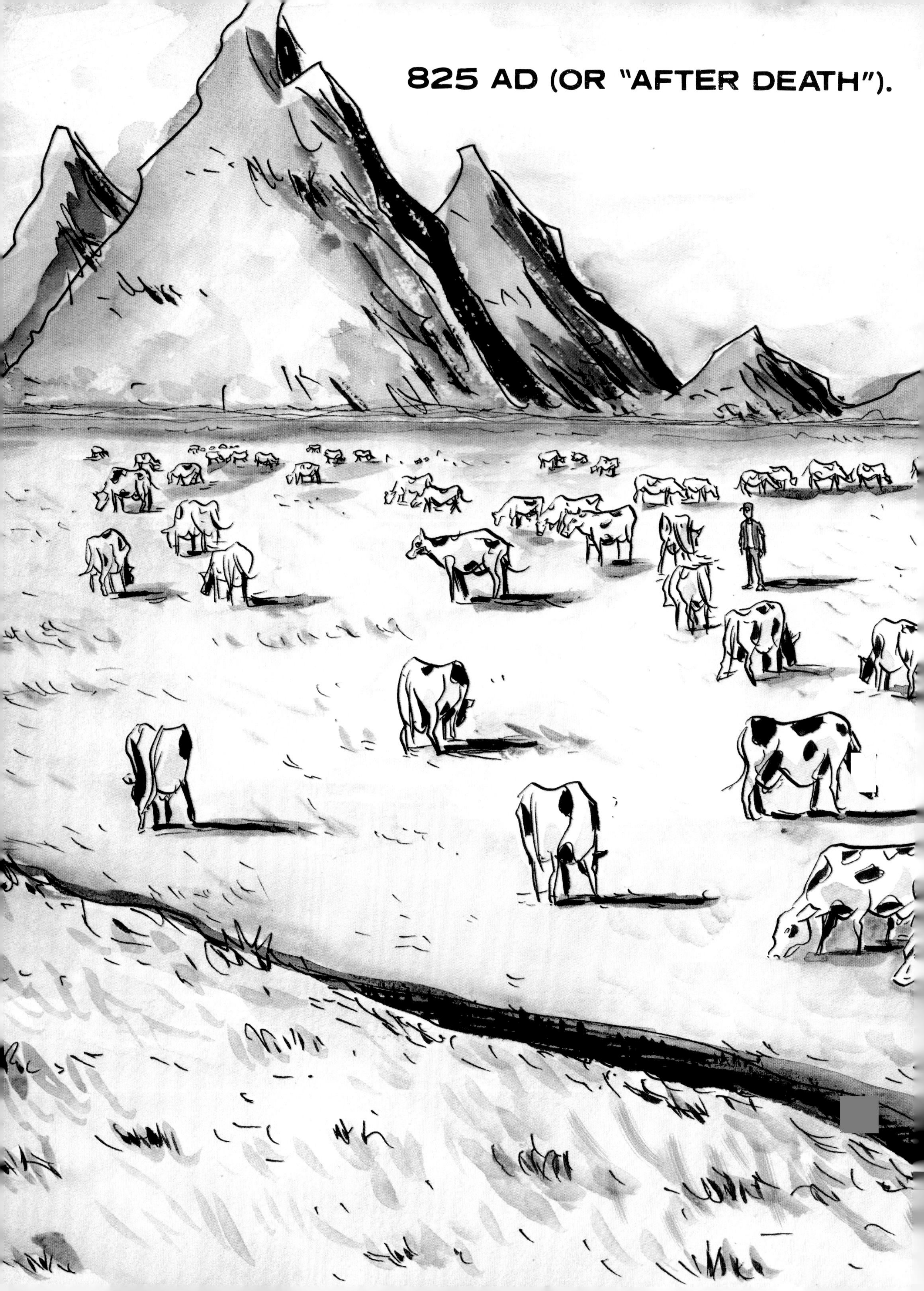
825 AD (OR "AFTER DEATH").

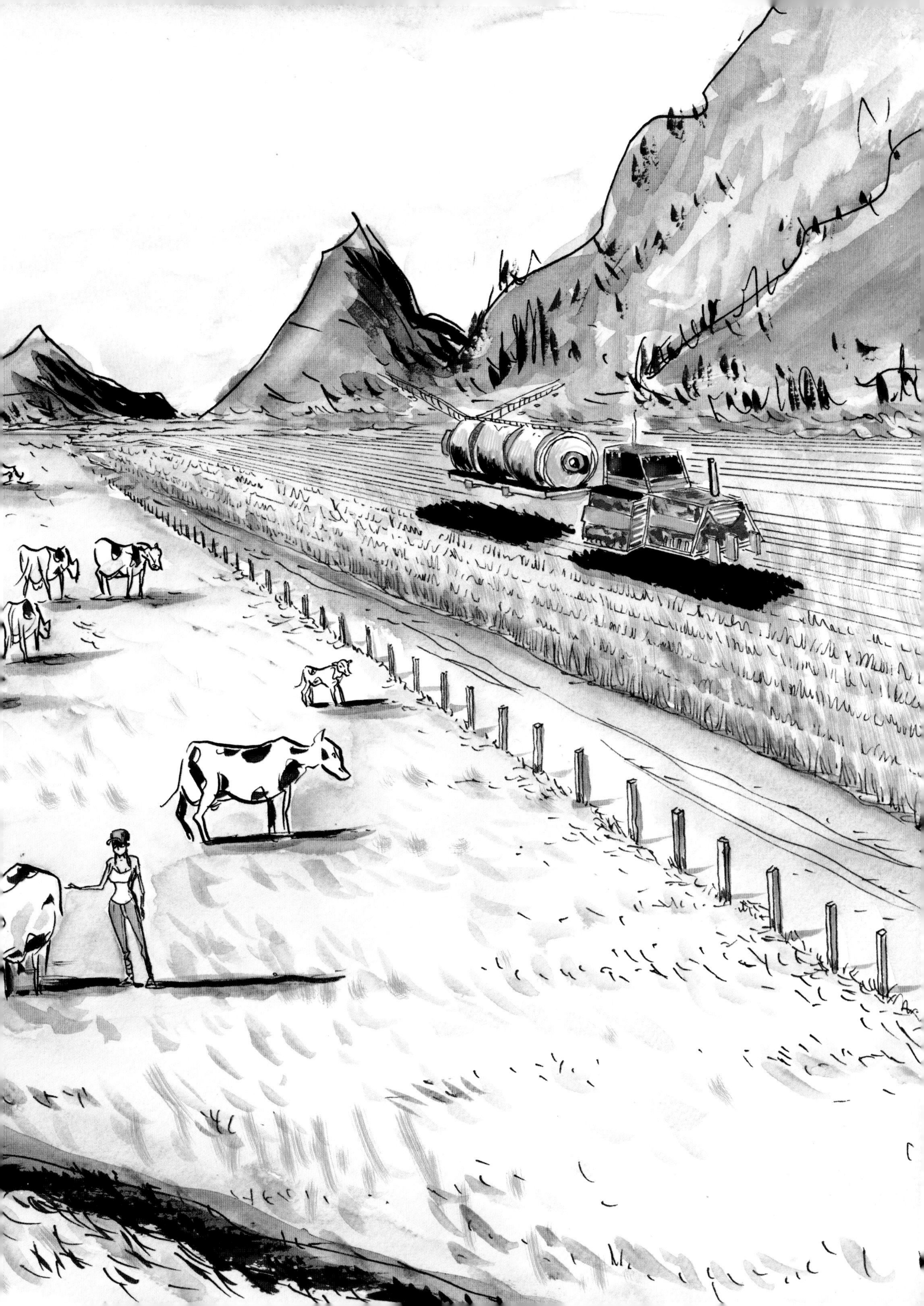

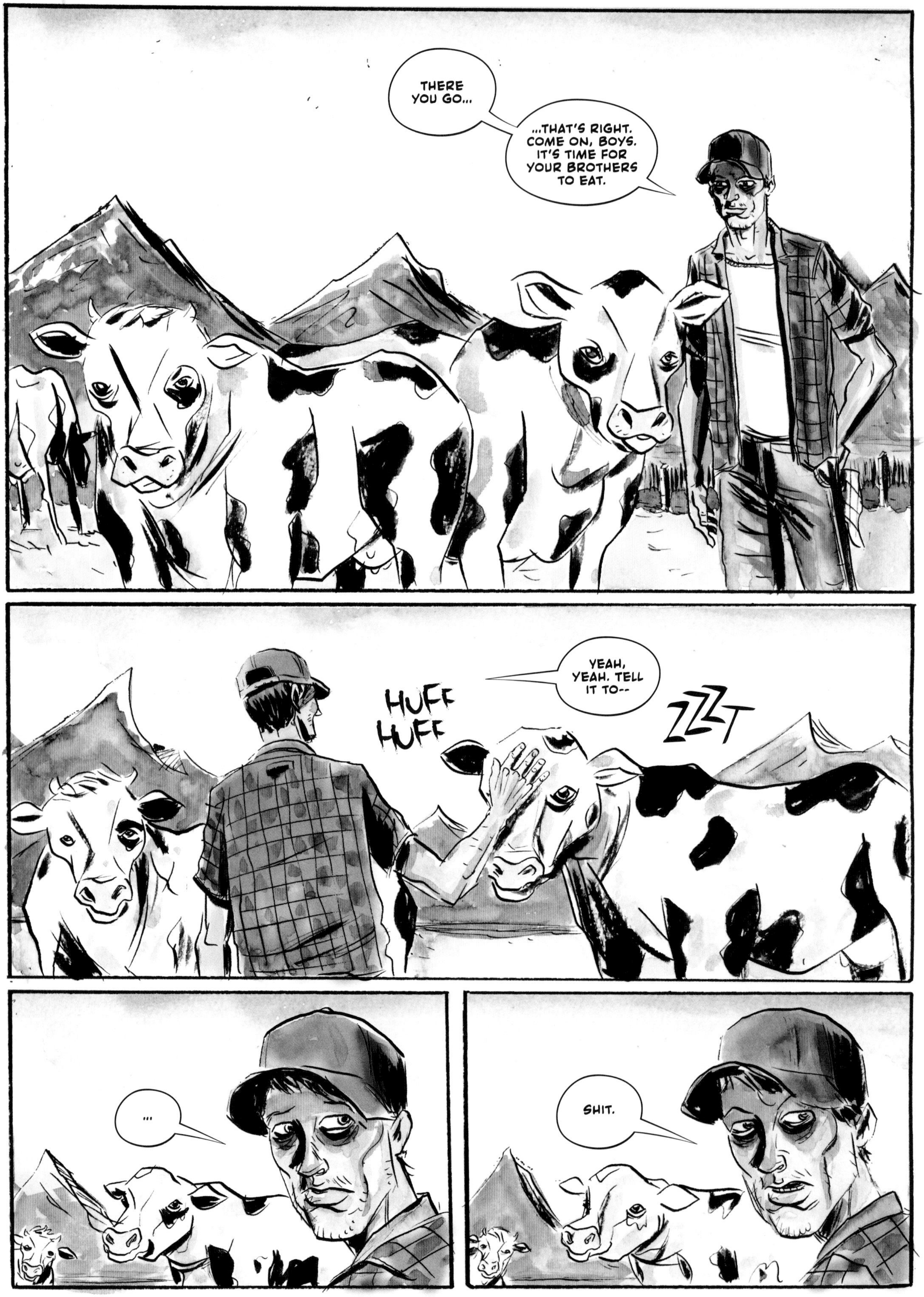
THERE YOU GO...
...THAT'S RIGHT. COME ON, BOYS. IT'S TIME FOR YOUR BROTHERS TO EAT.
HUFF HUFF
YEAH, YEAH. TELL IT TO--
ZZZT
...
SHIT.

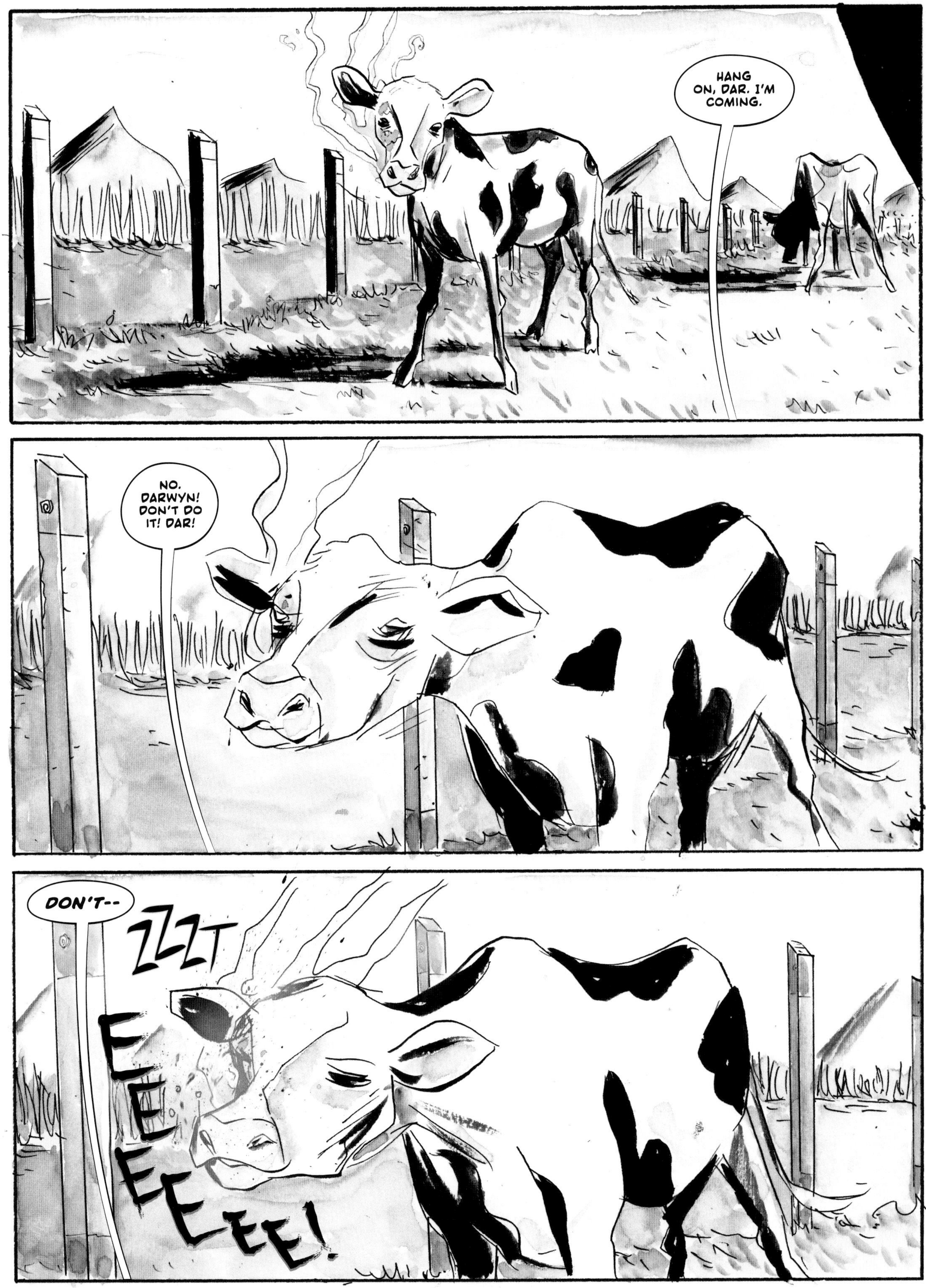
HANG ON, DAR. I'M COMING.
NO. DARWYN! DON'T DO IT! DAR!
DON'T--
ZZZT
EEEEEEEE!

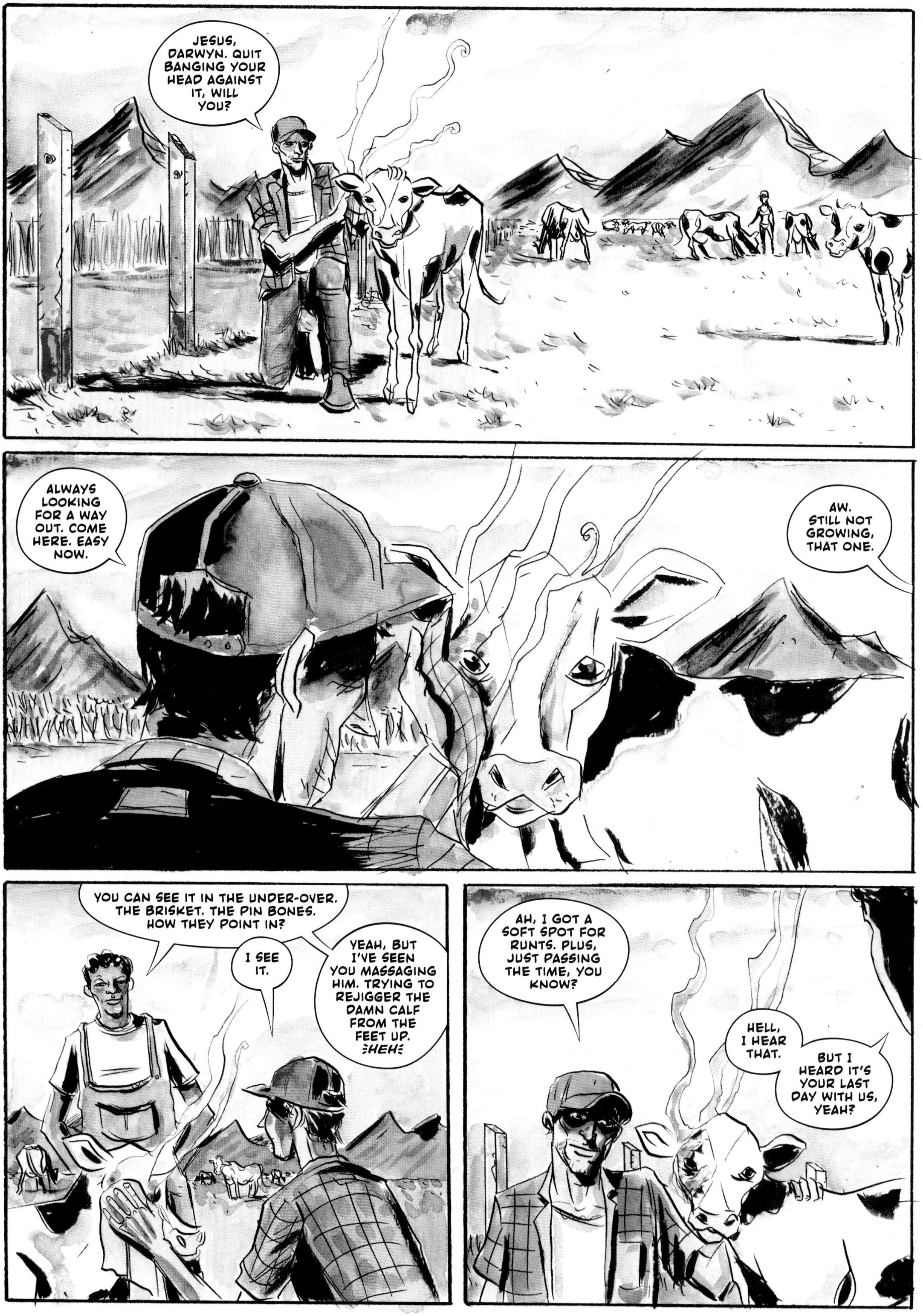
JESUS, DARWYN. QUIT BANGING YOUR HEAD AGAINST IT, WILL YOU?
ALWAYS LOOKING FOR A WAY OUT. COME HERE. EASY NOW.
AW. STILL NOT GROWING, THAT ONE.
YOU CAN SEE IT IN THE UNDER-OVER. THE BRISKET. THE PIN BONES. HOW THEY POINT IN?
I SEE IT.
YEAH, BUT I'VE SEEN YOU MASSAGING HIM. TRYING TO REJIGGER THE DAMN CALF FROM THE FEET UP. HEH
AH, I GOT A SOFT SPOT FOR RUNTS. PLUS, JUST PASSING THE TIME, YOU KNOW?
HELL, I HEAR THAT.
BUT I HEARD IT'S YOUR LAST DAY WITH US, YEAH?

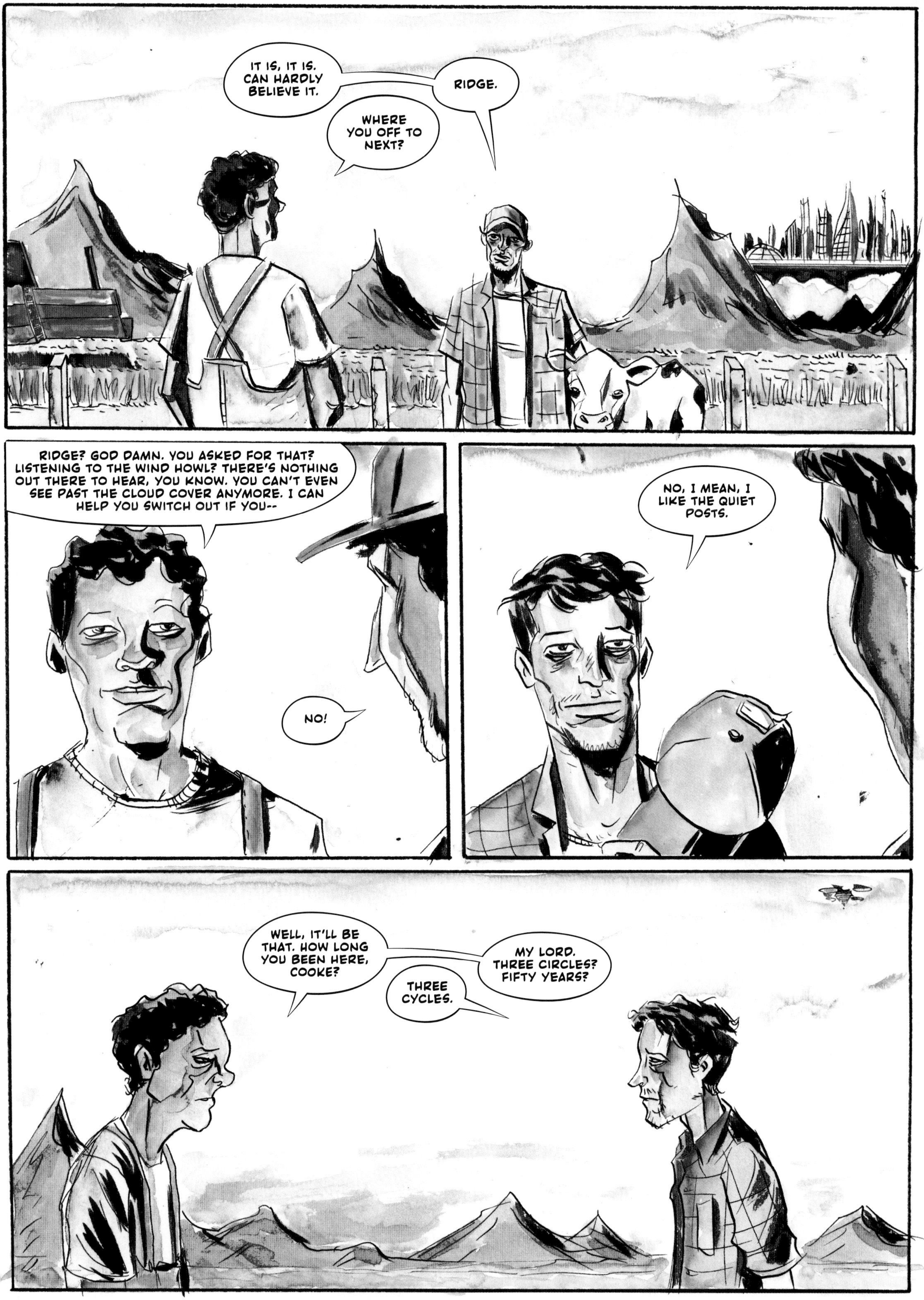
IT IS, IT IS. CAN HARDLY BELIEVE IT.
WHERE YOU OFF TO NEXT?
RIDGE.
RIDGE? GOD DAMN. YOU ASKED FOR THAT? LISTENING TO THE WIND HOWL? THERE'S NOTHING OUT THERE TO HEAR, YOU KNOW. YOU CAN'T EVEN SEE PAST THE CLOUD COVER ANYMORE. I CAN HELP YOU SWITCH OUT IF YOU--
NO!
NO, I MEAN, I LIKE THE QUIET POSTS.
WELL, IT'LL BE THAT. HOW LONG YOU BEEN HERE, COOKE?
THREE CYCLES.
MY LORD. THREE CIRCLES? FIFTY YEARS?

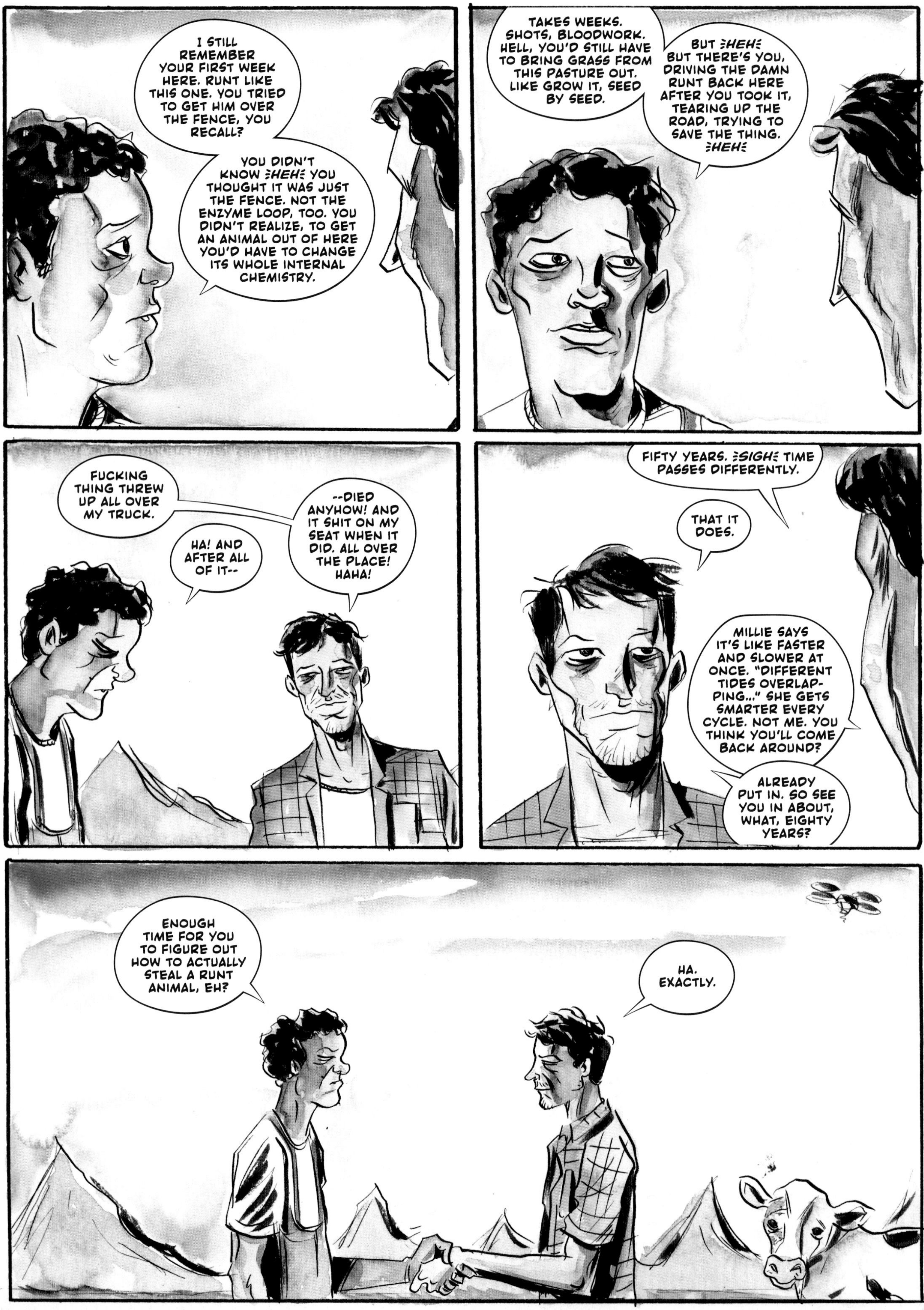
I STILL REMEMBER YOUR FIRST WEEK HERE. RUNT LIKE THIS ONE. YOU TRIED TO GET HIM OVER THE FENCE, YOU RECALL?
YOU DIDN'T KNOW ≡HEH≡ YOU THOUGHT IT WAS JUST THE FENCE. NOT THE ENZYME LOOP, TOO. YOU DIDN'T REALIZE, TO GET AN ANIMAL OUT OF HERE YOU'D HAVE TO CHANGE ITS WHOLE INTERNAL CHEMISTRY.
TAKES WEEKS. SHOTS, BLOODWORK. HELL, YOU'D STILL HAVE TO BRING GRASS FROM THIS PASTURE OUT. LIKE GROW IT, SEED BY SEED.
BUT ≡HEH≡ BUT THERE'S YOU, DRIVING THE DAMN RUNT BACK HERE AFTER YOU TOOK IT, TEARING UP THE ROAD, TRYING TO SAVE THE THING. ≡HEH≡
FUCKING THING THREW UP ALL OVER MY TRUCK.
HA! AND AFTER ALL OF IT--
--DIED ANYHOW! AND IT SHIT ON MY SEAT WHEN IT DID. ALL OVER THE PLACE! HAHA!
FIFTY YEARS. ≡SIGH≡ TIME PASSES DIFFERENTLY.
THAT IT DOES.
MILLIE SAYS IT'S LIKE FASTER AND SLOWER AT ONCE. "DIFFERENT TIDES OVERLAPPING..." SHE GETS SMARTER EVERY CYCLE. NOT ME. YOU THINK YOU'LL COME BACK AROUND?
ALREADY PUT IN. SO SEE YOU IN ABOUT, WHAT, EIGHTY YEARS?
ENOUGH TIME FOR YOU TO FIGURE OUT HOW TO ACTUALLY STEAL A RUNT ANIMAL, EH?
HA. EXACTLY.

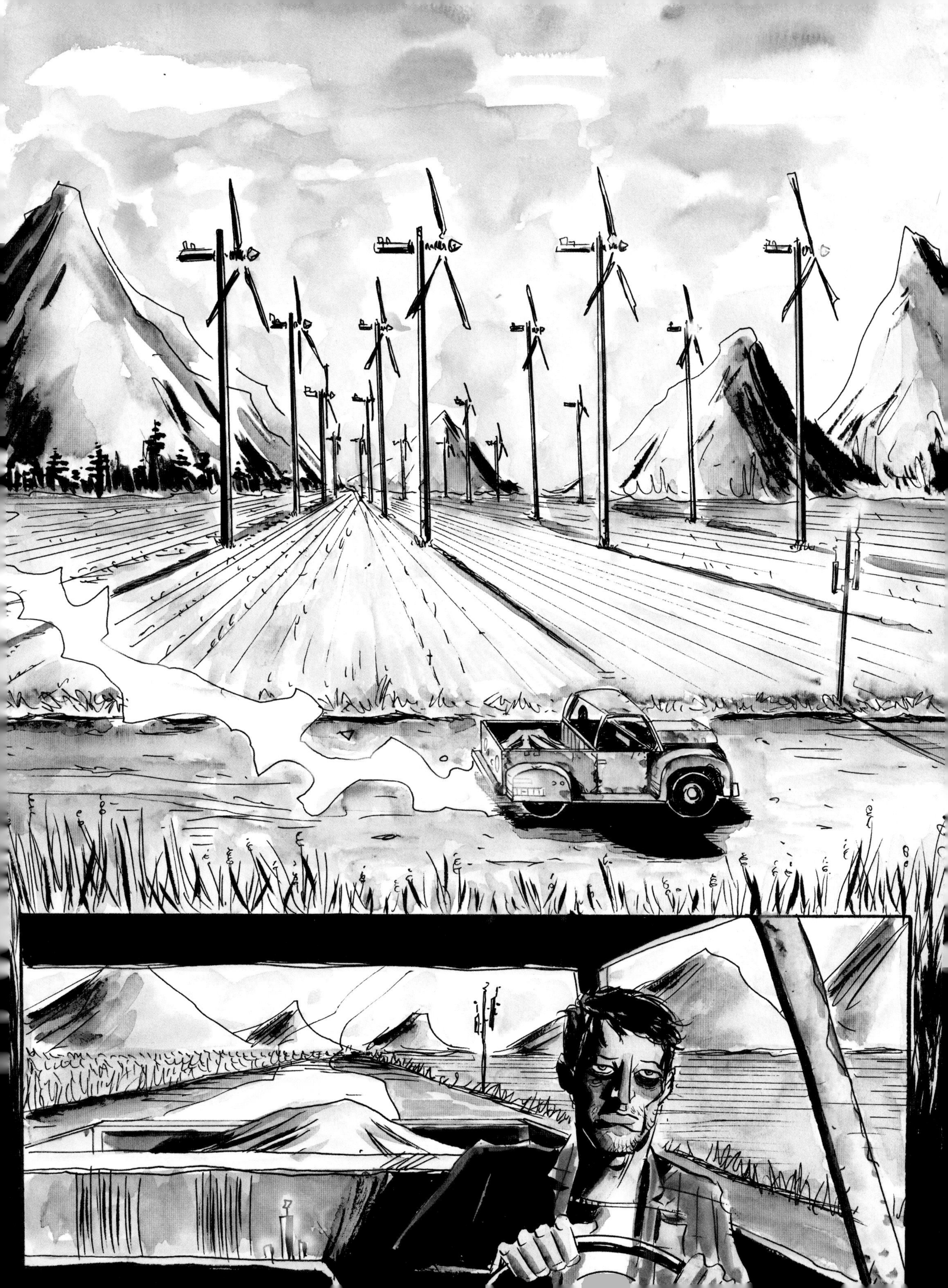

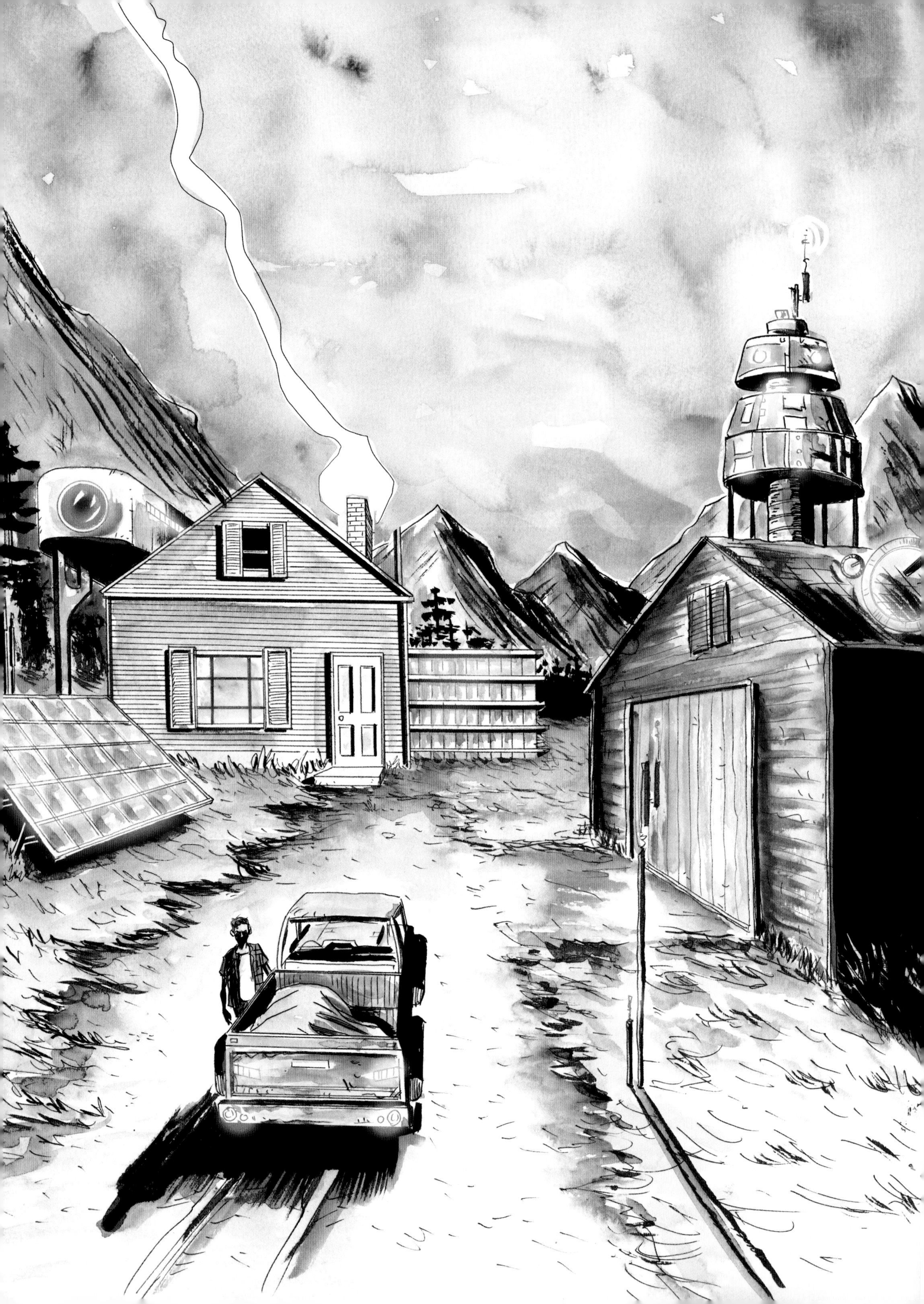

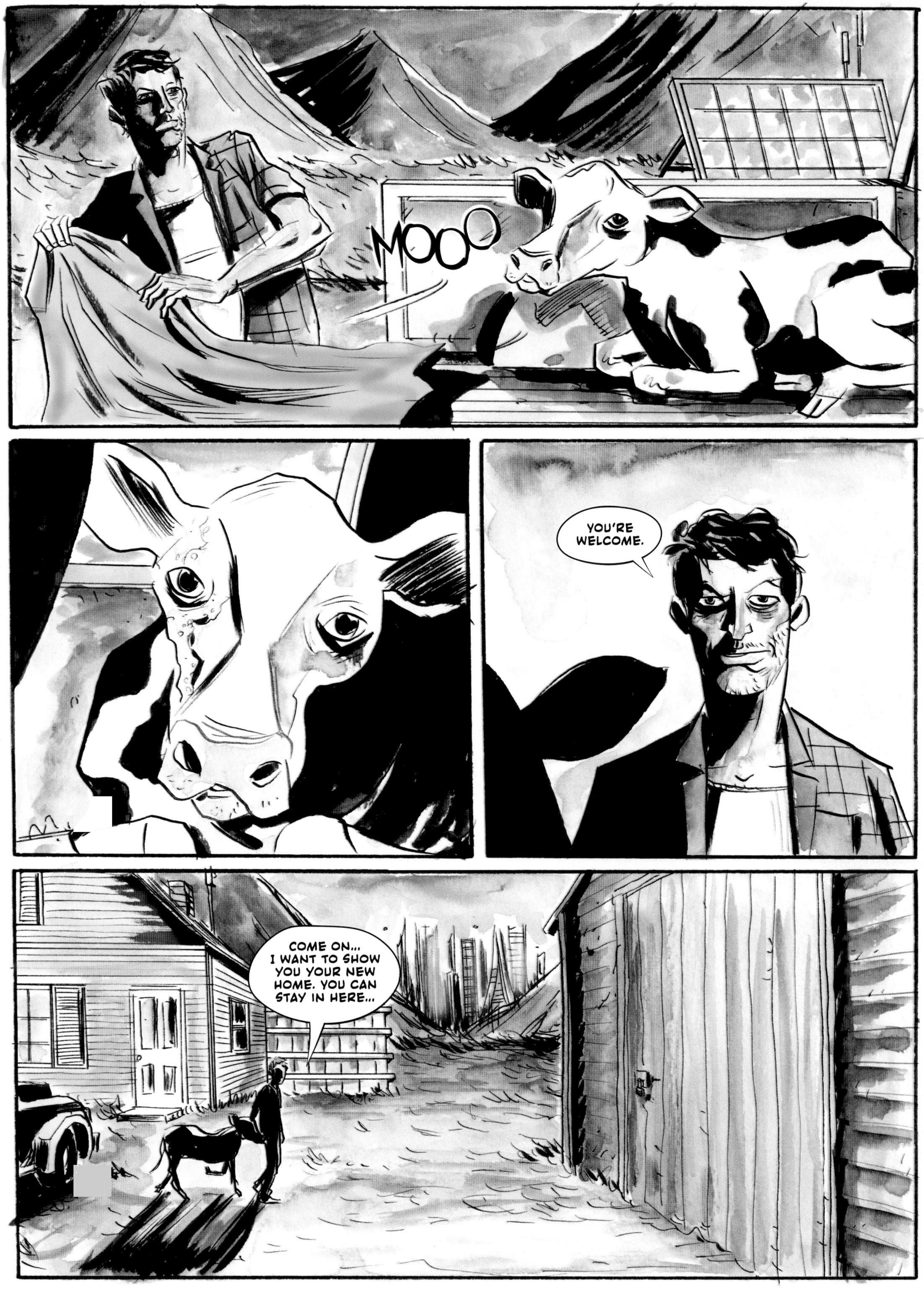
MOOO
YOU'RE WELCOME.
COME ON... I WANT TO SHOW YOU YOUR NEW HOME. YOU CAN STAY IN HERE...

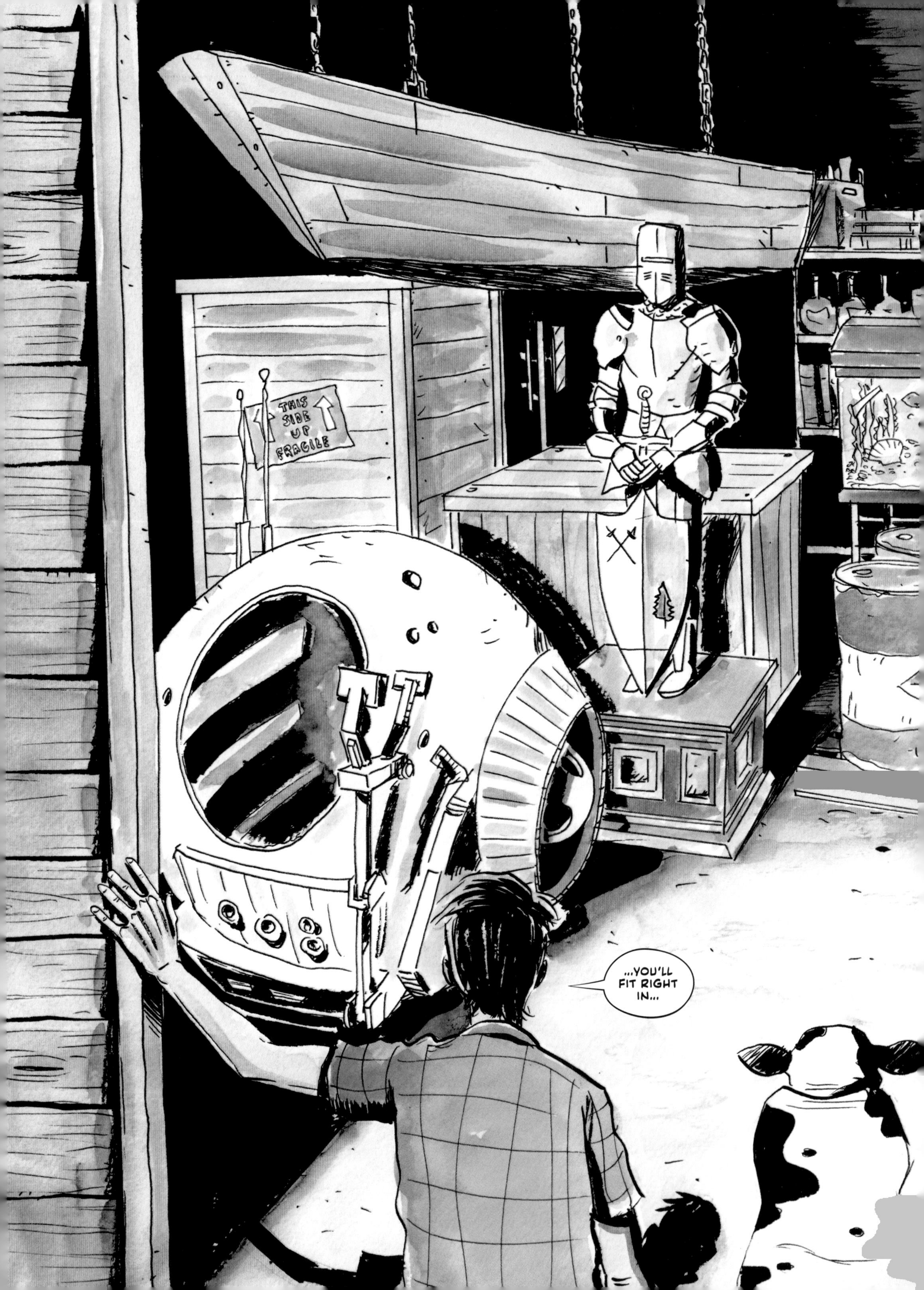
THIS SIDE UP FRAGILE
...YOU'LL FIT RIGHT IN...

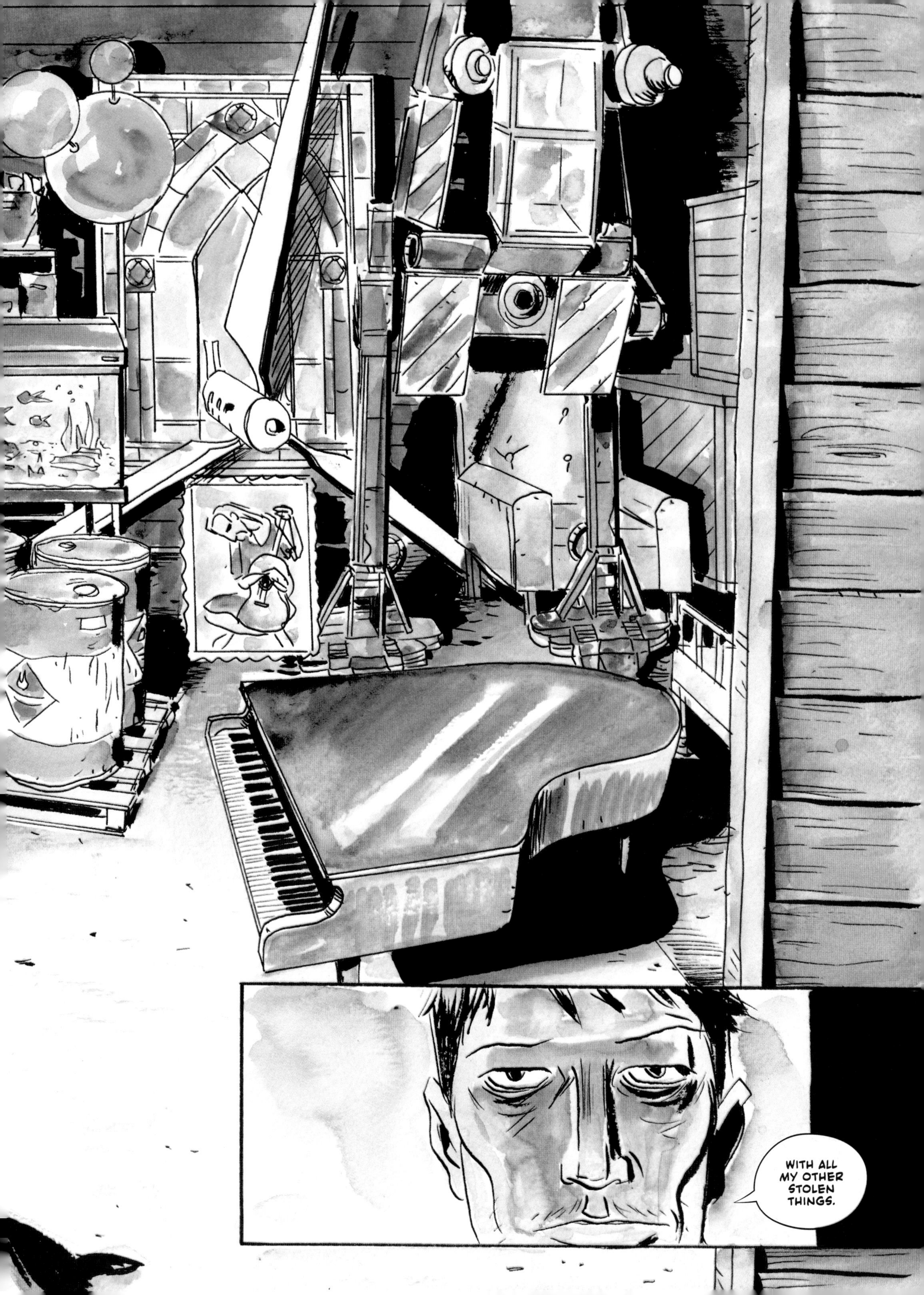
WITH ALL MY OTHER STOLEN THINGS.

Imagine something for me.

Imagine for a moment that you are a pygmy. You are part of the Aku tribe in West African Congo. You are dark skinned and very small, about four-foot-eleven. I am, too. You and I, we're together. We're walking through some of the lushest, greenest earth. We're part of that group--the famous one.

The one that found the first signs of it.

It's morning in the rainforest, and we're making our way through the brush. Above us, the leaves chatter with rain. There are five of us (or so the reports said), and we've known this place our whole lives--every tall, dark oil palm tree is familiar, every flesh-pink okoume. We have a goat with us. We're exercising the animal because it has been sick, but now it's well, and excited to be well, pulling at the braided tether, splashing through puddles. We pass mahogany trees and kapoks, talking and laughing, and then, suddenly, we stop.

Because on the ground in front of us lies something odd. This...small patch of gray. A pale, splintery spot about ten feet across. At the center, a tomato frog lies dead, curled in on itself like a pointless question mark. The understory is dead as well.

What really makes us stop, though, is the dryness. The ground in this patch is dry as bone. We watch the rain drum against the dirt inside the patch. It hisses and disappears, and the ground is dry again.

Before we can stop it, you or I, the goat pulls free and runs across the patch. Our leader yells and tries to grab it, knowing instinctively--knowing as we all know--that something is terribly, terribly wrong with this spot. It already seems to have grown by a yard on all sides (how could it have done that? Are we imagining?). But the goat is inside now, rushing ahead, just happy to be alive.

The thing is, I am not someone you'd expect to have been important to the story of the cure for death. This book, it's compiled from my notes. Notes hundreds of years old. My name is Jonah Cooke, and before it all happened, I was...no one extraordinary. I was nearly forty years old and lived on the north shore of Long Island, in a small condominium, the kind of place that didn't allow you to paint the walls or hammer into them. To hang pictures, you had to use a sticky gum that melted in the heat. The hedges were always full of cobwebs and punched-in wasps' nests. I worked at a modular-home company, about ten minutes down the freeway from the complex. We sold high-end free-build homes and additions. My office overlooked the showroom floor, where we kept an array of homes to tour, houses standing shoulder to shoulder like an army waiting to invade your neighborhood. I was unmarried when it all started.

The point is, I wasn't special. I was a no one.

But it's all my fault.

This place in the mountains.

The way things are.

All of it.

Because I stole the wrong thing.

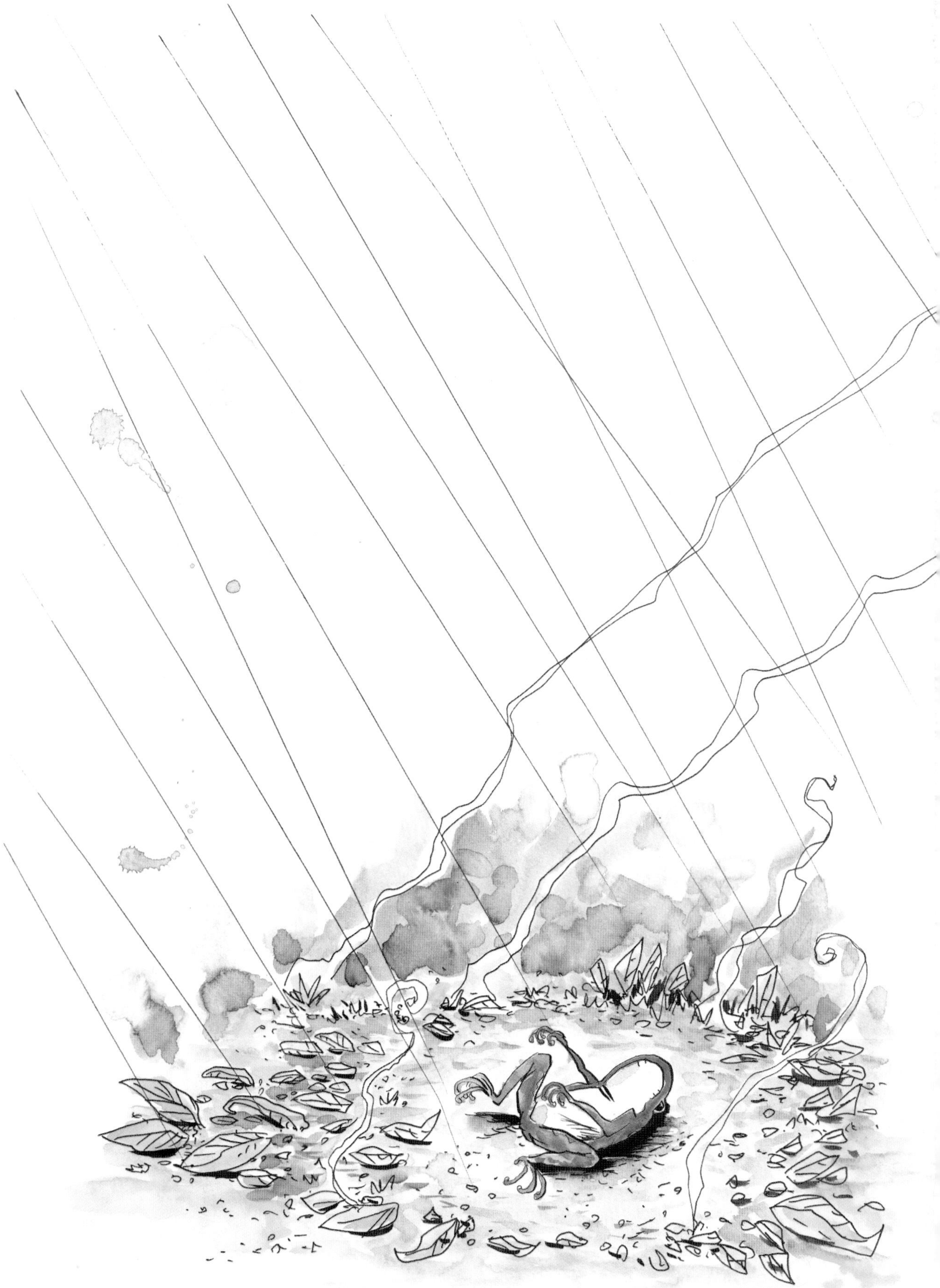

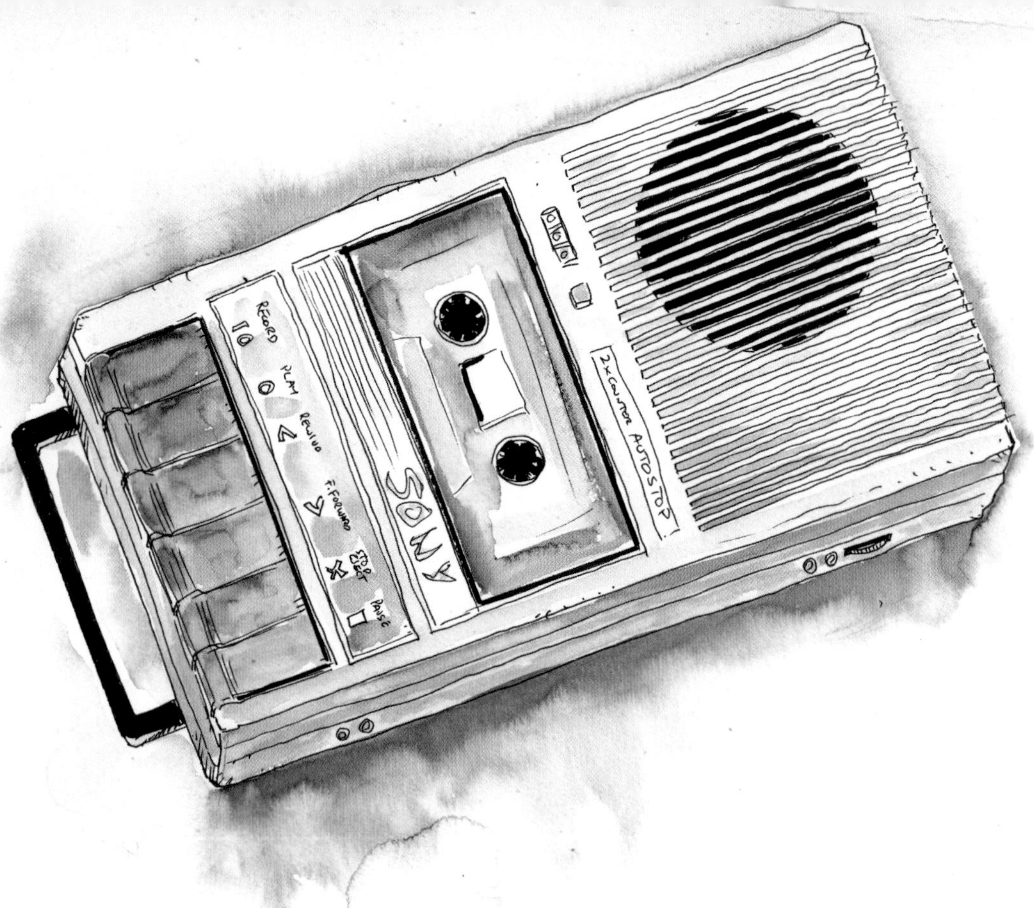
SONY
AUTOSTOP

The first thing I ever stole was a tape recorder. A 1990 Sony Quad. It cost $34.99 at the B and D Superstore and came with twelve cassettes for sixty hours of recording, more than any other tape recorder on the market. I was twelve years old and just about to start junior high. I'd never stolen anything before in my life--I'd never even thought about stealing anything, not a piece of candy or a comic book. Nothing. Sometimes I think I can trace everything that's happened since back to that tape recorder. Not just what's happened to me, in my life, but everything. All the death. All the lives spared... all of it. $34.99 at B and D.

At twelve years old, I couldn't really have told you why I wanted the tape recorder so badly. I could have told you what I wanted it for, just not why my need for it was so great. What I wanted it for was simple. I wanted the thing to record dinners with my mother and father. Ever since my mother's fall that day in Florida, I'd taken to recording my family life. I kept a journal at night, marking down the mundane things that happened each day. "Went to school. Argued with Frank Tsu about whether it's better to get unlimited lives before facing the boss on level..." And so on. I'm sure many kids do this, keep journals and such. But for me, there was something imperative about it.

See, in the weeks after my mother's first fall, back in Florida, she'd fallen two more times. Once at work and once in the pharmacy. The second time, she'd fractured her skull and come home with part of her head shaved bald. The months following those three falls had been awful, full of tests, CAT scans, and MRIs. Blood tests. I developed all sorts of ticks. Nervous behaviors not worth getting into here. The testing went on for a year, and despite the reassuring things we told each other, we all expected the worst--even me, at six years old. It was as though we'd crossed the border into some terrible country, my mother, father, and me, some hidden, brutal place that would never let us back home.

And then, miraculously, it all turned out to be nothing.

Test after test came back clear. My mother simply had a blood deficiency. It was easily fixable. She needed to take vitamin D, change her diet.

Her diet.

That was it.

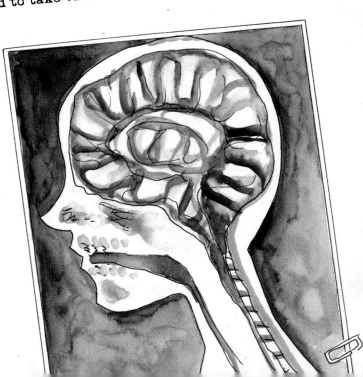

For a
while, she
and my father seemed
dazed by the news;
they literally looked
like they'd been roughed
up by the blast of good
fortune--their faces
slack and pale, hair askew.
Then the reality settled
in, and life between the
three of us became happier
than it had ever been.

Every Wednesday,
my father took my
mother out to a
Mexican chain
place they'd gone on
their first date
They'd come home tipsy,
sometimes wearing the
paper sombreros that
came in their
drinks strapped
to their
chins.

My mother cut hours and spent more time with me. Fridays, after school, we made a point to go exploring together along the coast, past the old farmlands out to the big houses on the water. The New England, shingle-style houses all sea gray and white trim. These were multi-million-dollar homes--compounds, really--but now that the storms were getting worse, and the shoreline was vulnerable and devalued, they were left abandoned most of the year. There'd been a big project to build a barrier out of defunct train cars, sinking them to make a reef--but it'd only just started when one of the first big storms rolled through and proved how useless the whole thing would be. Some of the houses were lifted and moved farther from the water, put on stilts. Others were left where they were.

My mother and I would drive around these properties, and if anyone came out to check on us, the help or whoever, we'd say we were lost, or even just peel away. When no one was home, we'd picnic on the lawns, maybe even go inside, if the doors were unlocked (which, stunningly, they often were, as nearly all had live-in help who ran errands most of the day). There was something sad and wonderful about these homes, these lonely palaces along the water with their huge glass walls reflecting the violent, rising coast. Standing in the surf on their stilts like sea captains' wives holding their skirts above their ankles as they watched the ocean. They were full of art, too, some notable, some brand new, none of it looked at.

Each home was a different story we were part of. In the oldest, most classical of them, my mother and I were heirs to oil fortunes. We penned letters to relatives in Europe, obscure aunts and uncles who were all after our money. In more contemporary homes, we were mother and son architects who built strange and misunderstood buildings around the world.

The one we both liked best we called the EGG HOUSE.

It was an ultra contemporary, curving glass walls lined with steel and marble, floating staircases everywhere. The library was an actual elevator shaft of books. The whole place was pale and filled with light and it somehow felt at once utterly complete and totally unformed, like the inside of a cleaned-out egg.

The house had a single caretaker, an older, stooped man my mother and I called "the Russian," for the fur hat he wore when it was chilly out. He lived in quarters at the west edge of the property and kept a strict routine for himself during the week. He always went to town on the same day, at the same time (Tuesday at noon), and, strangely, though he locked the front door with a key ring he kept on his belt, he always left the sliding glass doors wide open, and my mother and I went in through the screens.

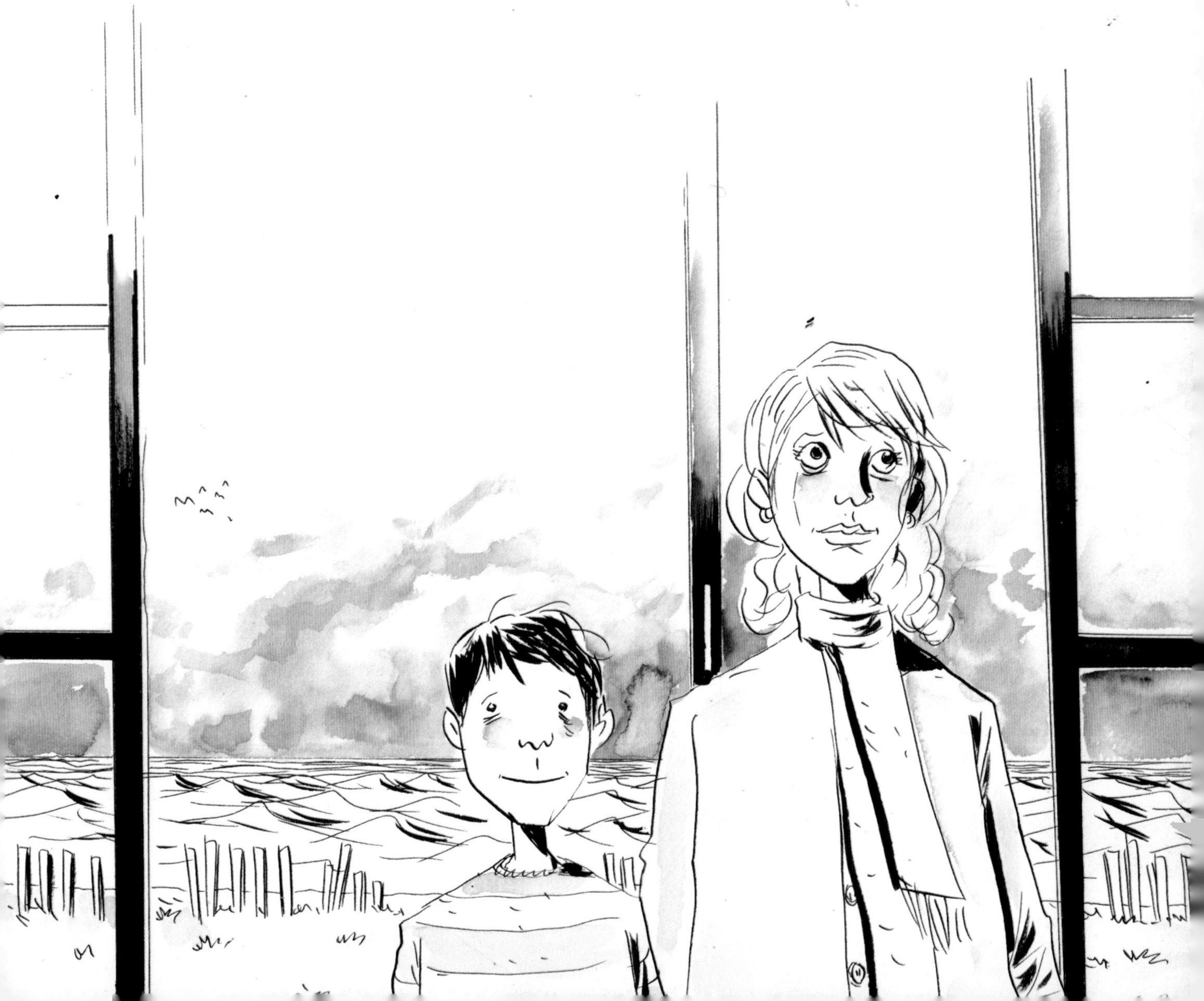

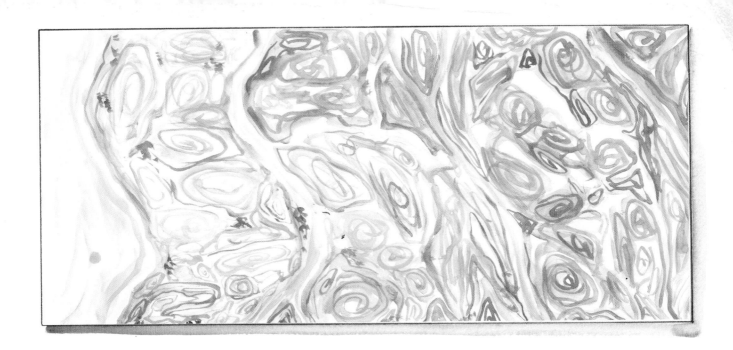

The house had great art, too. The best was a series of big pieces in the dining room. They looked like paintings, but were made with a kind of layered resin epoxy and depicted different aerial views of what looked like a hilly, ancient desert landscape. Golden sands cut through with white, winding rivers. There were three in the series, which was called "The land of milk and honey," and the trick to them was that they were actually made with milk and honey and ground-up human bone--bone ground to a sand-like texture...All of these things mixed and sculpted into something that should have been grim, but was instead shimmering beautiful. My mother and I visited that house at least once a month. Here we were always inventors--genius inventors! A mother-and-son team that had recently forged a new super-elastic material made from transitory, radioactive elements at the farthest, hidden end of the periodic table. Or the team that had just designed a new kind of computerized houseplant that would produce any bloom you requested. Sometimes my father joined us, too--he'd drive out after he was done and meet us at this house and we'd sit as a family in a home that wasn't ours and pretend to be the same people but different, people about to start.

We were safe and happy and this went on for years. Years.

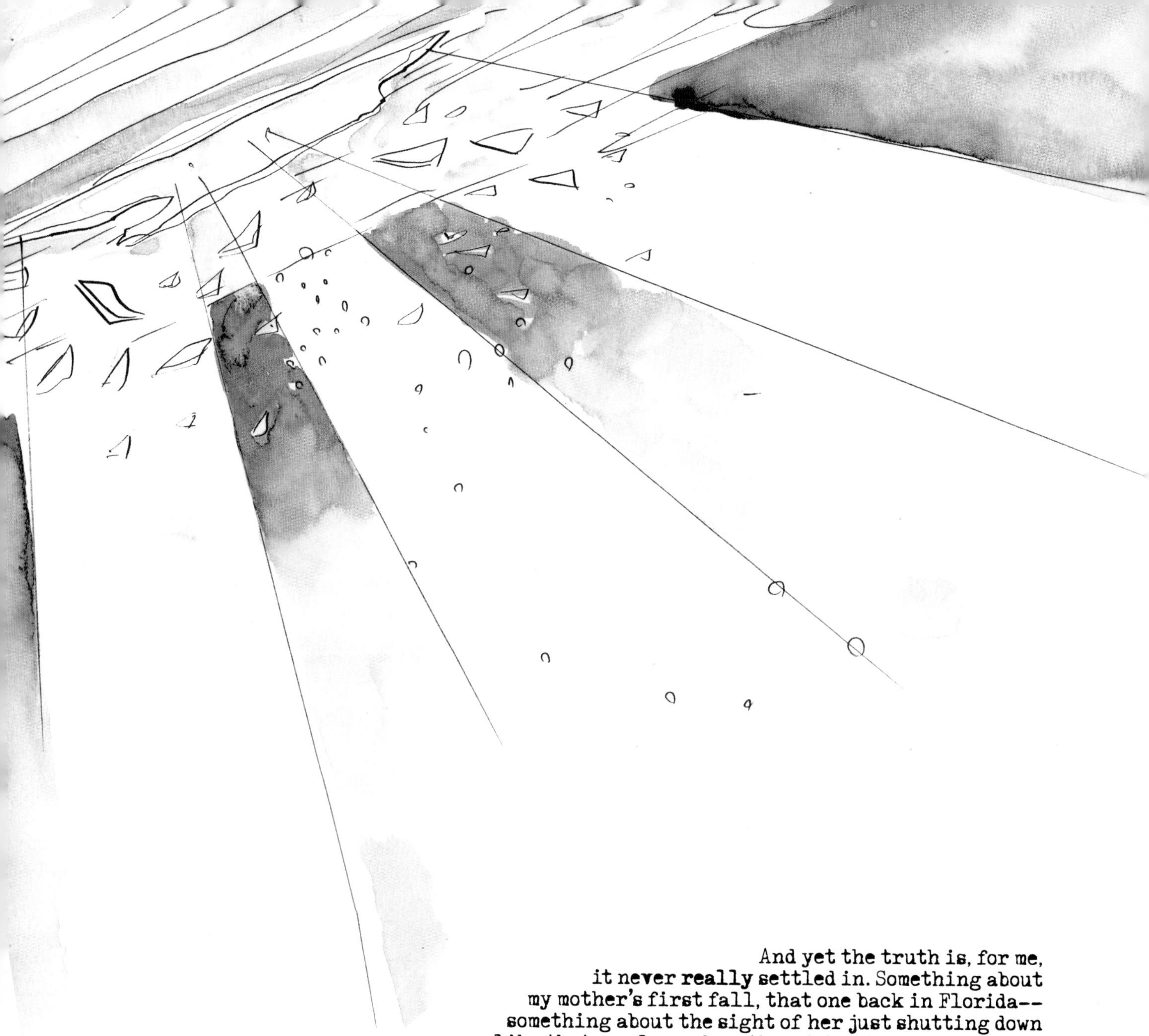

And yet the truth is, for me,
it never **really** settled in. Something about
my mother's first fall, that one back in Florida--
something about the sight of her just shutting down
like that, unplugged, as though her brain had simply
been turned off; seeing her body just go limp, go lifeless;
seeing her fall with no regard for injury, no hands out
to dull the impact, no bracing for the hit...just:
boom, down. A sack of bones. An empty
thing in the grasp of physics...

Something had gotten under my skin and just...**dug in.**
No matter how happy things were, even at that favorite house
of ours, I could never shake the fear that the other shoe was about to drop. I
remember being afraid when the phone rang that it was the doctors, all of them
at once, dozens, hundreds, calling from a single sterile room somewhere--
all the doctors in the whole state--to admit their big mistake together
and all at once: my mother was sick. Dying. Actually, my father was, too.
We all were, and nothing would ever be all right again.

I was happy, but always I was afraid that it wouldn't last. The best way I can describe the feeling is like being out on a big frozen lake with the people you know--your friends, your family. You're out there together, and everyone is enjoying the ice, laughing as they teeter and slide about. Kids chase each other. Older folks shuffle forward, arm in arm. And you're enjoying yourself, too--you are! You take a running start and drop to your knees, pinwheeling across the ice, and it's thrilling and hilarious, but who cares, because there's some part of you, some deep part, that cannot stop thinking about the freezing water beneath the ice. Stop it, you say to yourself.

STOP IT.

But you can't stop it. Because that part of you refuses to ignore what's beneath, to ignore the fact that at some point--maybe in seconds, maybe in weeks, maybe years, if it stays cold and you're lucky--but sometime in the foreseeable future, the ice will give way to the cold, black water below it. And, one by one, your friends, your family, and you, will all fall in.

Shut up, you think, as you spin across the ice, laughing.

SHUT UP.

There's your father, rushing toward you, about to drop to his belly and slide at you like a goofball. You're laughing and he's laughing, and here he comes, and it's--

But the water is there below you.

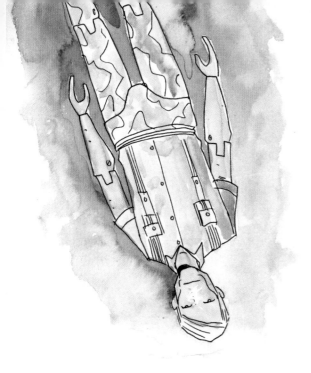

Will it **ever** go away, you wonder?
Or will it always be there, that shadow at the edge of
things? But, even at a young age, you know the answer to
that question, don't you? You know it: of course not.
Because it's just **there**, so close to the surface.

It's there at school, in the sickening way
the cellophane peels off your sandwich.

Or there, in a shattered vein on your teacher's calf.

Or there, in the scuffed nose of your action figure.

And there, in the weakening grip of the magnets on the
board. In the erasures on your homework. In pens running
out. In new sneakers that squeak so loudly, but go silent by
end of day. In the small tear in the backseat of the bus, the
wisp of stuffing you can't push back in all the way. In the
parade of blinking turn signals on the cars lined up at
the red light by your house, on and off, on and off, ticking
in some pattern that means nothing at all. And as the day
ends, you feel it deepening, that shadow, becoming material.
The blackness pooling below your nightlight. The deepest
dark of that hallway that separates your room from your
parents'.

All of it speaks to that same fucking water beneath the
crust of things, moving and shifting and waiting, and you
wonder, DOES ANYONE ELSE FEEL LIKE THIS?!

Are you alone?

Are you just messed up? Were you born missing something,
some protective layer, some membrane that's supposed to
shield you from the sight of it--that water, right here,
inches below.

By that year--by twelve years old--the fears had become more pronounced. It was a time of change for me and for my family. My body was certainly changing, becoming more and more foreign to me. Strange whorls of hair were growing under my arms and at my crotch, but not really, not fully; it was more like I was becoming someone's clumsy sketch of an adult. And my family was changing, too. My mother was pregnant. I was going to have a brother. My parents were elated. And I was happy about this, too, but more and more, my need to record life as it was right then--before anything changed--was unstoppable.

It was a Tuesday I made my play for the Quad. I'd scoped the B and D too many times at this point. Something had to happen. So I went for it. I had my puffy winter coat folded in my arms, and my plan was to lay it on top of a Quad box, act like I'd done this to tie my shoe, then stand up, take my coat, and inadvertently scoop up the Quad beneath it. The hitch in my plan occurred when I was just about to make my move and an old woman I didn't know stopped me. "Your shoe is untied," she told me. And so I had to tie my shoe, the shoe I'd left untied in order to snap up the Quad. The whole incident had me terrified, though. I was sure someone was onto me. Some employee behind a one-way mirror in some backroom. Still, it was too late to turn back now. I had to try. So I went for it, and less than two minutes later, I was biking home, furiously, joyously, with the stolen Quad under my arm.

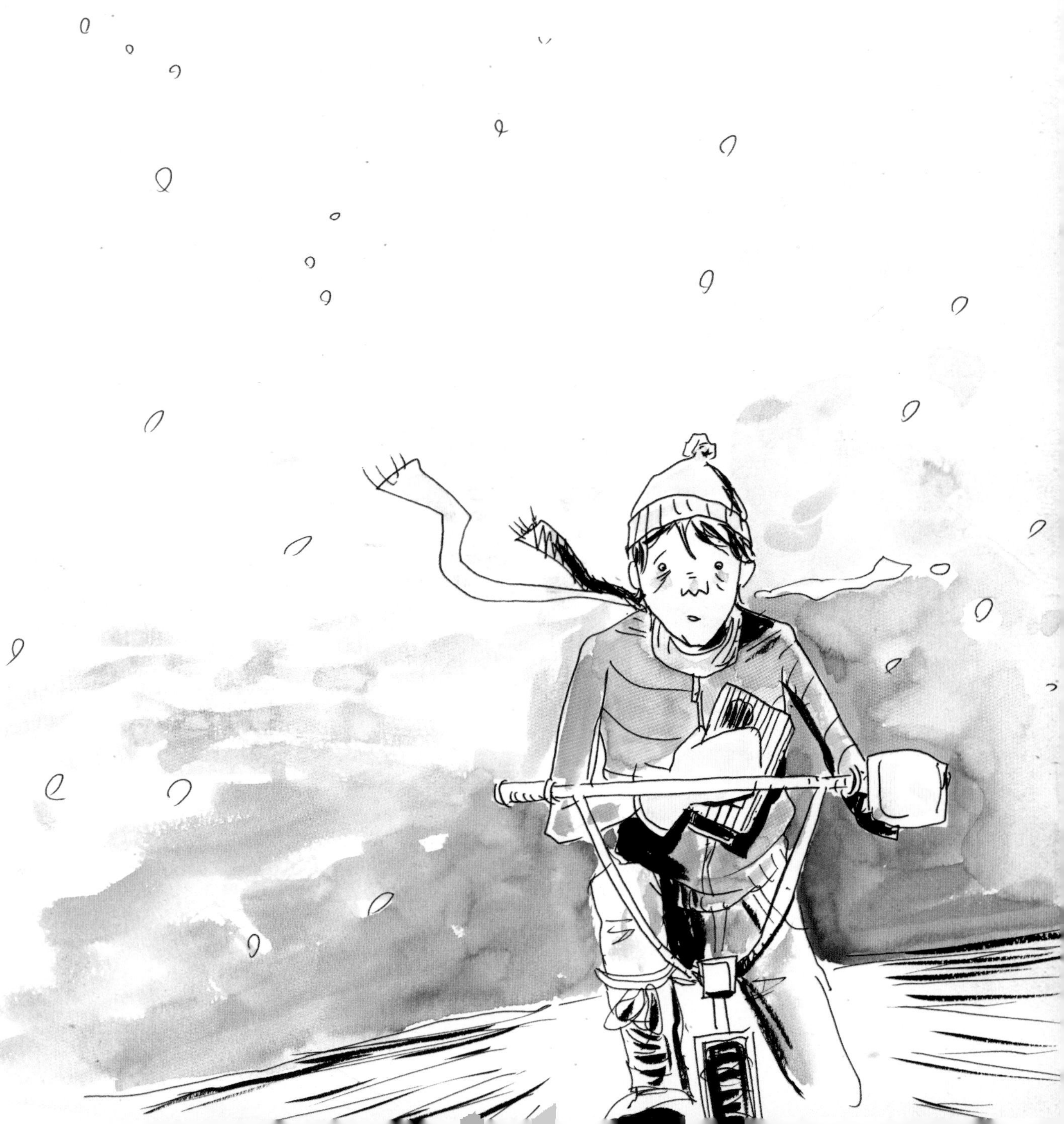

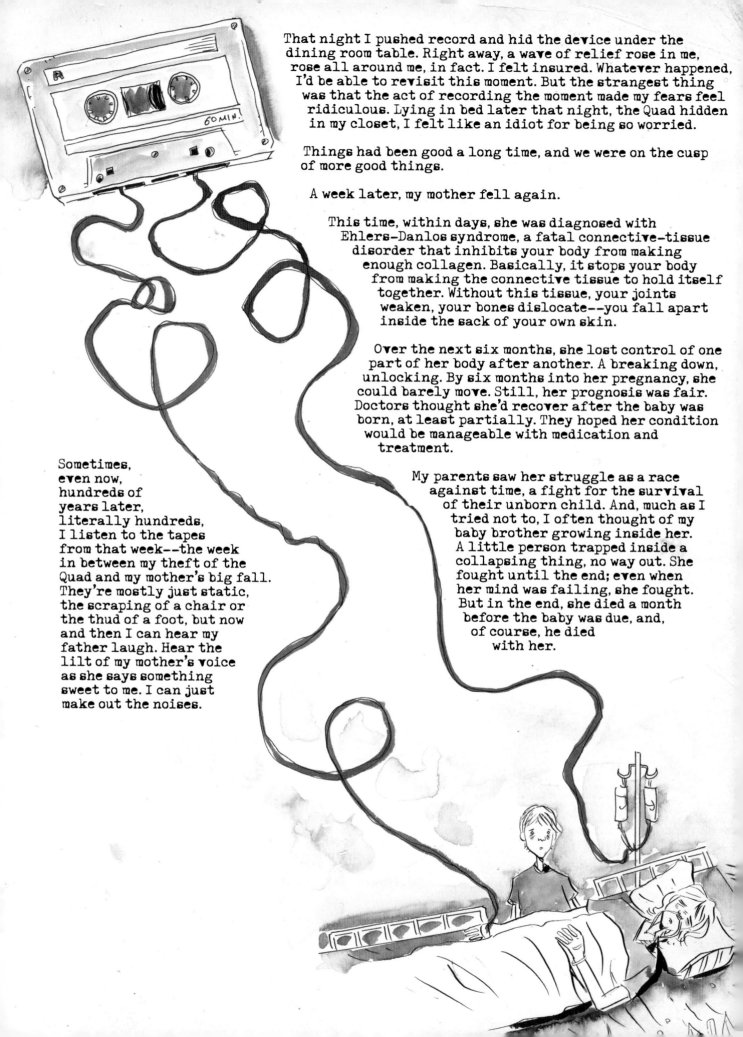

That night I pushed record and hid the device under the dining room table. Right away, a wave of relief rose in me, rose all around me, in fact. I felt insured. Whatever happened, I'd be able to revisit this moment. But the strangest thing was that the act of recording the moment made my fears feel ridiculous. Lying in bed later that night, the Quad hidden in my closet, I felt like an idiot for being so worried.

Things had been good a long time, and we were on the cusp of more good things.

A week later, my mother fell again.

This time, within days, she was diagnosed with Ehlers-Danlos syndrome, a fatal connective-tissue disorder that inhibits your body from making enough collagen. Basically, it stops your body from making the connective tissue to hold itself together. Without this tissue, your joints weaken, your bones dislocate--you fall apart inside the sack of your own skin.

Over the next six months, she lost control of one part of her body after another. A breaking down, unlocking. By six months into her pregnancy, she could barely move. Still, her prognosis was fair. Doctors thought she'd recover after the baby was born, at least partially. They hoped her condition would be manageable with medication and treatment.

My parents saw her struggle as a race against time, a fight for the survival of their unborn child. And, much as I tried not to, I often thought of my baby brother growing inside her. A little person trapped inside a collapsing thing, no way out. She fought until the end; even when her mind was failing, she fought. But in the end, she died a month before the baby was due, and, of course, he died with her.

Sometimes, even now, hundreds of years later, literally hundreds, I listen to the tapes from that week--the week in between my theft of the Quad and my mother's big fall. They're mostly just static, the scraping of a chair or the thud of a foot, but now and then I can hear my father laugh. Hear the lilt of my mother's voice as she says something sweet to me. I can just make out the noises.

But the goat...the one that escaped us, you and me, here in the jungle. It's looking at us from the other side of the gray patch on the ground, which has grown bigger yet. Carefully, we make our way around the patch and get the goat--I get him and shake his tether, pull his ear. We get him out of there, take him back to the village. But somewhere, deep down, we both know, you and I, that it is too late for the goat. That there is no taking him out of this place--that this place has trapped him somehow, and he will die as it dies. Less than a day later, he's screaming as his rotten hooves split open and fall away, revealing only horror underneath.

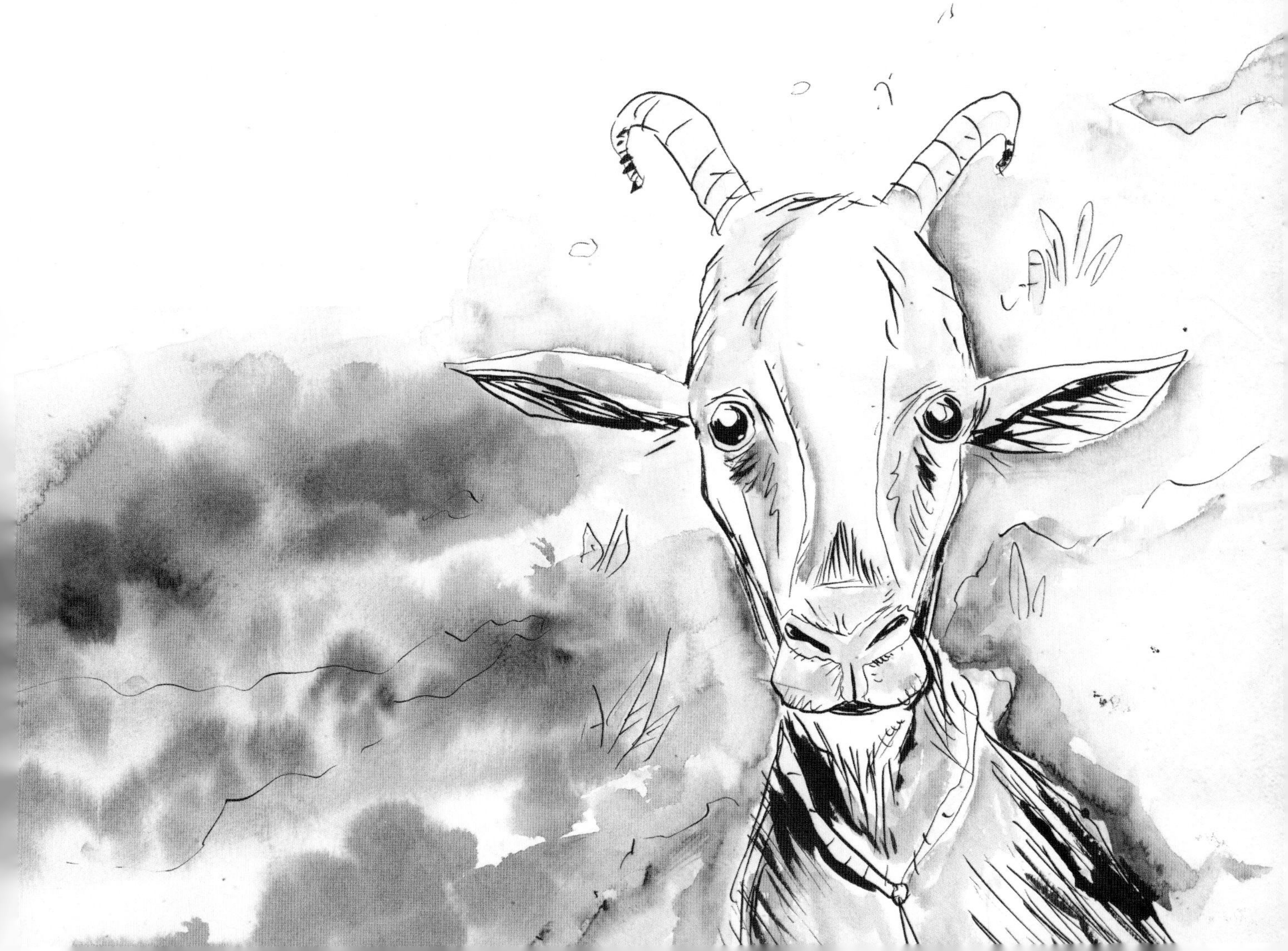

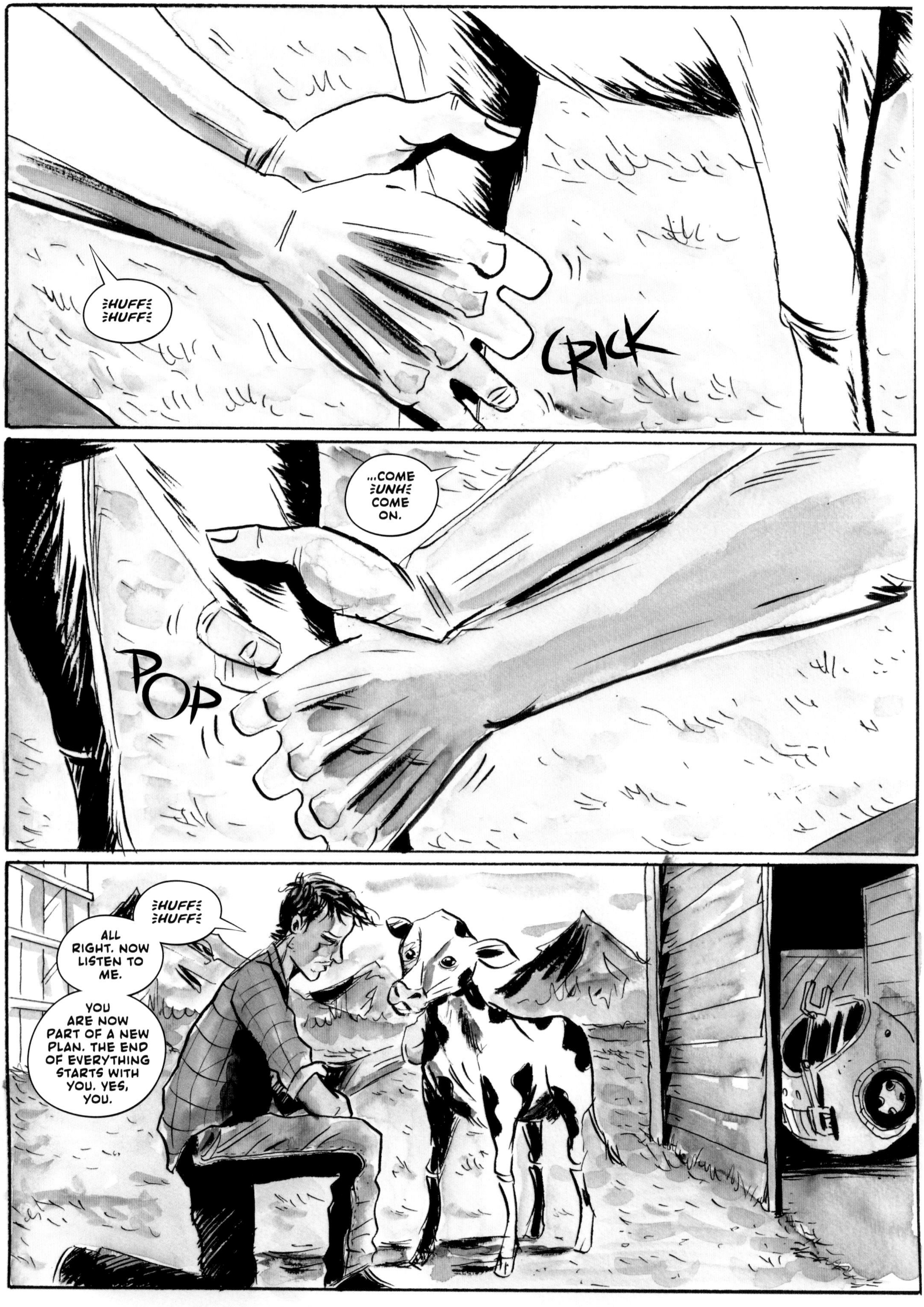
HUFF HUFF
CRICK
...COME UNH COME ON.
POP
HUFF HUFF
ALL RIGHT. NOW LISTEN TO ME.
YOU ARE NOW PART OF A NEW PLAN. THE END OF EVERYTHING STARTS WITH YOU. YES, YOU.

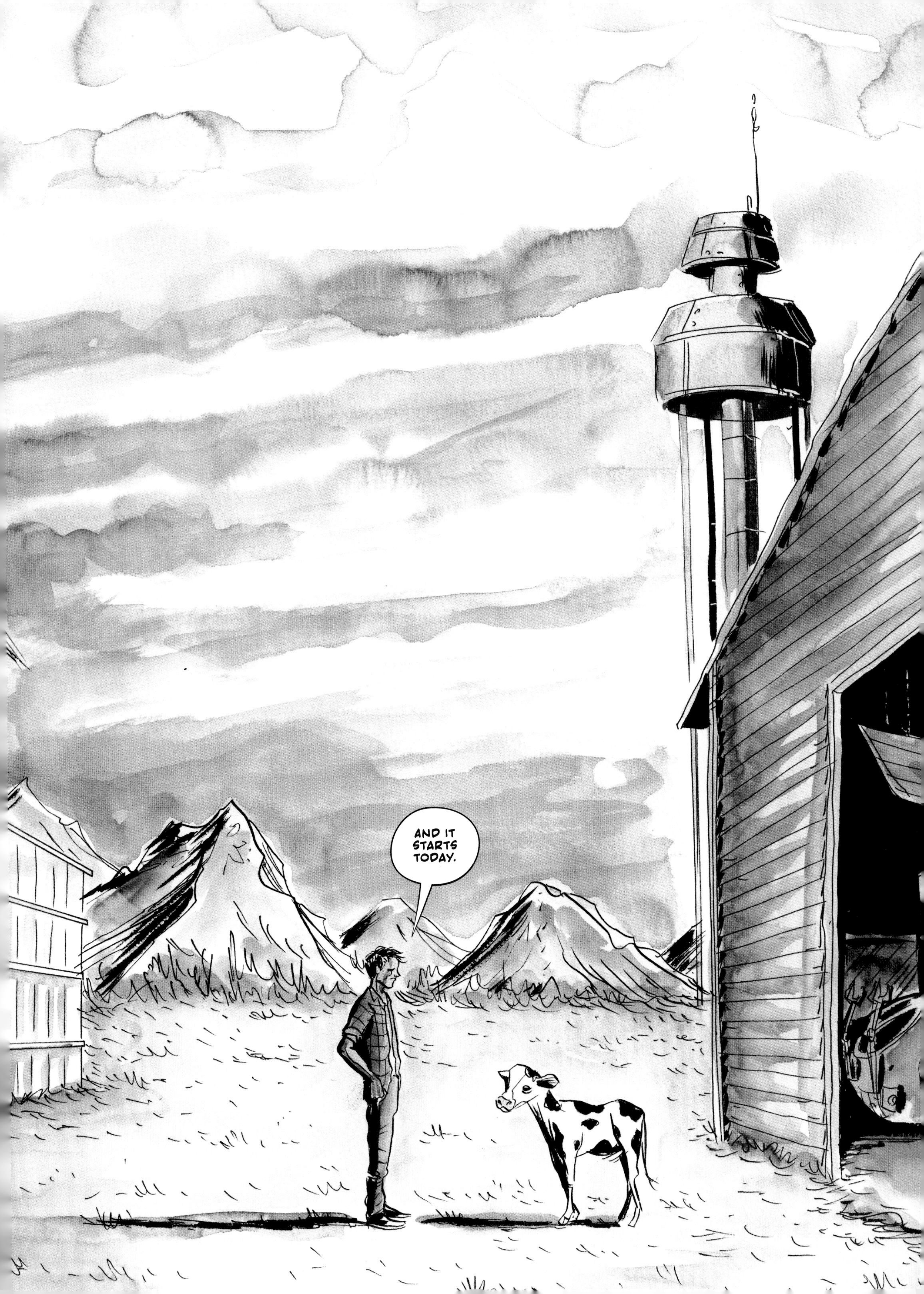
AND IT STARTS TODAY.

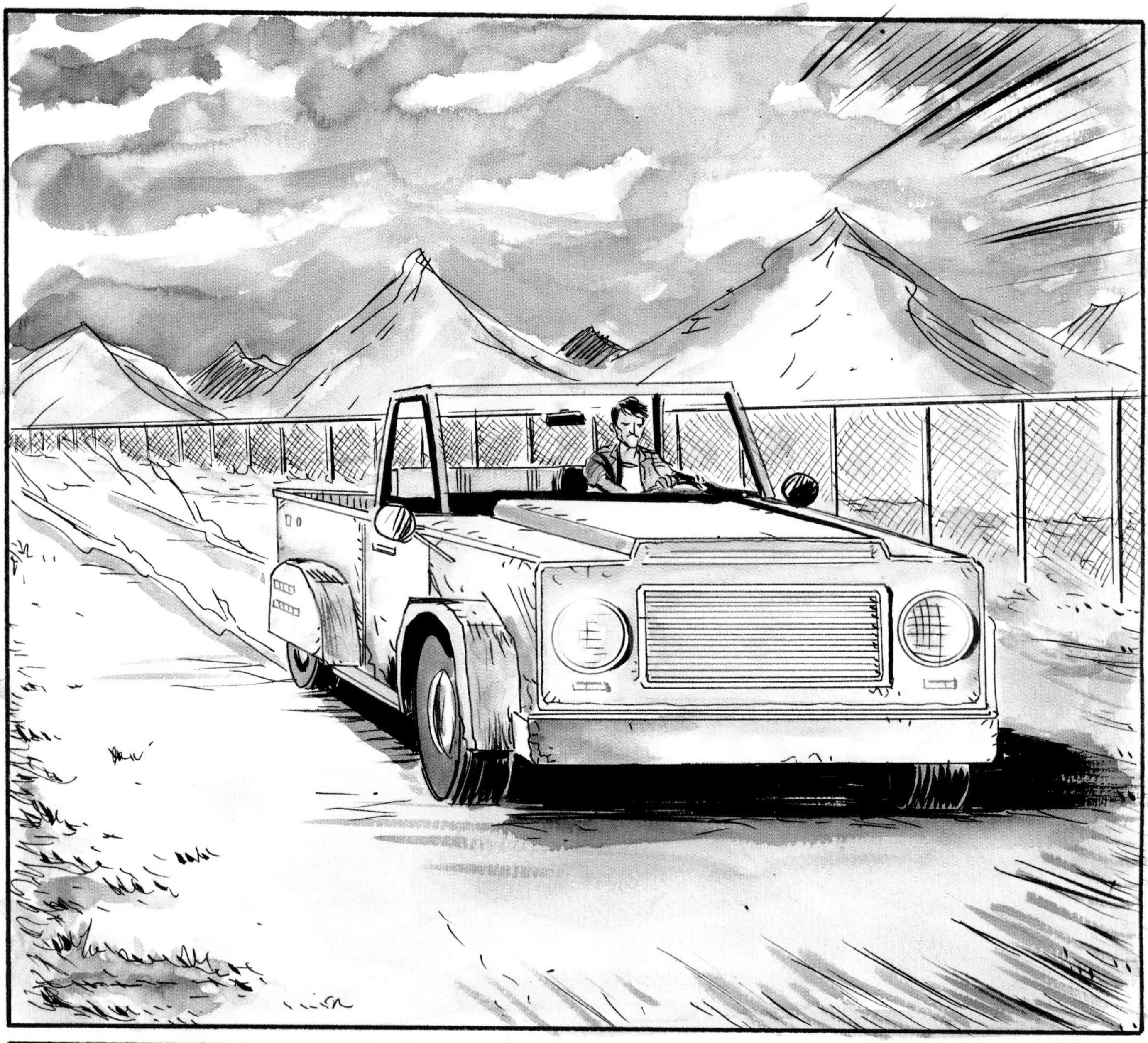

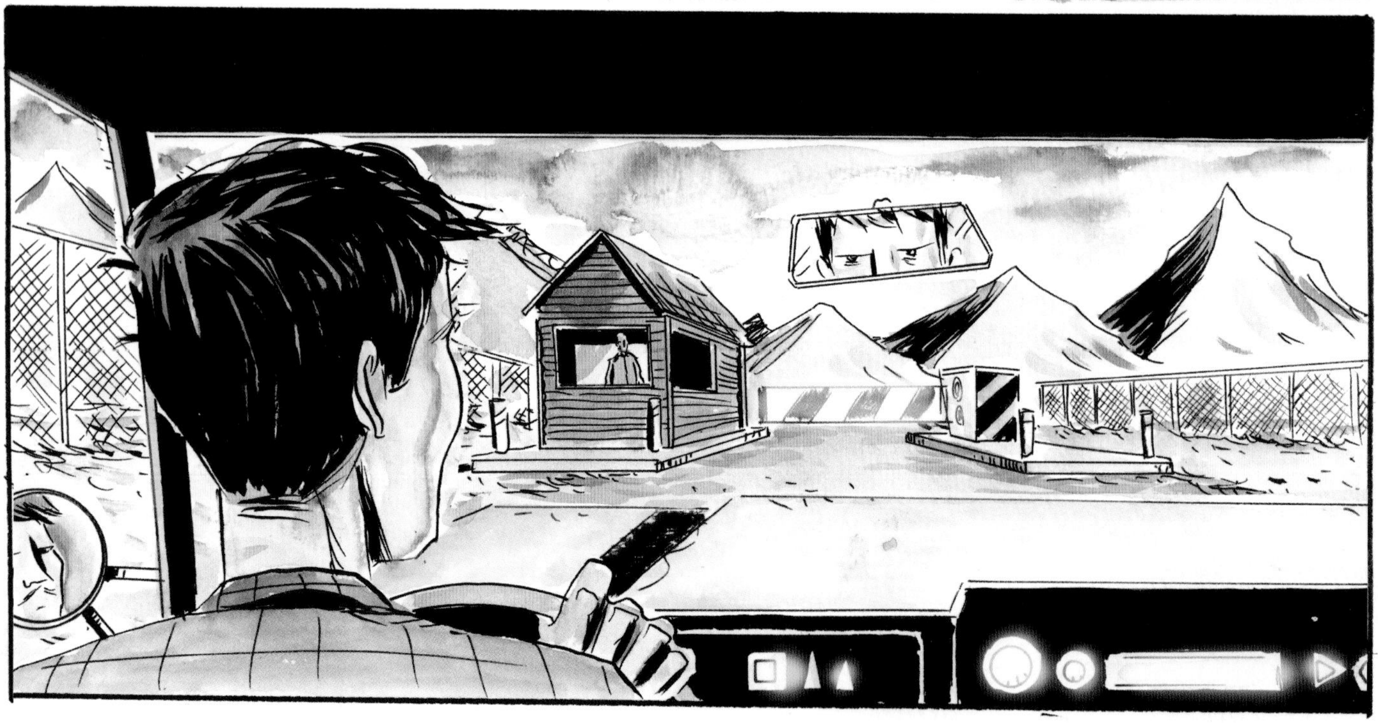

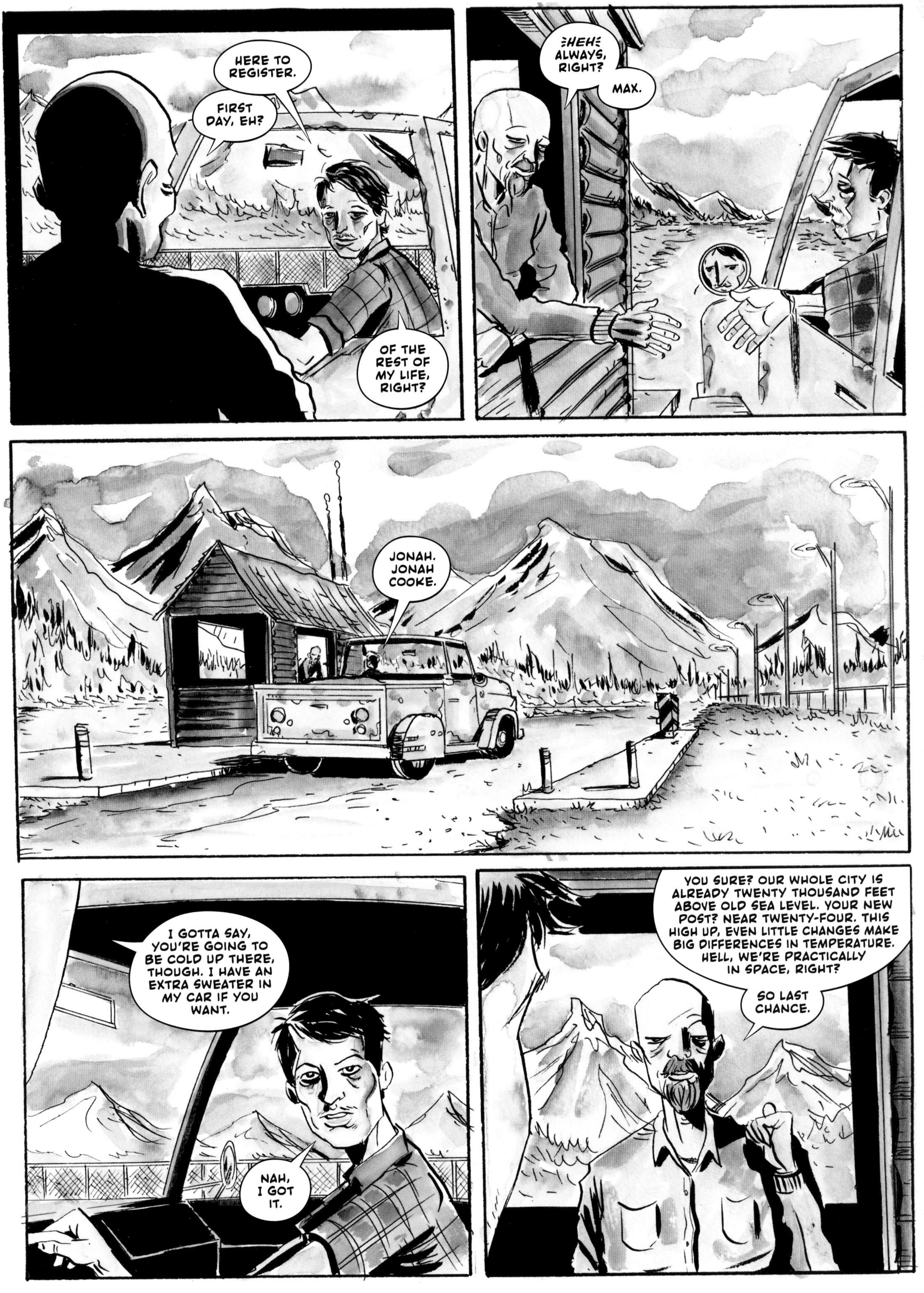

HERE TO REGISTER.
FIRST DAY, EH?
OF THE REST OF MY LIFE, RIGHT?
HEH ALWAYS, RIGHT?
MAX.
JONAH. JONAH COOKE.
I GOTTA SAY, YOU'RE GOING TO BE COLD UP THERE, THOUGH. I HAVE AN EXTRA SWEATER IN MY CAR IF YOU WANT.
NAH, I GOT IT.
YOU SURE? OUR WHOLE CITY IS ALREADY TWENTY THOUSAND FEET ABOVE OLD SEA LEVEL. YOUR NEW POST? NEAR TWENTY-FOUR. THIS HIGH UP, EVEN LITTLE CHANGES MAKE BIG DIFFERENCES IN TEMPERATURE. HELL, WE'RE PRACTICALLY IN SPACE, RIGHT?
SO LAST CHANCE.

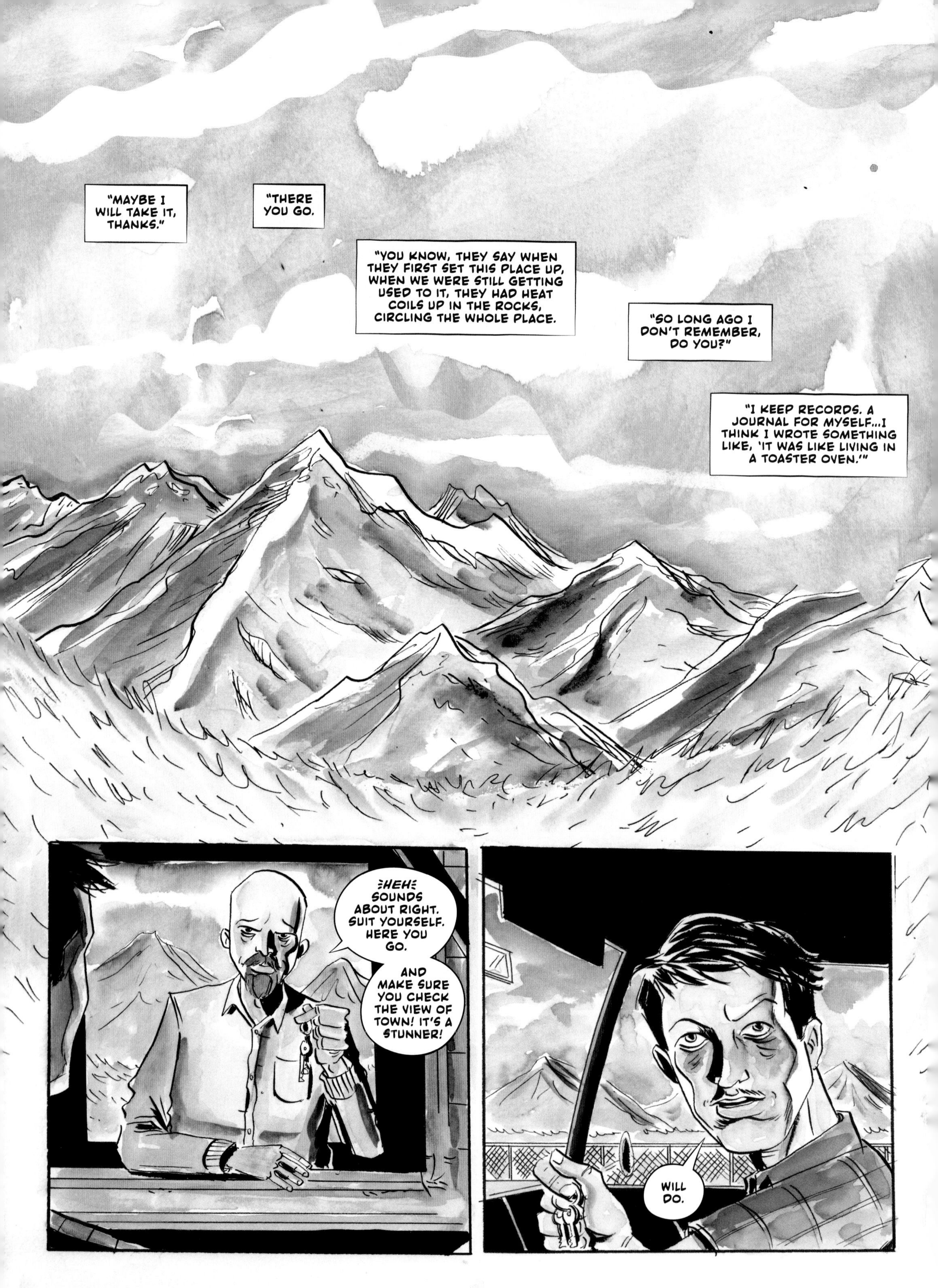
"MAYBE I WILL TAKE IT, THANKS."
"THERE YOU GO.
"YOU KNOW, THEY SAY WHEN THEY FIRST SET THIS PLACE UP, WHEN WE WERE STILL GETTING USED TO IT, THEY HAD HEAT COILS UP IN THE ROCKS, CIRCLING THE WHOLE PLACE.
"SO LONG AGO I DON'T REMEMBER, DO YOU?"
"I KEEP RECORDS. A JOURNAL FOR MYSELF...I THINK I WROTE SOMETHING LIKE, 'IT WAS LIKE LIVING IN A TOASTER OVEN.'"
HEH SOUNDS ABOUT RIGHT. SUIT YOURSELF. HERE YOU GO.
AND MAKE SURE YOU CHECK THE VIEW OF TOWN! IT'S A STUNNER!
WILL DO.

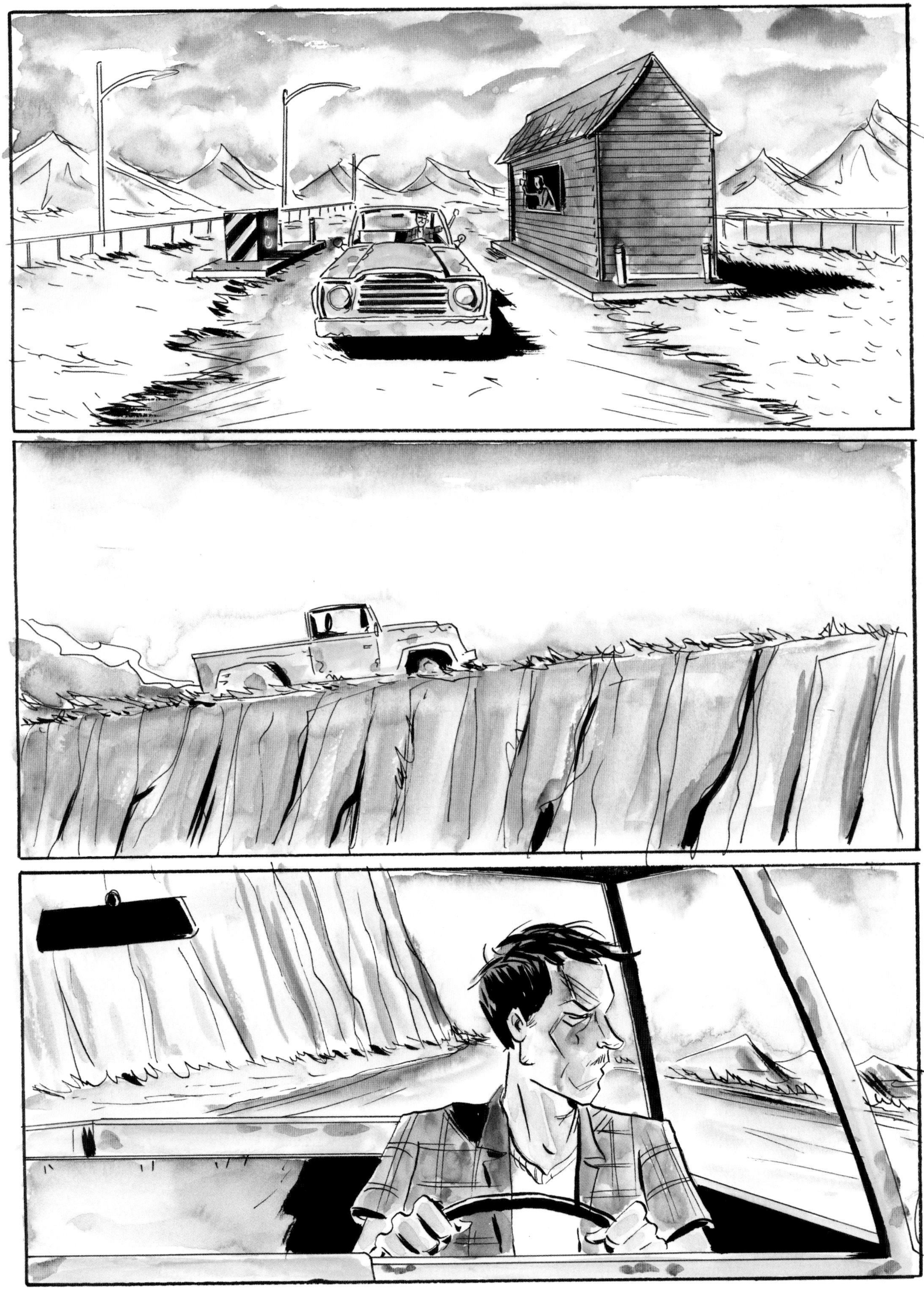

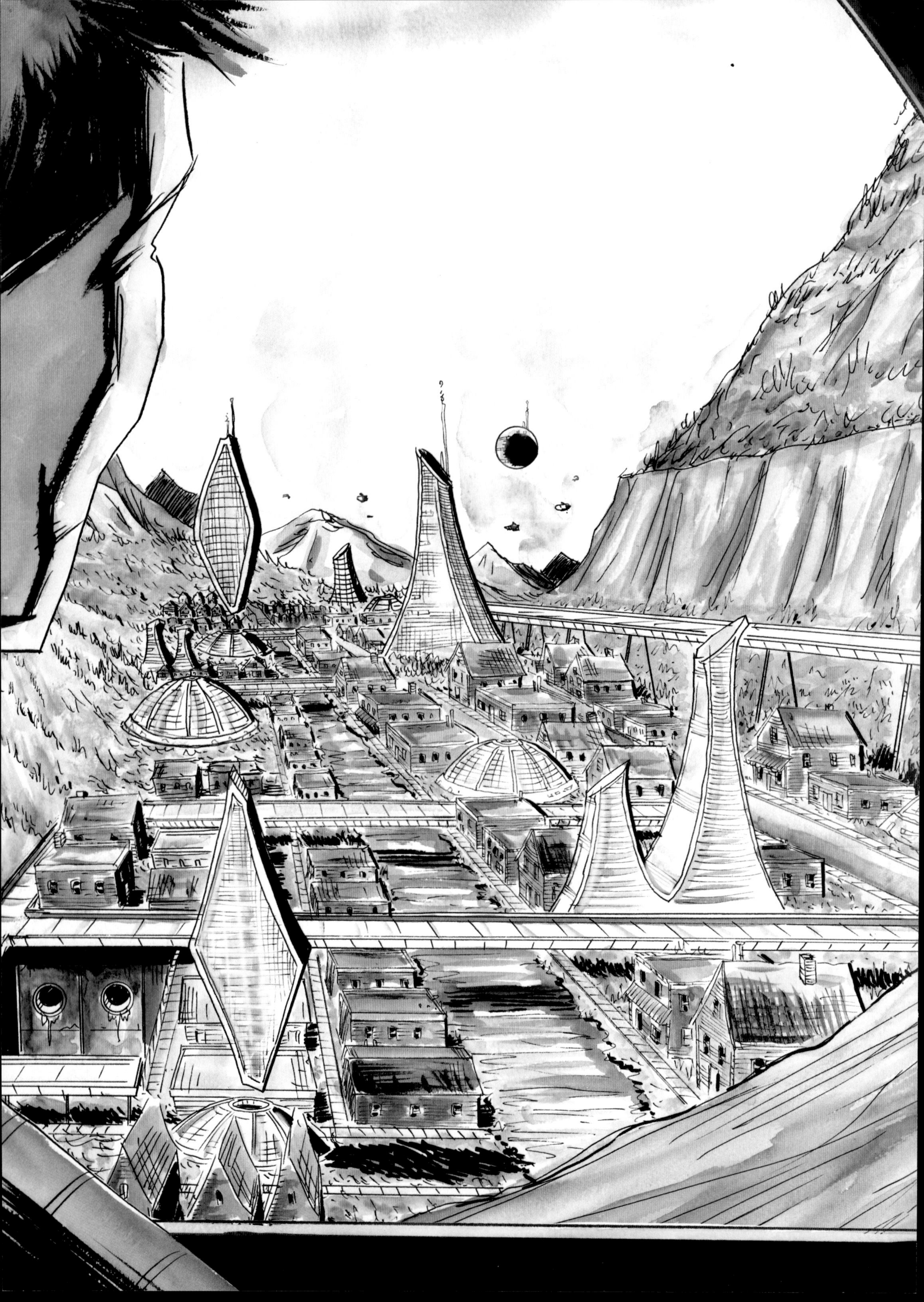

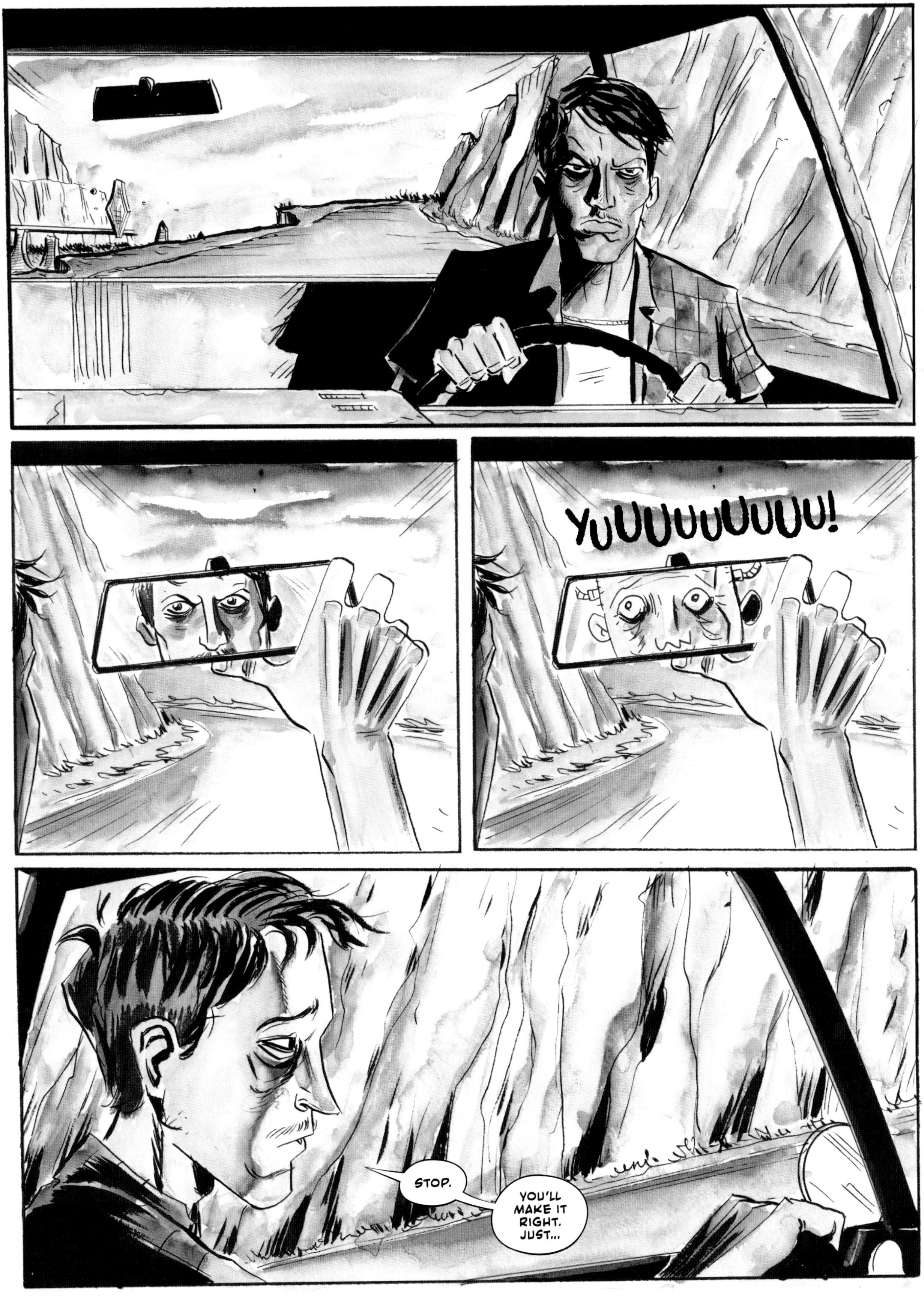
YUUUUUUUUU!
STOP.
YOU'LL MAKE IT RIGHT. JUST...

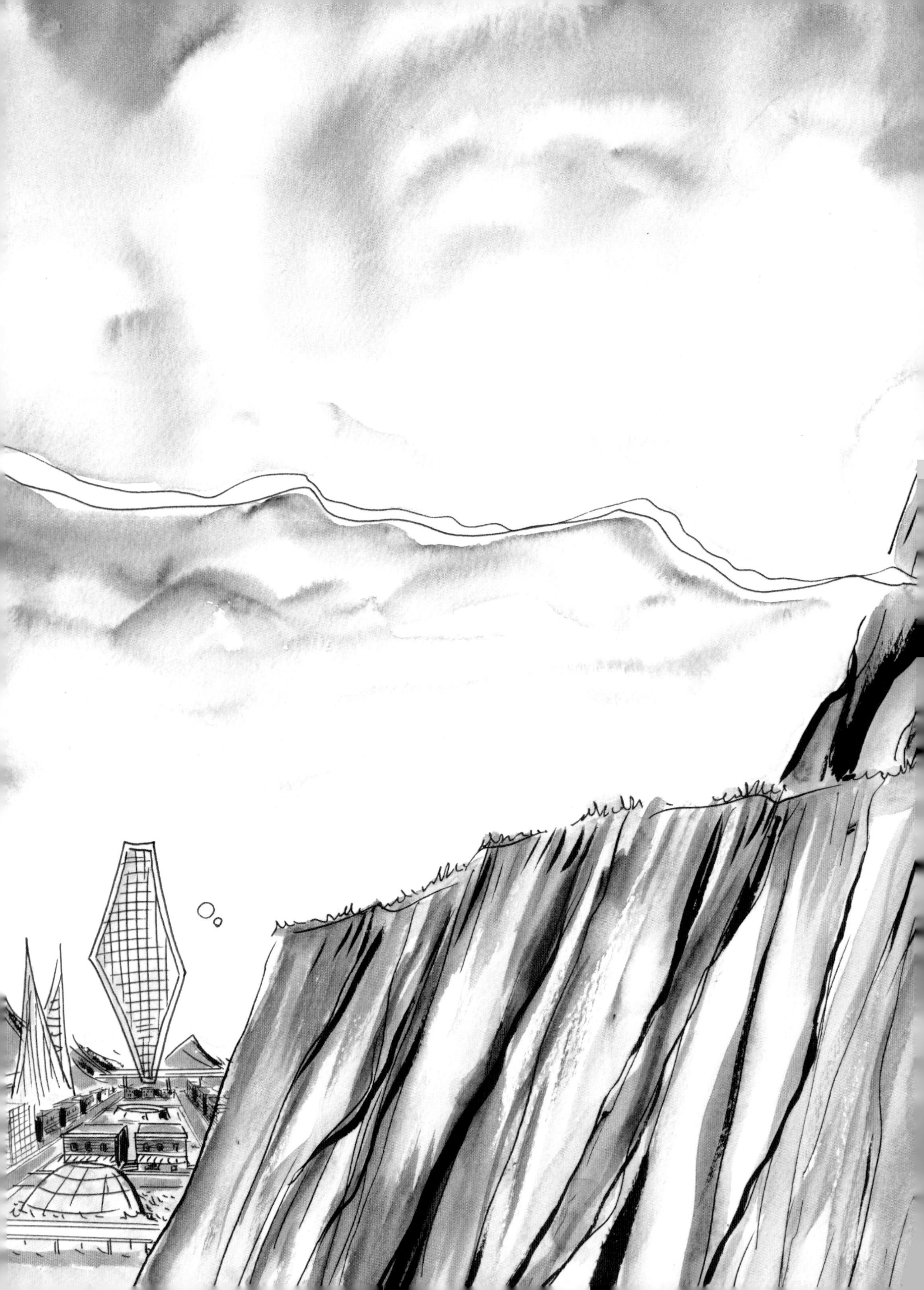

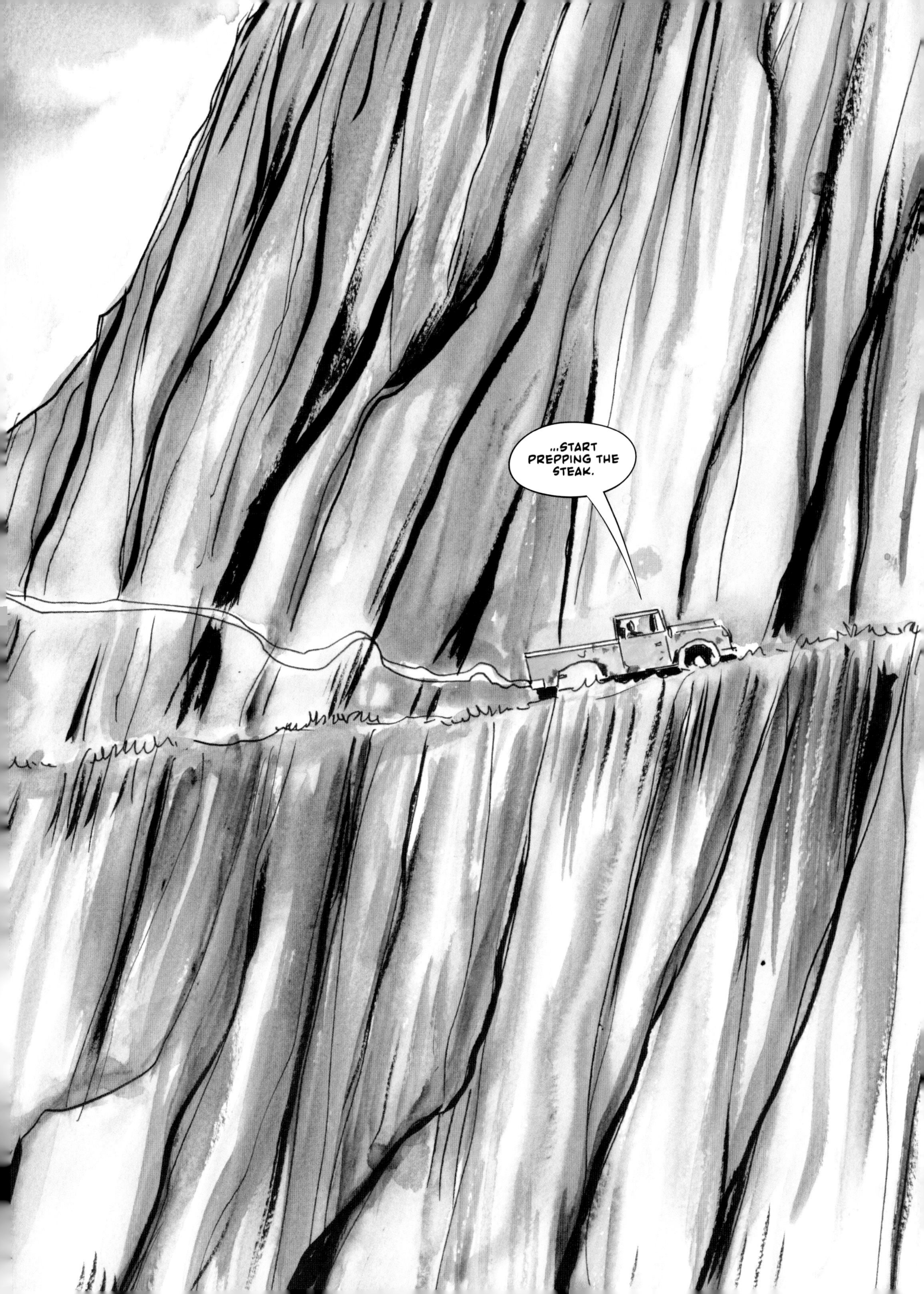
...START PREPPING THE STEAK.

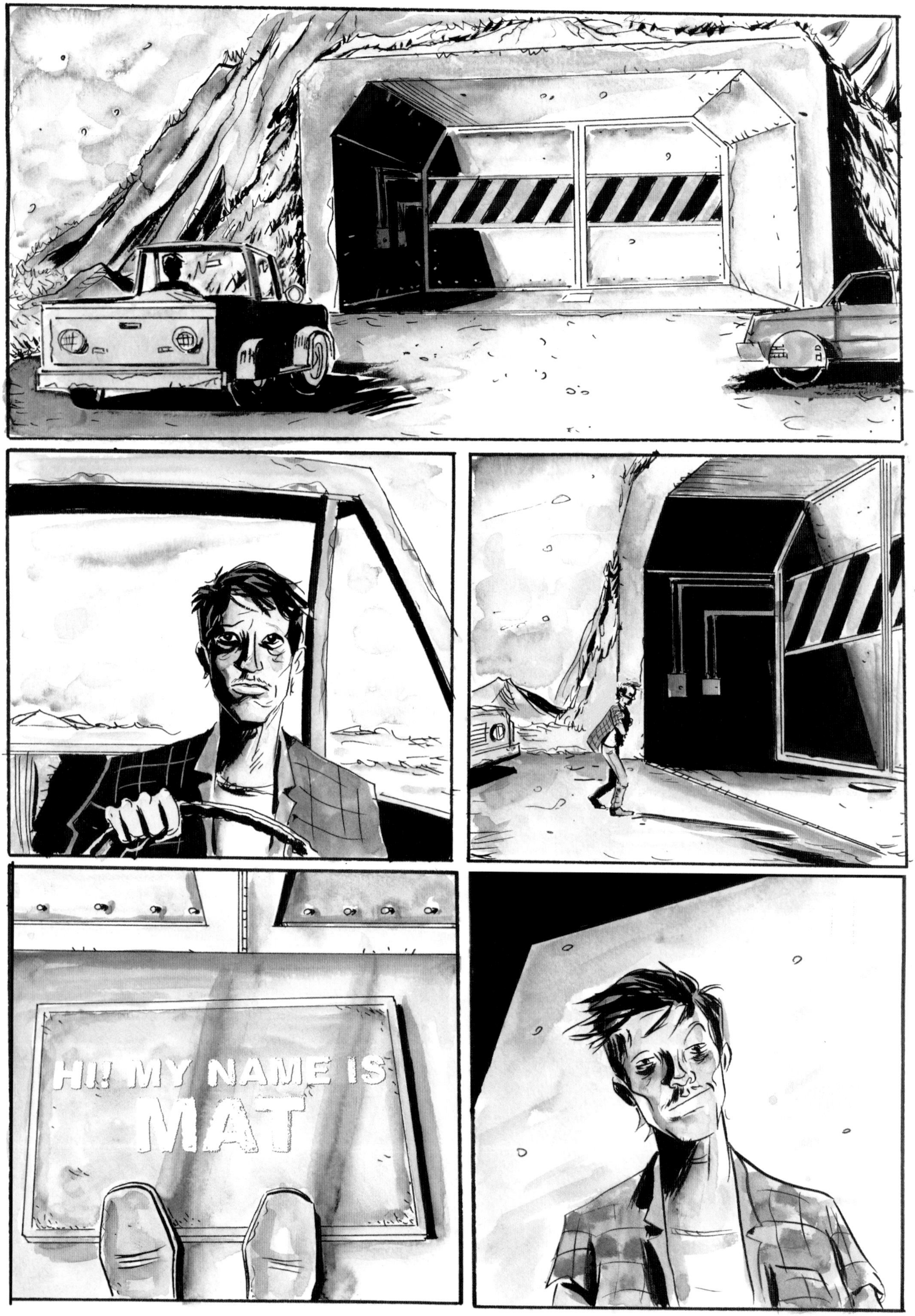
HI! MY NAME IS
MAT

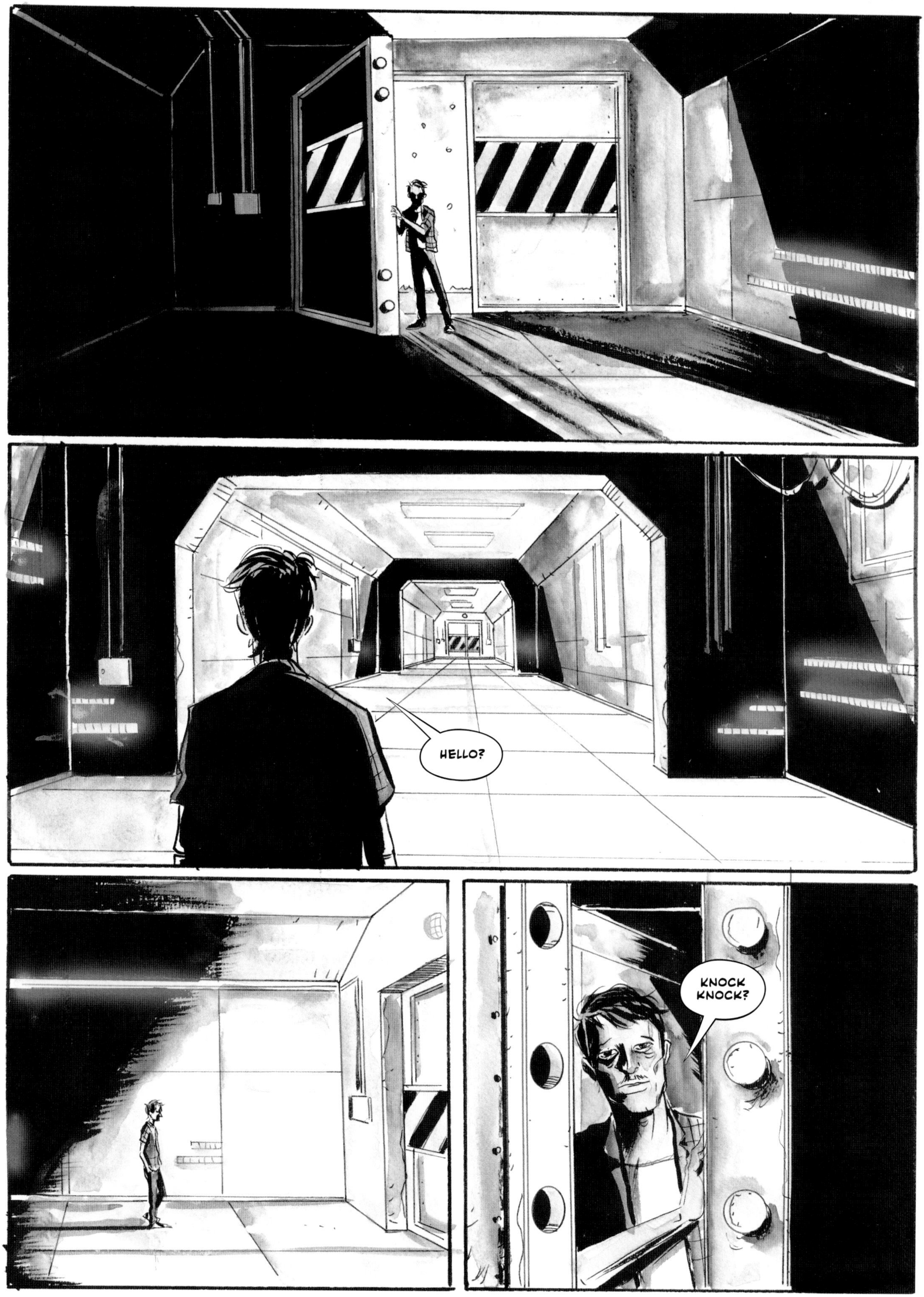
HELLO?
KNOCK KNOCK?

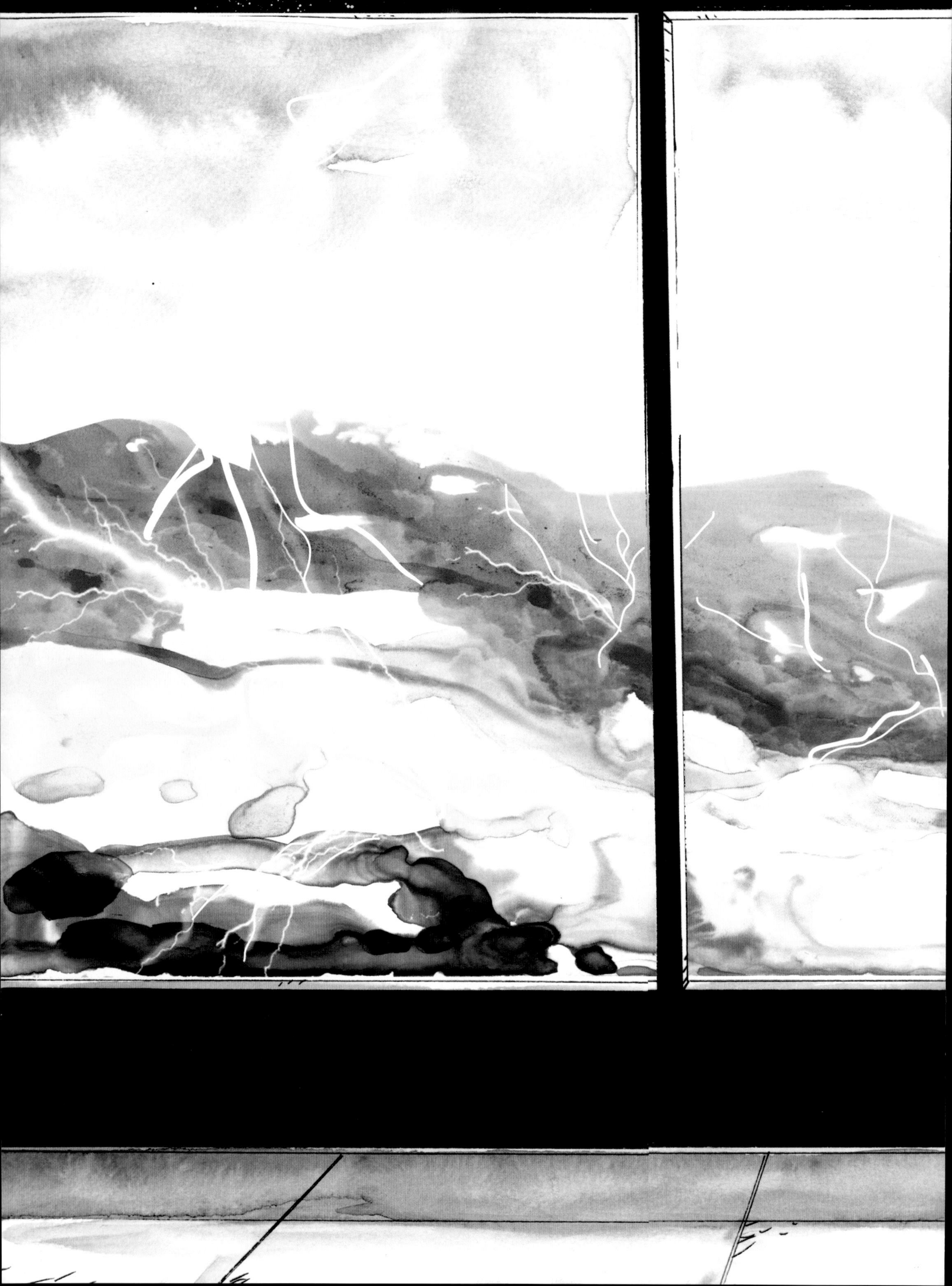

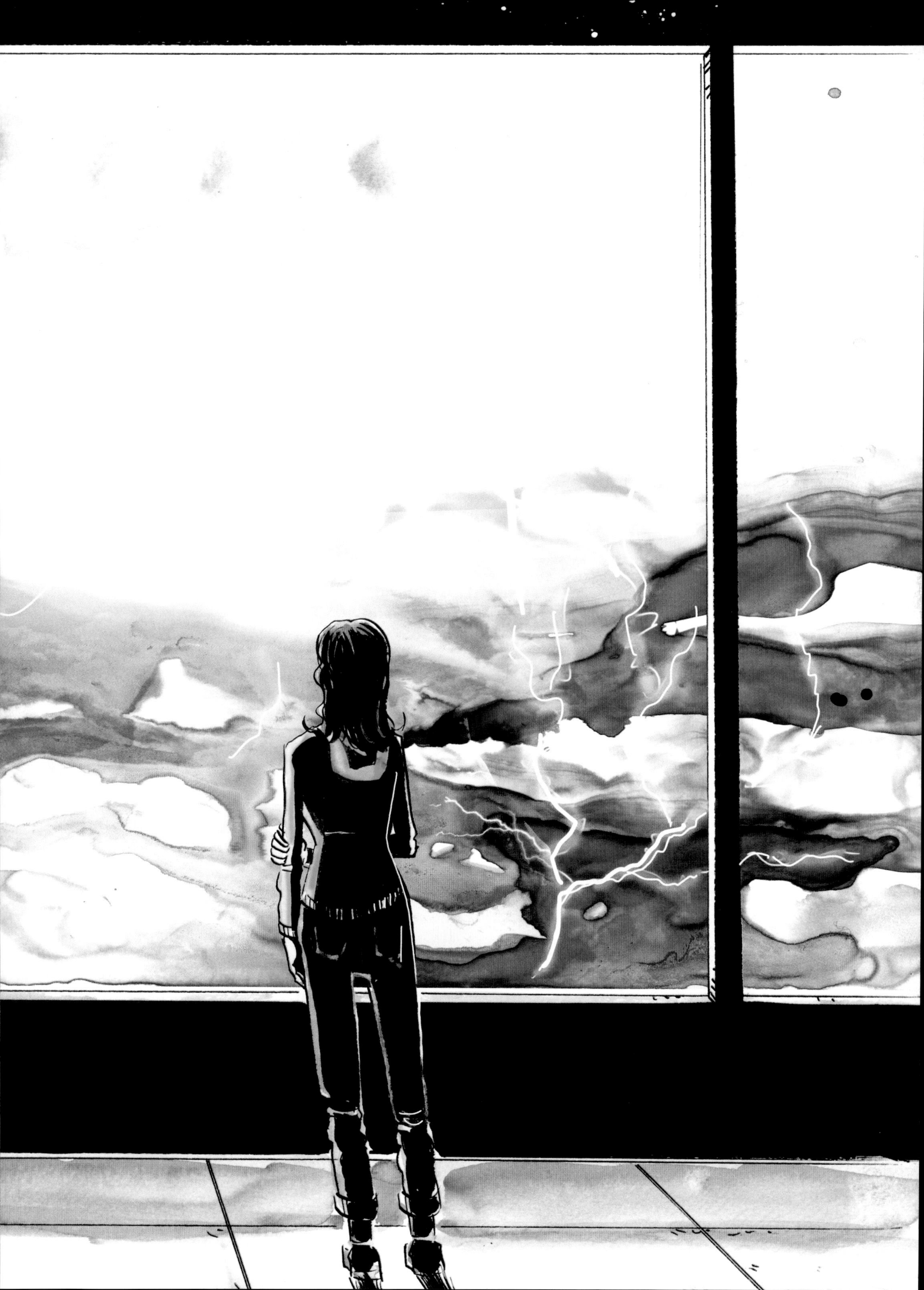

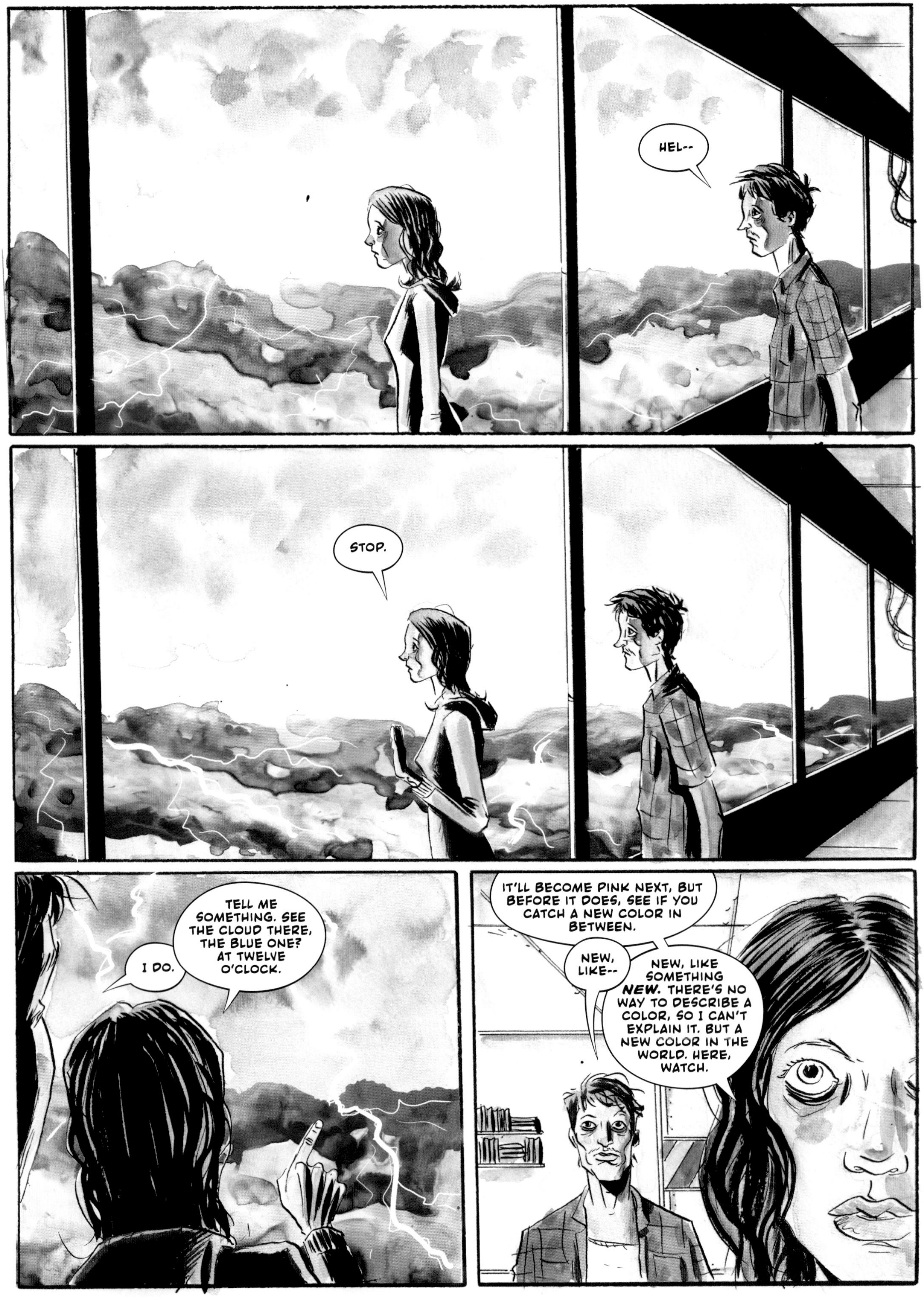
HEL--
STOP.
TELL ME SOMETHING. SEE THE CLOUD THERE, THE BLUE ONE? AT TWELVE O'CLOCK.
I DO.
IT'LL BECOME PINK NEXT, BUT BEFORE IT DOES, SEE IF YOU CATCH A NEW COLOR IN BETWEEN.
NEW, LIKE--
NEW, LIKE SOMETHING **NEW.** THERE'S NO WAY TO DESCRIBE A COLOR, SO I CAN'T EXPLAIN IT. BUT A NEW COLOR IN THE WORLD. HERE, WATCH.

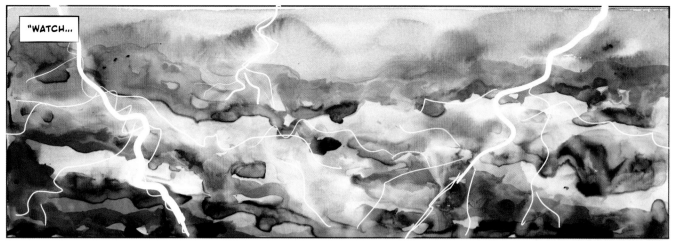

"WATCH...

"WATCH.

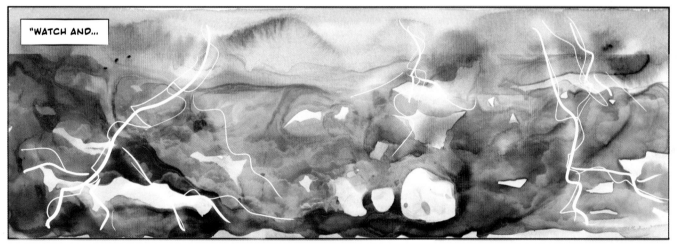

"WATCH AND...

"THERE. RIGHT THERE."

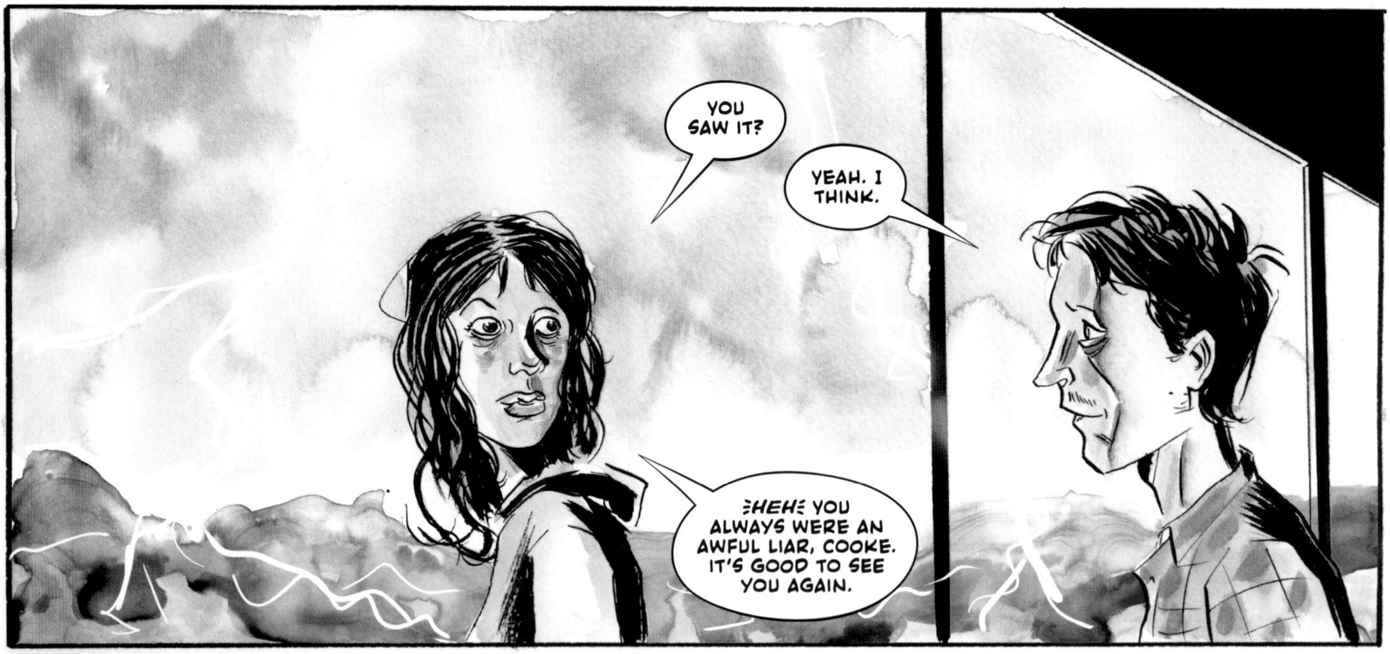
YOU SAW IT?
YEAH. I THINK.
HEH YOU ALWAYS WERE AN AWFUL LIAR, COOKE. IT'S GOOD TO SEE YOU AGAIN.

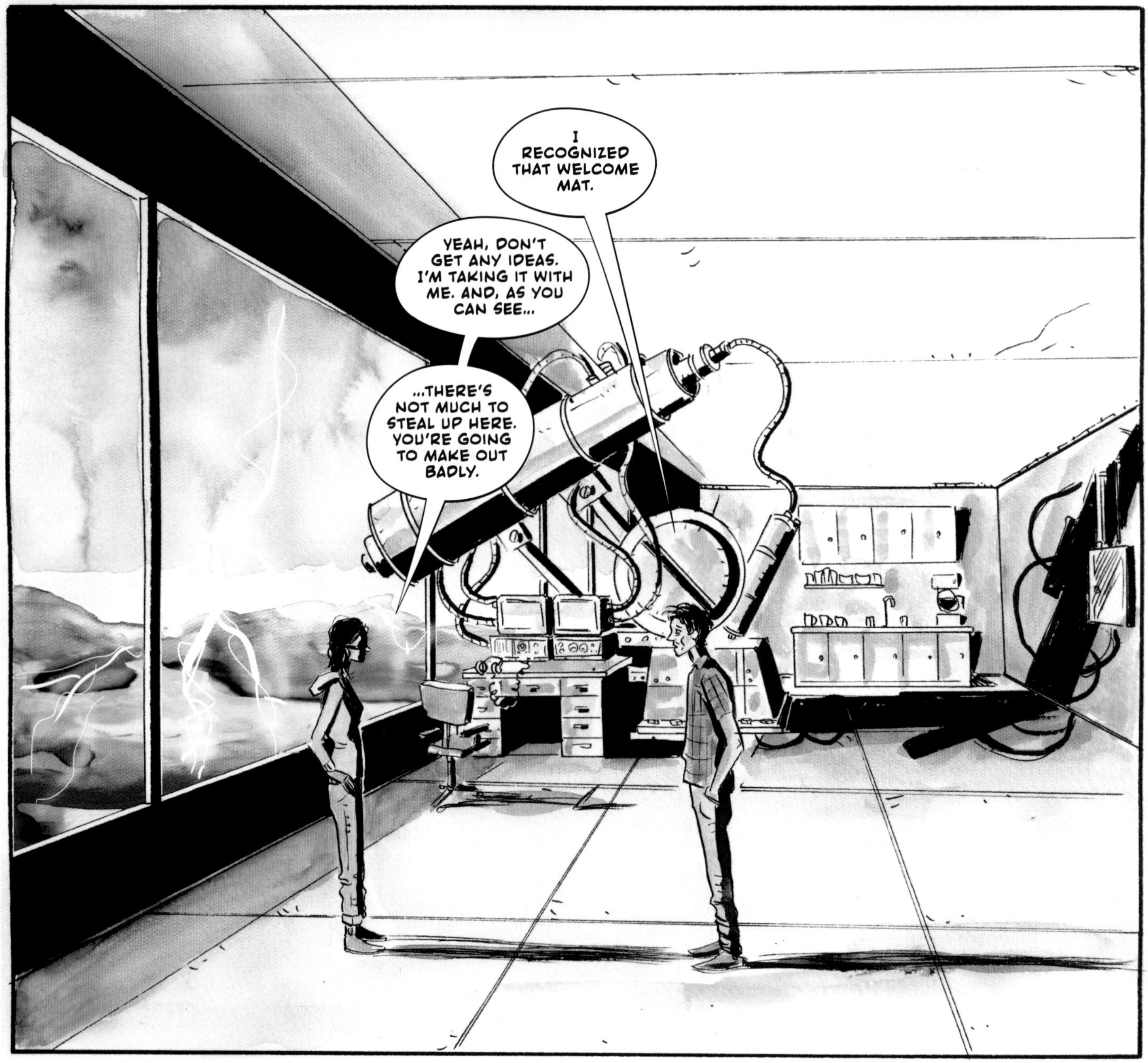
I RECOGNIZED THAT WELCOME MAT.
YEAH, DON'T GET ANY IDEAS. I'M TAKING IT WITH ME. AND, AS YOU CAN SEE...
...THERE'S NOT MUCH TO STEAL UP HERE. YOU'RE GOING TO MAKE OUT BADLY.

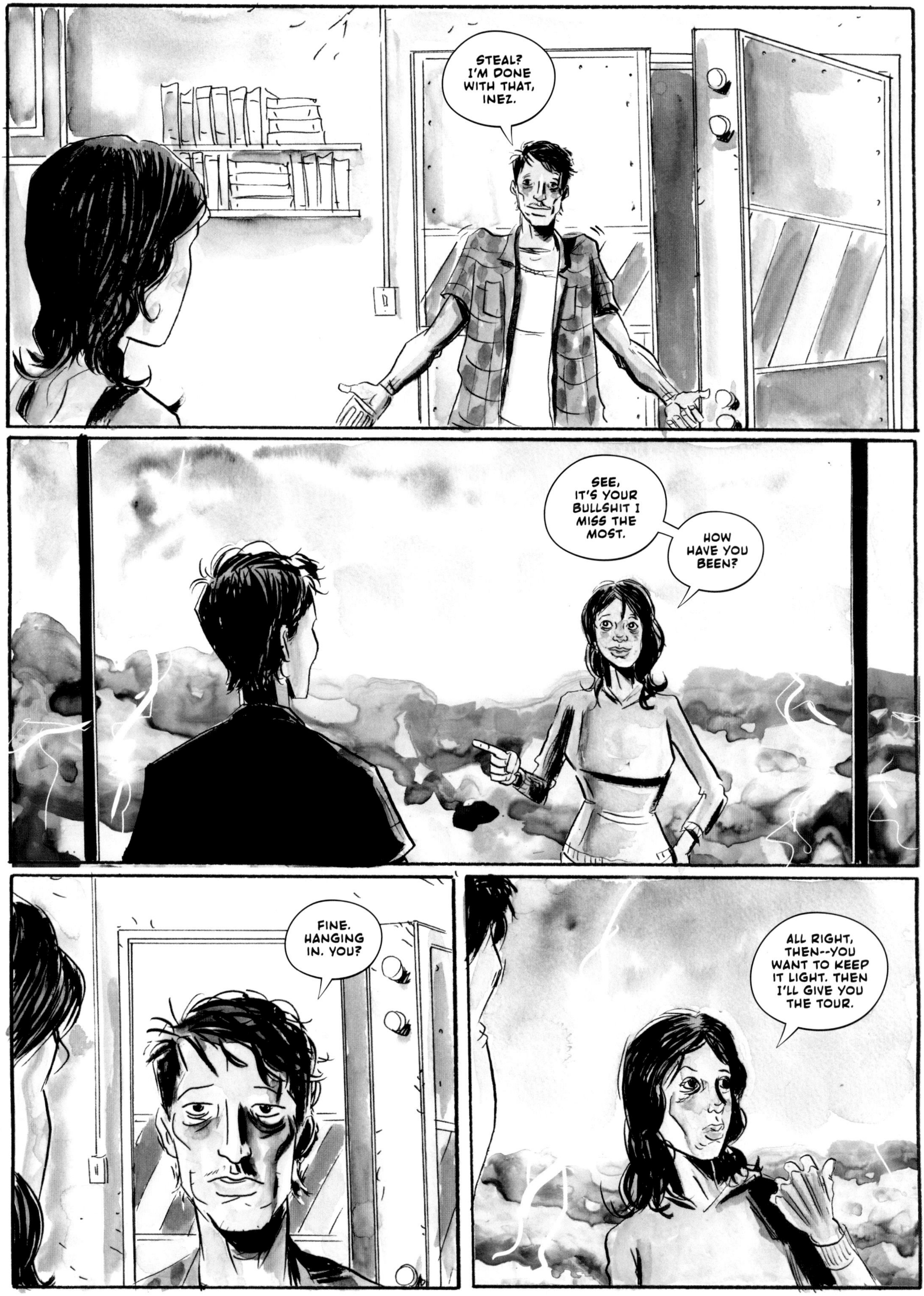
STEAL? I'M DONE WITH THAT, INEZ.
SEE, IT'S YOUR BULLSHIT I MISS THE MOST.
HOW HAVE YOU BEEN?
FINE. HANGING IN. YOU?
ALL RIGHT, THEN--YOU WANT TO KEEP IT LIGHT. THEN I'LL GIVE YOU THE TOUR.

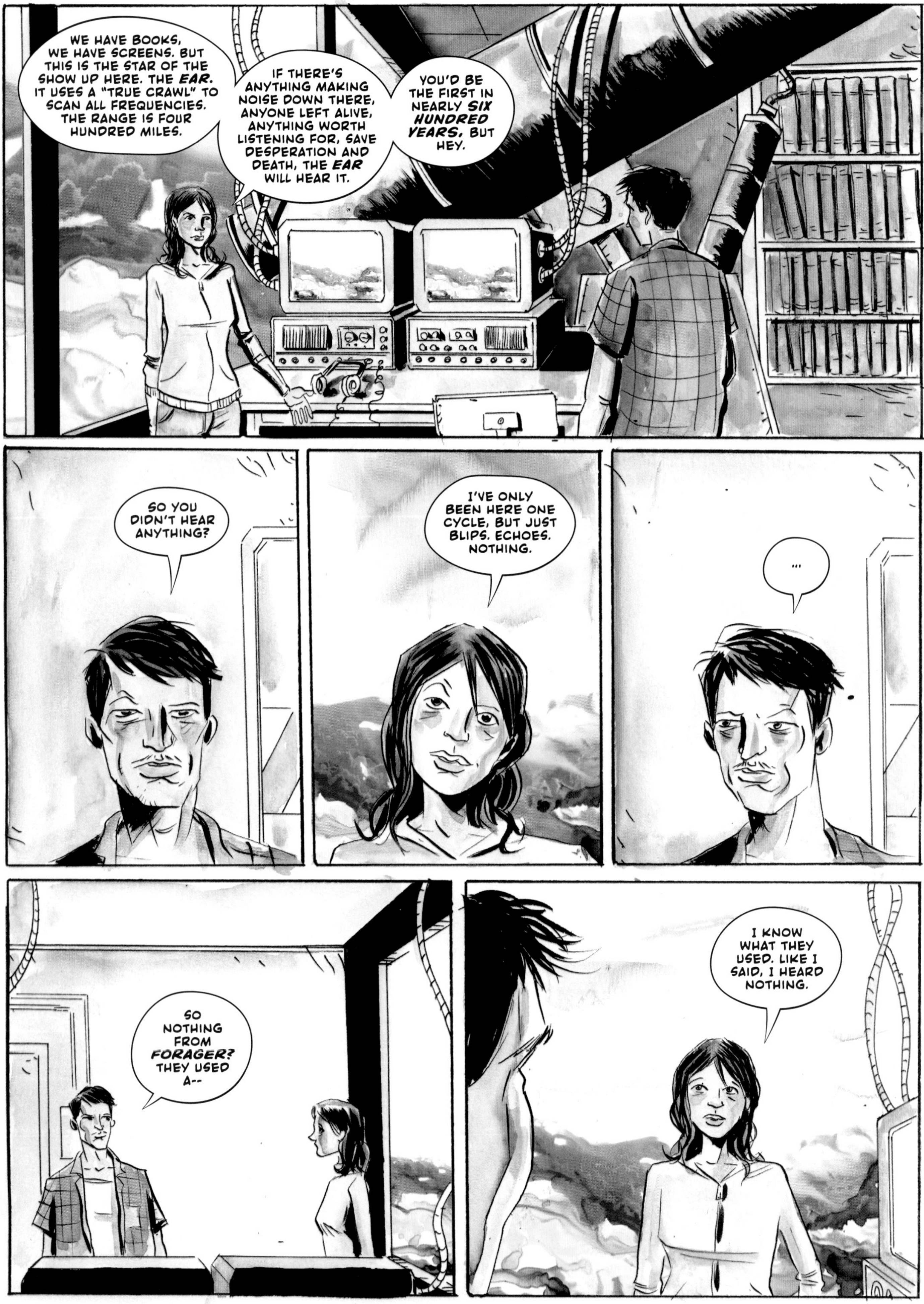
WE HAVE BOOKS, WE HAVE SCREENS. BUT THIS IS THE STAR OF THE SHOW UP HERE. THE *EAR.* IT USES A "TRUE CRAWL" TO SCAN ALL FREQUENCIES. THE RANGE IS FOUR HUNDRED MILES.
IF THERE'S ANYTHING MAKING NOISE DOWN THERE, ANYONE LEFT ALIVE, ANYTHING WORTH LISTENING FOR, SAVE DESPERATION AND DEATH, THE *EAR* WILL HEAR IT.
YOU'D BE THE FIRST IN NEARLY *SIX HUNDRED YEARS,* BUT HEY.
SO YOU DIDN'T HEAR ANYTHING?
I'VE ONLY BEEN HERE ONE CYCLE, BUT JUST BLIPS. ECHOES. NOTHING.
...
SO NOTHING FROM *FORAGER?* THEY USED A--
I KNOW WHAT THEY USED. LIKE I SAID, I HEARD NOTHING.

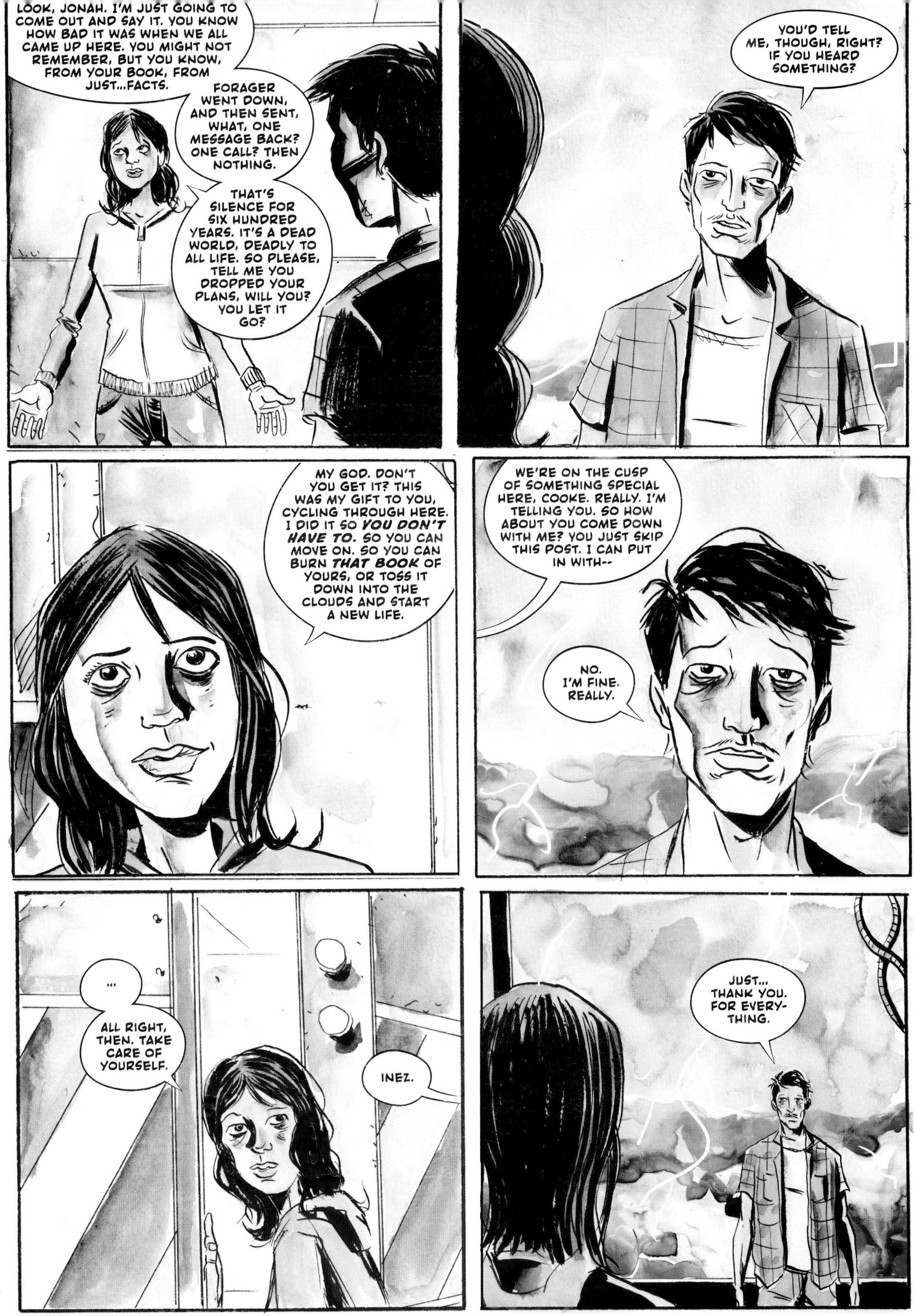
LOOK, JONAH. I'M JUST GOING TO COME OUT AND SAY IT. YOU KNOW HOW BAD IT WAS WHEN WE ALL CAME UP HERE. YOU MIGHT NOT REMEMBER, BUT YOU KNOW, FROM YOUR BOOK, FROM JUST...FACTS.
FORAGER WENT DOWN, AND THEN SENT, WHAT, ONE MESSAGE BACK? ONE CALL? THEN NOTHING.
THAT'S SILENCE FOR SIX HUNDRED YEARS. IT'S A DEAD WORLD, DEADLY TO ALL LIFE. SO PLEASE, TELL ME YOU DROPPED YOUR PLANS, WILL YOU? YOU LET IT GO?
YOU'D TELL ME, THOUGH, RIGHT? IF YOU HEARD SOMETHING?
MY GOD. DON'T YOU GET IT? THIS WAS MY GIFT TO YOU, CYCLING THROUGH HERE. I DID IT SO *YOU DON'T HAVE TO.* SO YOU CAN MOVE ON. SO YOU CAN BURN *THAT BOOK* OF YOURS, OR TOSS IT DOWN INTO THE CLOUDS AND START A NEW LIFE.
WE'RE ON THE CUSP OF SOMETHING SPECIAL HERE, COOKE. REALLY. I'M TELLING YOU. SO HOW ABOUT YOU COME DOWN WITH ME? YOU JUST SKIP THIS POST. I CAN PUT IN WITH--
NO. I'M FINE. REALLY.
...
ALL RIGHT, THEN. TAKE CARE OF YOURSELF.
INEZ.
JUST... THANK YOU. FOR EVERY-THING.

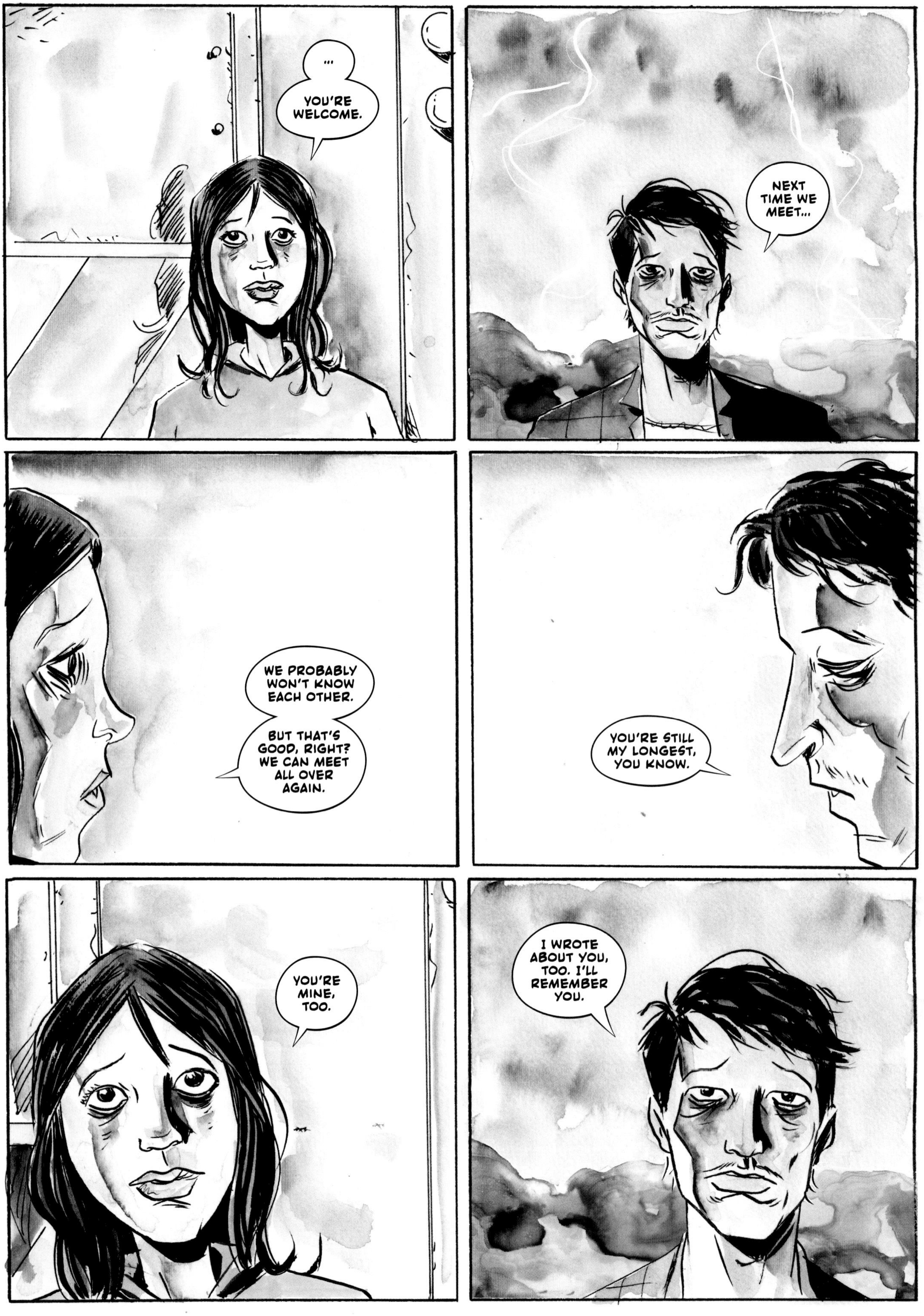
...
YOU'RE WELCOME.
NEXT TIME WE MEET...
WE PROBABLY WON'T KNOW EACH OTHER.
BUT THAT'S GOOD, RIGHT? WE CAN MEET ALL OVER AGAIN.
YOU'RE STILL MY LONGEST, YOU KNOW.
YOU'RE MINE, TOO.
I WROTE ABOUT YOU, TOO. I'LL REMEMBER YOU.

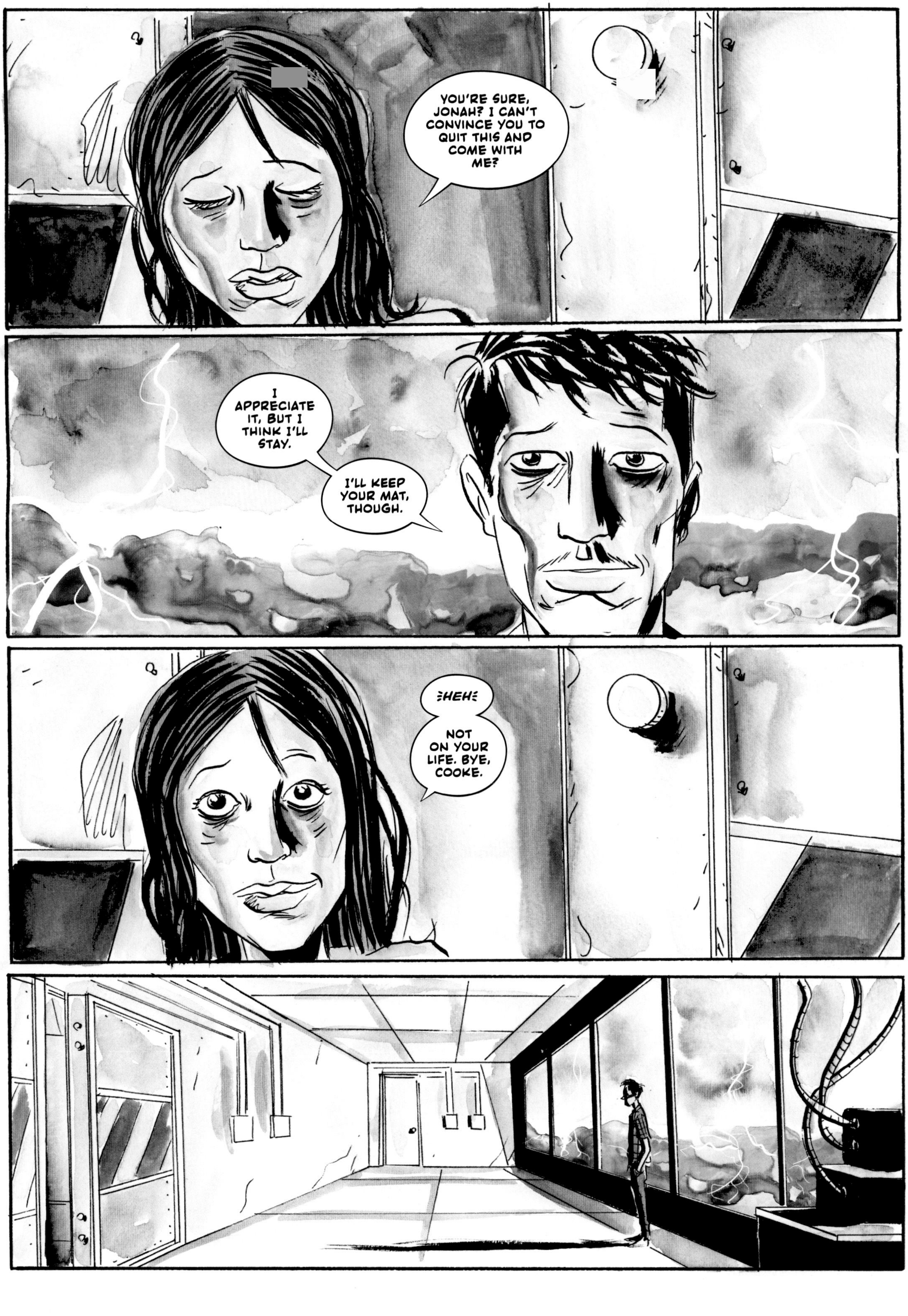
YOU'RE SURE, JONAH? I CAN'T CONVINCE YOU TO QUIT THIS AND COME WITH ME?
I APPRECIATE IT, BUT I THINK I'LL STAY.
I'LL KEEP YOUR MAT, THOUGH.
HEH
NOT ON YOUR LIFE. BYE, COOKE.

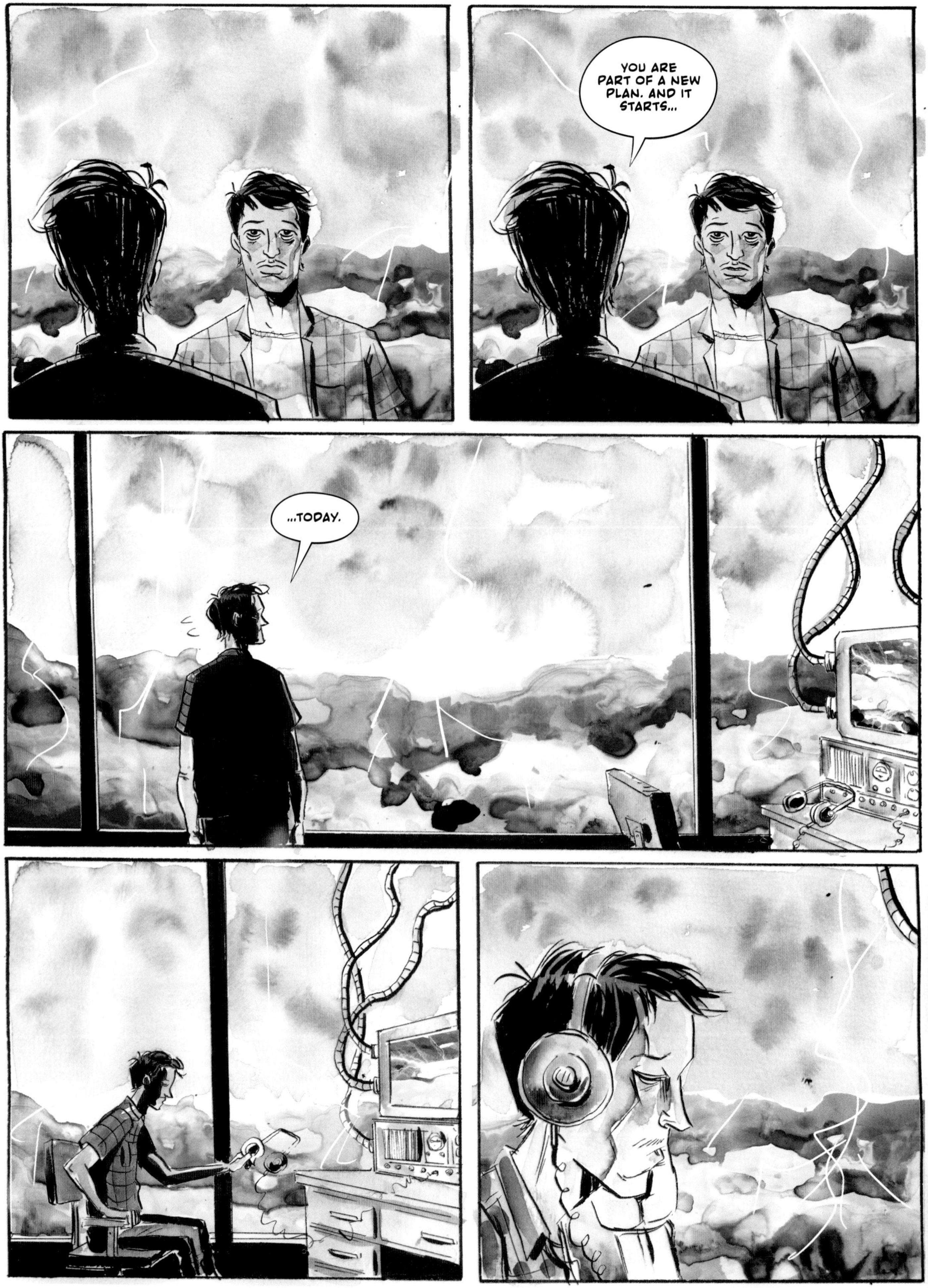
YOU ARE PART OF A NEW PLAN. AND IT STARTS...
...TODAY.

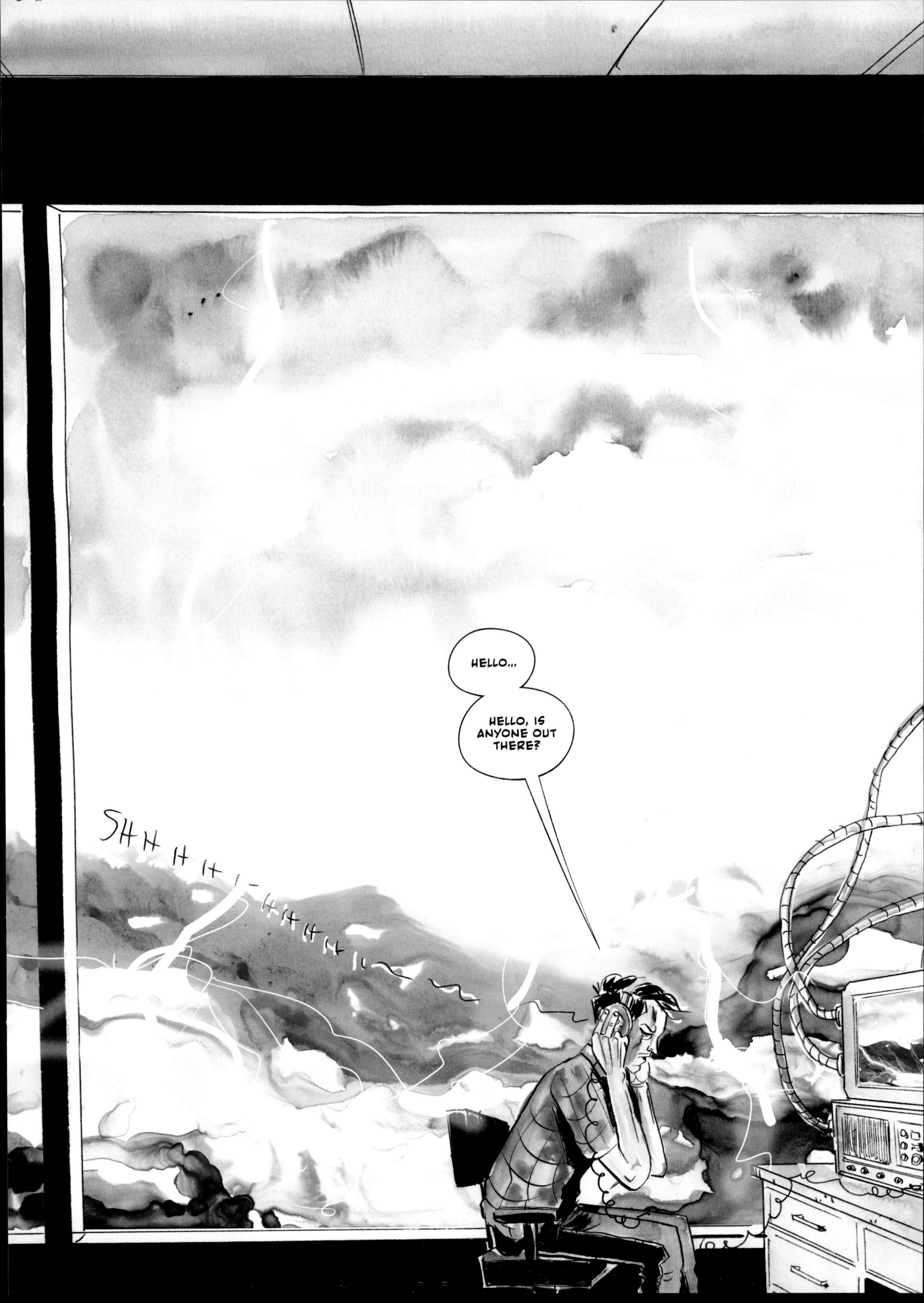
HELLO...
HELLO, IS ANYONE OUT THERE?
SHHHHH-HHHHHH~~

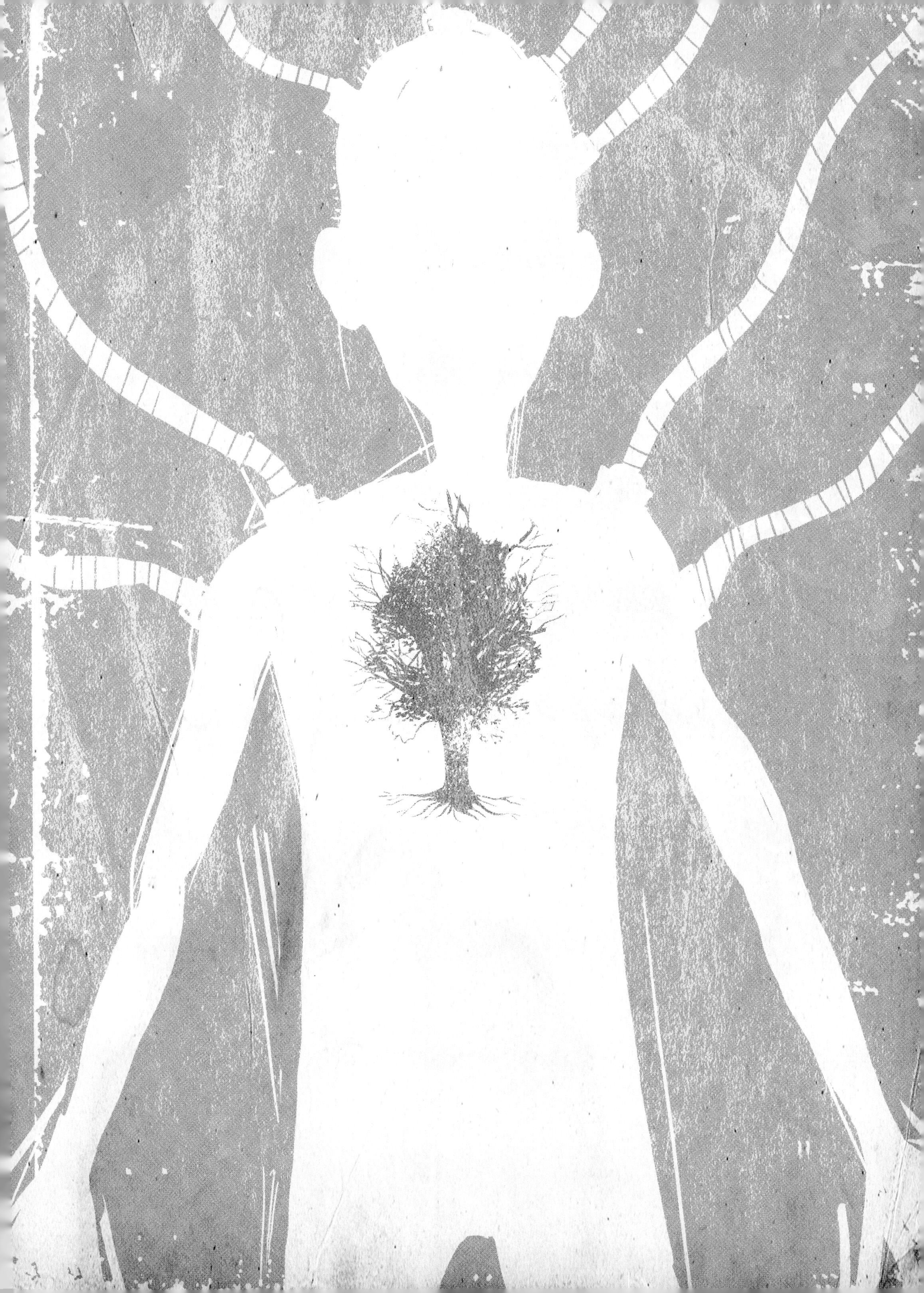

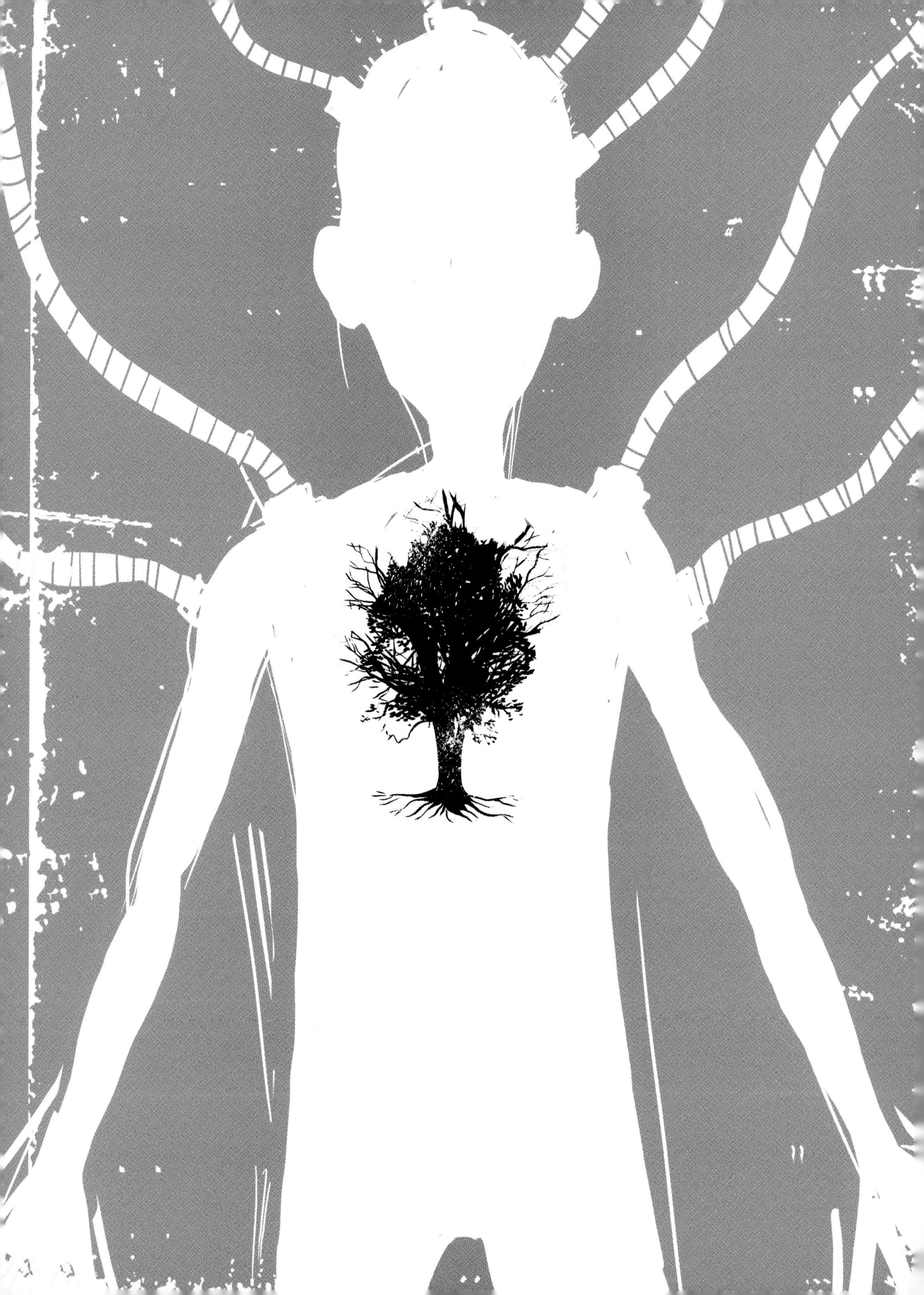

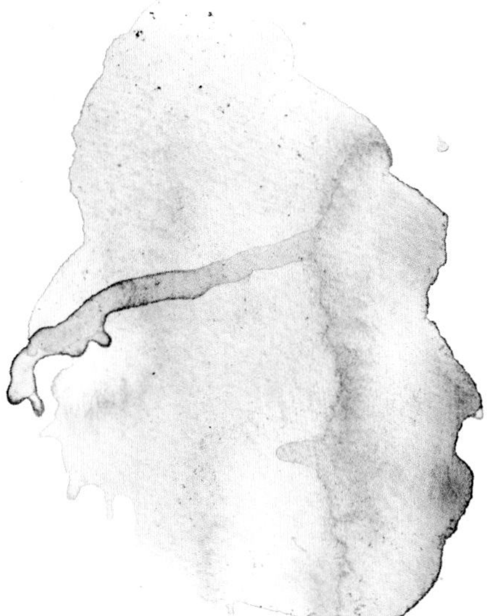

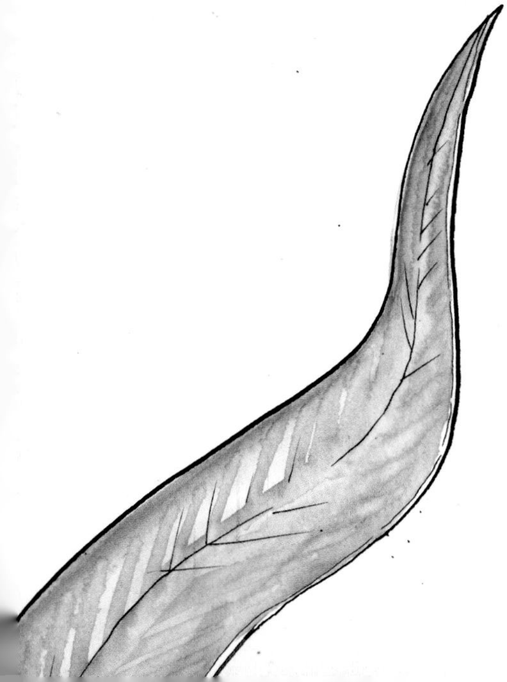

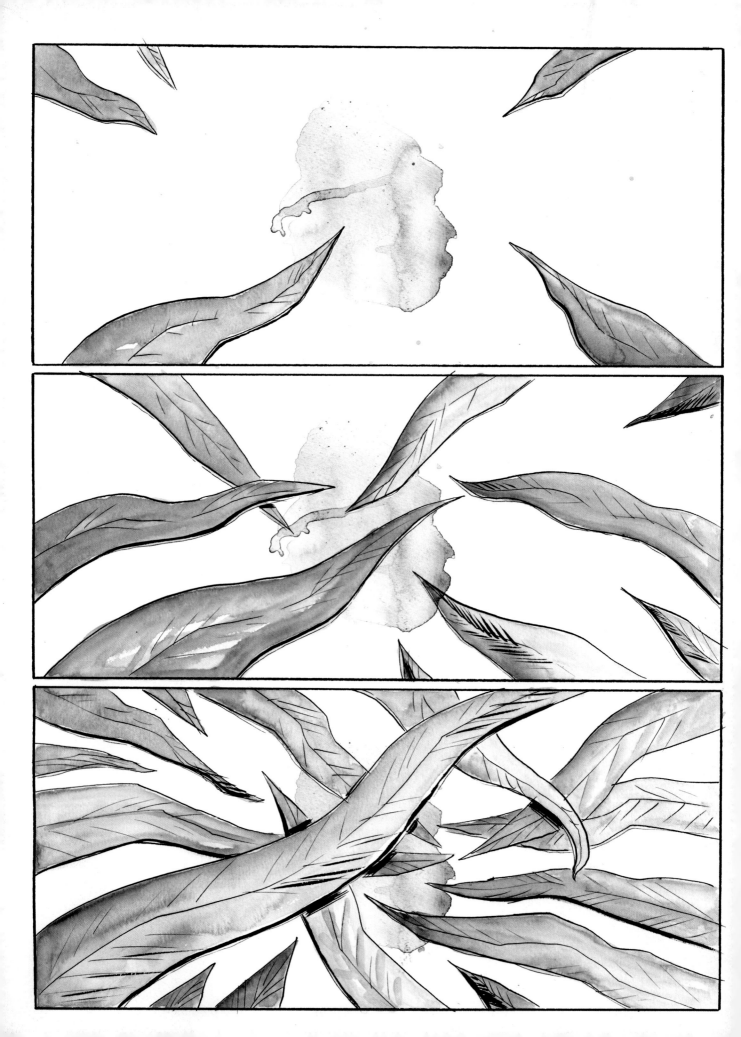

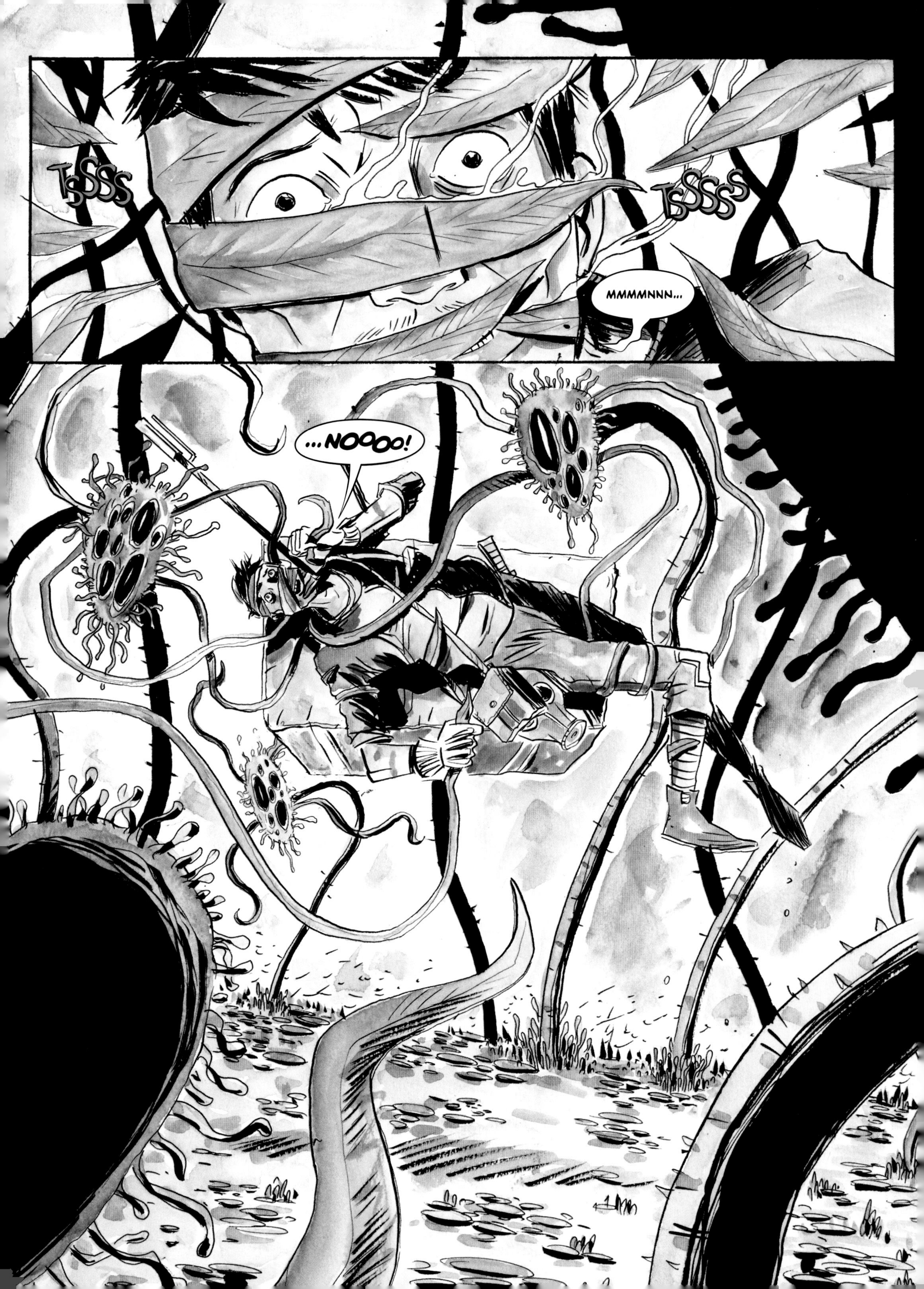
TSSSS
TSSSSS
MMMMNNN...
...NOOOO!

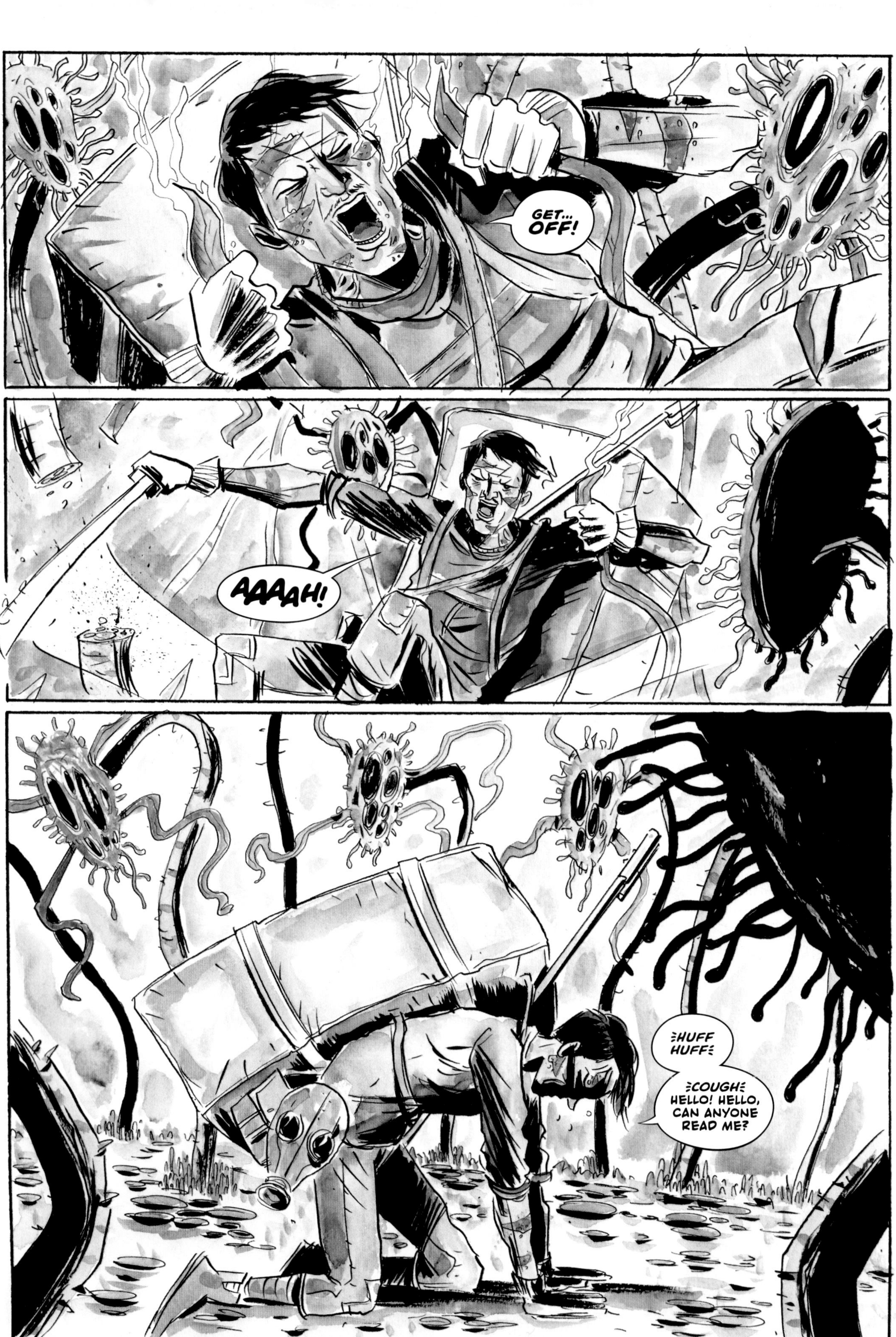
GET... OFF!
AAAAH!
HUFF HUFF
COUGH HELLO! HELLO, CAN ANYONE READ ME?

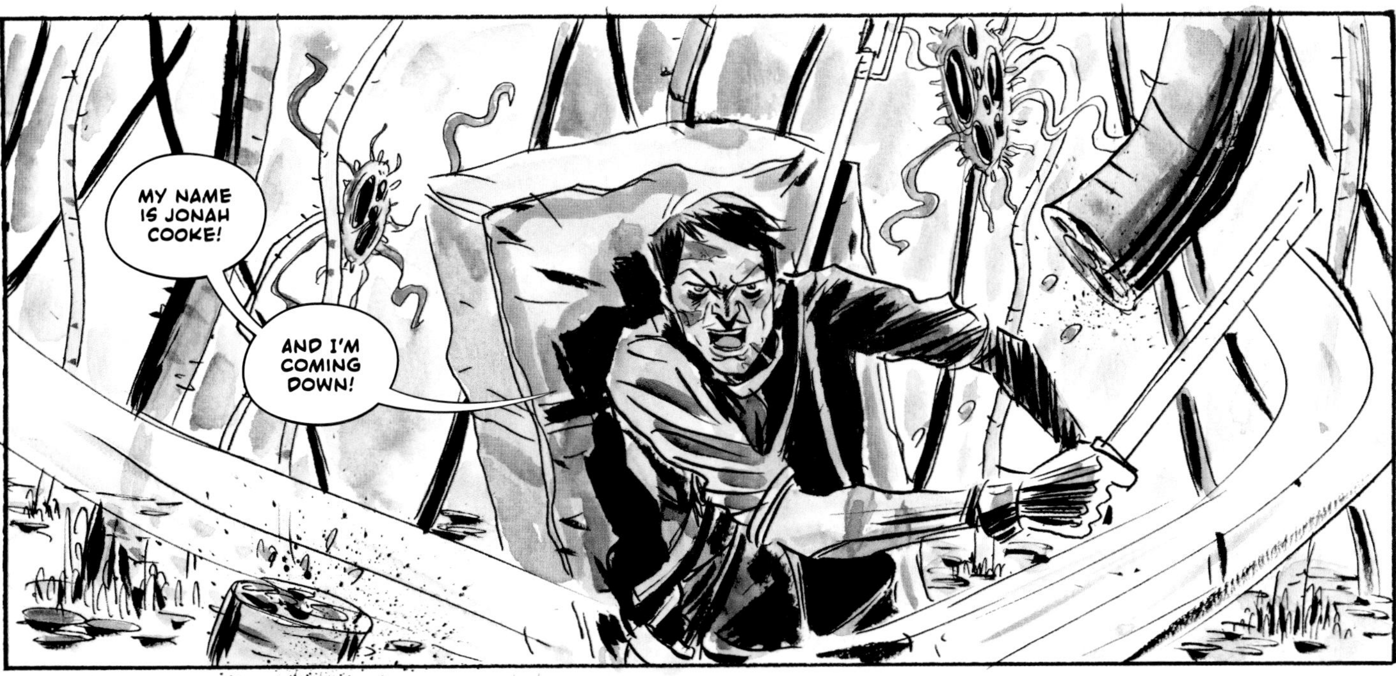
MY NAME IS JONAH COOKE!
AND I'M COMING DOWN!

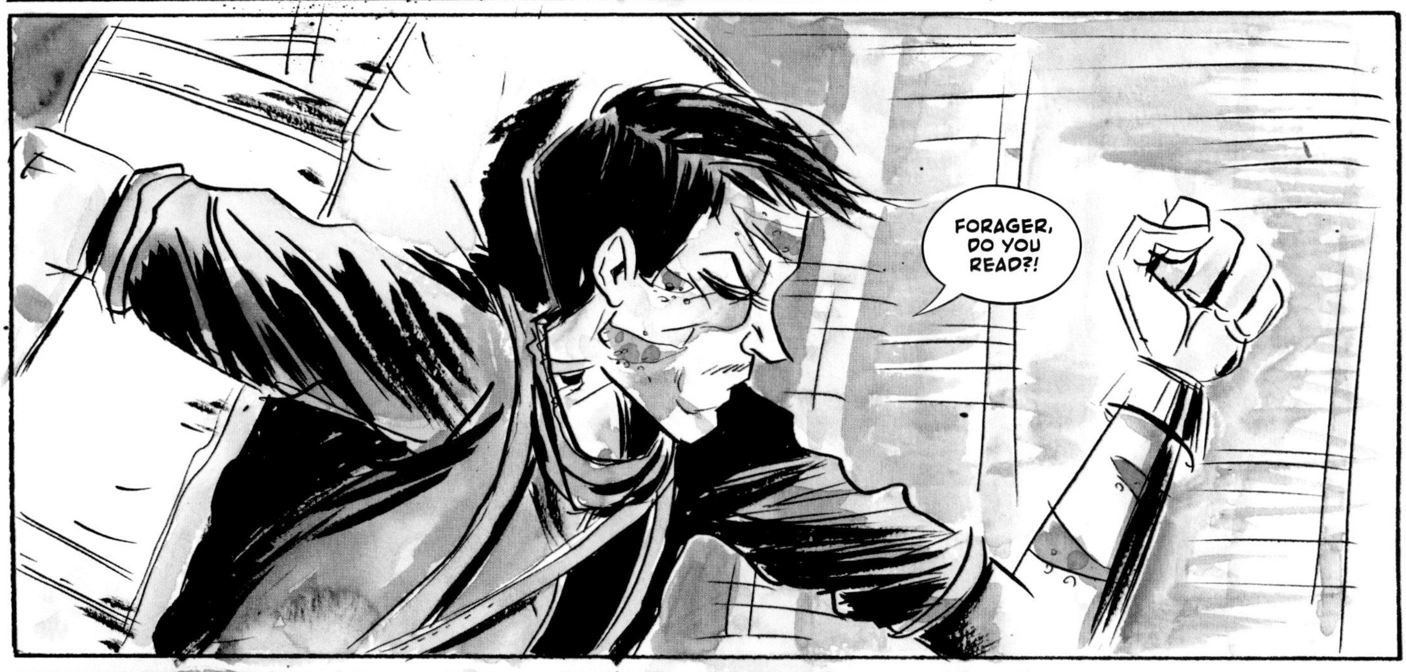
FORAGER, DO YOU READ?!

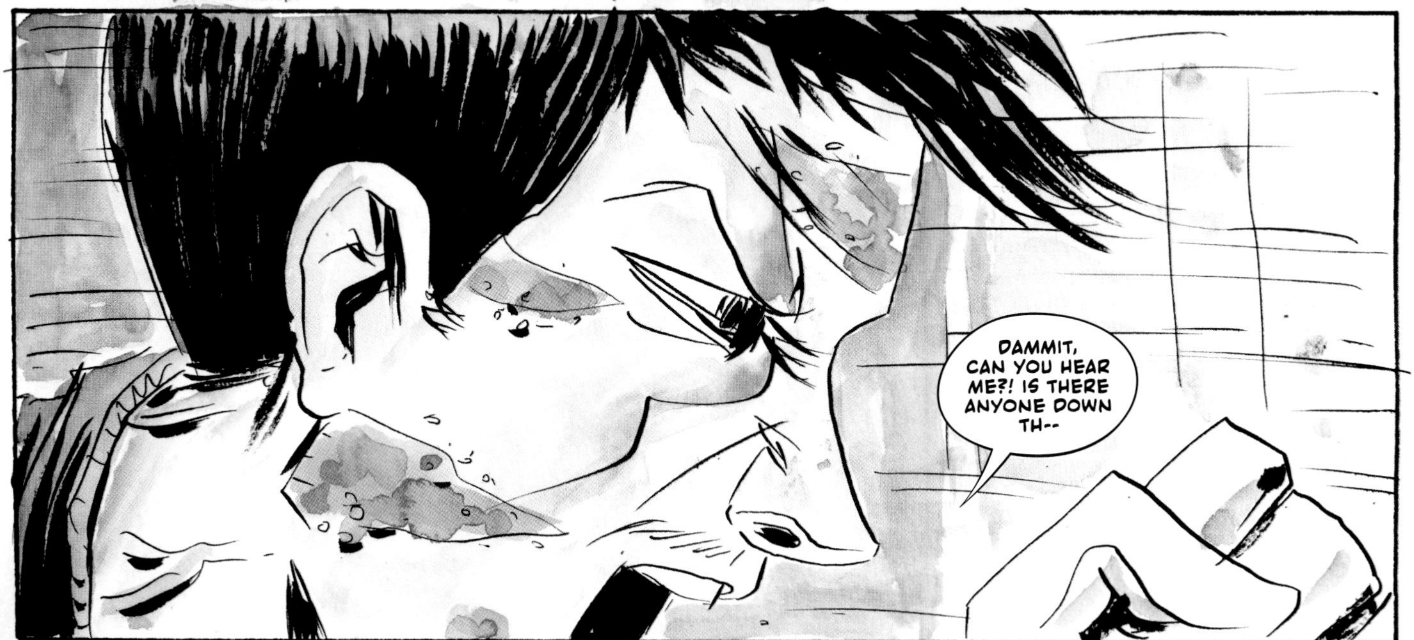
DAMMIT, CAN YOU HEAR ME?! IS THERE ANYONE DOWN TH--

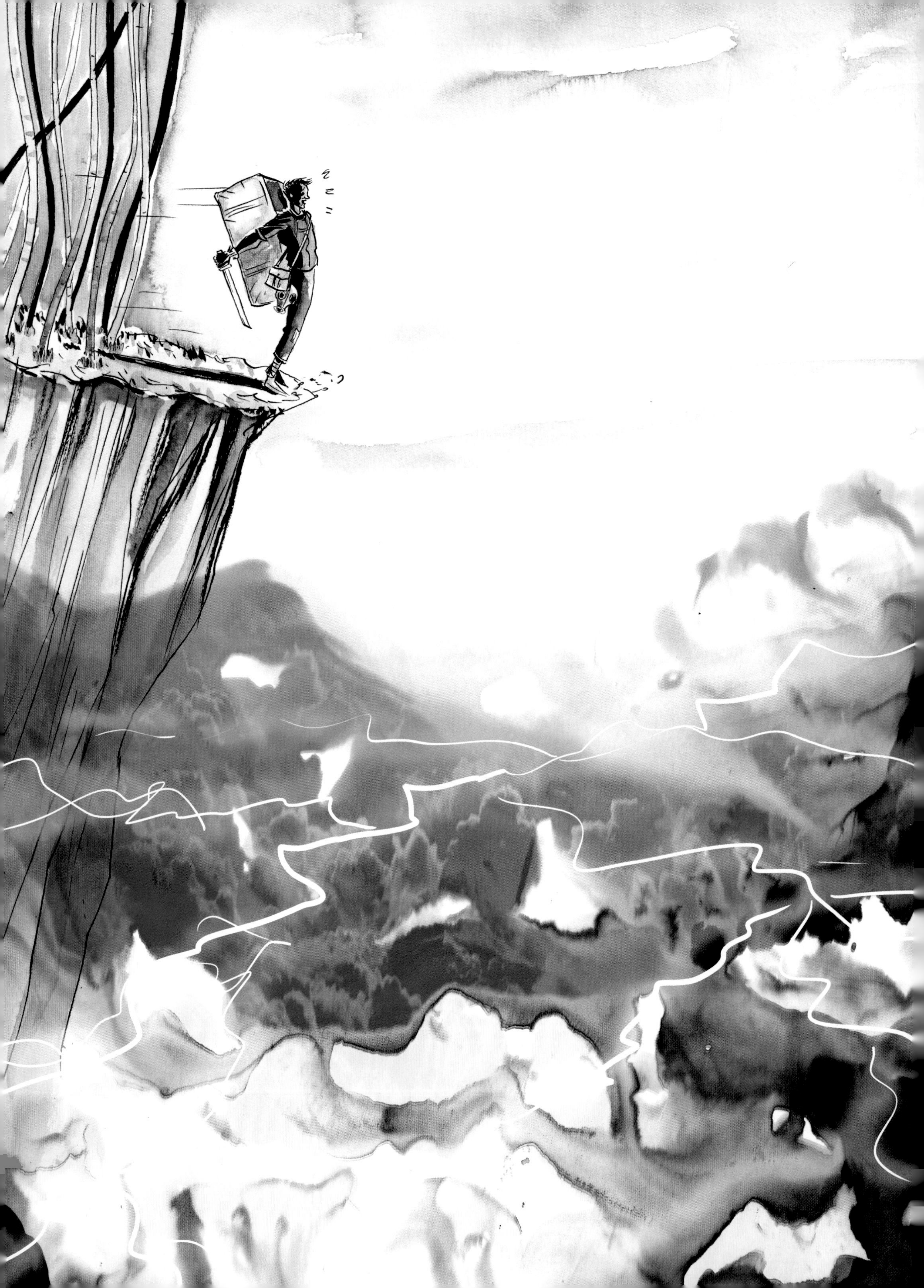

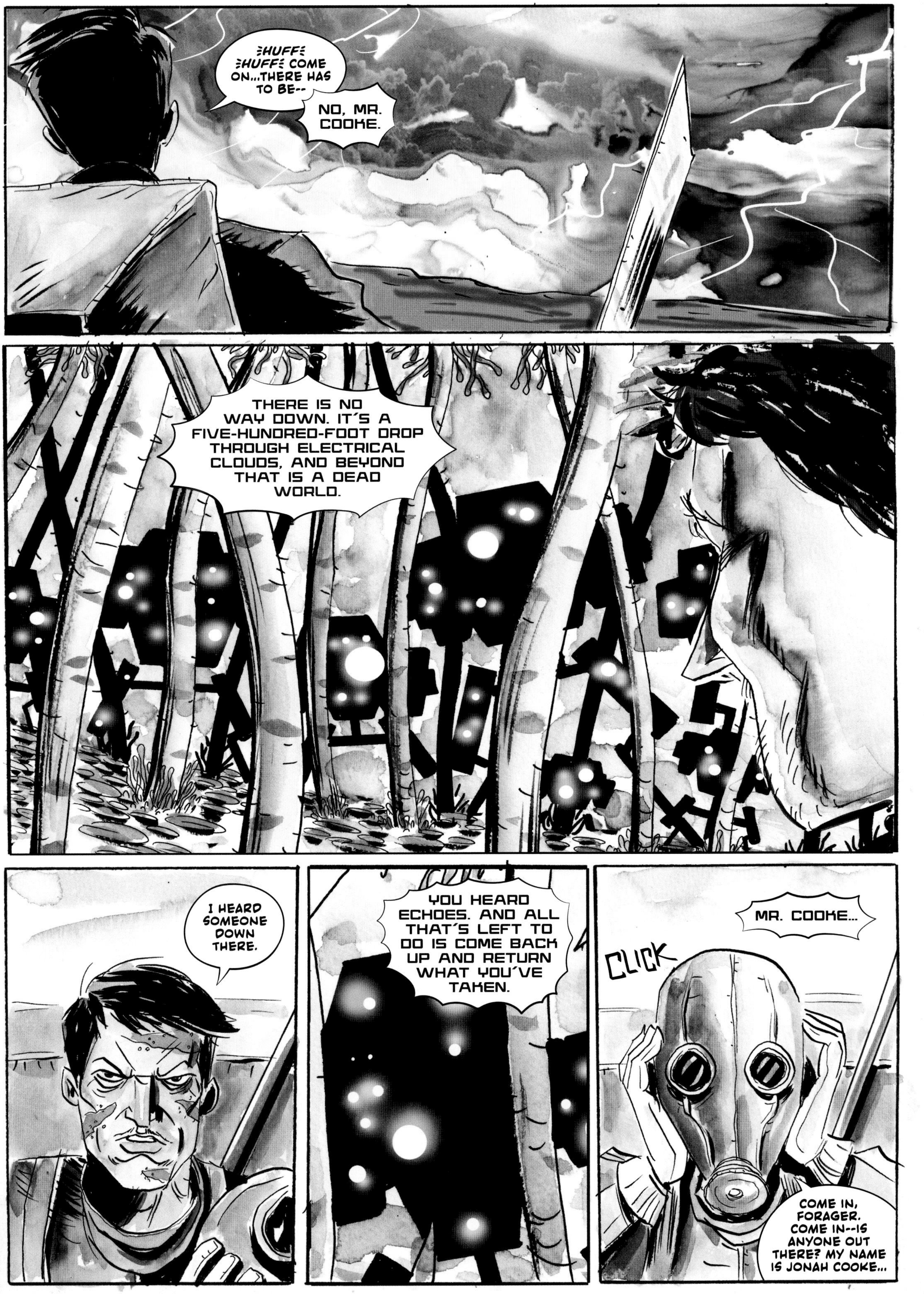

HUFF HUFF COME ON...THERE HAS TO BE--
NO, MR. COOKE.
THERE IS NO WAY DOWN. IT´S A FIVE-HUNDRED-FOOT DROP THROUGH ELECTRICAL CLOUDS, AND BEYOND THAT IS A DEAD WORLD.
I HEARD SOMEONE DOWN THERE.
YOU HEARD ECHOES. AND ALL THAT´S LEFT TO DO IS COME BACK UP AND RETURN WHAT YOU´VE TAKEN.
MR. COOKE...
CLICK
COME IN, FORAGER. COME IN--IS ANYONE OUT THERE? MY NAME IS JONAH COOKE...

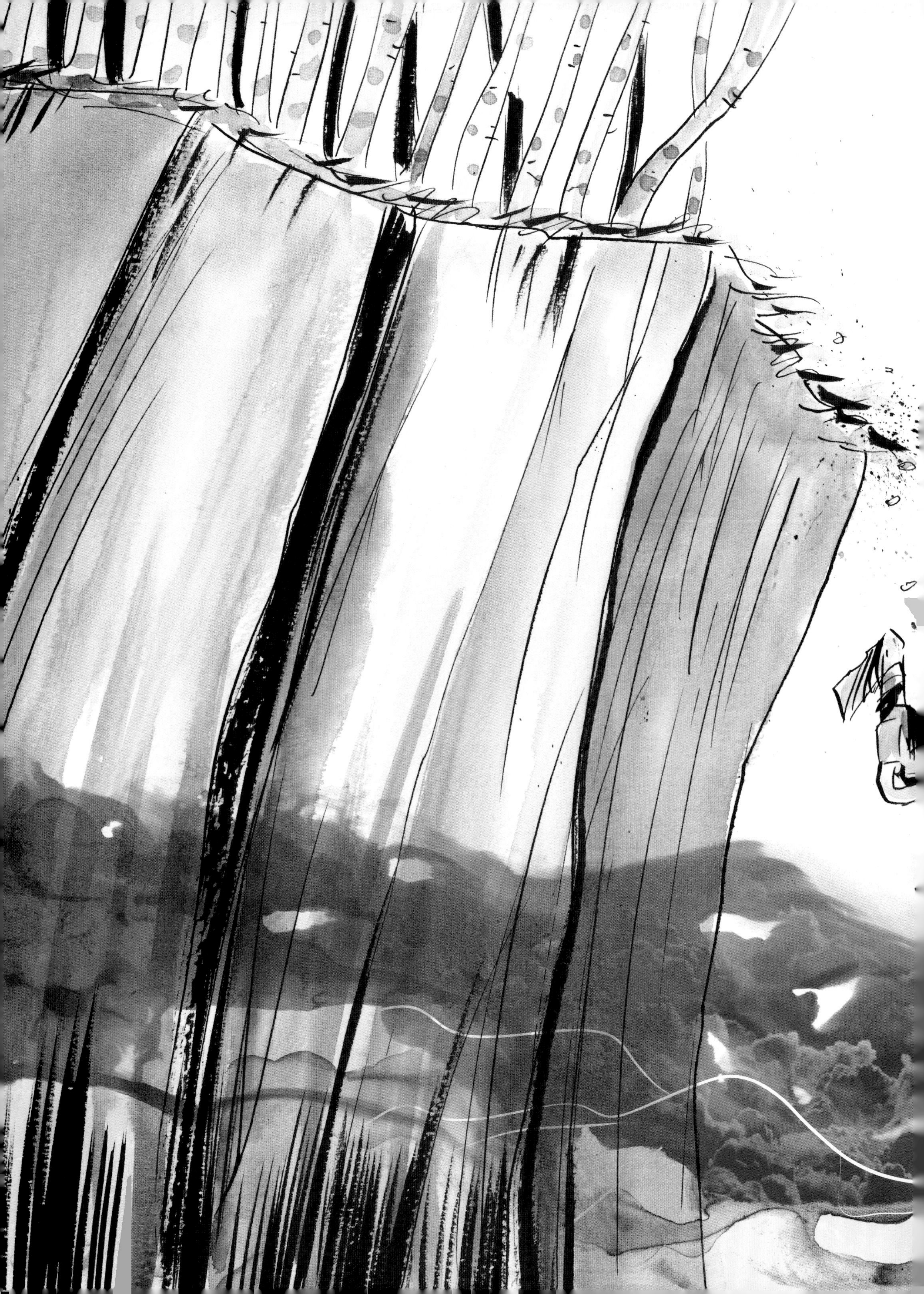

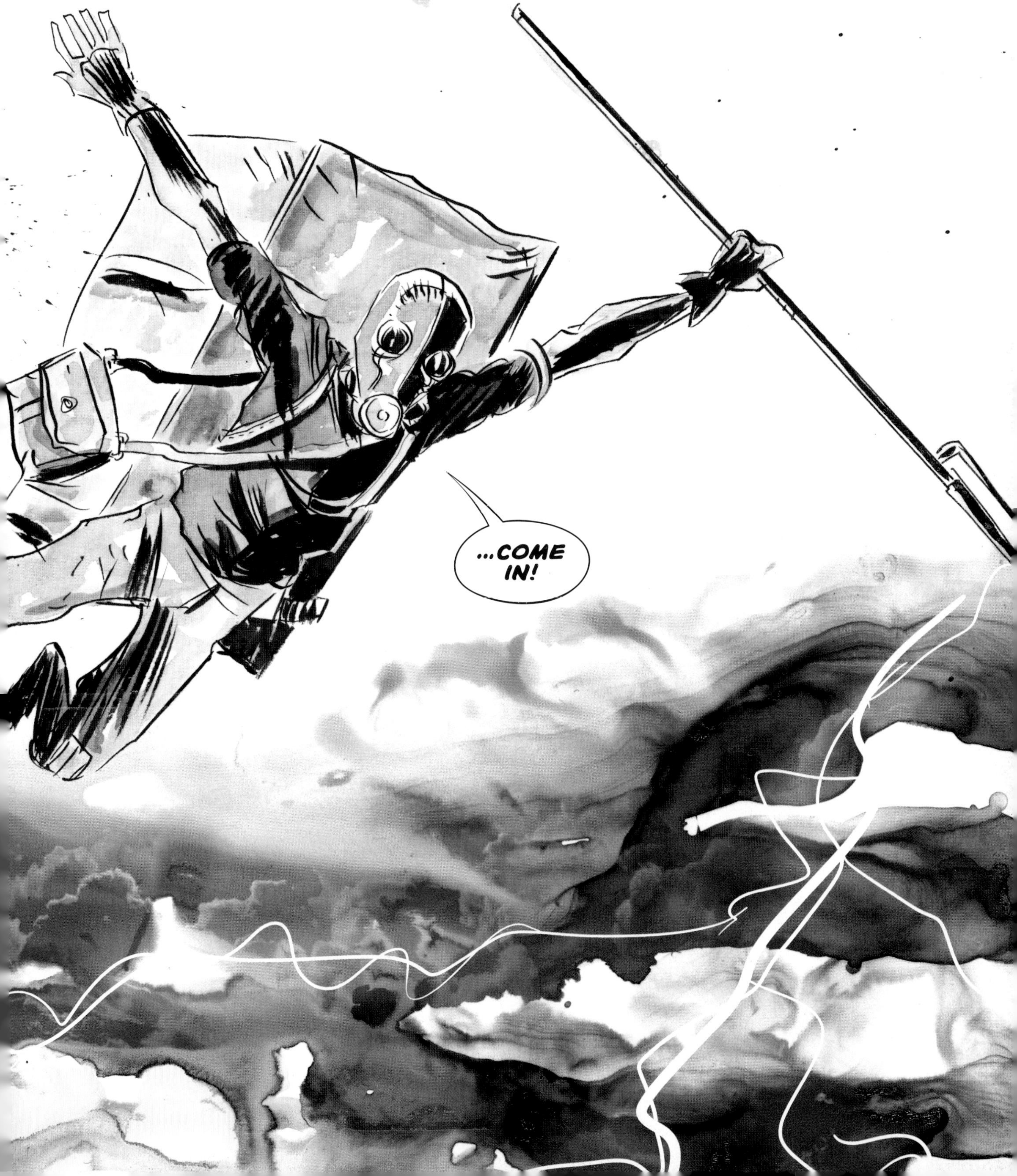
...COME IN!

PART TWO
THE GOODBYE SUIT

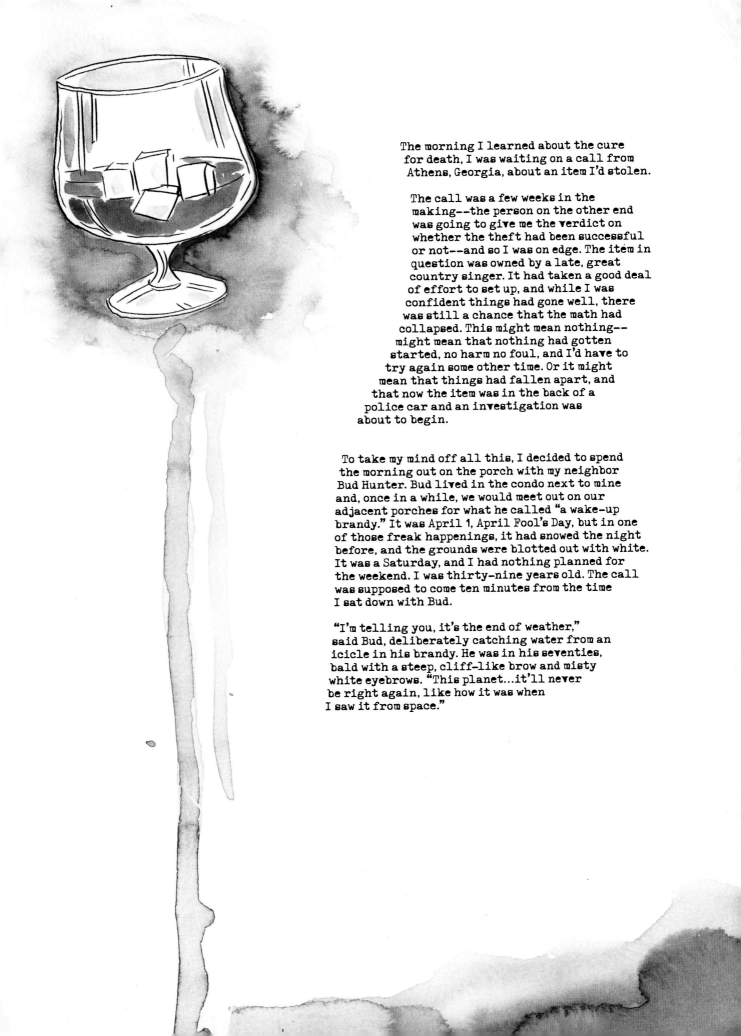

The morning I learned about the cure
for death, I was waiting on a call from
Athens, Georgia, about an item I'd stolen.

The call was a few weeks in the
making--the person on the other end
was going to give me the verdict on
whether the theft had been successful
or not--and so I was on edge. The item in
question was owned by a late, great
country singer. It had taken a good deal
of effort to set up, and while I was
confident things had gone well, there
was still a chance that the math had
collapsed. This might mean nothing--
might mean that nothing had gotten
started, no harm no foul, and I'd have to
try again some other time. Or it might
mean that things had fallen apart, and
that now the item was in the back of a
police car and an investigation was
about to begin.

To take my mind off all this, I decided to spend
the morning out on the porch with my neighbor
Bud Hunter. Bud lived in the condo next to mine
and, once in a while, we would meet out on our
adjacent porches for what he called "a wake-up
brandy." It was April 1, April Fool's Day, but in one
of those freak happenings, it had snowed the night
before, and the grounds were blotted out with white.
It was a Saturday, and I had nothing planned for
the weekend. I was thirty-nine years old. The call
was supposed to come ten minutes from the time
I sat down with Bud.

"I'm telling you, it's the end of weather,"
said Bud, deliberately catching water from an
icicle in his brandy. He was in his seventies,
bald with a steep, cliff-like brow and misty
white eyebrows. "This planet...it'll never
be right again, like how it was when
I saw it from space."

Bud had been an astronaut--an actual astronaut in the early 1970s.

He'd flown on two missions, one to the short-lived US space station Skylab in 1973,
where he'd helped discover coronal holes in the sun, and another in 1975, which had
almost killed everyone involved.

I have nothing in my notes on the name of this second mission--if I knew it I've
forgotten--but it was apparently well known at the time it happened. The reason is
that there'd been an freak accident on the way up. An oxygen tank had blown,
venting gas and crippling the command console, forcing the men to use the service
module as a kind of sealed-off life raft.

The accident caused a communications blackout with Earth as well. And, for a good
few hours, the men were adrift in the dark.

Three men sealed up in a compartment hardly bigger than an elevator, hurtling
deeper into space, with no end in sight.

To get back to Earth, Bud and his crew had to perform the same dangerous maneuver the crew of the Apollo 13 had executed--they had to slingshot around the dark side of the moon in order to get enough thrust to achieve a return trajectory.

They'd managed all this in relative darkness and radio silence, circling the farthest lunar curve on January 15, 1975. Their route actually took them farther out into space than any mission in human history--to this day, Bud and his crewmates hold the record for greatest distance from Earth by a manned spacecraft.

"I was at the south end of the module, too," Bud has said to me on many occasions. "Meaning, I was the farthest of us from Earth by a good five feet, the farthest distance any living thing has EVER traveled from this rock."

Once, I asked him if he was scared during that blacked-out period, the three of them alone in that steel bubble, adrift on a sea of death.

The biggest risk, he'd explained, was that they'd come around the moon so quickly that the momentum would fling them off course, causing them to miss the Earth and float off into darkness forever.

"Sure, we were scared," he'd said. "Tommy, though, he started this gag that we'd be LUCKY to float off. We'd wake up in a thousand years, on a planet of curvy green alien girls. We talked about it the whole way around, to take our minds off it."

Bud gets together with the men from that mission a couple times a year--Tommy Gunnerson and Will Webb. In fact, looking back, they were supposed to get together on the day in question, the day I learned about the cure for dying. Inside Bud's condo were chips and beer. Pictures from their flight, framed on the kitchen counter. They always wore their NASA windbreakers and hats when they got together. They'd call me over--they were friendly that way--and we'd get drunk and they'd tell me the story about flying past the dark side of the moon and how they came THIS CLOSE to being kings of a sexy female alien race.

"Think of it," Bud would say to us all, getting to his feet, spreading his arms..."They're all around us, women, eight feet tall and green."

"Five bosoms," Tommy would say through his oxygen tube, and laugh-cough.

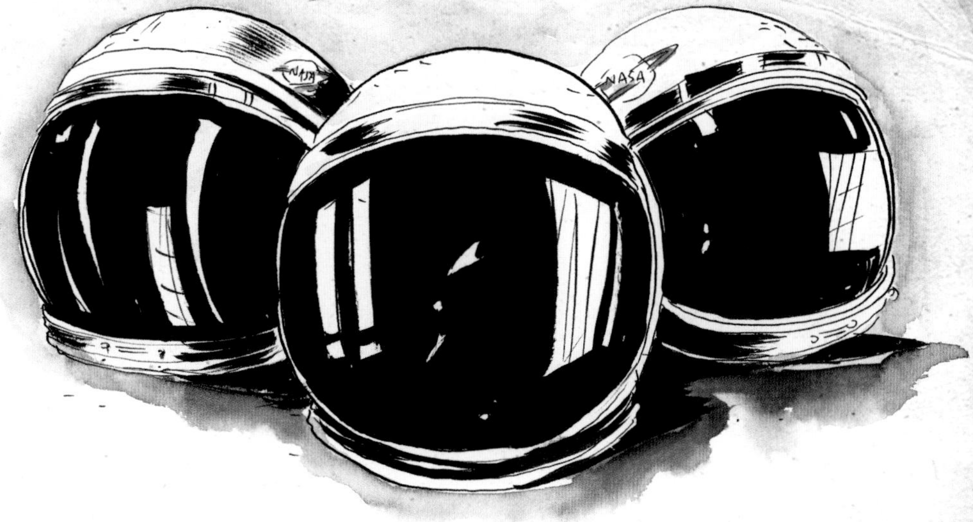
NASA
NASA

In my condo were the helmets Bud and his crew had worn on their failed mission. I'd acquired them a couple weeks earlier from a small museum in Texas near the old launch complex--stolen them, to be fair--and I'd been waiting to give them to the three men since their last visit. I thought about going in and giving them to Bud now, showing him his at least, which was in the best shape of the three, but I decided to wait. He knew I was a part-time thief, and he could get moral on me sometimes. With his friends there, drunk and happy, I was sure he'd simply be glad to be reunited with his helmet.

I checked my watch.

My call should have come by now.

Most people, when they
think of thieves,
picture all sorts
of adventure.

A man in black descending like a spider through a web of
lasers. Or someone in a speedboat holding a flute of
champagne, racing away from a moonlit wharf while the
police are left behind to curse and kick the pilings. In
the early twenty-first century, though, being a thief
wasn't about glamour or adventure. I wish it had been. I
wish it had been hushed conversations on some Italian
lake, or blueprints projected on the wall of a chalet.

But theft just before the
cure--before A.D. 1--was
nothing glamorous. It was
plain people behind plain
computer screens; it was
Post-its and mugs of old coffee.
Because theft back then was
largely theoretical--logic
problems and systems analyses.
For the most part, it took place
in temporary forums on the
darknet called "tables."

Momentary TOR/Torch
rooms that appeared and
vanished in minutes,
collapsing into code.

In these forums, the "head of table" would pose a problem to rest of the members, and those members would compete to solve the problem, sometimes for fun, sometimes for real. If you stole in theory, you were called "bread," on account of there being no risk, everything free. If you stole for real, you were "steak," as you had an investment, or stake in the transaction.

For example:
Head of table says: "A Touch of Class, Just a Touch Tho" a thoroughbred stud (registered closed book). Currently in Miami, Dream Breed Stables. Transport to Hawaii, port of Kawahee by April 19 of current year.

What the H.O.T. is asking is: Can you steal me a racehorse housed in Miami, and deliver it to Hawaii three days from now?

Or Head of table says: "Knockout Mouse" MUS Surditatem. Prevaris Lab. Salt Lake City. Corporate. Steal and destroy by below date.

Here the bread/steak is a laboratory animal being used in gene sequencing. H.O.T. needs it out and dead by tomorrow.

It was never something I set out to do, become a thief.

After my mother passed away, I finished high school and then went to community college near home to help take care of my father. I studied medicine. My mother's decline had been ugly, the way her body had loosened up part by part, like a spring toy unlocking, all the while the baby trapped inside...Studying medicine felt right at first. I would help find a cure for what she had, too. I would push the thing back by a bit--an inch, maybe a fraction of an inch.

But by the second term, I was falling behind. I couldn't concentrate. Not on organic or bio. It all felt like studying maps and guides to a country I never wanted to visit, and little by little I started slipping away. I visited with my father, who'd moved to an apartment not far from our old house. We'd talk politics, he'd go on about the dismal slide of everything toward resignation, the lack of activism in the kids in his classes. I dated, had some girlfriends, but nothing ever took.

The black water was just always...there. A transparency. I'd be with someone I liked, really liked, sitting with them on the couch, watching some dumb show, and she'd put her head on my chest and I'd kiss the top of her hair and I'd feel good, but then it'd come over me, this chill, and I'd look down and not see the head of the girl I liked but a physical thing, hair and scalp and blood and bone and electricity--a collection of cells and mechanisms, which was what I was, too, a thing, ending at my nose, my feet, my fingertips. A shock from a socket could change me. A knife through my eye would change me. Something could already be malfunctioning. Something could be unlocking inside and then boom, down, any second now and my heart would race and I'd start to sweat and grind my teeth, and say to myself you are a whole, not parts, but parts is what I felt like, a tiny being driving some huge, failing machine of a body, staring through the portals of my eyes.

Some nights, I took to driving out to the houses I'd visited with my mother years before--the mansions on the water. A couple had been torn down and rebuilt, a few had been dragged even farther back from the shore. The beach had receded farther, and on certain evenings I could see what looked like the tops of two, maybe three train cars poking up through the surf. Now and then, I'd go into a house, walk around, open a fridge.

The egg house hadn't changed much. They'd added a pool in the basement, a narrow lane of water cut through marble, but overall, the house looked the same as it had years before. The Russian was still there, following his routine.

It was on my second or third visit I started taking things from the egg house.

I told myself I was taking them to remember happier times, as mementos, but really, even then I knew it was about something else.

At first I stole small objects.

A box of shells from the bathroom.

A blown glass tumbler from the bar cart.

It took me a while to get up the courage to steal THE LAND OF MILK OF AND HONEY.

I knew I could likely just take it and run, let the alarm go off behind me (if there was an alarm at all), but that wasn't what I wanted. My idea was to create a replica of the piece and switch it out. As I said, though, the work wasn't really a painting so much as a sculptural diorama, so the challenge was reproducing it. I researched 3D printing and found that if I scanned the dimensions of the canvas, I could create a mold of its general topography--not perfect, but still--and print a copy out of a wood polymer filament. From there, I could hire a student from the graduate art department to create the right epoxy, paint the mold in, grind, and so on. In hindsight, all this seems insanely clumsy and sloppy. Had I known then how easy it was to replicate paint hues--how even complicated or unevenly mixed colors can be mirrored perfectly by the same basic programs used in home improvement stores, and brushstrokes can literally be "written" on to a canvas by simple software and an operating brush--I would have done it myself, but like I said, I was new to it all.

By October I had a working replica of the piece and was ready to try for the original. I was twenty-two years old and, looking back, I should have been nervous, like I had been with the Quad so many years earlier, but I simply wasn't. That first time at B and D, I'd been terrified, I was sweating, my heart was pounding hard enough that my pulse actually hurt, the blood throbbing in my hands, my feet. This time, I was nervous, but above all, I was just curious to see if I could pull it off.

I drove out to the house with my replica wrapped in bubble tape and walked in through the same glass doors my mother and I always used. By now I'd learned that the art in this room was not alarmed after all, and I removed THE LAND OF MILK AND HONEY without incident.

I was just hanging my replica on the wall when the Russian walked in.

In all the time I'd been to this house, he had never, ever entered. But now here he was.

He'd followed me in through the glass doors and was standing there in the midday sun in his fur hat. He was leaning on a cane, something I'd never seen him do, and he was breathing hard, like he'd hurried here. I had the strange feeling he'd been waiting for this moment for a long time.

I looked down at the painting, the real one, THE LAND OF MILK AND HONEY. I went to pick it up but the Russian stopped me.

"The real one," he said, pointing to the replica of the painting. "You leave it and get out."

I tried to explain. "I'm sorry, the real one is--"

But the Russian hissed and jabbed the cane at the air between us, as though stabbing my words dead, mid-flight. I noticed for the first time that his fur hat had a small brim in front, like a visor. He was still breathing hard.

"Leave that one where you found it," he said, meaning, leave the fake painting in place of the real one, "and just...leave."

I nodded, grateful that he was letting me go.

I took the real painting from the ground and left. As I hurried across the lawn, a thrill rose in me. I'd done it. By luck, sure, but I'd done it anyway! And right there, crossing the grass to my car, it suddenly hit me, why I'd done what I'd done.

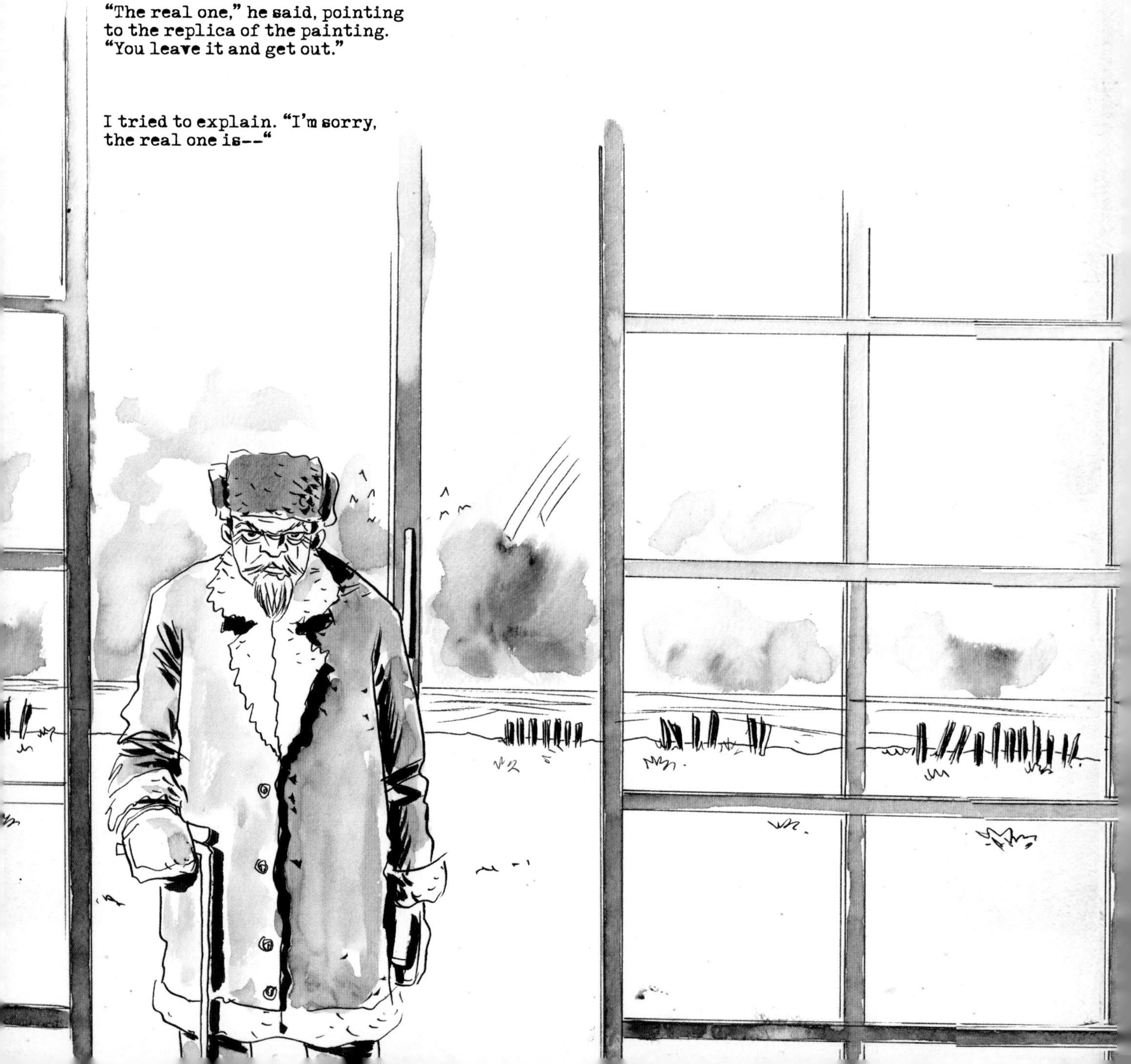

I understood in that moment that I hadn't stolen the painting for memories, or out of
nostalgia. That was all an excuse. I had stolen it for the deep, specific thrill of
removing the thing from the intractable, steel system that contained it--not just
contained it, but imbued it with meaning, gave it its role in the world. I was removing it
from the rules of its life, like taking a word out of a paragraph without anyone knowing,
replacing it with a stand-in. The real thing had escaped, had been rescued, and no one
knew. I saw now that even the Quad I'd taken--even that--hadn't been about the Quad
itself. It had been about secretly recording my life; the theft was about squirreling
away precious moments, hiding them from the slide of time, or slide of memory, keeping
them safe under my bed from the math of the universe.

Theft was a form of magic--I saw that now; a theft was a feat that eluded common perception and, more than this, hinted at the fallibility of the physical bonds of this world.
We're escapists, in essence, thieves and magicians, testing for holes in the system. We
look for ways out of boxes, locked, sinking, air-tight boxes headed deeper into the dark.
Perhaps it's no surprise then that so many magicians throughout history had obsessions
with death. Houdini swore to be the first to give evidence of life after death. David
Copperfield purchased an island in the Archepelgros that's supposedly home to a
fountain of youth for vegetation. Put a dead leaf in, and it comes back to life.

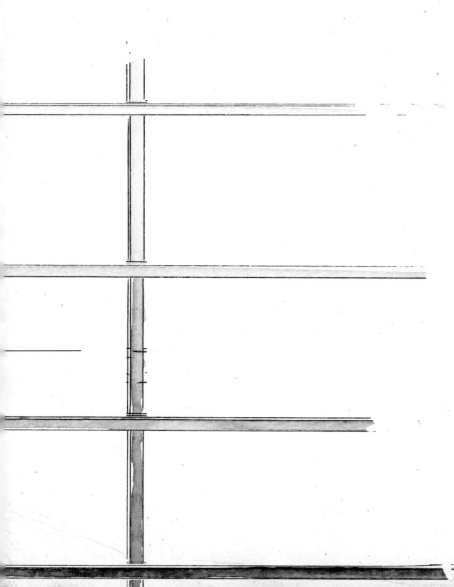

From there, stealing just
became something I did for
myself.

I ended up learning about
moving the art I stole (at
first, it was all art) from the
graduate student who'd helped
me replicate THE LAND OF MILK
AND HONEY. She told me about the
right places to go, the sites and
rooms where people trafficked in
all things stolen. And when I say
all things, I mean all things.

See, people always assume what the head
of table most often challenged thieves like
me to steal were priceless works of art. Some
painting under heavy guard in a museum in a remote
corner of the world. But, in fact, these sorts of prizes were never
that hard to get. Look at the Isabella Stewart Gardner Museum theft, or the Musée
d'Art Moderne de la Ville de Paris heist. Really, all you had to do was pay some guard fifty, maybe
fifty-five thousand Euros AT MOST, and they'd let you know which shipping facility was holding
the work--and there were only three main ones, two in Switzerland; they'd tell how to disable the
tag, tear the cornia, all of it. For under a million, you could get a hired hand to cut paintings
from their frames with a thumb razor, roll them up, and drive away. If the hand was caught but
didn't have the painting anymore because he'd burned it (not really), he'd get seven years. Maybe
ten. That meant seven hundred thousand at most for a ten-million-dollar painting.

The true challenges were tougher. The ones for real thieves, thieves in the rooms I ended up
frequenting.

They went more like this:

Head of table says: a pound of butter from A Glace in Callais. Butter there is made with
hyper-fresh milk. Composition of butter changes within hours. Challenge is to preserve butter
(no freezing, as this will expand moisture in the cellular channels and compromises integrity)
and deliver to Miami as-is.

And everyone at the table had a certain amount of time to pose his or her solution to that problem.
You used what you could to learn about the system that pound of butter belonged to. Who in the
restaurant could help you get that butter fresh--the melatonin levels in the milk were what
made it precious. Who could get a vehicle with a vacuum chamber inside. Who could ship or fly that
vacuum chamber across the Pacific in the amount of time allotted, and so on.

You did it by learning about each and every link in the process. It was a living, breathing
mechanical engineering project done in your own home.

After a while, you started bumping into the same people in these rooms. It was a small set, to say the least, and, soon enough, you sought each other out. You looked to find rooms set up by the same head of table; he or she looked for you.

My life went on, too. I tried going back to school, and I finished, though it took time. I cared for my father, who passed from a stroke while I was in my thirties. I started working for a former student of his, who sold real estate, then moved into modular homes.

All the while, I kept up in thieving rooms, sometimes as bread, sometimes as steak. I never met the people I trafficked with, neither the heads nor the thieves, but I became well known in that world as CAPCOOK. Sometimes I worked with other thieves I knew. Runnid or Loki. The head of table I worked with most called himself R'overknight.

Like with most heads of table, R'overknight's marks were usually utilitarian things--a mini-server from a small blood bank in Sao Paolo, a sample of an experimental paint-on solar panel from a facility in Wisconsin. But he also made an effort to get to know us a bit, the men and women on the other side of the calculus.

Maybe it was the way he liked to ask us about our lives while setting a mark. He'd ask out of nowhere, too. White words on a black screen at night. He always started with the same phrase: "Forgive me for asking, but..."

As I said, the item I was after for R'overknight the morning I learned of the cure for death was a memento from a famous musician's collection. It was a suit this singer's wife had made him. A spangly thing with arrows and sequins. It had never been worn, but had stayed in his private holdings, never been donated. Apparently it was something special.

"Forgive me for asking, but are you married?"

"Forgive me for asking, Capcook, but how are things?"

Sometimes I'd chat with him in one room, then, when it folded, in the next room, a conversation appearing and disappearing.

I talked to him openly. Once I even told him about my mother, about the last moments of her life...

There was a moment, I typed, just before she died, with my
brother inside her, when she...forgot who she was for moment.
Where she was. Her mind was going, and she had this conversation with me where she thought I was my brother, the baby
inside her, all grown up. She was talking to me like I was him.
I was Nathan--that was the name they'd chosen--Nathan about
to go to college. She mentioned me, too, Jonah, and how I'd
married, had children. She talked to me like we were twenty
years down the line, and she was so happy. I played along,
acting the part. But then, suddenly, midsentence, her mind
snapped back and she realzied what was happening. It all
rushed back to her. She was dying. Nathan would die. We were in
a different life. And the look on her face, the terror...

I think about this now, how maybe my closest friend back then was a head of table, someone asking me to prep steaks, prep bread, a ghost I'd never meet, called R'overknight, and it makes me angry at my younger self.

I want to tell that young man to turn back, that only horrors lie ahead.

You would never guess the things missing from the world, by the way. Shakespeare's skull was stolen long ago. Look it up. It's true. They used ground-penetrating radar to check.

The actual letters of Benjamin Franklin and the key used in the lightning storm are gone. All replaced with stand-ins.

Not to mention three astronaut helmets from a sea and air museum in Texas.

"I wonder where they are," said Bud now, looking out over the parking lot for his friends.

"None of us are ever late, except when coming back to Earth, of course," he said. It was an old joke he used, but he said it mirthlessly now. He looked at his phone--a flip-phone with a brown, insectoidile shell.

"I'm sure they'll be along," said Bud.

I decided to give him his helmet now.

I got up to do it when the pohone rang.

A private number.

My call. R'overknight.

I answered.

"Jonah?" Right away I recognized the voice as Brooke's. She was front of office at the company where I worked.

I felt a pang of worry over the theft, but pushed it away. I asked Brooke what the issue was. It was the weekend, and I had no obligation to the office.

"Someone's here to see you."

"It's Saturday, and--"

"Just come down, Jonah," she said. "You're going to want to take this call."

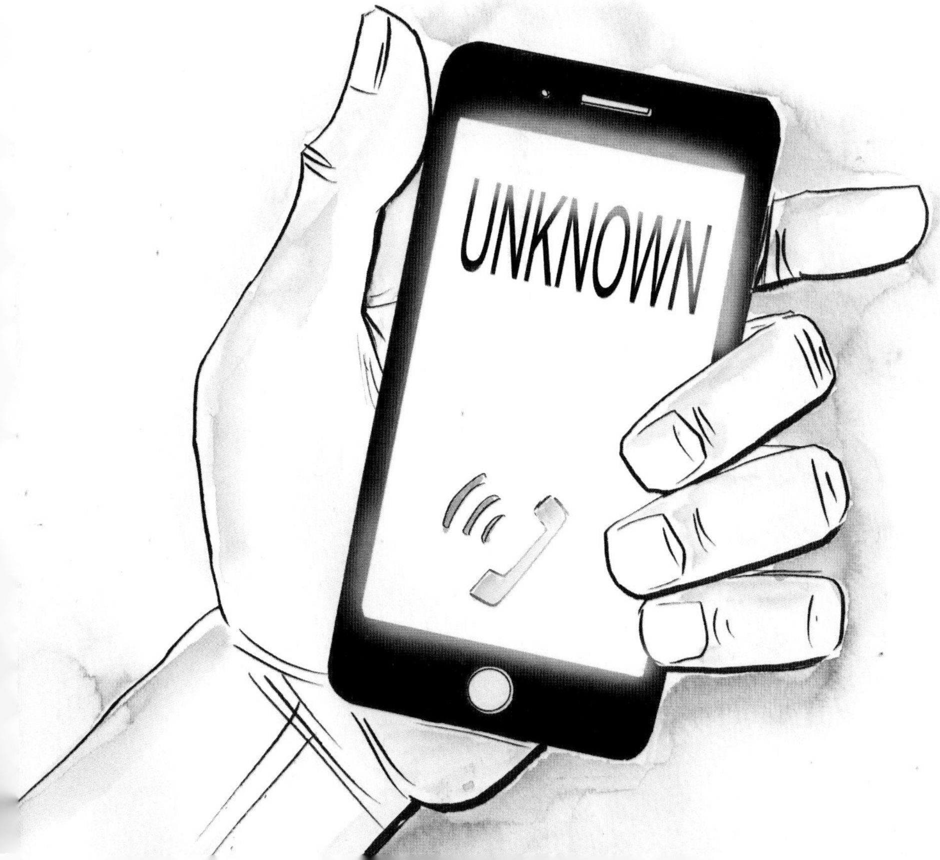
UNKNOWN

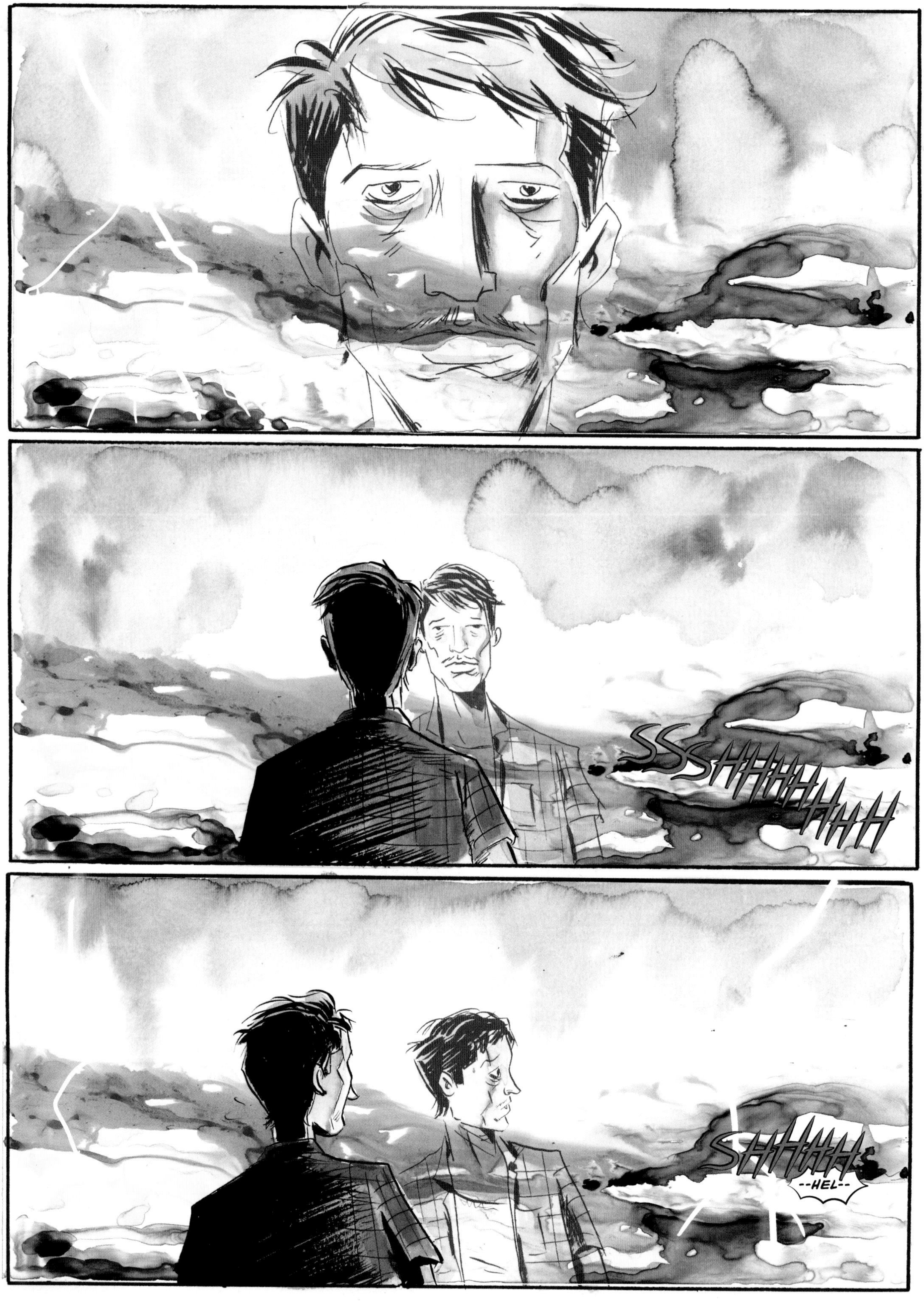
SSSHHHHHHHHH
SHHHHH
--HEL--

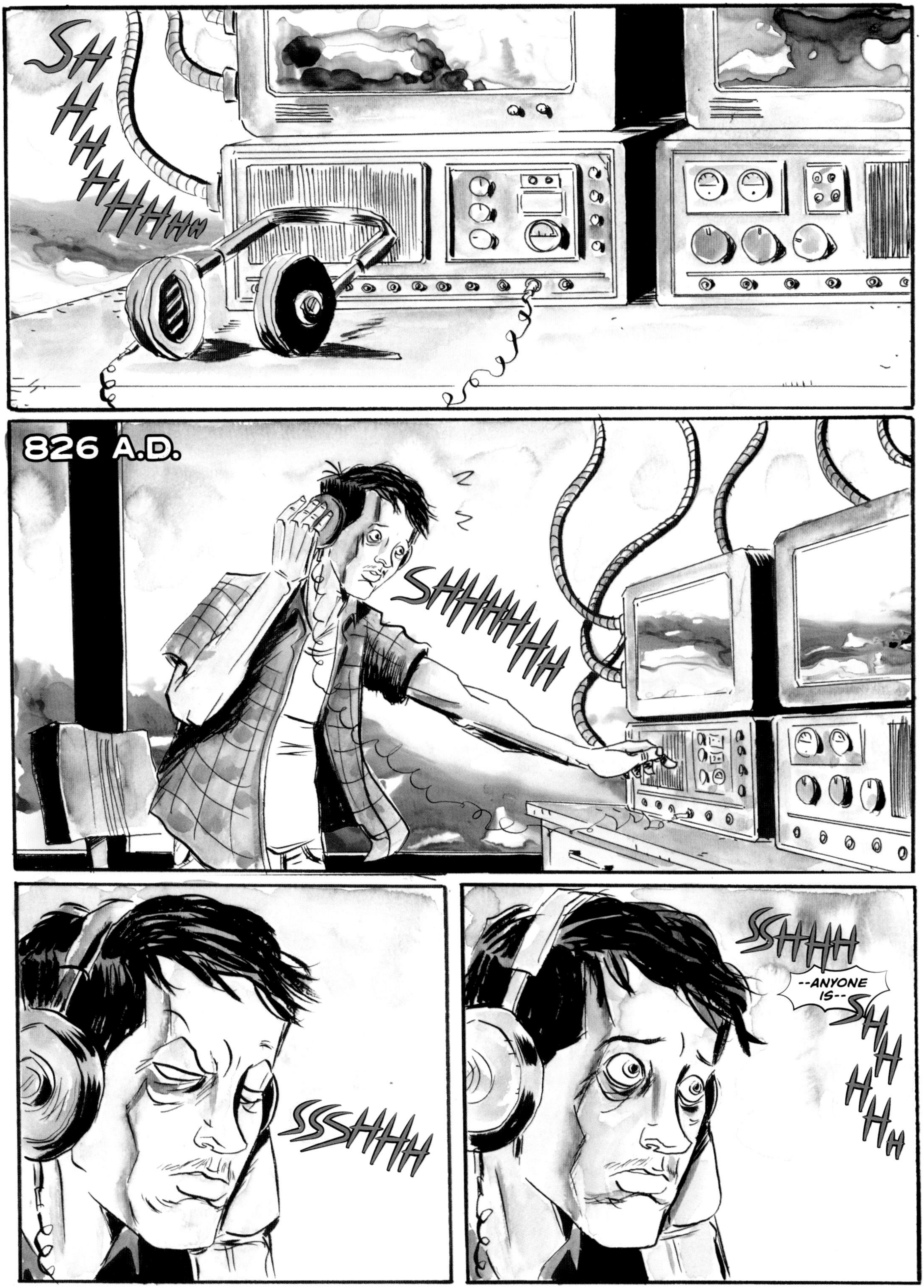
SHHHHHHHH
826 A.D.
SHHHHHHHH
SSSHHHH
SSHHH
--ANYONE IS--
SHHHHHH

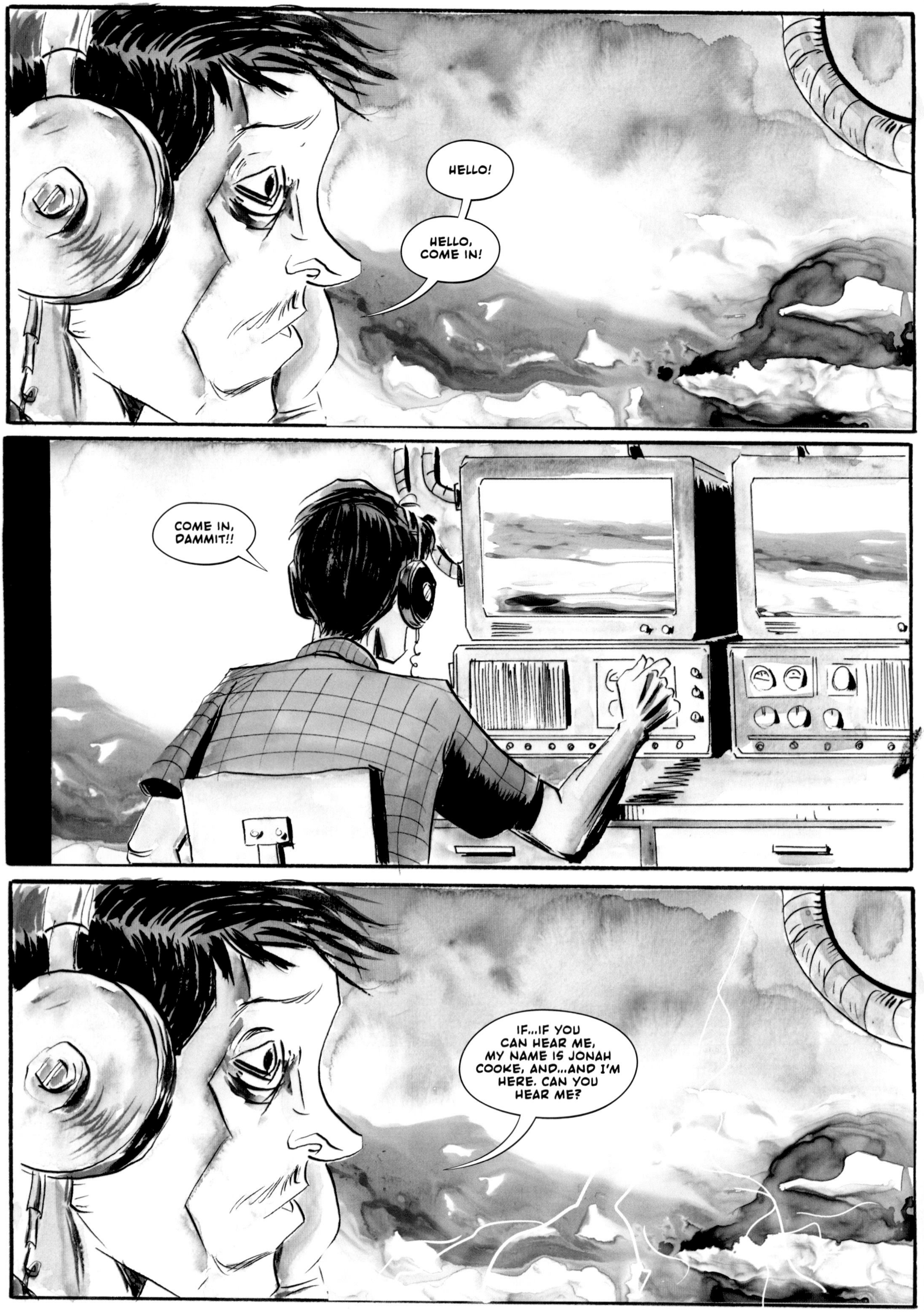
HELLO!
HELLO, COME IN!
COME IN, DAMMIT!!
IF...IF YOU CAN HEAR ME, MY NAME IS JONAH COOKE, AND...AND I'M HERE. CAN YOU HEAR ME?

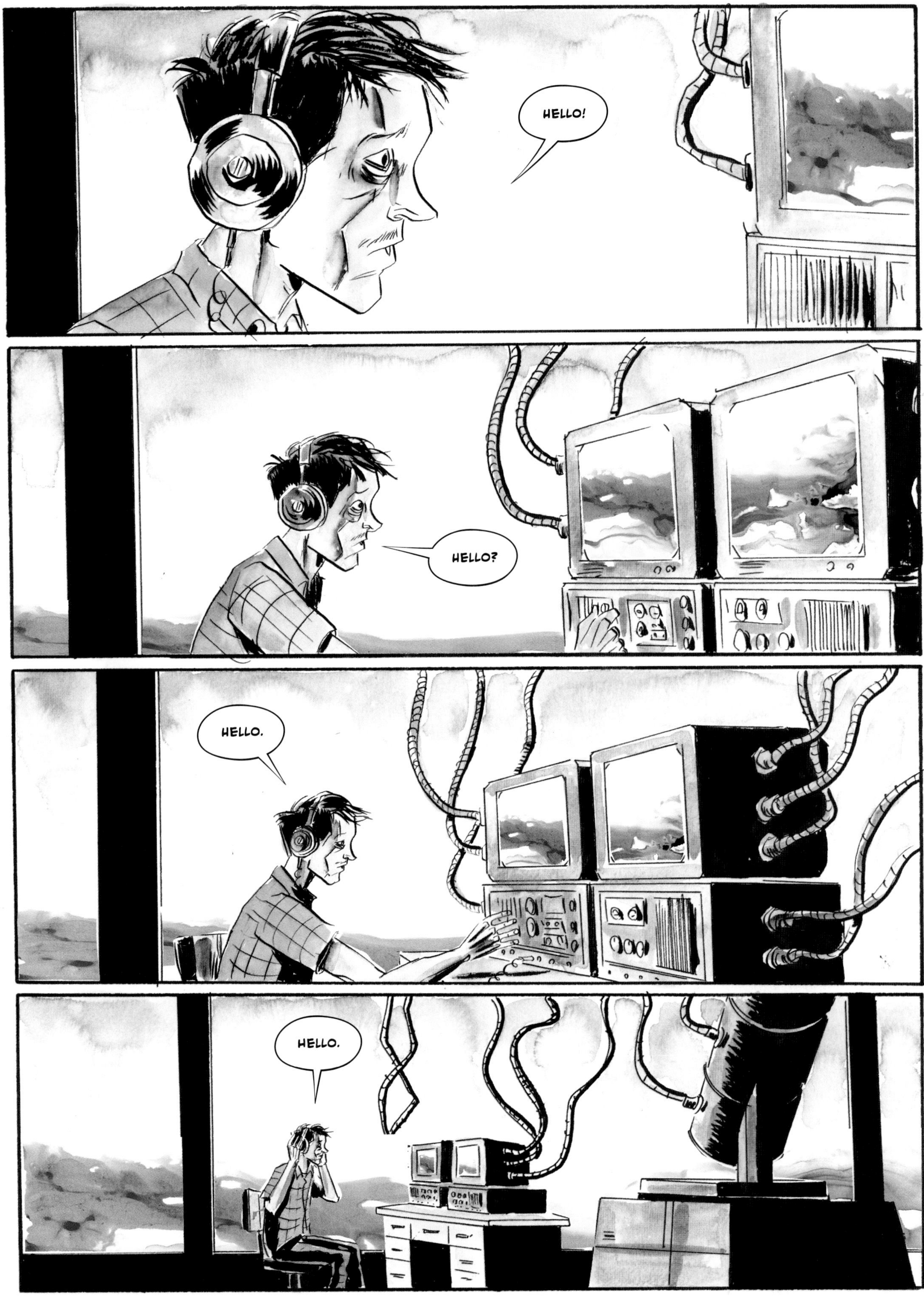
HELLO!
HELLO?
HELLO.
HELLO.

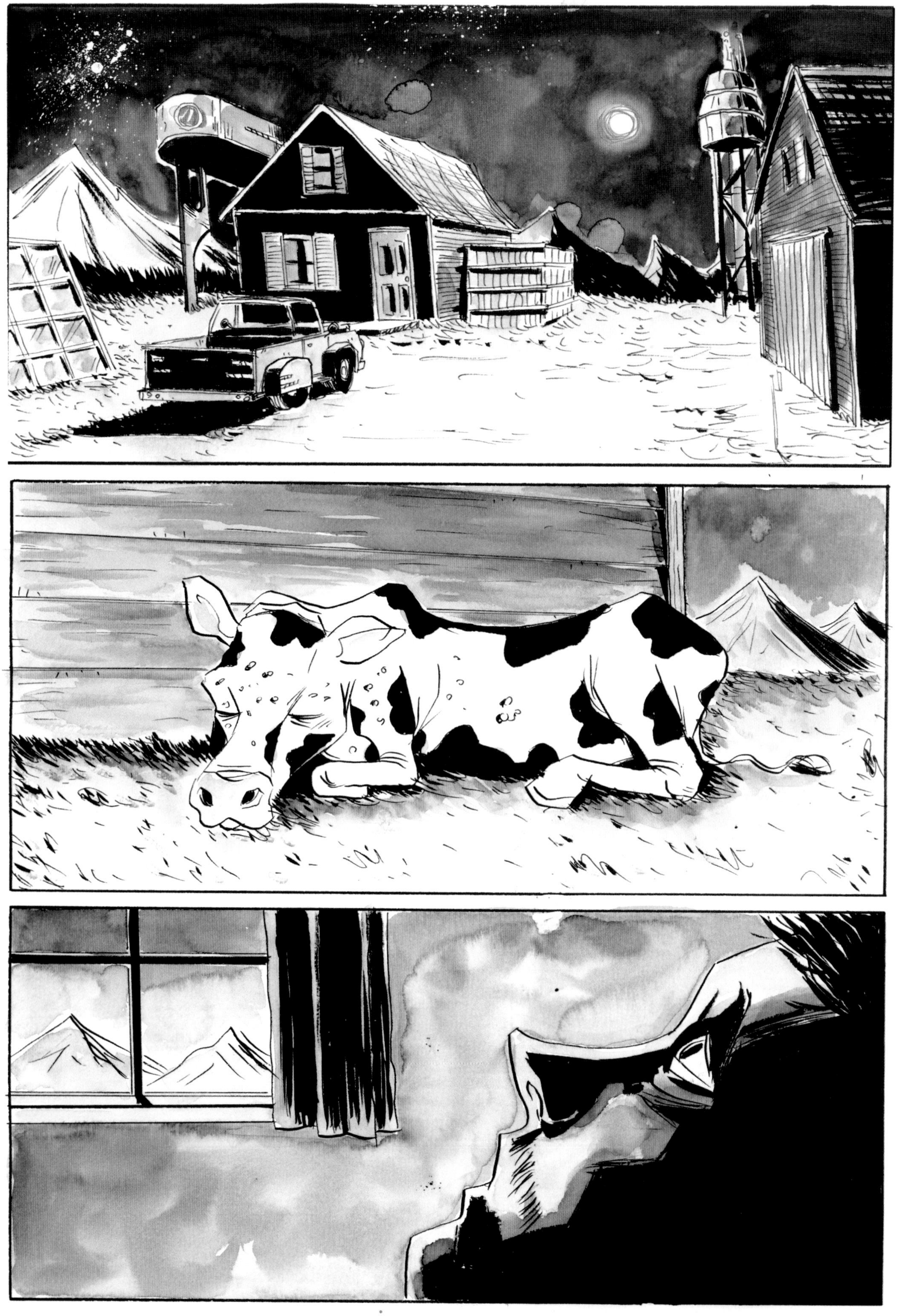

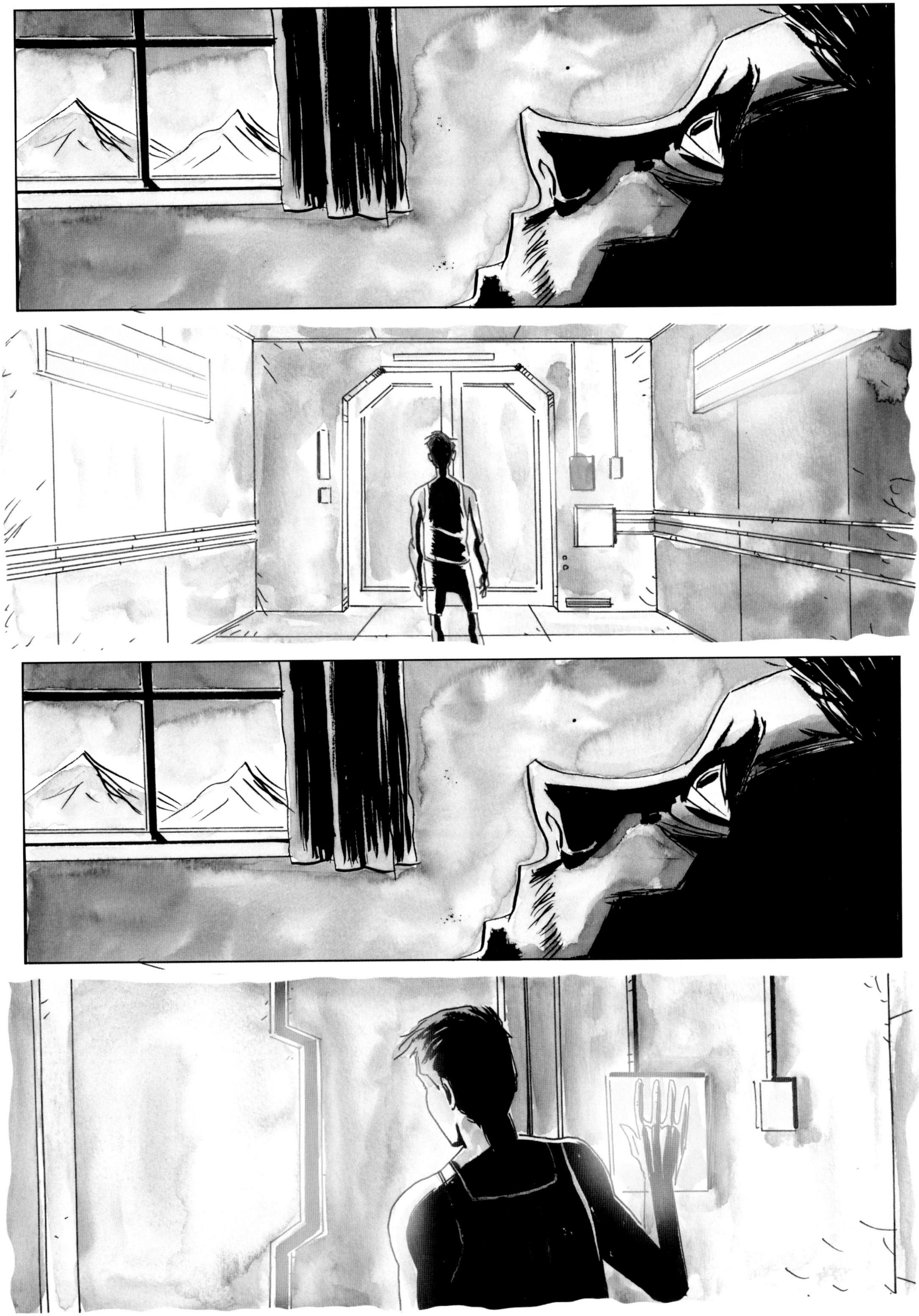

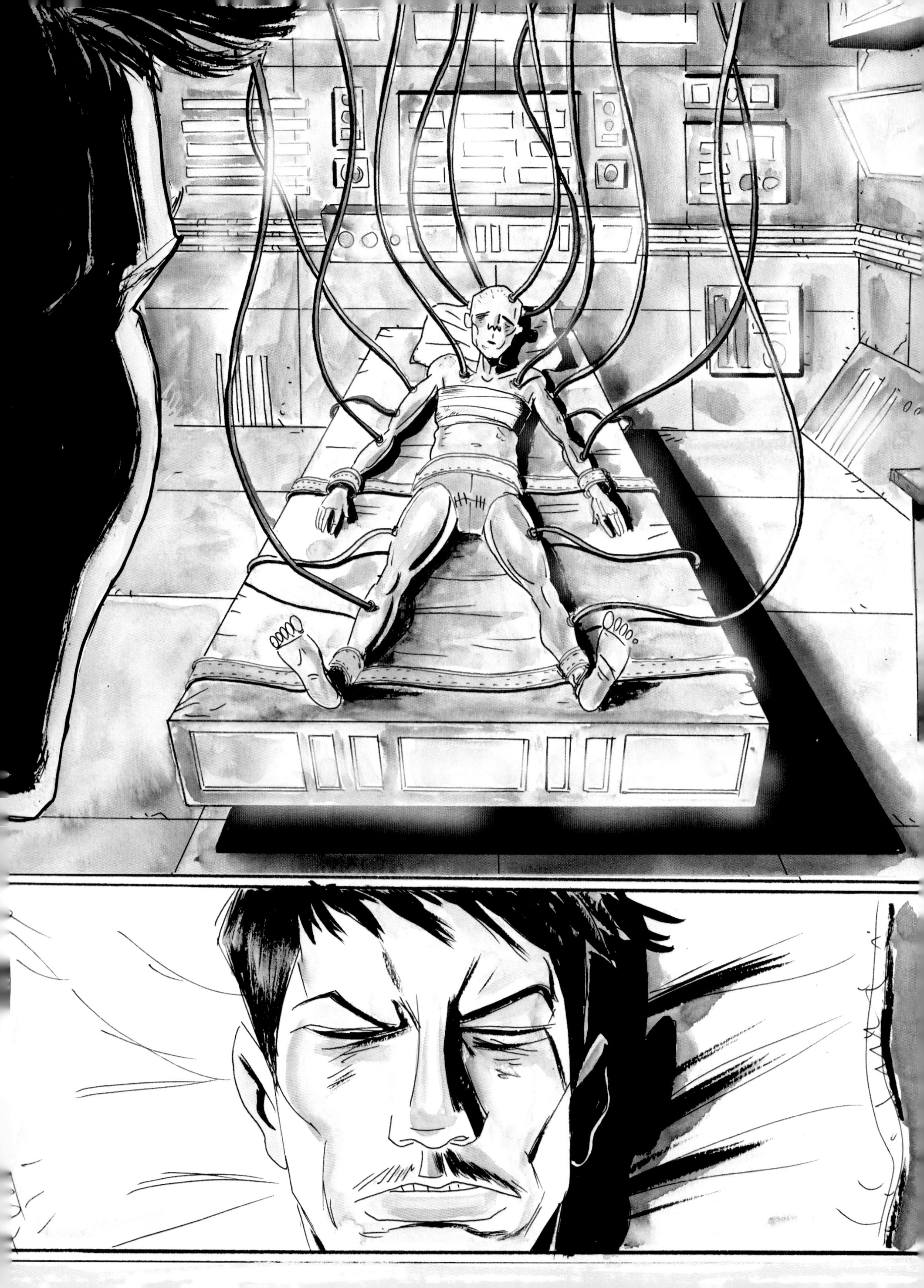

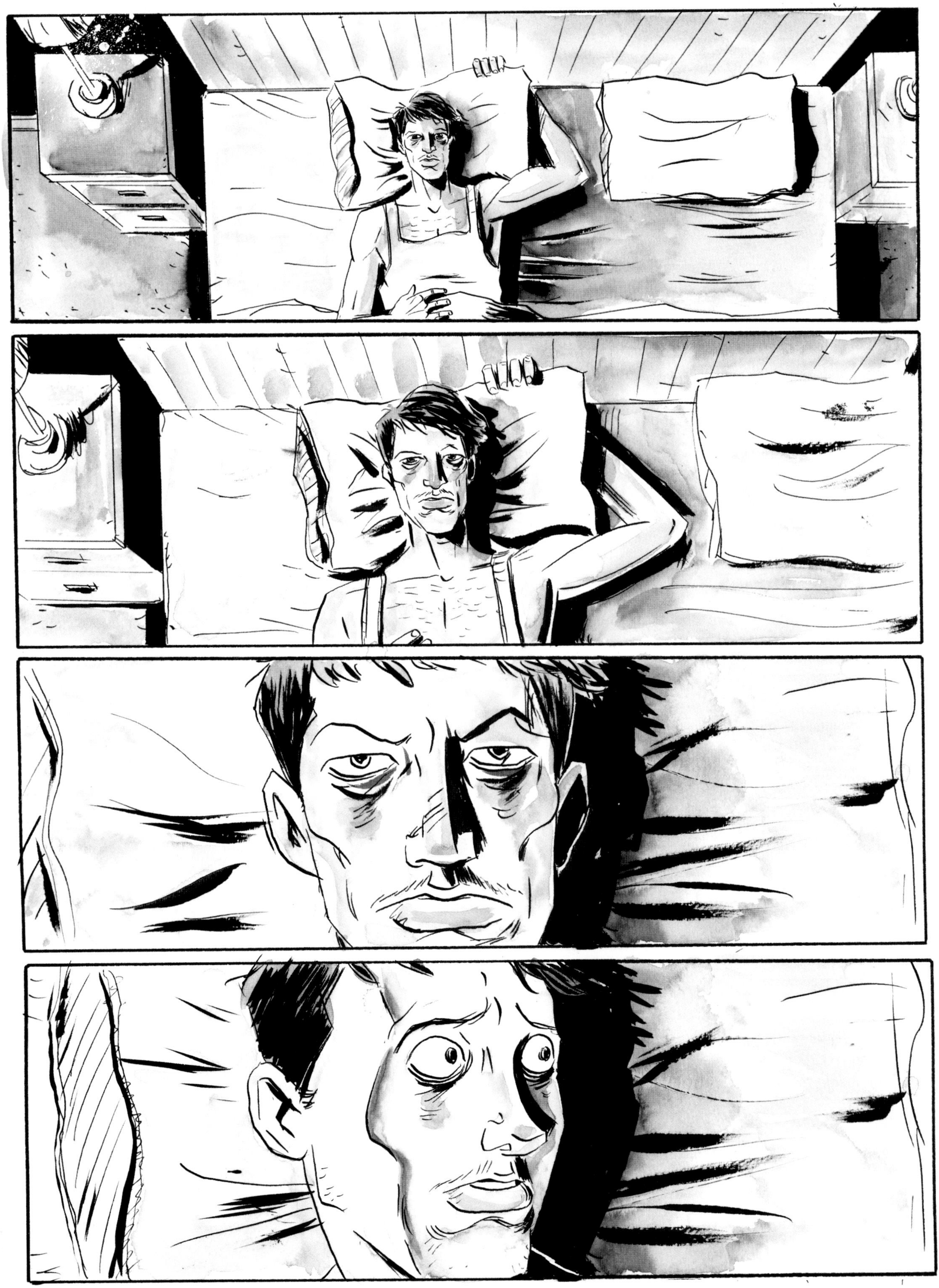

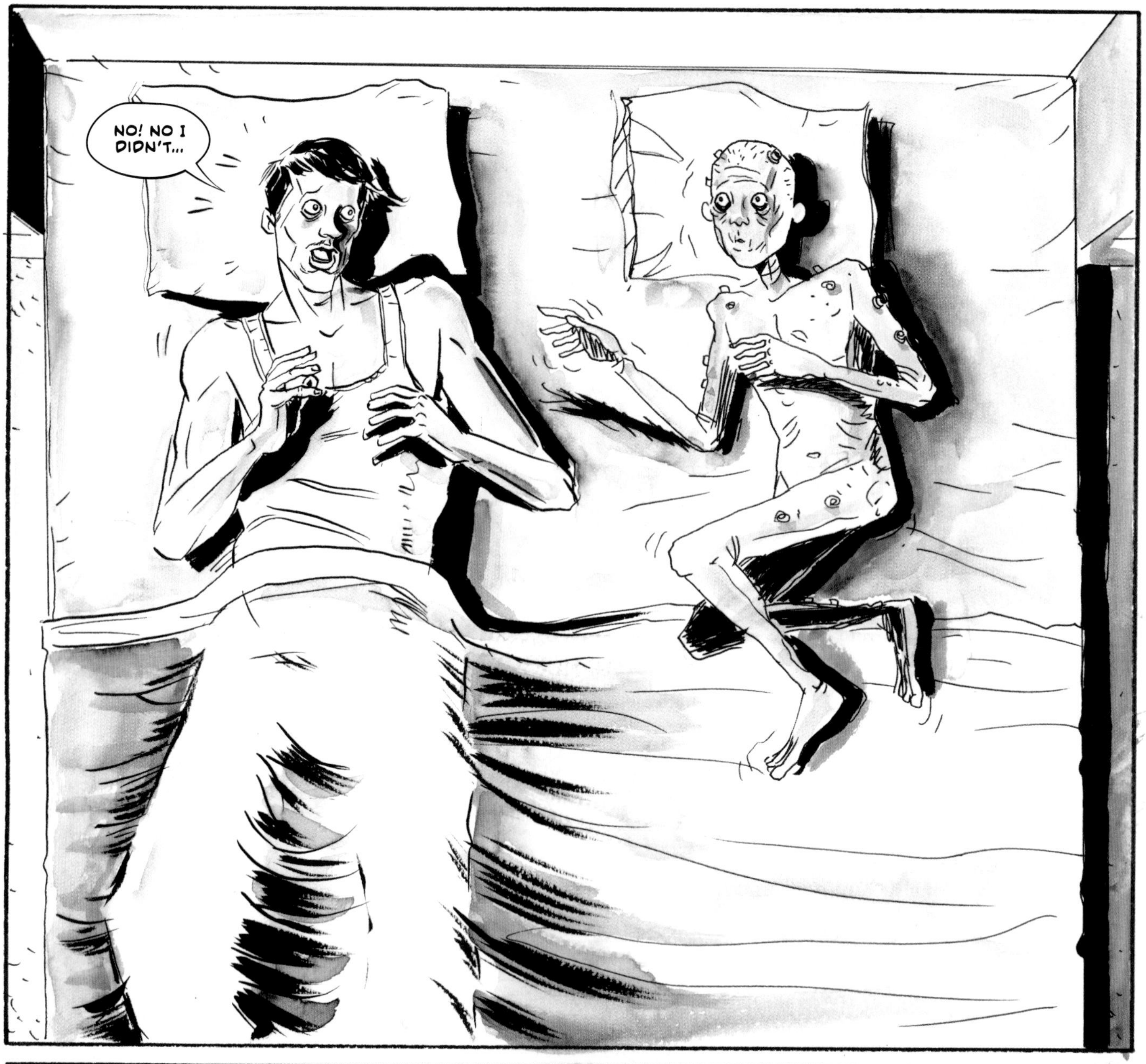
NO! NO I DIDN'T...

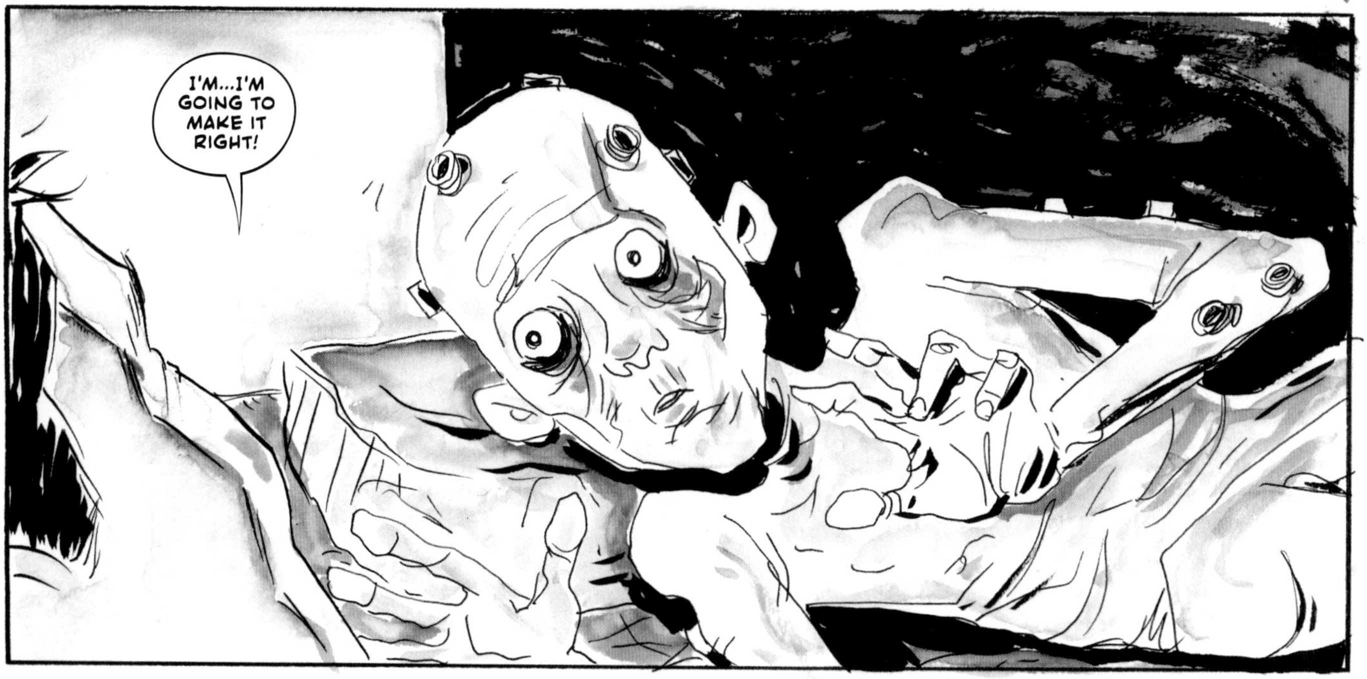
I'M...I'M GOING TO MAKE IT RIGHT!

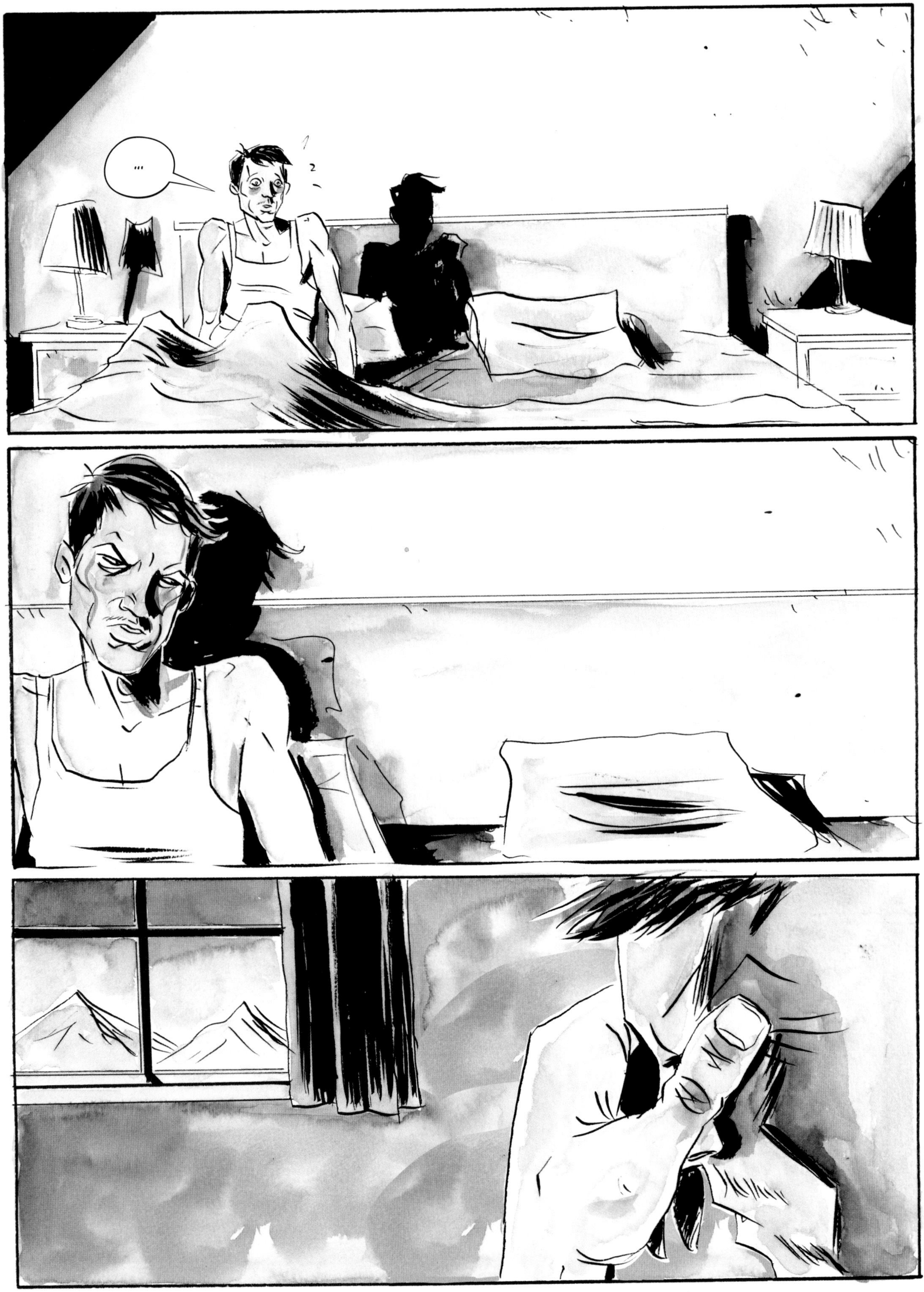
...

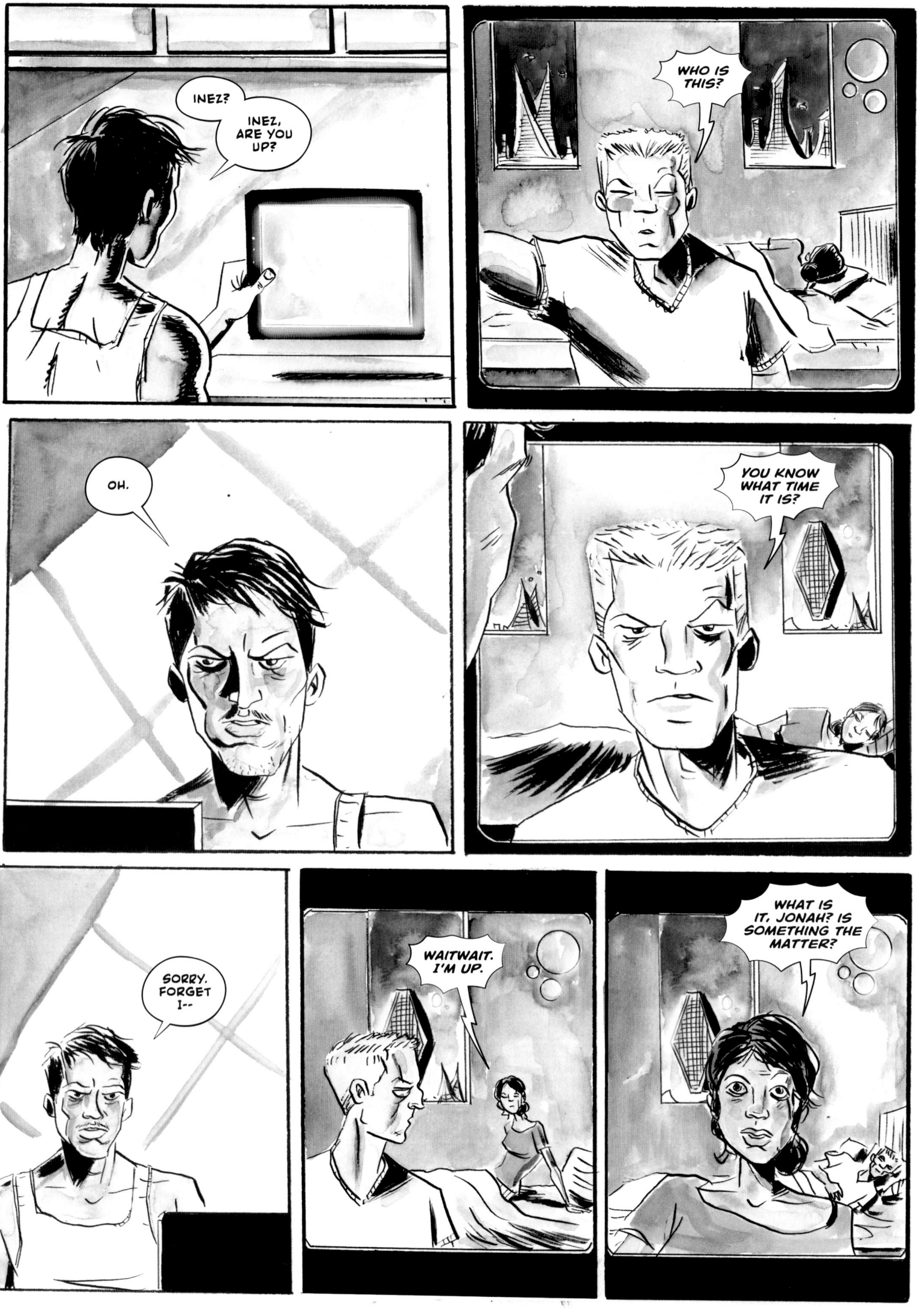
INEZ?
INEZ, ARE YOU UP?
WHO IS THIS?
OH.
YOU KNOW WHAT TIME IT IS?
SORRY. FORGET I--
WAITWAIT. I'M UP.
WHAT IS IT, JONAH? IS SOMETHING THE MATTER?

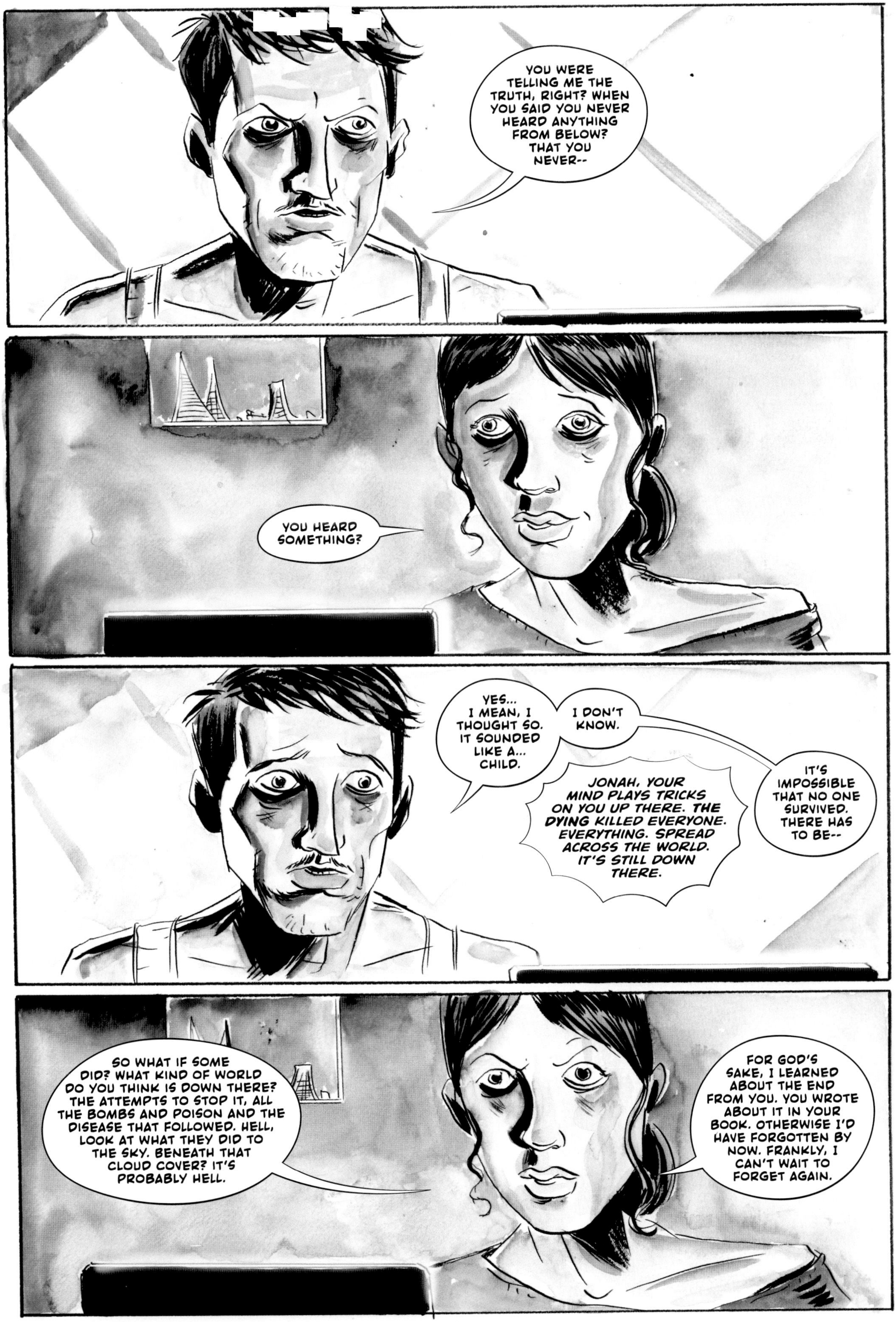

YOU WERE TELLING ME THE TRUTH, RIGHT? WHEN YOU SAID YOU NEVER HEARD ANYTHING FROM BELOW? THAT YOU NEVER--
YOU HEARD SOMETHING?
YES... I MEAN, I THOUGHT SO. IT SOUNDED LIKE A... CHILD.
I DON'T KNOW.
JONAH, YOUR MIND PLAYS TRICKS ON YOU UP THERE. THE DYING KILLED EVERYONE. EVERYTHING. SPREAD ACROSS THE WORLD. IT'S STILL DOWN THERE.
IT'S IMPOSSIBLE THAT NO ONE SURVIVED. THERE HAS TO BE--
SO WHAT IF SOME DID? WHAT KIND OF WORLD DO YOU THINK IS DOWN THERE? THE ATTEMPTS TO STOP IT, ALL THE BOMBS AND POISON AND THE DISEASE THAT FOLLOWED. HELL, LOOK AT WHAT THEY DID TO THE SKY. BENEATH THAT CLOUD COVER? IT'S PROBABLY HELL.
FOR GOD'S SAKE, I LEARNED ABOUT THE END FROM YOU. YOU WROTE ABOUT IT IN YOUR BOOK. OTHERWISE I'D HAVE FORGOTTEN BY NOW. FRANKLY, I CAN'T WAIT TO FORGET AGAIN.

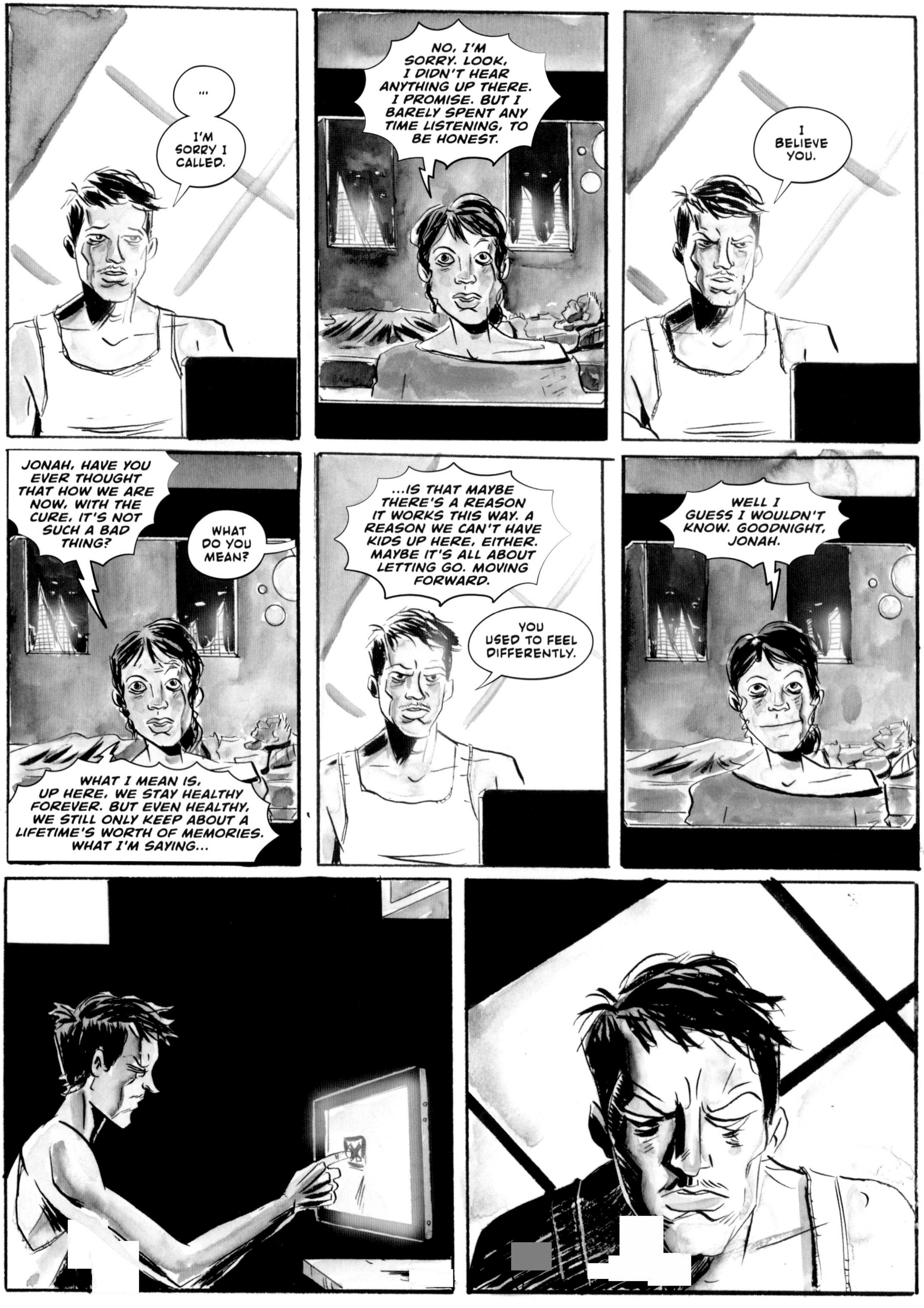
...
I'M SORRY I CALLED.
NO, I'M SORRY. LOOK, I DIDN'T HEAR ANYTHING UP THERE. I PROMISE. BUT I BARELY SPENT ANY TIME LISTENING, TO BE HONEST.
I BELIEVE YOU.
JONAH, HAVE YOU EVER THOUGHT THAT HOW WE ARE NOW, WITH THE CURE, IT'S NOT SUCH A BAD THING?
WHAT DO YOU MEAN?
WHAT I MEAN IS, UP HERE, WE STAY HEALTHY FOREVER. BUT EVEN HEALTHY, WE STILL ONLY KEEP ABOUT A LIFETIME'S WORTH OF MEMORIES. WHAT I'M SAYING...
...IS THAT MAYBE THERE'S A REASON IT WORKS THIS WAY. A REASON WE CAN'T HAVE KIDS UP HERE, EITHER. MAYBE IT'S ALL ABOUT LETTING GO. MOVING FORWARD.
YOU USED TO FEEL DIFFERENTLY.
WELL I GUESS I WOULDN'T KNOW. GOODNIGHT, JONAH.

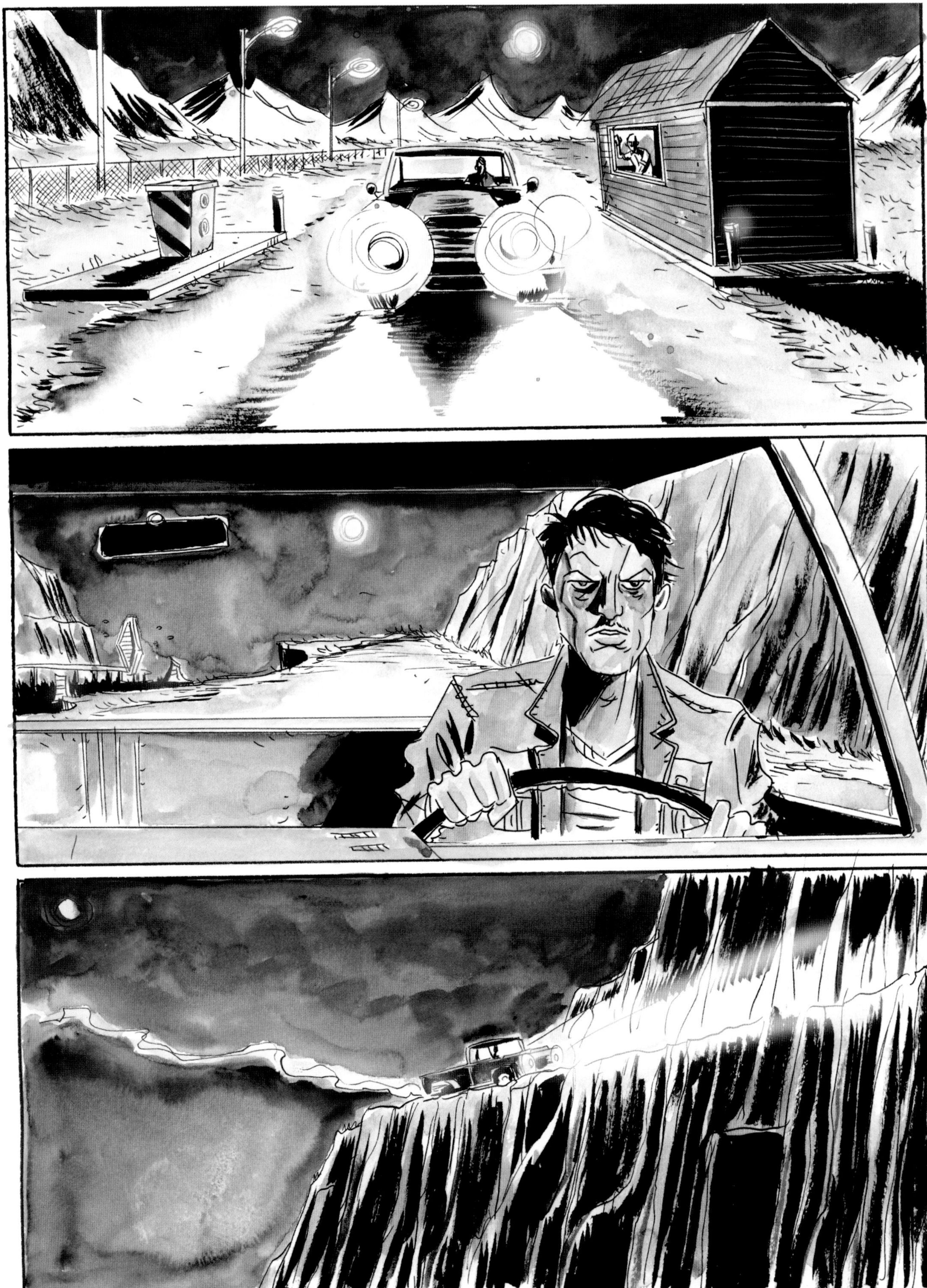

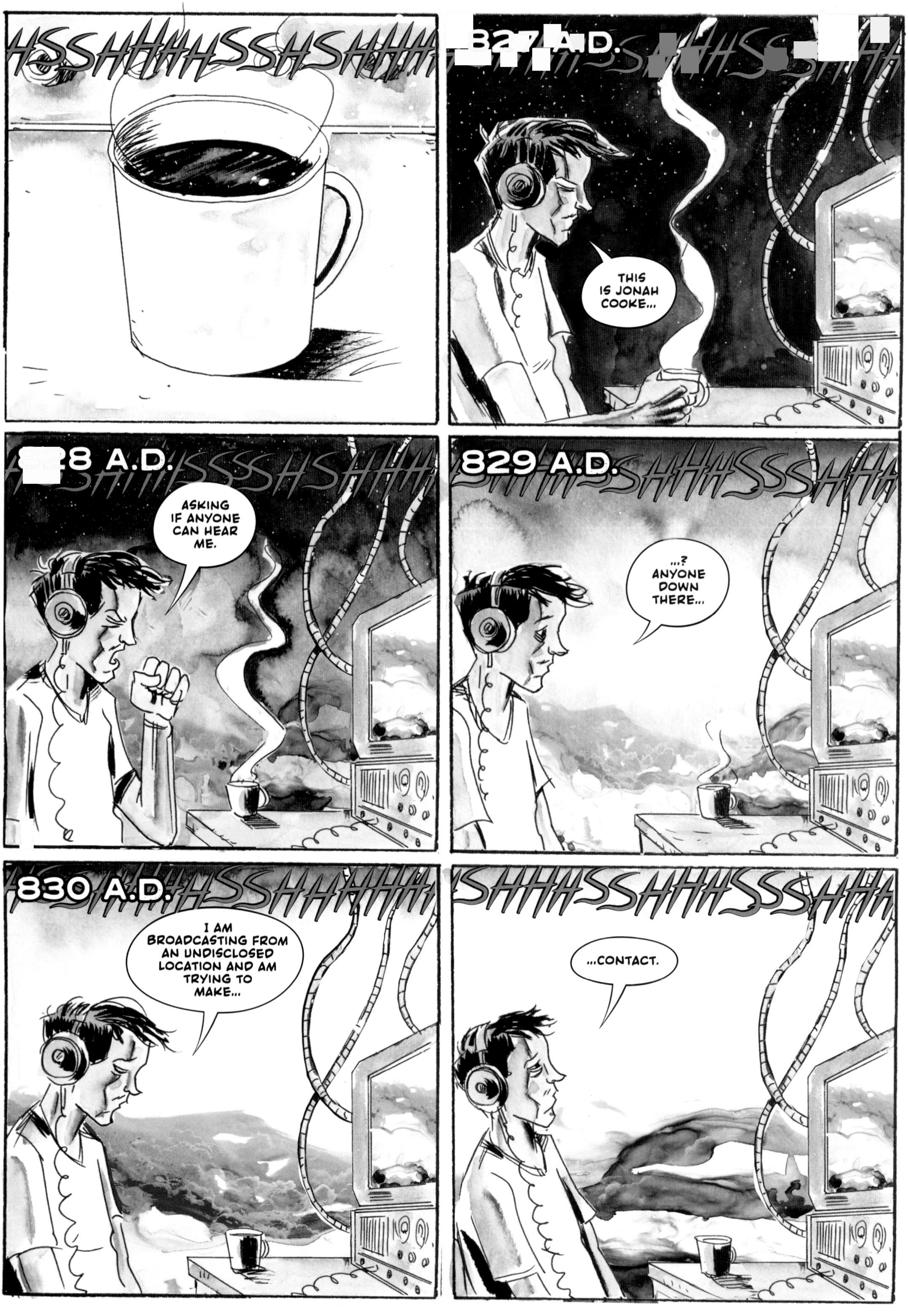
827 A.D.
THIS IS JONAH COOKE...
828 A.D.
ASKING IF ANYONE CAN HEAR ME.
829 A.D.
...? ANYONE DOWN THERE...
830 A.D.
I AM BROADCASTING FROM AN UNDISCLOSED LOCATION AND AM TRYING TO MAKE...
...CONTACT.

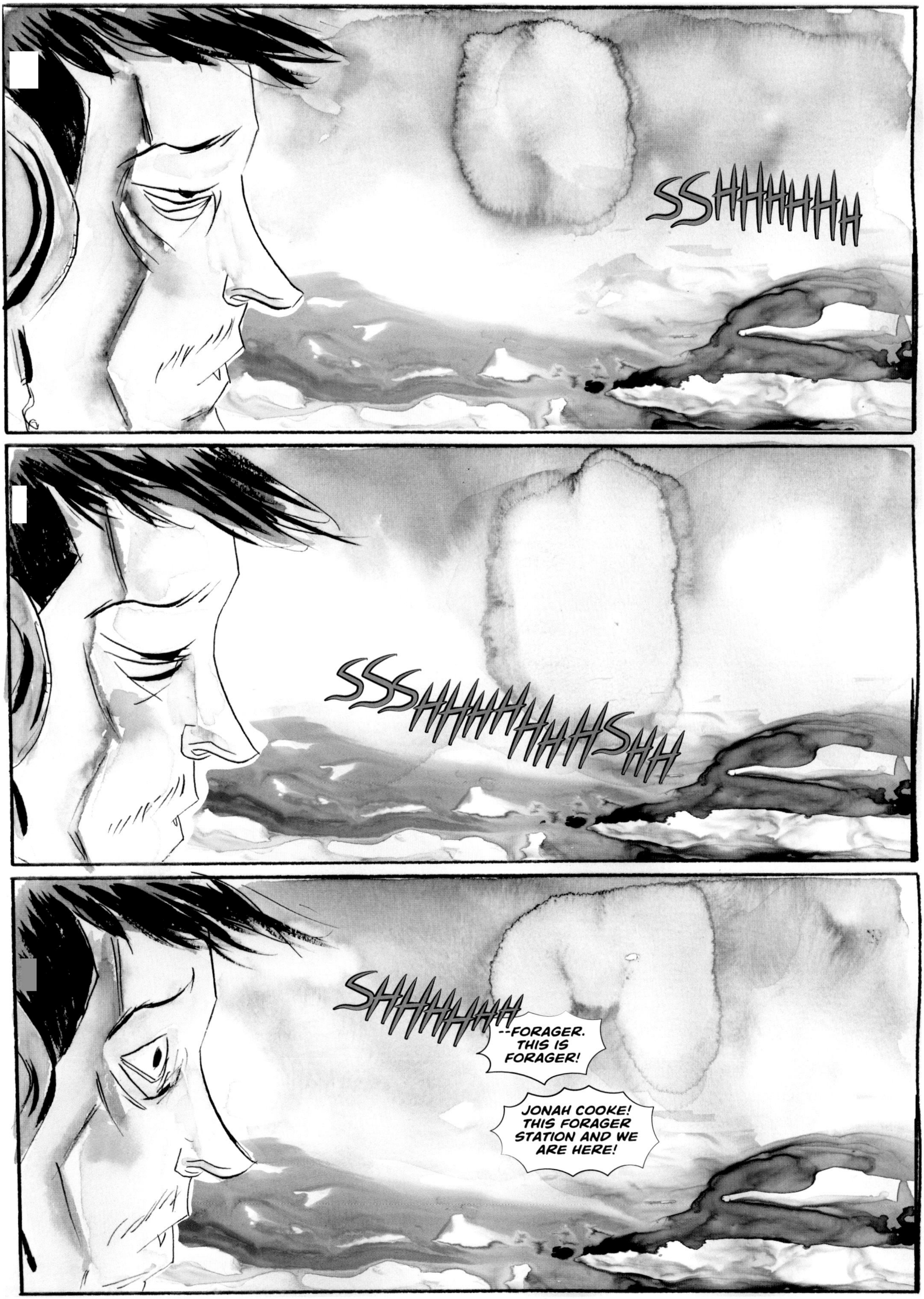
SSHHHHHHH
SSSHHHHHHHHHSHH
SHHHHHHH
--FORAGER. THIS IS FORAGER!
JONAH COOKE! THIS FORAGER STATION AND WE ARE HERE!

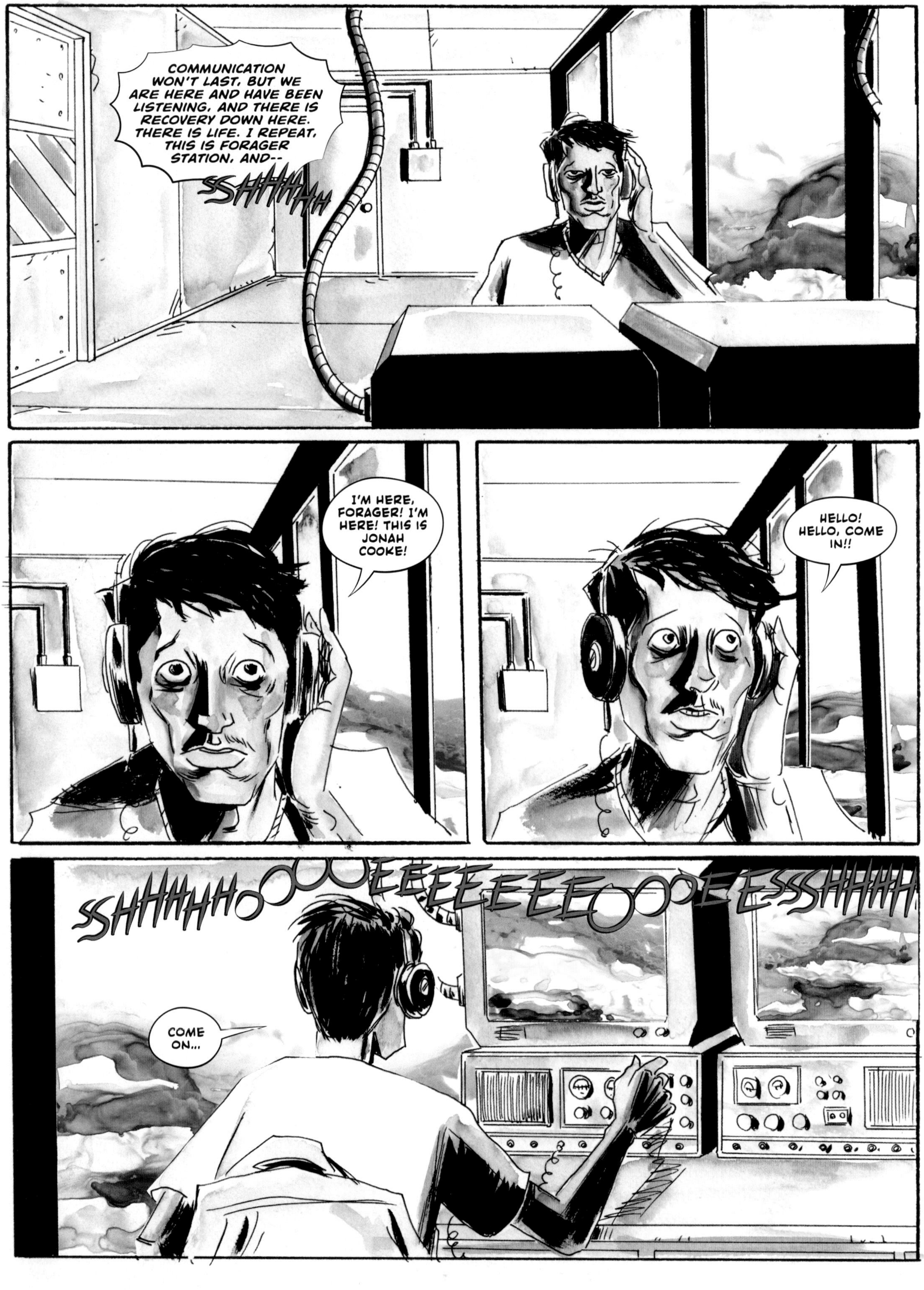
COMMUNICATION WON'T LAST, BUT WE ARE HERE AND HAVE BEEN LISTENING, AND THERE IS RECOVERY DOWN HERE. THERE IS LIFE. I REPEAT, THIS IS FORAGER STATION, AND--
SSHHHHHH
I'M HERE, FORAGER! I'M HERE! THIS IS JONAH COOKE!
HELLO! HELLO, COME IN!!
SSHHHHHOOOEEEEEEEEOOOEESSHHHH
COME ON...

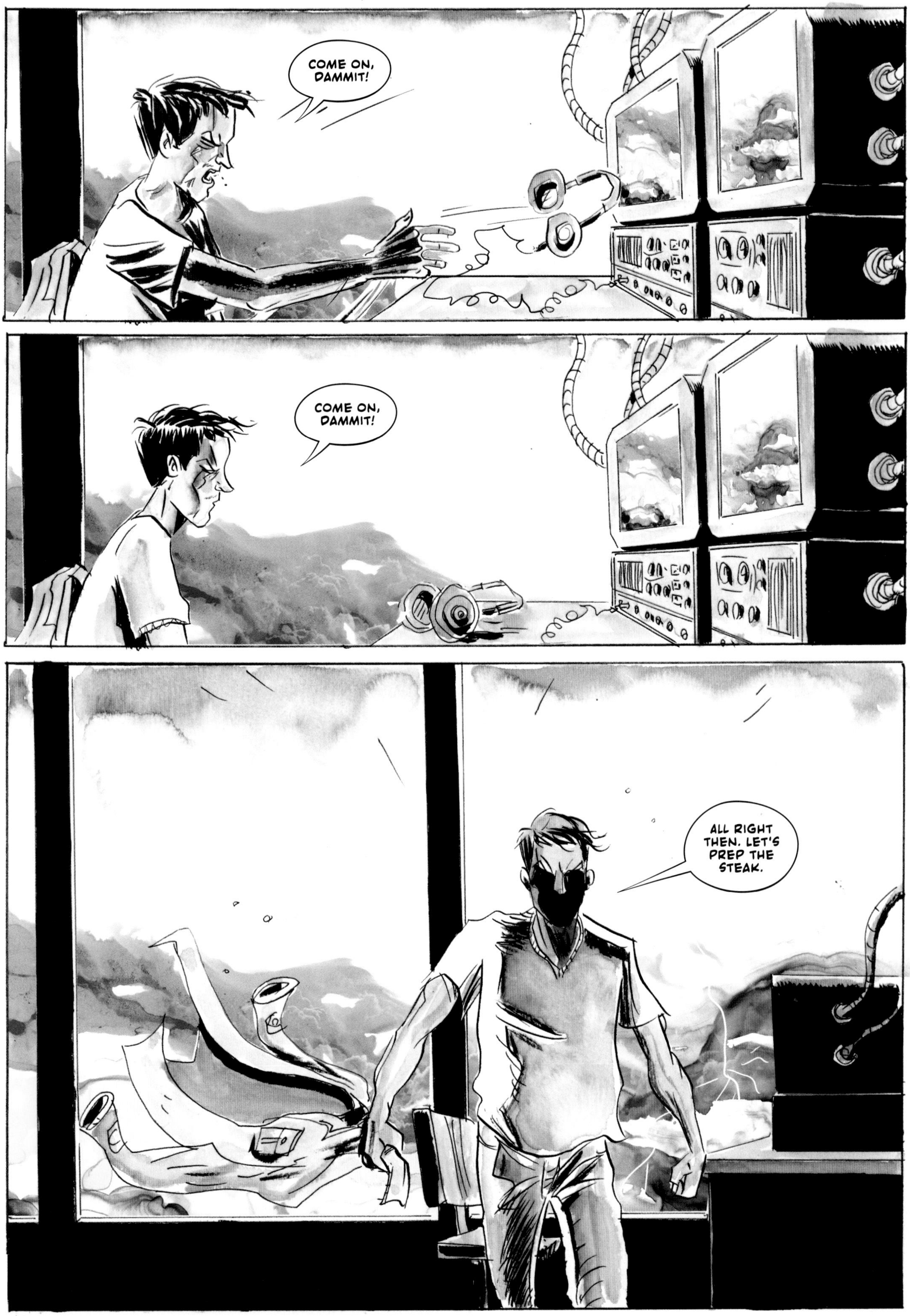
COME ON, DAMMIT!
COME ON, DAMMIT!
ALL RIGHT THEN. LET'S PREP THE STEAK.

MODERN HOME

JONAH COOKE
SALES ASSOCIATE

The company where I worked, Modern Home, was housed in a lot about ten minutes from my condo. The lot was part of a loosely designed strip mall. A furniture liquidation place stood about a hundred meters to the west, and to the east lay a series of cheap takeout places, a row of seven in one long structure, like a pill planner.

By the time I arrive, my call from R'overknight is an hour late, and I'm getting concerned. It's nothing, I think, but the truth is that it's uncommon, and I can feel that something is very off.

I think of the mistakes I might have made, the details I might have bungled. A theft often feels like one of those intricate, fragile equations written on blackboards in movies about geniuses--a looping and delicate causal latticework, every part balanced on its predecessor. What if some variable had changed along the way? What if the storage facility was having random maintenance that day? What if a guard had called in sick, or what if the street outside the place was closed for a burst pipe? Hell, there'd been another shooting a few miles from the facility just days before. Three dead in the DMV, the shooter dead, too. Maybe that had affected things. The point is, there are events you can't plan for, and now, as I approach Modern Home, my head is full of them.

Brooke is in my office when I enter. She's looking down at the showroom floor through the big glass wall at the back of the room, but she's doing it cautiously, like she's trying not to be seen by whomever she's observing, craning her neck and standing on tiptoes.

"What's the emergency?" I say.

She jumps.

"Jesus, you scared me," she says, her hand over her chest. She waves me over. "Come here. Check it out. Brody called me in to see if it was a joke. Look and see, and tell me if it is."

I walk to the window. There are four of us agents at Modern Home, and each of our offices is backed with a glass wall that looks down on the showroom floor below, a massive hangar designed to look like a suburban street, with five different model homes lined up beside one another. The first house is a geometric contemporary, all glass, corrugated steel and wood laminate. The second home is a classic gray and white Colonial. The third is a standard ranch, and the fourth an example of a custom, a cape with add-ons like an enclosed porch, a playroom...Our specialty is customization, our ability to configure a home however the client wants. Modular isn't just a single structure; it's every component of a structure. Room by room.

The houses have small fake lawns out front, bordered by a sidewalk that runs around the whole fake block. Behind the row stands a theatrically lit backdrop of a summer sky. For a brief period, the manager, my father's old student, had tried placing mannequins along the sidewalk and inside the homes, but the consensus among the staff and customers was that they gave the place a creepy feel, reminiscent of those model homes used in doomsday blast tests of the 1950s. Behind the sky backdrop, the hangar turns into a materials warehouse, like front of stage and backstage.

I scan the floor but see nothing of interest.

Brooke sighs and takes my arm, pulling me closer. She points with her chin, all of this clearly embarrassing to her. "Right there. On the custom."

And then I see what she's gesturing at: a man standing on the balcony of the custom home. He's older, I can see that much from here, maybe in his late sixties, thin and very tall, with a wisp of blond-white hair. He's wearing a T-shirt and jeans, nothing fancy, and he looks relaxed.

As I watch, he gives the house a gentle once-over, running a hand over the balcony railing.

"Brody says he's some kind of billionaire," says Brooke, scanning my face for a reaction. "Please, please tell me he's here to make us all rich."

I look again.

Suddenly I know who he is. I recognize him because of my second profession, and all at once his name appears in my mind--appears like a logo more than a name, a stamped, visual thing. He is Warner Errant, and, yes, he's a billionaire. Not one of those billionaires out in front of the cameras, doing shows or socializing, though. From what I know, Errant was from money to begin with, but made an even bigger fortune in music production--producing popular songs, then founding a company called SIGIL, which led to all sorts of projects to improve recording technologies. Within the music industry, people say he has "diamond ears," both for hit songs and for miniscule but significant improvements to the recording process itself. He has extensive art and sculpture collections, and so has come up over the years in the rooms I frequent.

"So?" says Brooke.

"He's no one. Calm yourself," I tell her, and start walking downstairs to meet him.

On any other day I'd take a real curiosity in someone like Errant, but today, my mind is on that suit. It's over ninety minutes after I was supposed to get the call from R'overknight, and I'm pretty sure something has gone very, very wrong. While I know there's no reason to panic, I can't quell my fears. I've set up thefts where things have gone wrong before, of course, but not in a long time, and not for R'overknight, AND not when the steak was an object of public interest. A botched attempt at stealing a piece of country western history is entertainment news, and that means visibility, which means pressure, and so on.

I walk up the steps to the custom, and find Mr. Errant still there on the porch.

He doesn't see me at first. He's got his back to me, and his hands are planted on the railing and he's looking out over the showroom like a man staring out at his neighborhood in the small, quiet hours. I almost feel like I'm interrupting something speaking to him.

"Morning," I finally say.

He turns to face me.

"Ah," he says, and smiles. "There you are."

He's tall and thin, with white-blue eyes, and the first thing that strikes me is his voice. He has a deep, smooth voice, a radio voice--this dark mixture of the fatherly and gracious that eases you into conversation. I'm caught by how handsome he is, too, even at his age, how the scaffolding is still there beneath the surface, a sharp Nordic angularity. He's old, sure, but his features have that burnished and wind-sharpened quality you see in people who spend a lot of time at high altitudes.

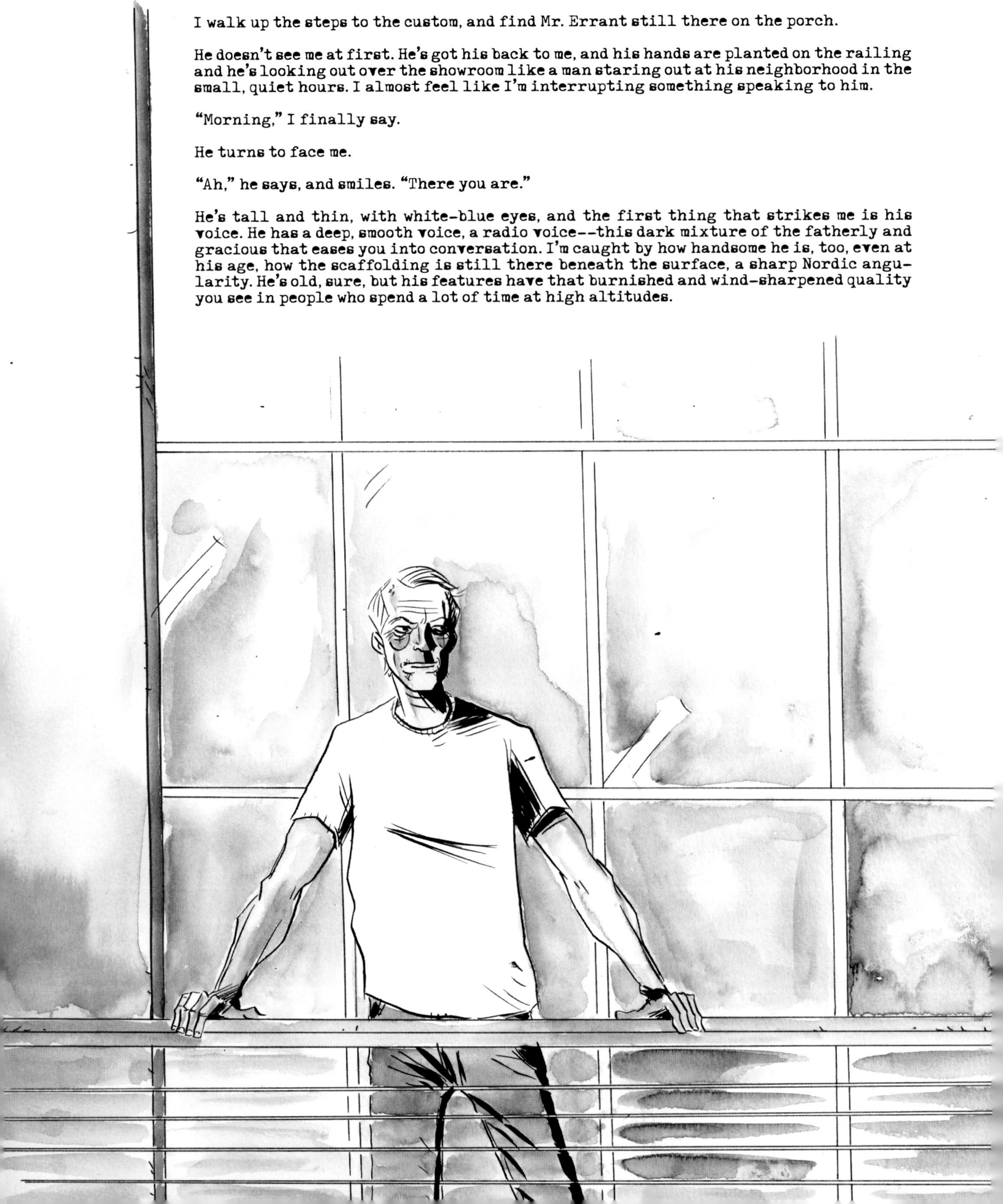

I introduce myself, and he shakes my hand. His grip is large and firm, and again a feeling comes over me like I'm in his home here, like this all belongs to him.

I ask him how I can help.

"First, you can tell me what this wondrous stuff is made of," he says, running a hand over the balcony railing. He seems completely at ease with himself.

I explain that it's a treated wood laminate over a melamine resin. It's used in much of our siding, too, and here I go into my pitch, telling him how our agents work with customers to guide them to make their choices work within their budget.

The whole time, he's smiling at me in this kind, gentle way, nodding. He asks appropriate questions about the process for creating this poly-fiber, or about how we determine if a site is viable for construction. He seems genuinely interested, and yet I have no idea why this is so, and this makes things doubly frustrating, unnerving even; it's like we're playing roles...or rather, like I'm playing a role in front of someone assessing my ability to play it. I keep waiting for him to turn away, to look at anything other than me so I can check my phone again, but he's entirely involved.

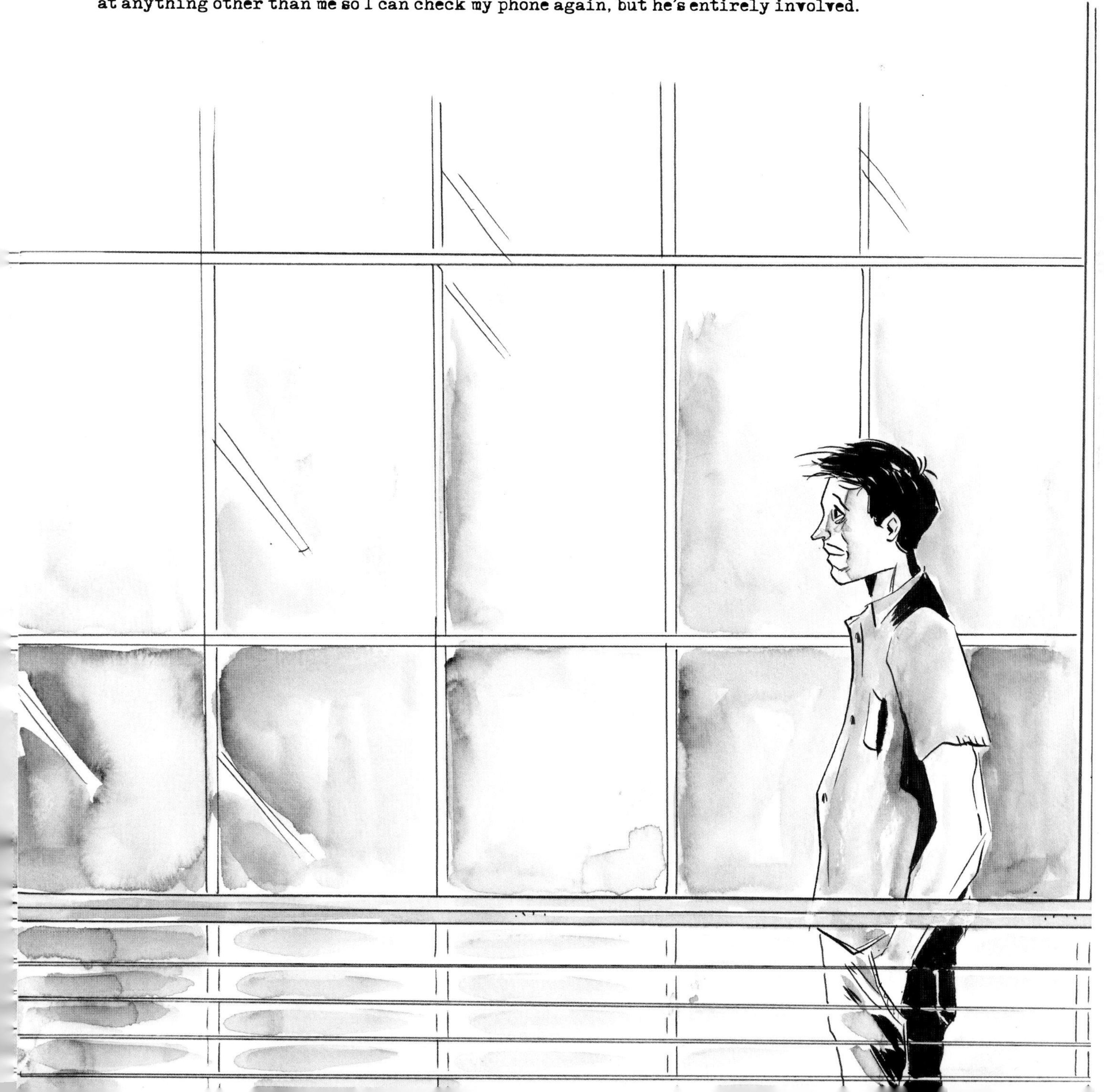

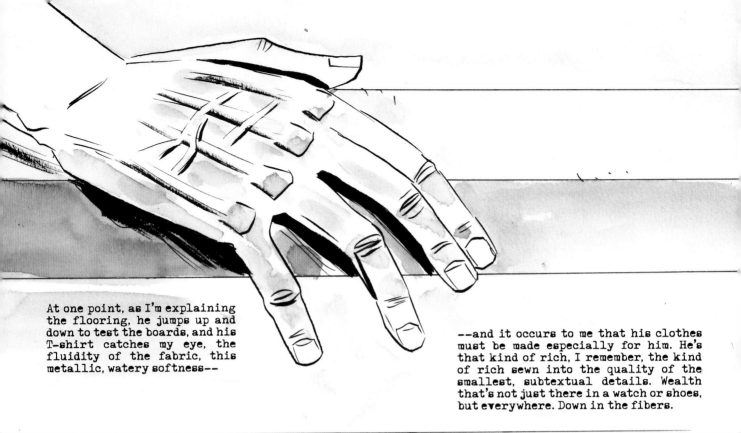

At one point, as I'm explaining the flooring, he jumps up and down to test the boards, and his T-shirt catches my eye, the fluidity of the fabric, this metallic, watery softness--

--and it occurs to me that his clothes must be made especially for him. He's that kind of rich, I remember, the kind of rich sewn into the quality of the smallest, subtextual details. Wealth that's not just there in a watch or shoes, but everywhere. Down in the fibers.

See, THAT'S "custom," I think to myself. And, suddenly, I'm frustrated by the situation, by the cheapness of the custom house we're standing in, the chasm between his version of custom and ours. And more than this, I'm frustrated by whatever game this rich man is playing with me.

I finish my pitch and ask him if he's interested in coming up to my office, or if he's got enough to go on.

"Sure, I'd like to come up to your office," he says. "There's a lot more to discuss." His eyes are twinkling.

"Great," I say, trying to hide my chagrin. "It's just up here." I gesture to the stairs.

"Terrific," he says. But he doesn't move.

"If you just follow me..." I say.

"Uh-huh," he says, but still he doesn't move, just stands there, and I wonder if there's something wrong with him. His eyes are fixed on me.

I try again. "Sir, if you'll just--"

"Do you know who I am?" he says. And while his smile is constant, there's something a bit hard in this question, a directness that sets me back a bit.

I tell him that I do, actually.

"Good," he says, never taking his eyes off of me. "I'd like to place a big order with you."

Above us, I see Brooke peeking through the window, no shame anymore.

"Wonderful," I say. "How big are you thinking?"

"Pretty...substantial," he says, finally turning away, toward the room.

As he turns, I quickly check my phone for word from R'overknight. Nothing. My stomach tightens. Two hours late.

"I'm working on a project with some people," says Errant. "A clinic, or retreat. It's nowhere near here, though. It's far, far away."

"Well, I'm afraid we only work locally," I tell him, listing the farthest towns we accommodate.

"I see," he says, turning back to me, looking serious now. "Well, I brought something to change your mind."

I start to tell him that I'm just a manager, but he just keeps going, taking a small suitcase from beneath the porch furniture. He puts it on the chair between us. The suitcase is a simple wheel board bag, black, nothing special.

As he works the bag onto the chair, I check my phone again.

Still nothing.

The DMV shooting, I think. It had to be. The beefed-up police presence. And now the fiercer worries swarm in. My mind attacks me, citing everything I did wrong on this one. Everything I've done wrong dating back to the Quad. Back to the balloon...Everything wrong with my life.

"I tried to put together a plan for earlier," says Errant, unzipping the suitcase.
"I asked you if you knew who I was."

"Right," I say. I'm trying to put together a plan for approaching the suit situation. Most connections in theft are all done through collapsible rigs. I'm trying to figure out how to protect the people I've paid, and how to get word to the ones paid through proxies. A cracking sort of sound interrupts my thoughts, and I realize it's me, grinding my teeth.

"And?" says Errant. He's clearly said something I've missed.

"I'm sorry. What?"

Errant smiles in that gentle way. "I said," he says, "forgive me for asking again, Jonah, but do you know who I am?"

"Yes. I told you already." I'm losing my patience here. R'overknight is likely waiting somewhere for his steak, thinking I screwed him over, or simply screwed this up, and--

Errant unzips the bag. "Well, then, forgive me for asking a third time, but..."

And suddenly I hear it: that phrase. Forgive me for asking.

The bag opens and I know what's going to be inside before it does, but there it is...

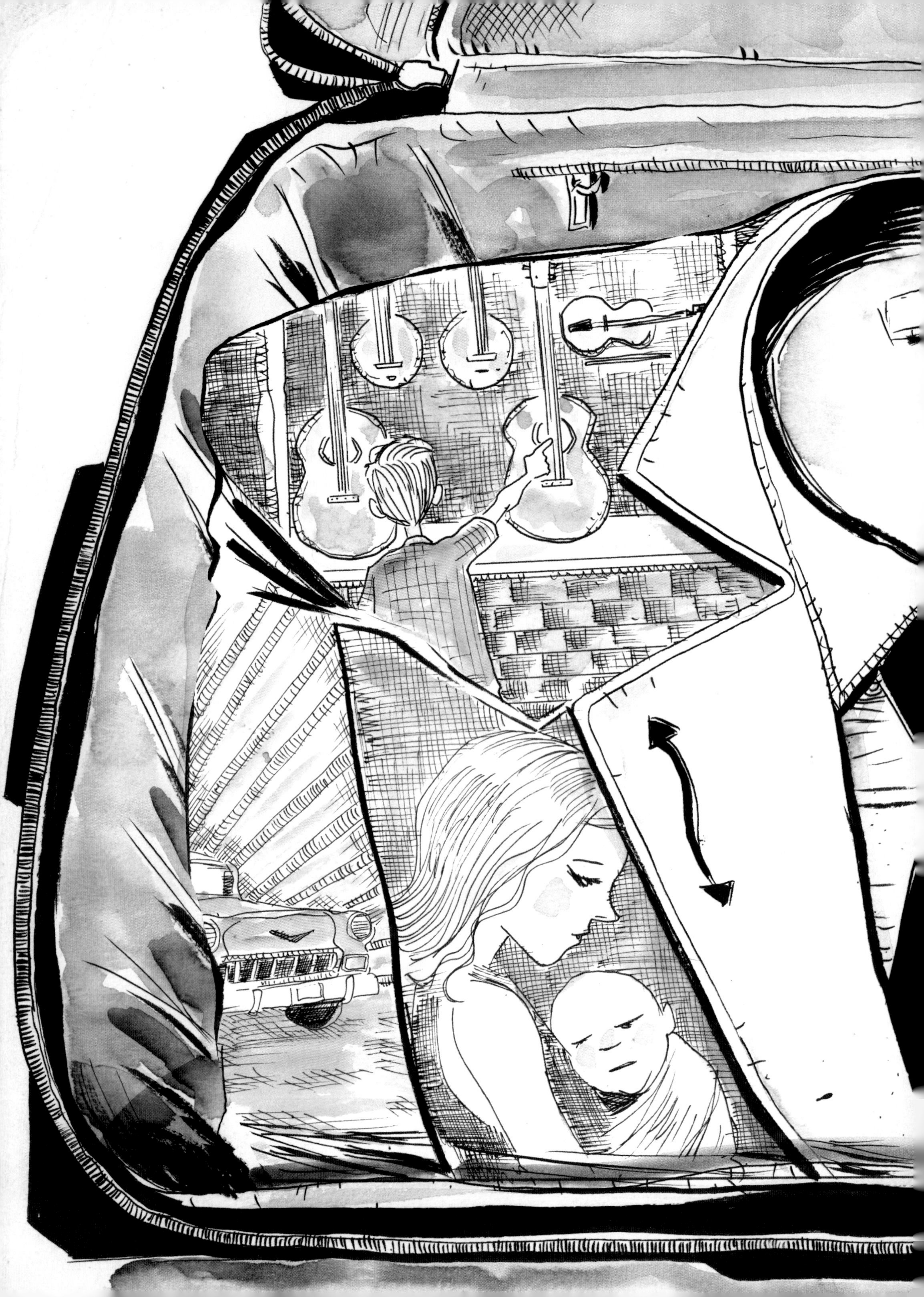

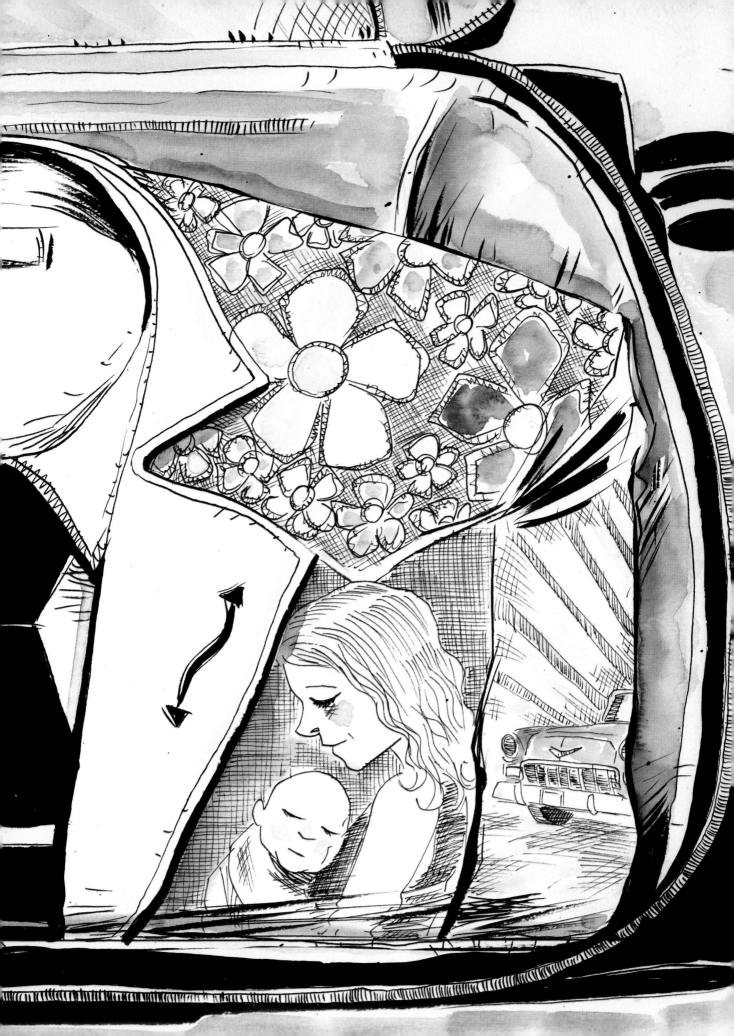

I look at Errant, and then it all comes together.

ERRANT.

By definition the word means “traveling in search of adventure.”

An “errant knight” is a roving knight.

R’overknight. That’s who he is.

I notice Brooke staring at us openly now, no more caution. She has her face cupped to the window and her breath appears on the glass in tiny blooms of fog.

“You shouldn’t be here,” I say to Errant.

“I know,” he says, raising a hand in a gesture of calm, that radio voice soothing. “But like I said, I have a big order to place with you.”

I try to process this. I ask him if he means with Modern Home, or with me.

“With you, of course, Jonah,” he says. “I meant what I said. I’m working with people to set up a clinic. A special place. It’ll be far away from here, in the mountains.”

“What kind of clinic?”

“Jonah, right now, there are five corporations, all major corporations,” he says, “working on a cure for cellular senescence. A cure for aging. Really, though, it's a cure for death itself,” Errant says, putting his hands in his pockets, kicking at the wood floor with his toe. “See, the end of senescence also causes a kind of spasmodic, hyper immunity to illness and infection. Something no one expected, but still pretty revelatory. All this is stuff I can explain later, but the point is, SIGIL is close to a preliminary recipe.”

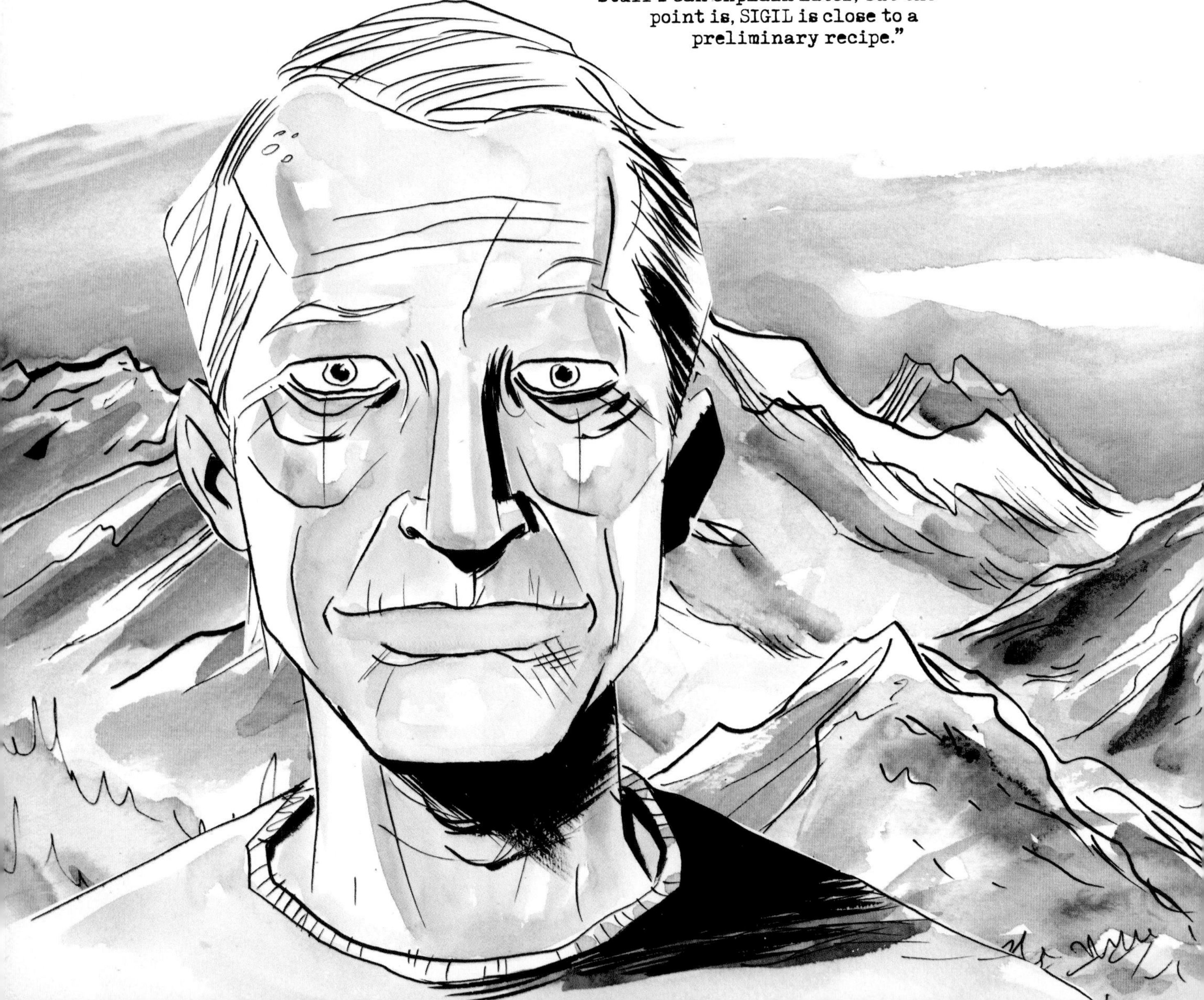

"A cure for death," I say. Have you ever found yourself in a moment you know will be important to the course of the rest of your life, but also a moment you were completely unprepared for that day?

"That's ridiculous," I say, just trying to slow the conversation down.

"No, it's not, and you know it's not. You're just trying to take in what I'm telling you, and, yes, I know it's a lot. But you follow the research at least a little--you've told me so."

He says this kindly, but there's that edge in his voice again, that small table corner that might catch you as you pass by. And, suddenly, all the late-night conversations with this man come rushing back to me. All the things I said to him about my mother, my fears, things I said precisely because I'd never meet him. Yet here he is. And more than ever before, I feel this overwhelming sensation of being trapped, and I just want to get away from Errant, from the situation, from this place, this fake neighborhood of manufactured homes and grass and this suburb, and my mind springs into action, starts working on the problem, on how I'm going to extricate myself from this, steal myself away--not just from the moment, but anything connected to it. The math starts going up on the board...

"Heh. Don't do that." Errant puts a hand on my shoulder, and it's heavier than I'd expect, a gentle anchor.

"Don't run. Just listen to me. Hear me out. You're a great thief. Look at this. Look at what you were able to steal."

He lifts the suit from its case. He does this carefully, respectfully.

In the light the colors radiate, the sequins flash. I'd thought of the thing as some kind of silly show costume. A spangly suit with arrows and boots on it. Pandering. But it's actually quite beautiful. The fabric is an ivory white, and instead of a consistent design, some repeating country and western pattern, the suit is covered in singular scenes. On the breast is a threaded portrait of a woman holding a baby. On the shoulder, a boy pointing to a guitar in a store window. On the arm, a young man driving a Cadillac. It's gorgeous, really. It makes me think of stained glass windows and tapestries.

"Do you know what it is, really?" he says. "You know it's a suit made for a country legend by his wife. Sure. But did you know it was the last suit she ever made for him? She worked on it for years. See, all his life his wife had made him these suits. Suits with designs and decorations and colors that spoke to where they were in their shared life. Each suit a moment in time. But this...this was meant to be the suit he wore to meet God. On it are all the important scenes from their life together, from his life alone. Here is his first communion. See? And here is the moment he learned to play guitar. Even the seams and decorative lines and arrows are significant...see here? And here? They're designed to look like the sheet music to his favorite compositions.

"His wife called this suit his goodbye suit. It was his story, everything that he'd accomplished and he'd loved and he'd been. He was supposed to be buried in it.

He puts the suit back in the suitcase. "She made me one, too," he says. "As a thank-you for helping the family. It's just as pretty as this one. Maybe prettier. It's got my life sewn into it, Jonah. And I'd have had you steal it instead of this one, but I had it burned."

"Burned?" I say.

"Burned to ash. So listen to me when I tell you are not alone."

"What are you talking--"

His hand tightens on my shoulder.

"I have lived a life fuller than any I expected as a man your age. I had a wife I loved. Jennifer. I have children and grandchildren I adore. John and Forrest and Adele. And I have tried to live a good life, making music that makes people happy. I have tried to affect the world in good ways, through our foundation. We have built schools in places that had none, and developed music education programs.

"I am seventy-two years old, Jonah. And my story is a good story. Do you understand me?

"My suit makes a good suit. But I don't want it to be over. I am supposed to be okay with it, but I'm not. I lay awake at night and I am screaming inside. I pass a mirror and see my face and think, who...the HELL...is that?

"A month ago, they had me dip my right ear in a plaster so they could make a mold of it. Look."

He puts a pinkie in his ear, wiggles it, and then shows it to me. The tip has blood on it.

"Ruptured something that won't heal all the way. I hear different now. There's a whistling."

He purses his lips and makes a noise, a whistle but shriller.

I remove his hand from my shoulder and step back.

"I don't understand what any of this has to do with me," I say, though I can feel what's coming. "In fact, I don't even get why you'd--"

"There's something I need you to steal. Period. If you steal it, SIGIL will have a great advantage in the research I'm telling you about. We'll have the advantage over our competitors. A huge jump on them."

I glance up, looking for Brooke, but she's gone.

"Why not just ask me the conventional way?" I say.

"Because it'll be a trickier job than normal, Jonah. And because... this is too big to ask of you that way. I wanted to see you, to tell you I feel the way you do. And that I know many people who do. In fact, I suspect more and more people do these days.

"Imagine how it was at the start. When humanity was young, a child. You lived among the same people every day, saw a small breadth of land. Your life was huge. Your story, and the stories of those you knew, were the only stories. But now, we're all connected. We know of each other. We affect each other all day, every day. We all feel it, that it's the end of something. The rising waters. The overlap of culture and war. The hot, intense, buzzing, buzzing, buzzing…it's like everything has come to this.

"Old age is being aware of yourself, your fragility; it's being scared, and humanity is in its old age now, is my belief. We are a frail old man, aware of our brittleness. All it'll take is a push. A fall and a broken hip. A plague. A bomb. A cataclysm. And we will start to fall apart, fast, just like your mother did."

At the mention of my mother, I feel my rage rising, but he stops me before I say anything.

"But it doesn't have to be that way, Jonah," he says. "Millions of years of history could change right here, on this porch. With you and me."

The whole situation is too much. I look away from him, at the fake sky behind us. The brushstrokes are visible in the clouds, in the swirls of white and gray. The blue is so bright in the floodlights it hurts my eyes.

"What is it you need me to steal?" I say.

"It's not a what," says Errant.

"It's a who."

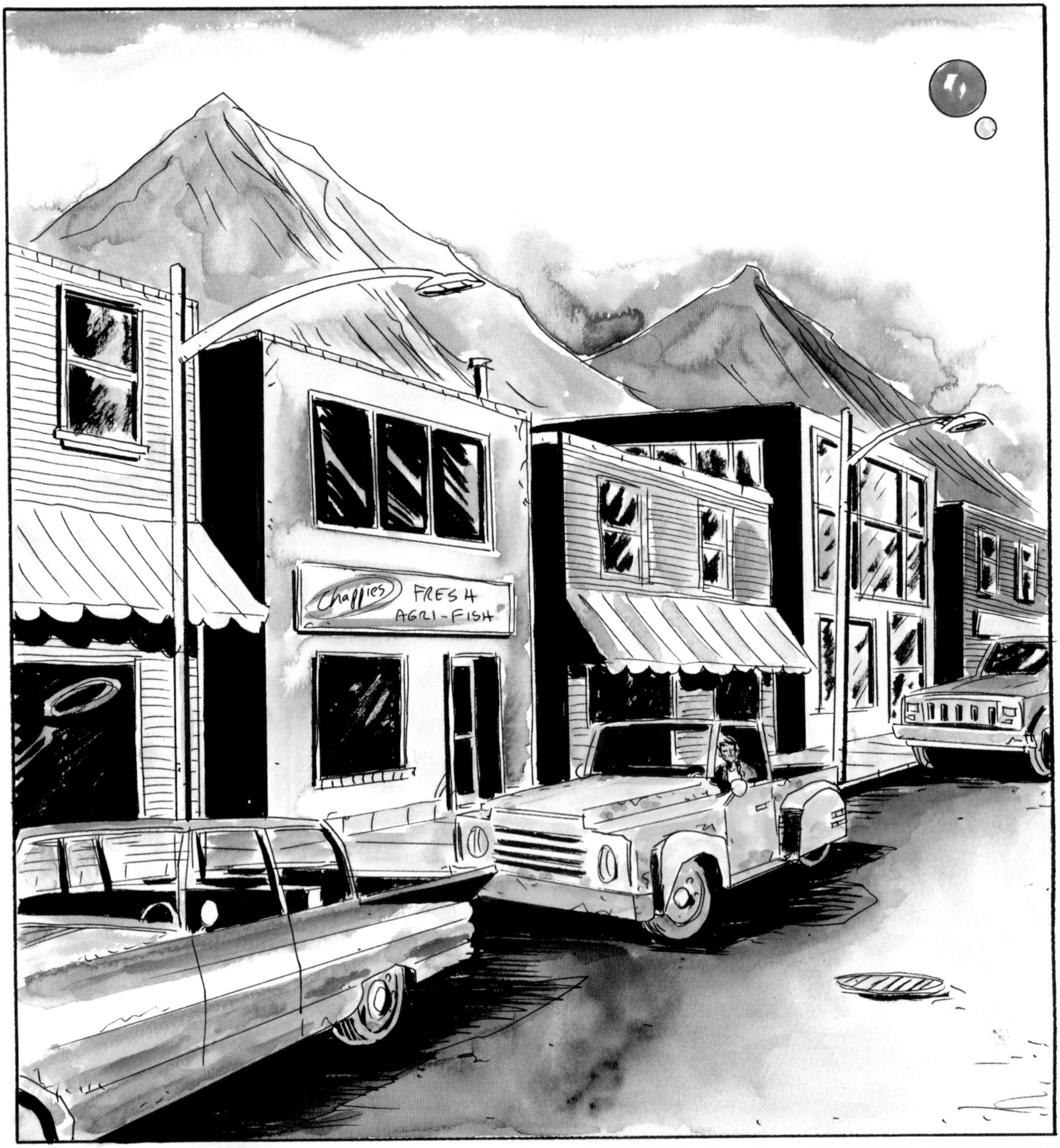
Chappies FRESH AGRI-FISH

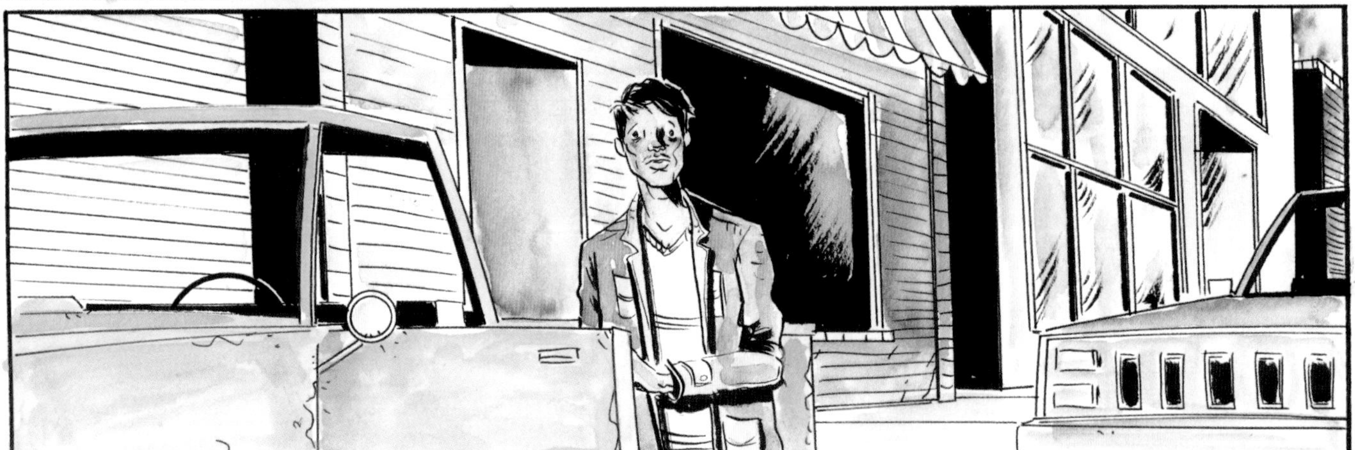

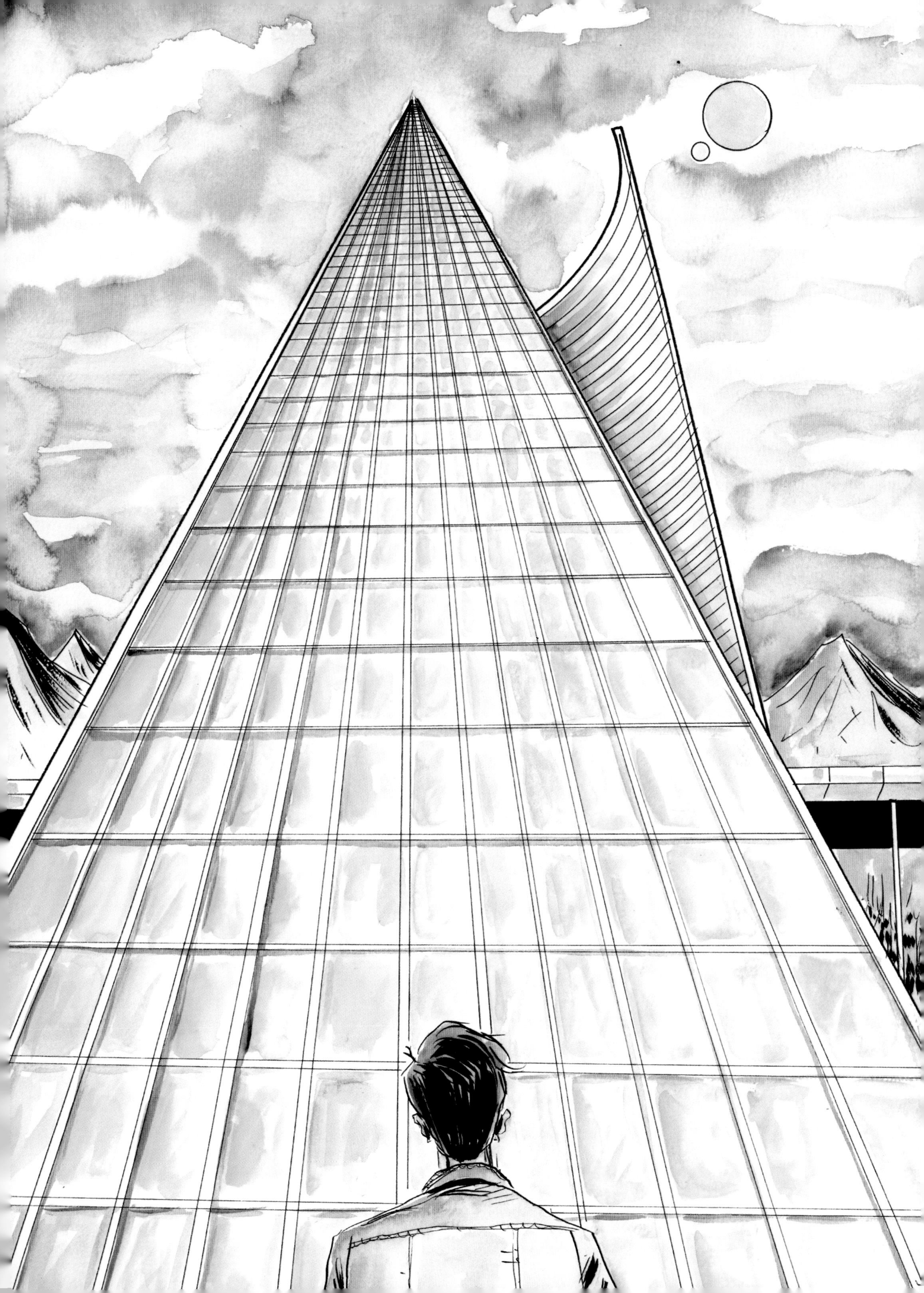

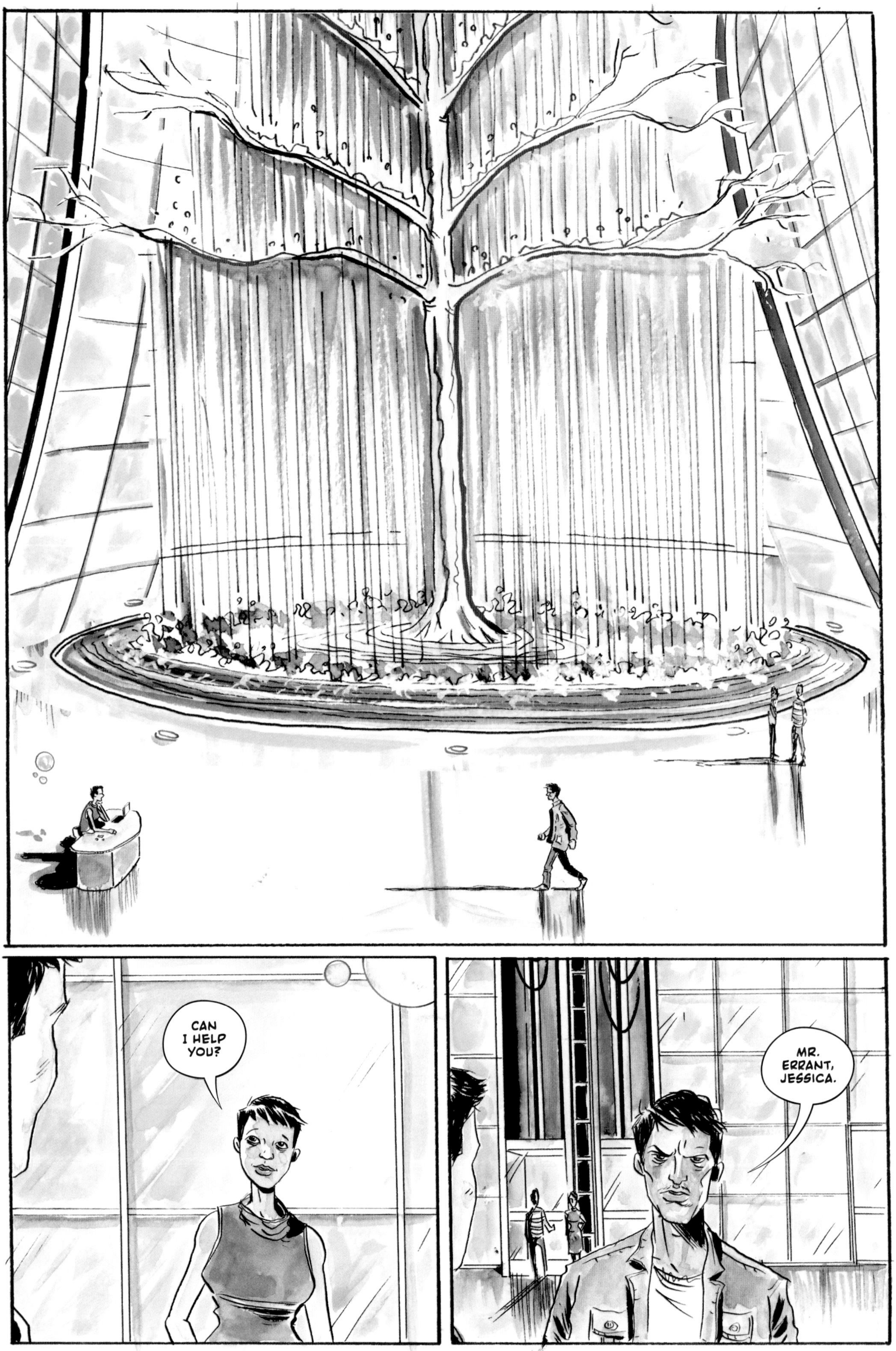
CAN I HELP YOU?
MR. ERRANT, JESSICA.

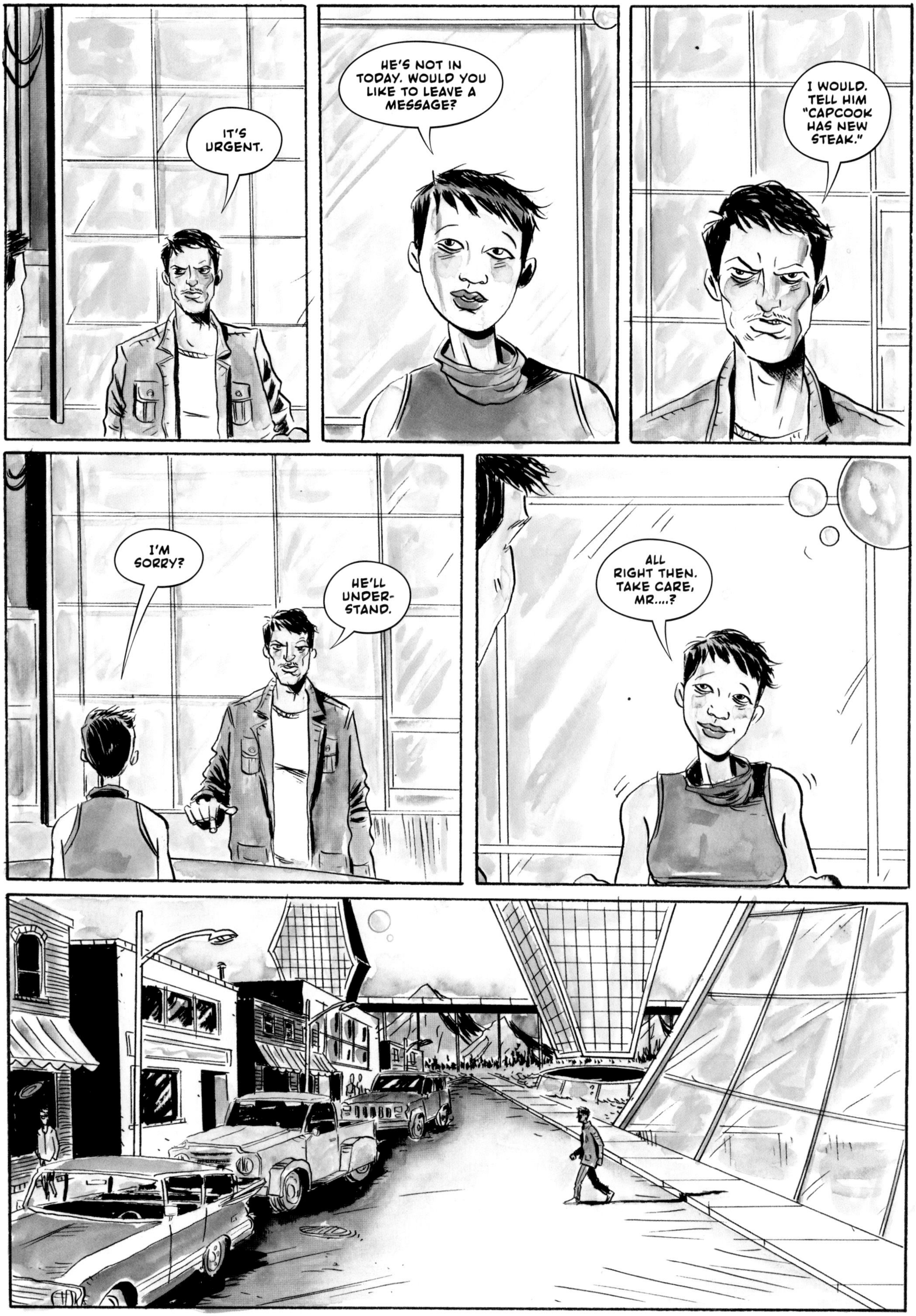
IT'S URGENT.
HE'S NOT IN TODAY. WOULD YOU LIKE TO LEAVE A MESSAGE?
I WOULD. TELL HIM "CAPCOOK HAS NEW STEAK."
I'M SORRY?
HE'LL UNDER-STAND.
ALL RIGHT THEN. TAKE CARE, MR....?

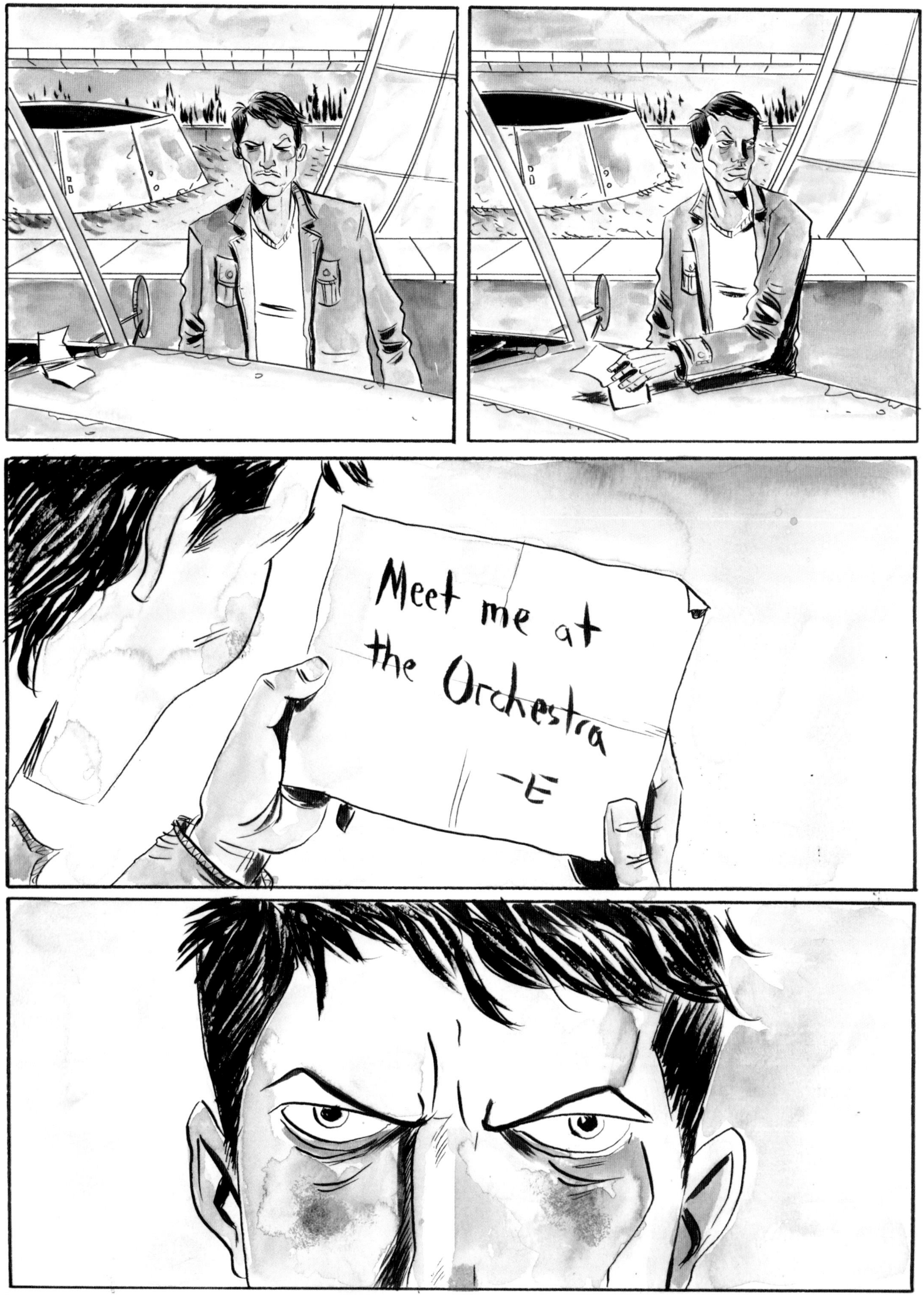
Meet me at the Orchestra
-E

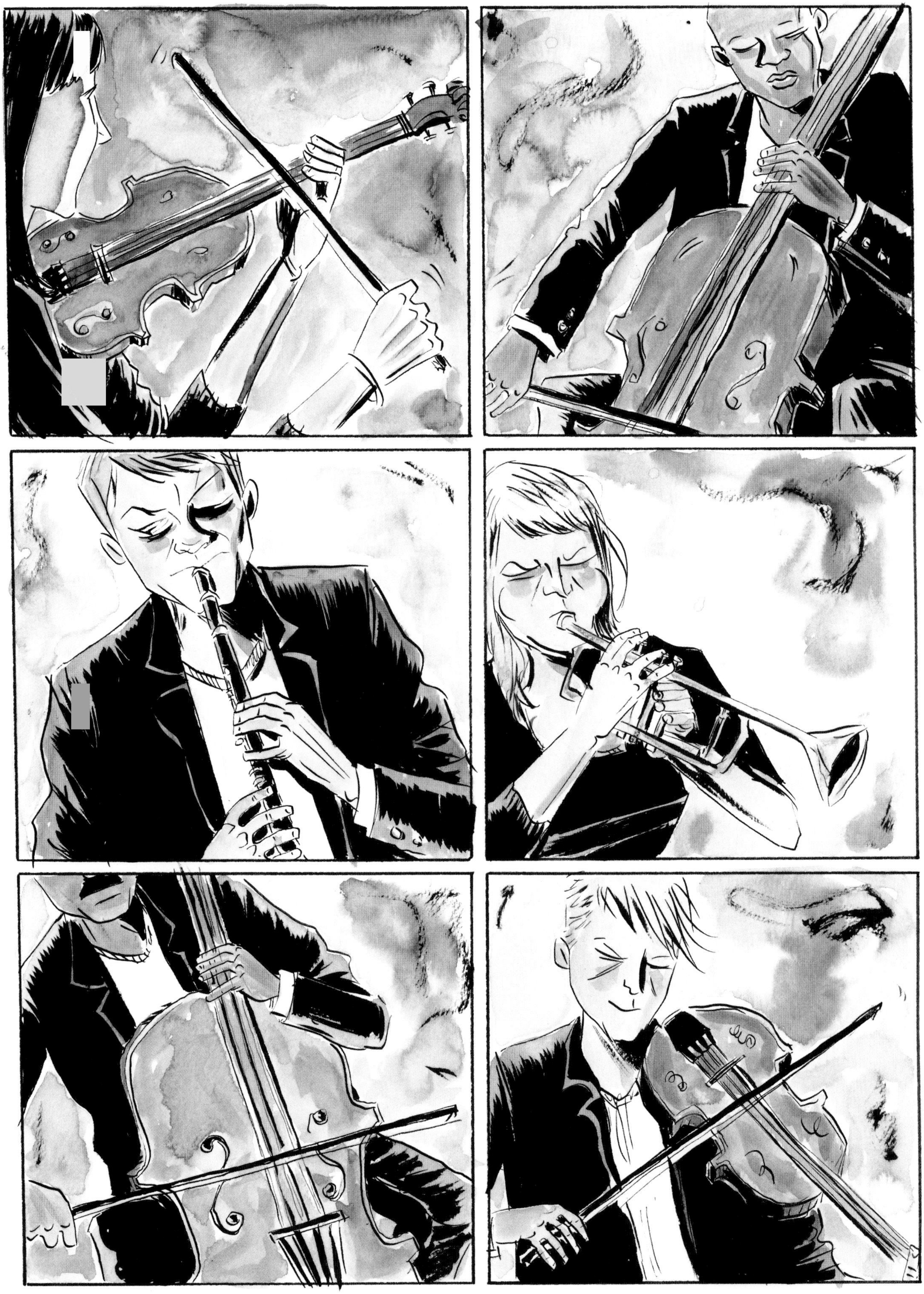

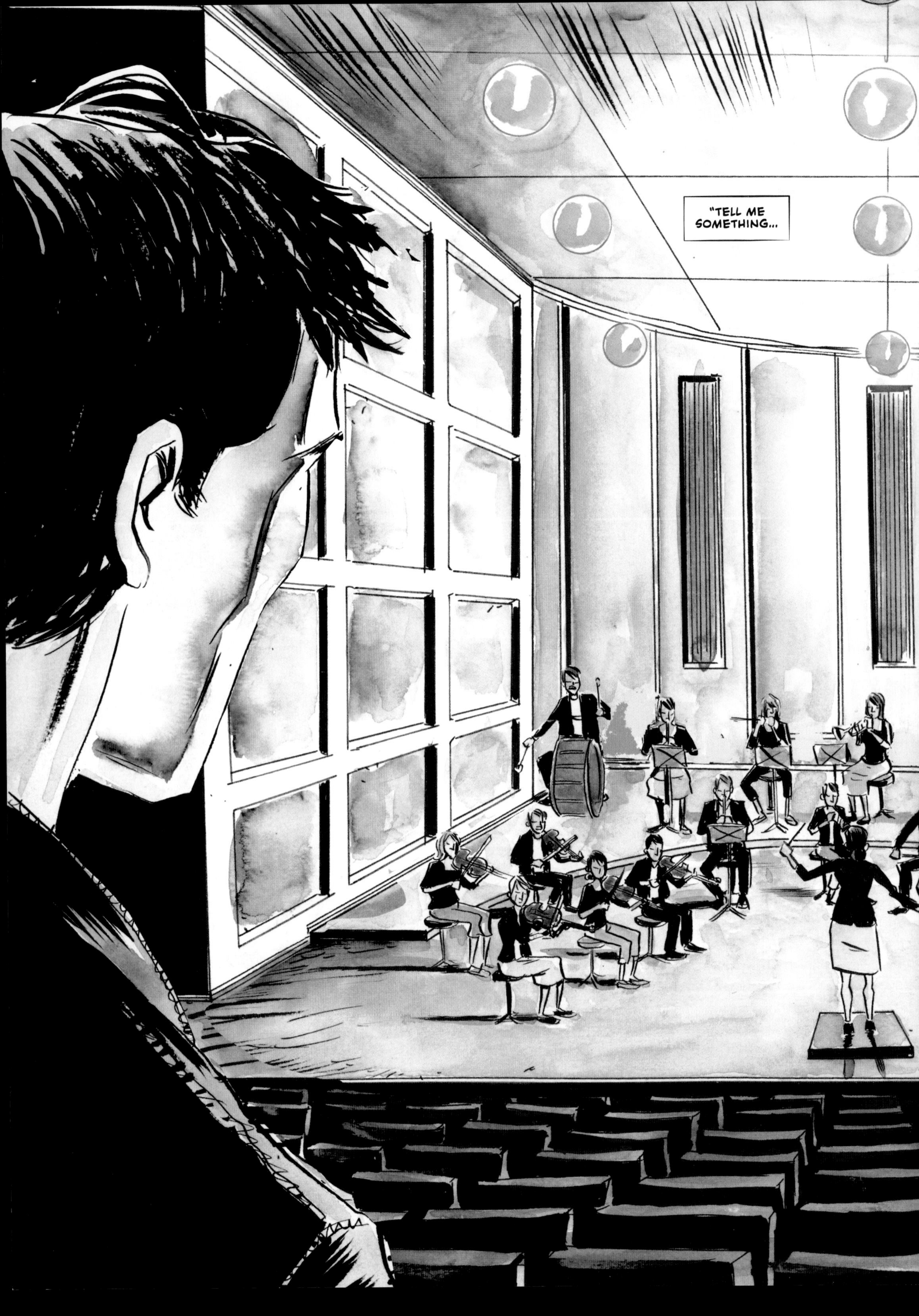
"TELL ME SOMETHING...

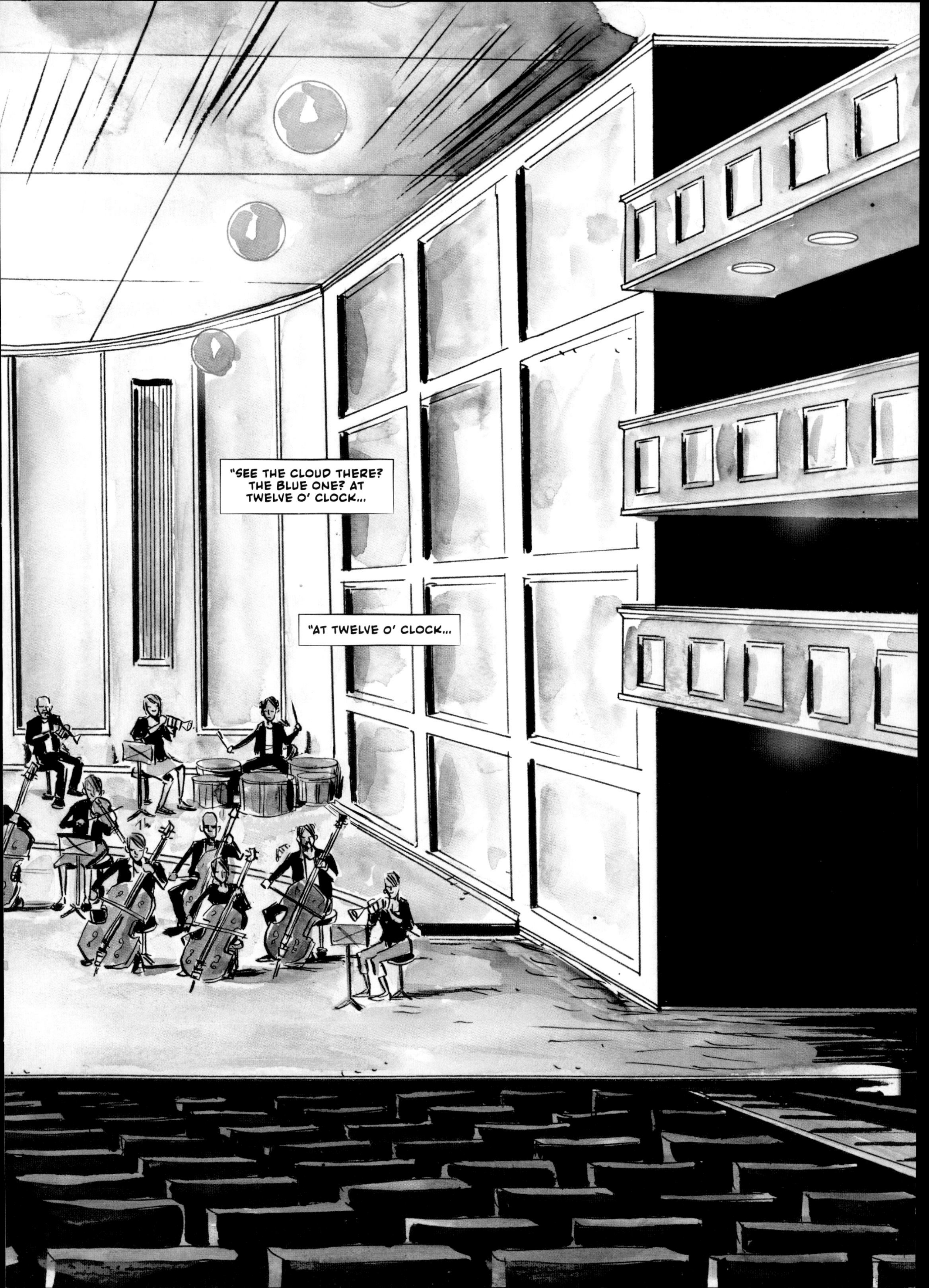
"SEE THE CLOUD THERE? THE BLUE ONE? AT TWELVE O' CLOCK...
"AT TWELVE O' CLOCK...

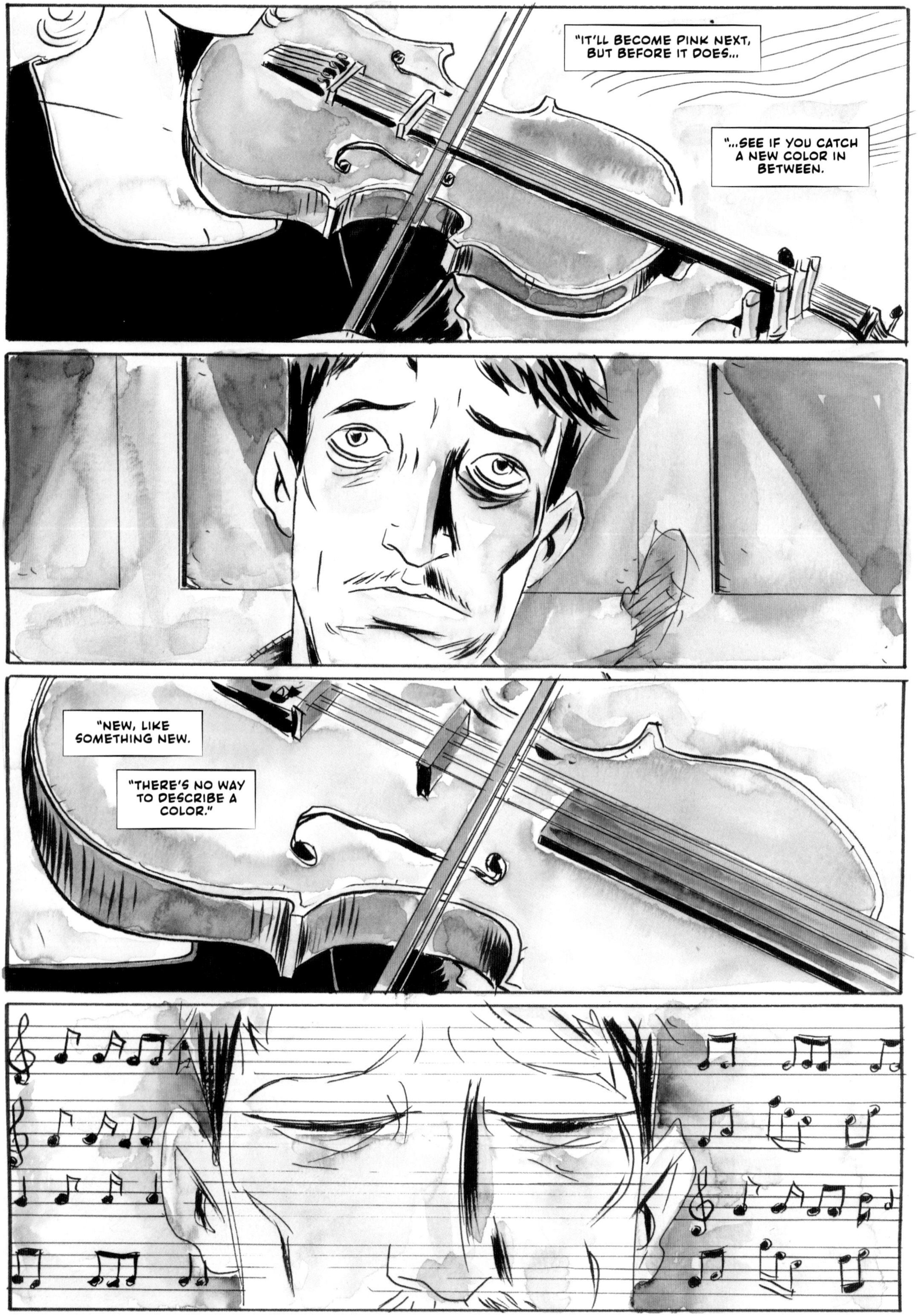
"IT'LL BECOME PINK NEXT, BUT BEFORE IT DOES...
"...SEE IF YOU CATCH A NEW COLOR IN BETWEEN.
"NEW, LIKE SOMETHING NEW.
"THERE'S NO WAY TO DESCRIBE A COLOR."

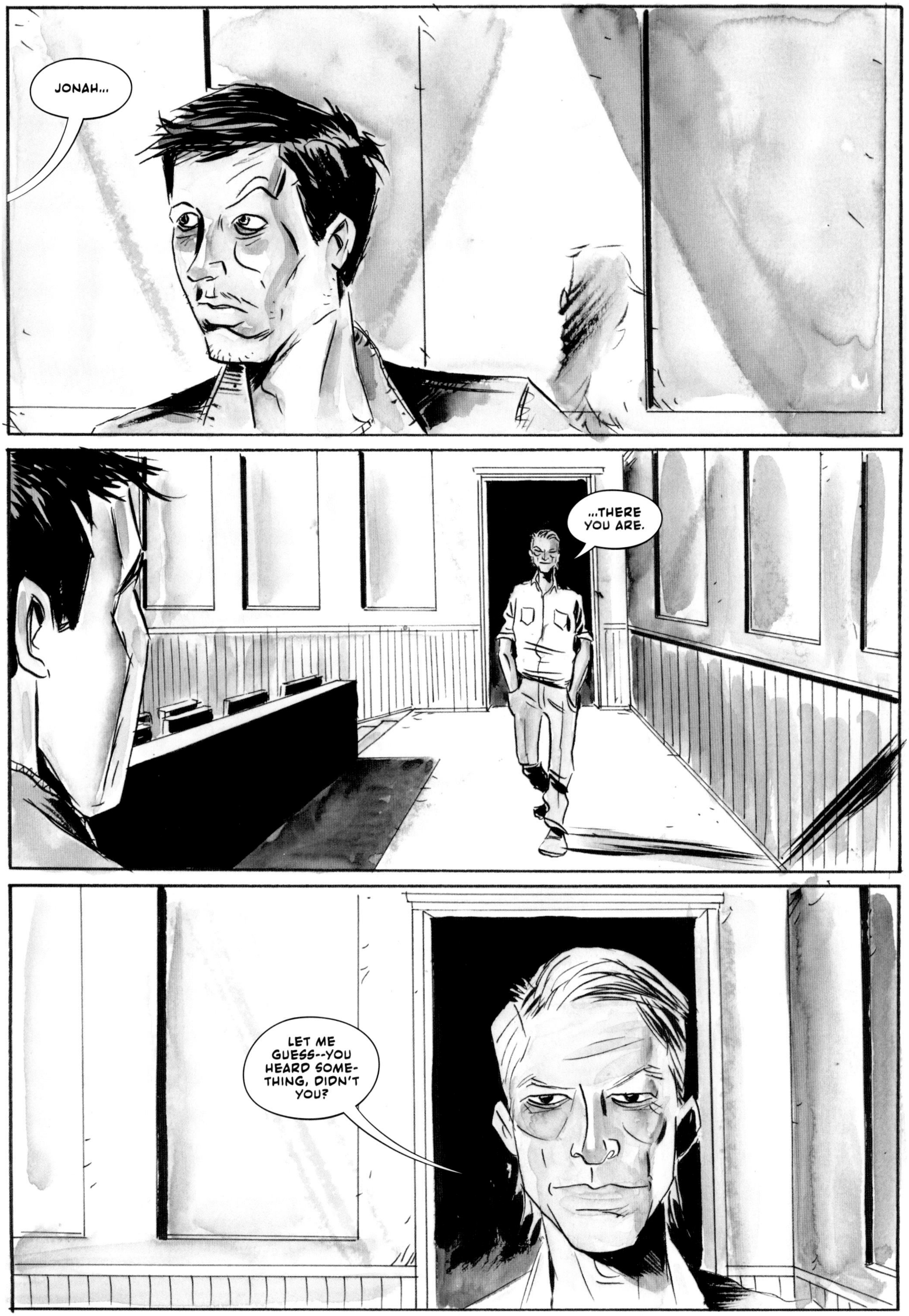
JONAH...
...THERE YOU ARE.
LET ME GUESS--YOU HEARD SOME-THING, DIDN'T YOU?

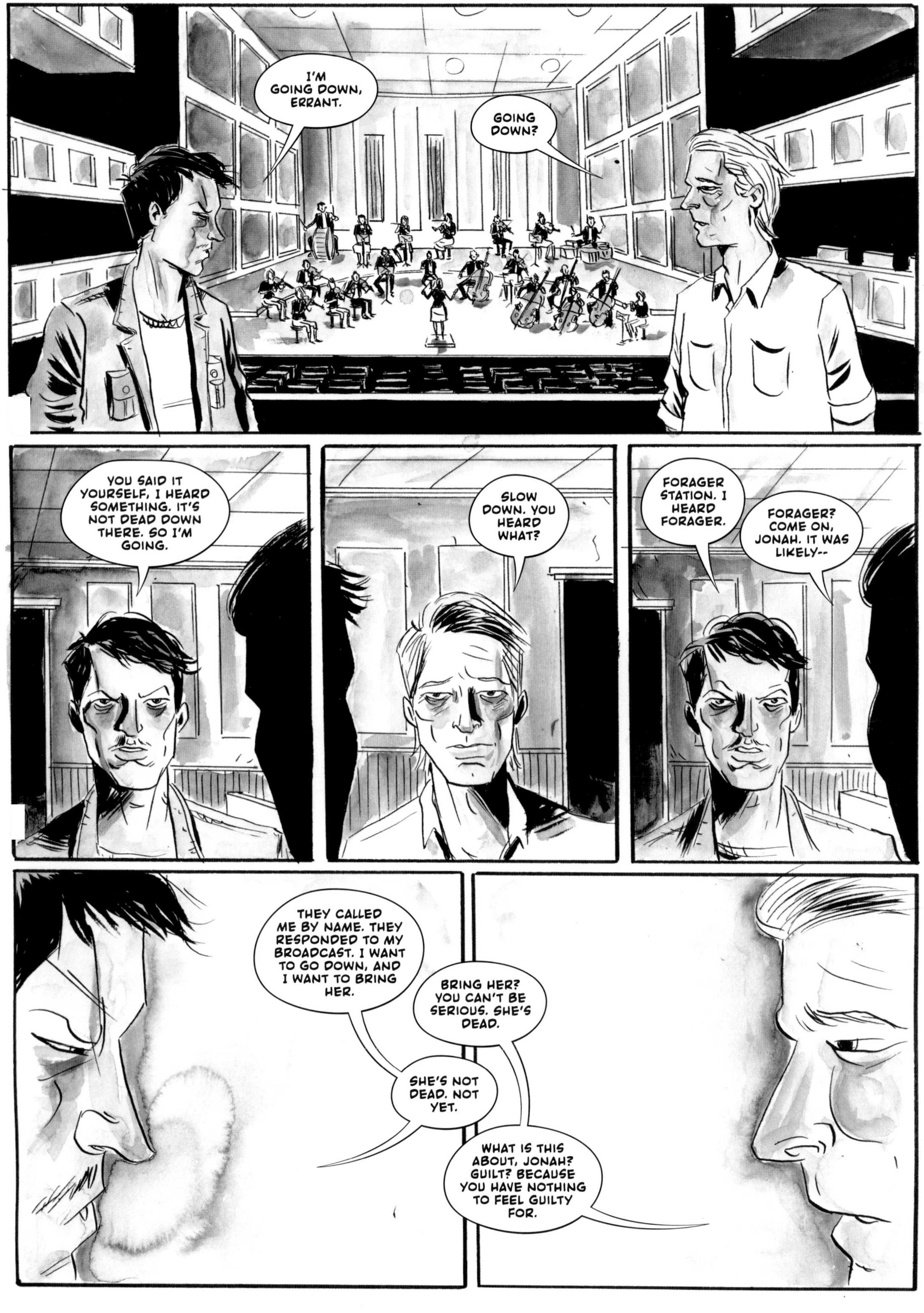
I'M GOING DOWN, ERRANT.
GOING DOWN?
YOU SAID IT YOURSELF, I HEARD SOMETHING. IT'S NOT DEAD DOWN THERE. SO I'M GOING.
SLOW DOWN. YOU HEARD WHAT?
FORAGER STATION. I HEARD FORAGER.
FORAGER? COME ON, JONAH. IT WAS LIKELY--
THEY CALLED ME BY NAME. THEY RESPONDED TO MY BROADCAST. I WANT TO GO DOWN, AND I WANT TO BRING HER.
BRING HER? YOU CAN'T BE SERIOUS. SHE'S DEAD.
SHE'S NOT DEAD. NOT YET.
WHAT IS THIS ABOUT, JONAH? GUILT? BECAUSE YOU HAVE NOTHING TO FEEL GUILTY FOR.

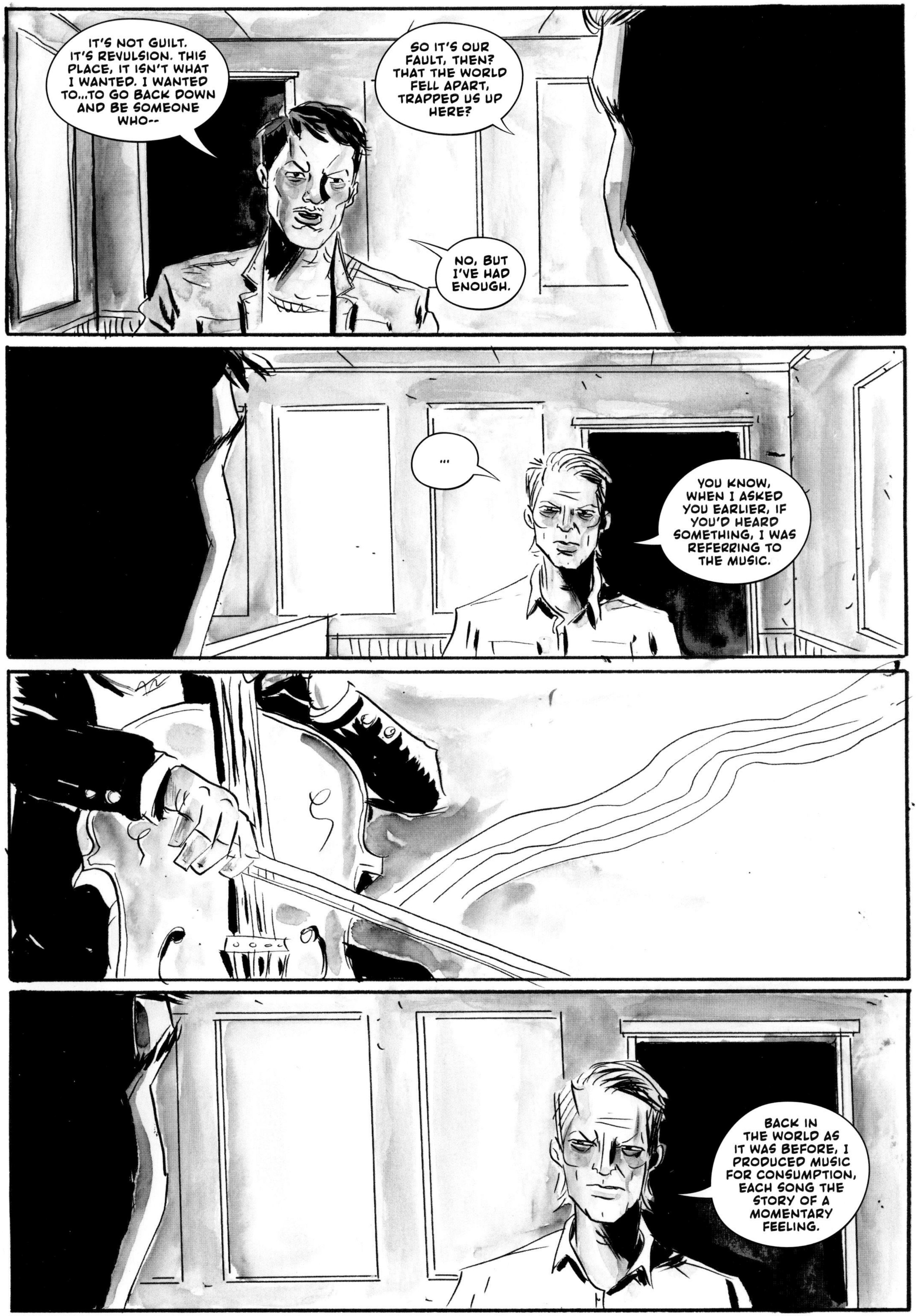
IT'S NOT GUILT. IT'S REVULSION. THIS PLACE, IT ISN'T WHAT I WANTED. I WANTED TO...TO GO BACK DOWN AND BE SOMEONE WHO--
SO IT'S OUR FAULT, THEN? THAT THE WORLD FELL APART, TRAPPED US UP HERE?
NO, BUT I'VE HAD ENOUGH.
...
YOU KNOW, WHEN I ASKED YOU EARLIER, IF YOU'D HEARD SOMETHING, I WAS REFERRING TO THE MUSIC.
BACK IN THE WORLD AS IT WAS BEFORE, I PRODUCED MUSIC FOR CONSUMPTION, EACH SONG THE STORY OF A MOMENTARY FEELING.

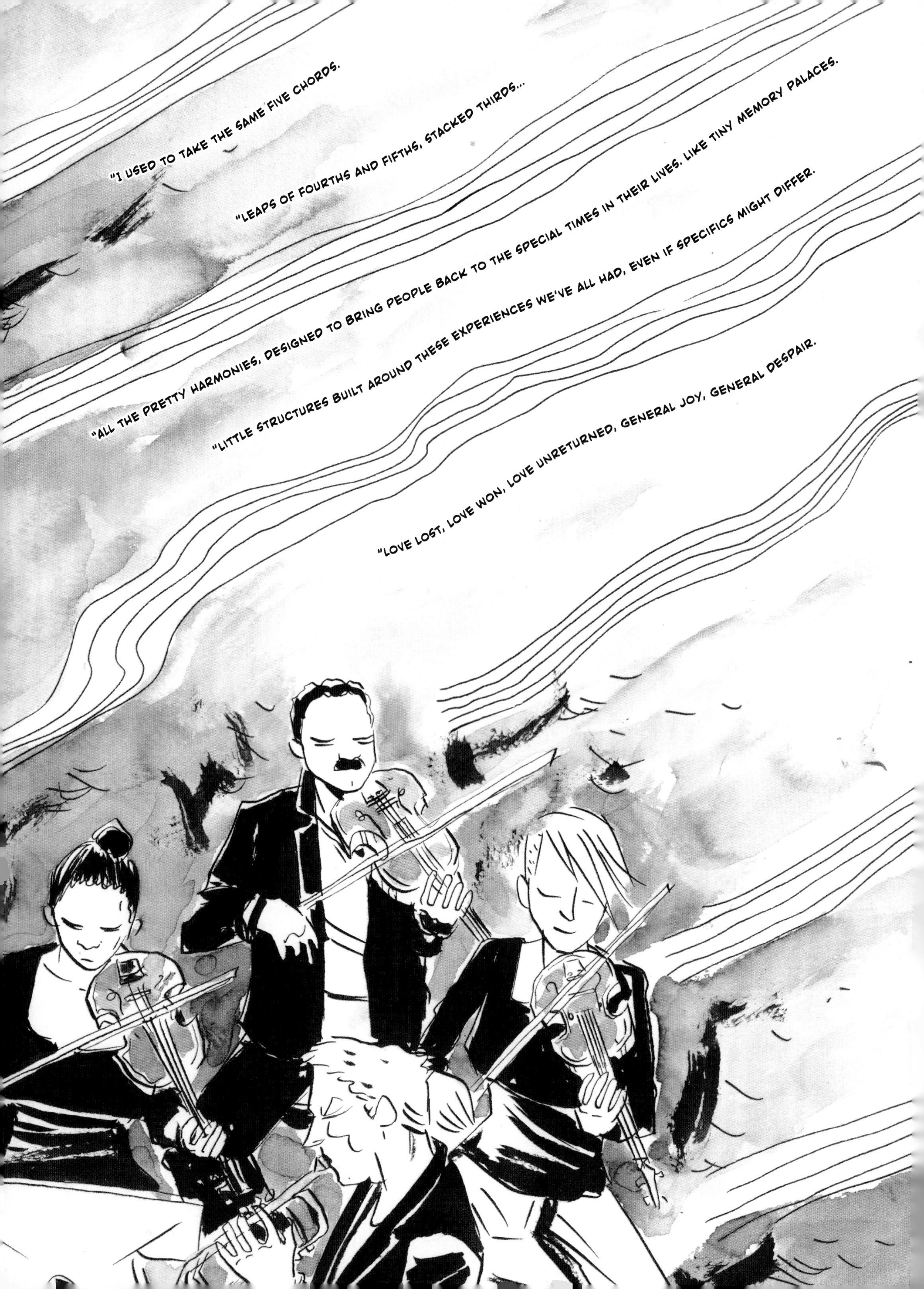
"I USED TO TAKE THE SAME FIVE CHORDS.
"LEAPS OF FOURTHS AND FIFTHS, STACKED THIRDS...
"ALL THE PRETTY HARMONIES, DESIGNED TO BRING PEOPLE BACK TO THE SPECIAL TIMES IN THEIR LIVES. LIKE TINY MEMORY PALACES.
"LITTLE STRUCTURES BUILT AROUND THESE EXPERIENCES WE'VE ALL HAD, EVEN IF SPECIFICS MIGHT DIFFER.
"LOVE LOST, LOVE WON, LOVE UNRETURNED, GENERAL JOY, GENERAL DESPAIR.

"HERE, THOUGH...IN THIS PLACE...

"I MAKE SOMETHING UNHEARD OF.

"MUSIC THAT CONNECTS WITH NOTHING THAT CAME BEFORE.

"MUSIC BUILT ON UNCOMMON INTERVALS, BIG LEAPS OUTSIDE THE OCTAVE. TRITONES AND TWELVE-TONES AND STRANGE TUNINGS.

"COMPOSITIONS THAT LAST MONTHS, EVEN YEARS, JONAH.

"THIS SONG YOU'RE HEARING, IT'S YEARS LONG.

"AND THERE ARE NEW NOTES BENT INTO IT. THINGS WE COULDN'T EVEN HEAR BEFORE.

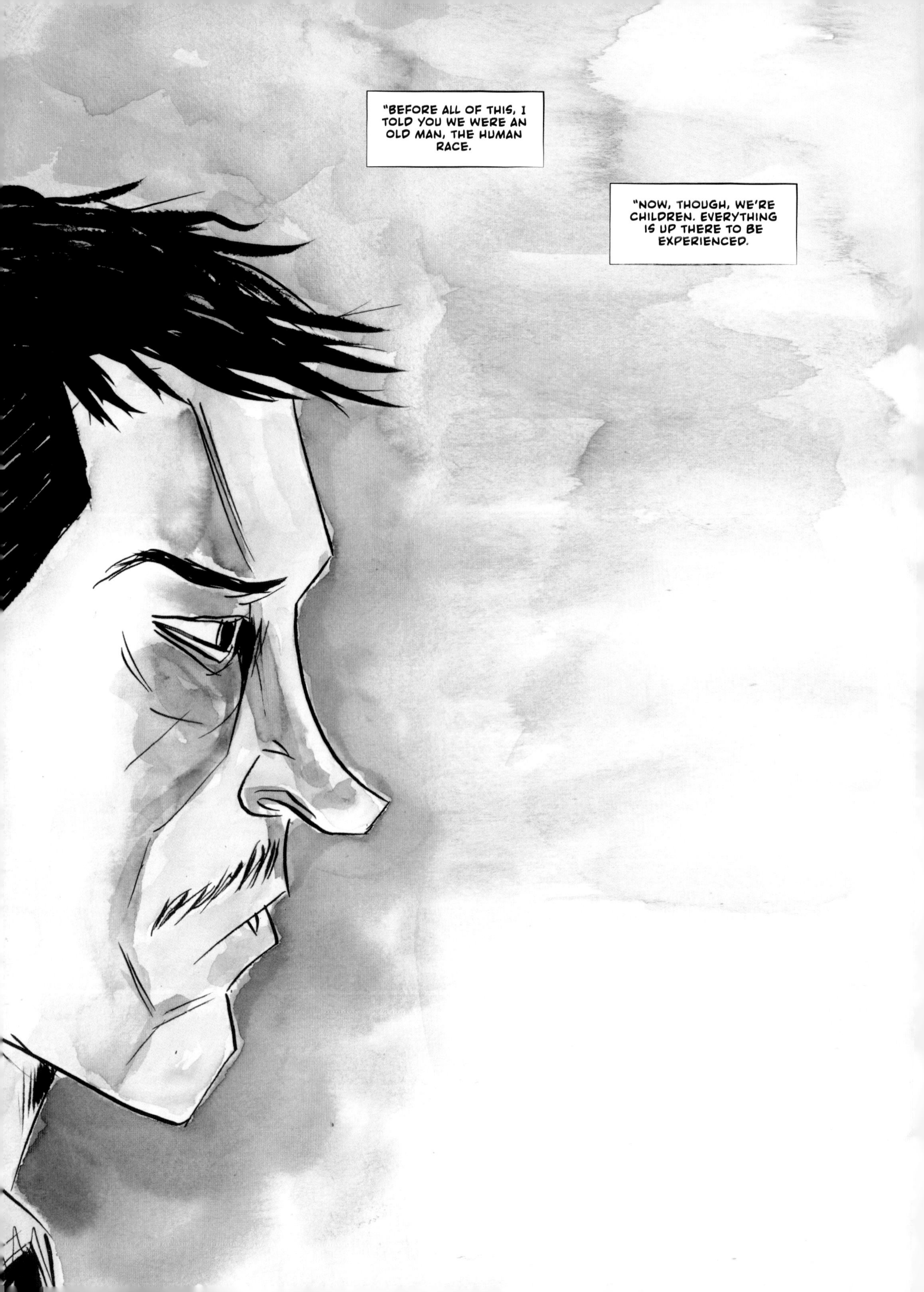
"BEFORE ALL OF THIS, I TOLD YOU WE WERE AN OLD MAN, THE HUMAN RACE.
"NOW, THOUGH, WE'RE CHILDREN. EVERYTHING IS UP THERE TO BE EXPERIENCED.

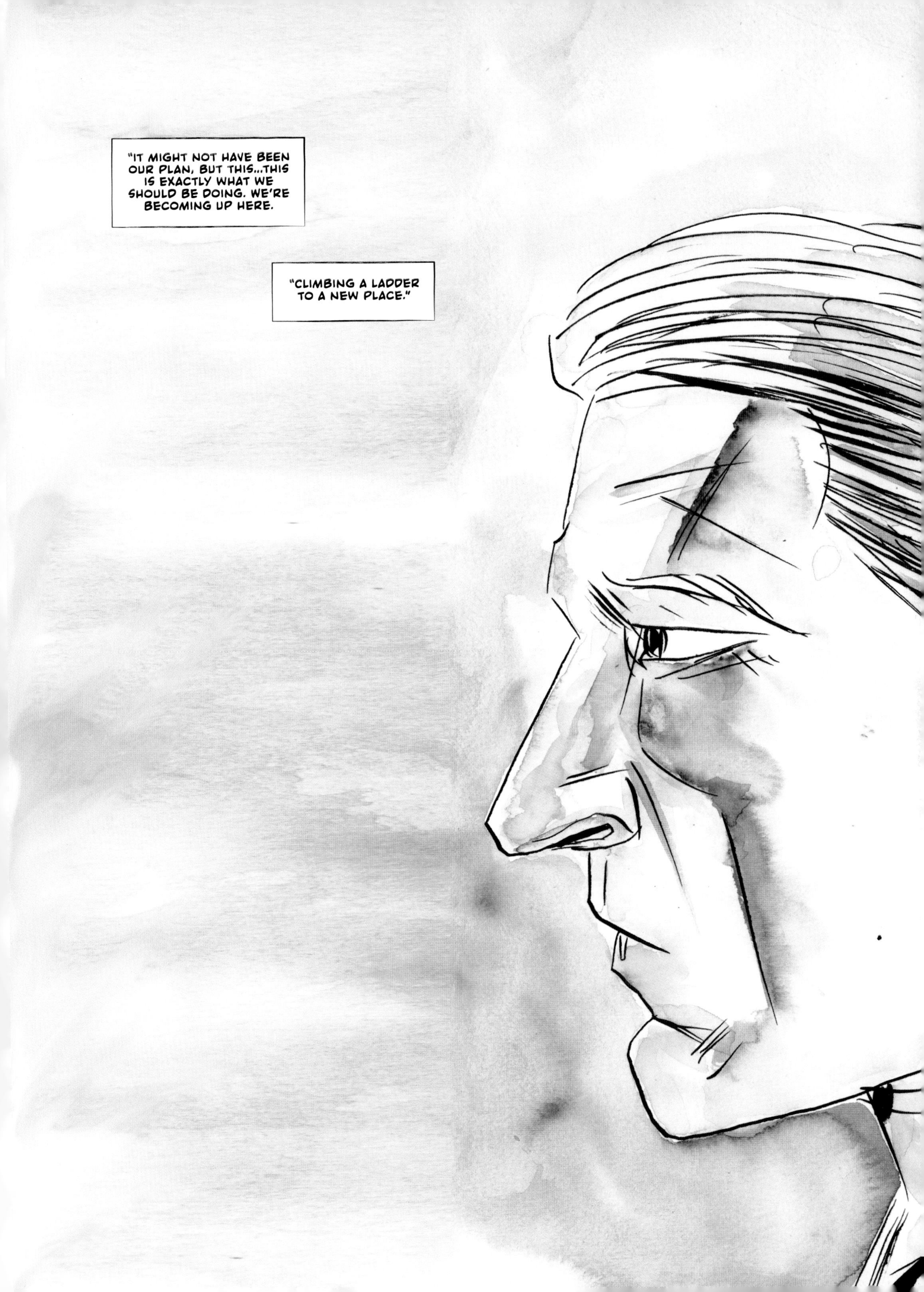
"IT MIGHT NOT HAVE BEEN OUR PLAN, BUT THIS...THIS IS EXACTLY WHAT WE SHOULD BE DOING. WE'RE BECOMING UP HERE.
"CLIMBING A LADDER TO A NEW PLACE."

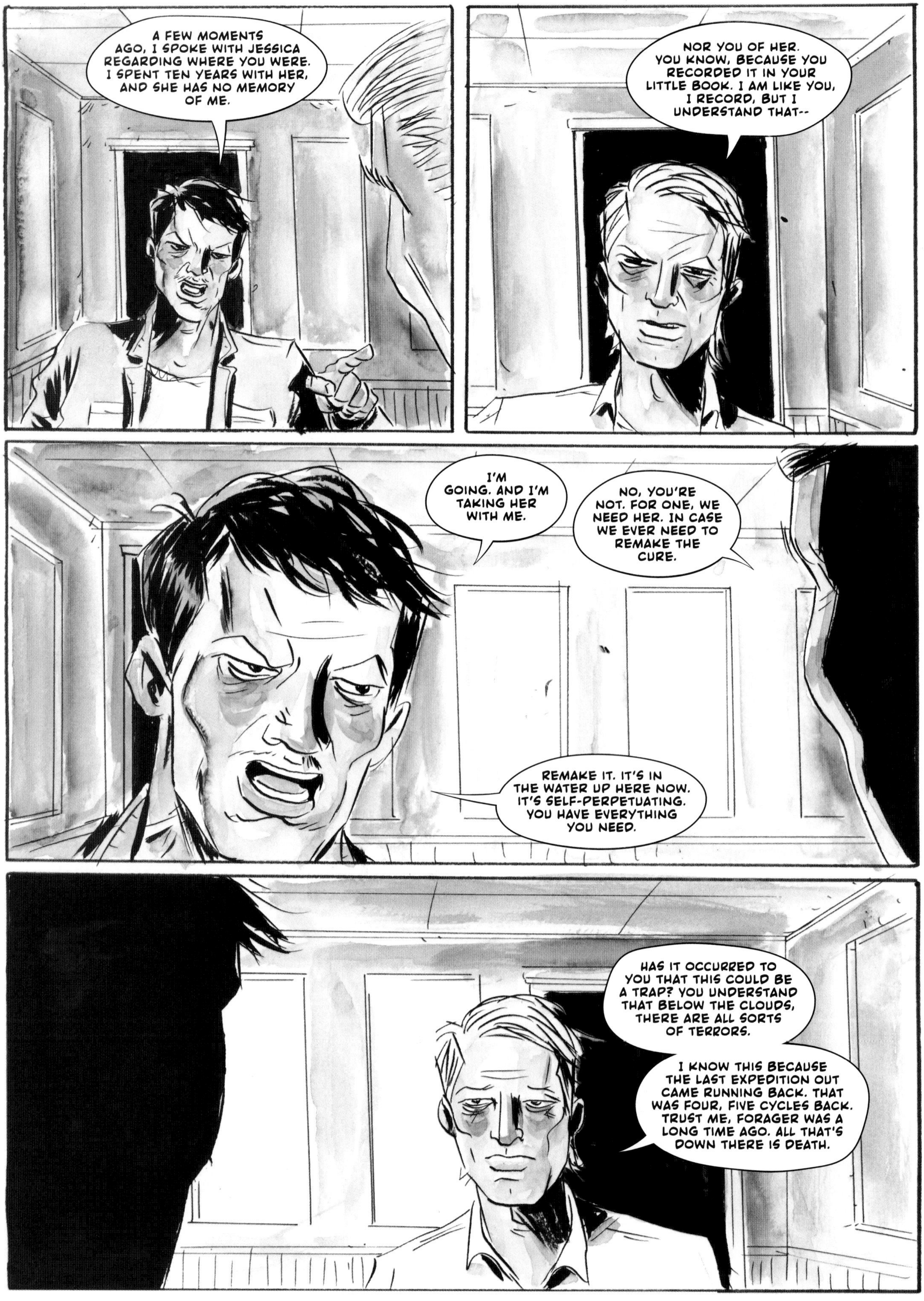
A FEW MOMENTS AGO, I SPOKE WITH JESSICA REGARDING WHERE YOU WERE. I SPENT TEN YEARS WITH HER, AND SHE HAS NO MEMORY OF ME.
NOR YOU OF HER. YOU KNOW, BECAUSE YOU RECORDED IT IN YOUR LITTLE BOOK. I AM LIKE YOU, I RECORD, BUT I UNDERSTAND THAT--
I'M GOING. AND I'M TAKING HER WITH ME.
NO, YOU'RE NOT. FOR ONE, WE NEED HER. IN CASE WE EVER NEED TO REMAKE THE CURE.
REMAKE IT. IT'S IN THE WATER UP HERE NOW. IT'S SELF-PERPETUATING. YOU HAVE EVERYTHING YOU NEED.
HAS IT OCCURRED TO YOU THAT THIS COULD BE A TRAP? YOU UNDERSTAND THAT BELOW THE CLOUDS, THERE ARE ALL SORTS OF TERRORS.
I KNOW THIS BECAUSE THE LAST EXPEDITION OUT CAME RUNNING BACK. THAT WAS FOUR, FIVE CYCLES BACK. TRUST ME, FORAGER WAS A LONG TIME AGO. ALL THAT'S DOWN THERE IS DEATH.

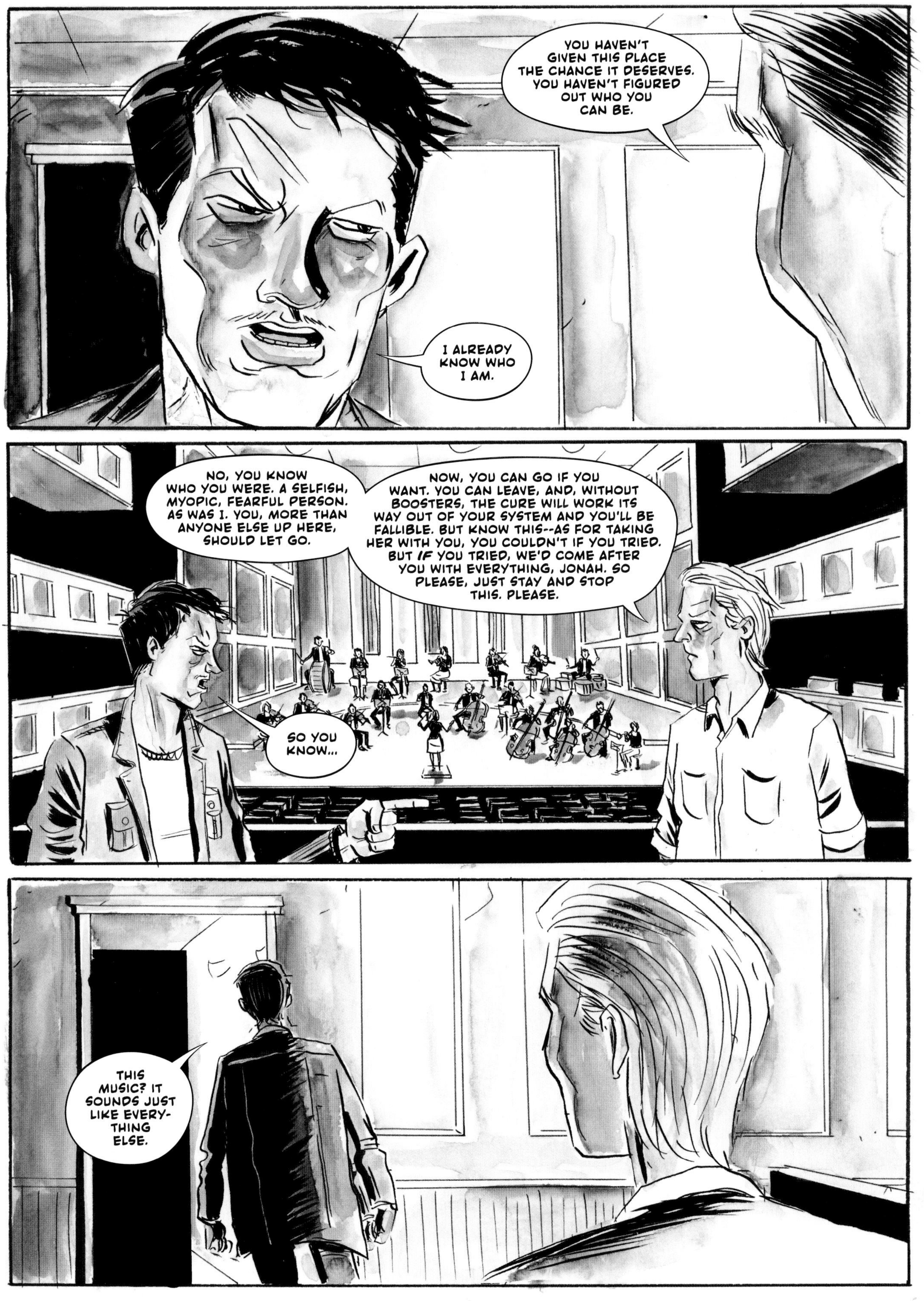

YOU HAVEN'T GIVEN THIS PLACE THE CHANCE IT DESERVES. YOU HAVEN'T FIGURED OUT WHO YOU CAN BE.
I ALREADY KNOW WHO I AM.
NO, YOU KNOW WHO YOU WERE. A SELFISH, MYOPIC, FEARFUL PERSON. AS WAS I. YOU, MORE THAN ANYONE ELSE UP HERE, SHOULD LET GO.
NOW, YOU CAN GO IF YOU WANT. YOU CAN LEAVE, AND, WITHOUT BOOSTERS, THE CURE WILL WORK ITS WAY OUT OF YOUR SYSTEM AND YOU'LL BE FALLIBLE. BUT KNOW THIS--AS FOR TAKING HER WITH YOU, YOU COULDN'T IF YOU TRIED. BUT *IF* YOU TRIED, WE'D COME AFTER YOU WITH EVERYTHING, JONAH. SO PLEASE, JUST STAY AND STOP THIS. PLEASE.
SO YOU KNOW...
THIS MUSIC? IT SOUNDS JUST LIKE EVERY-THING ELSE.

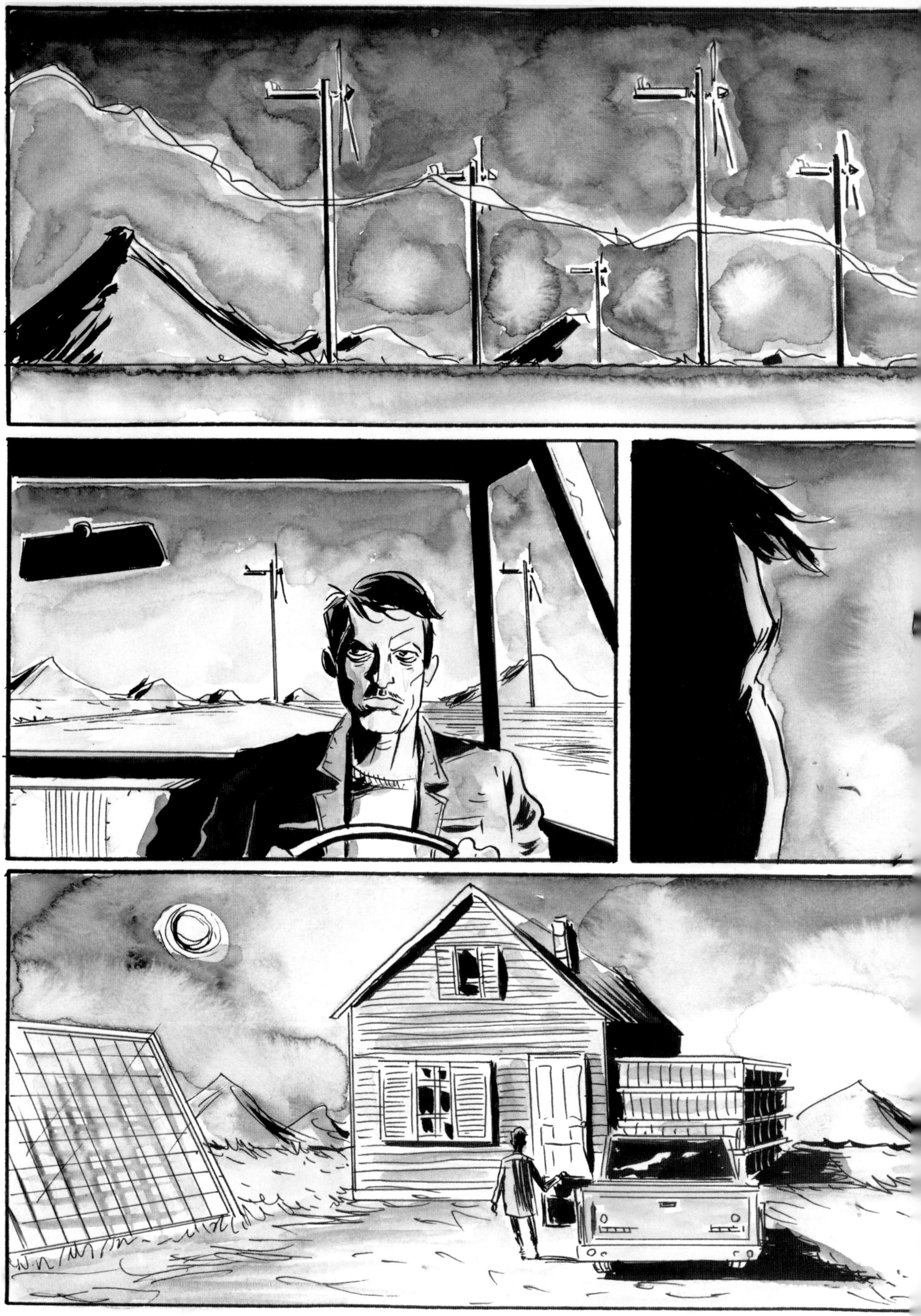

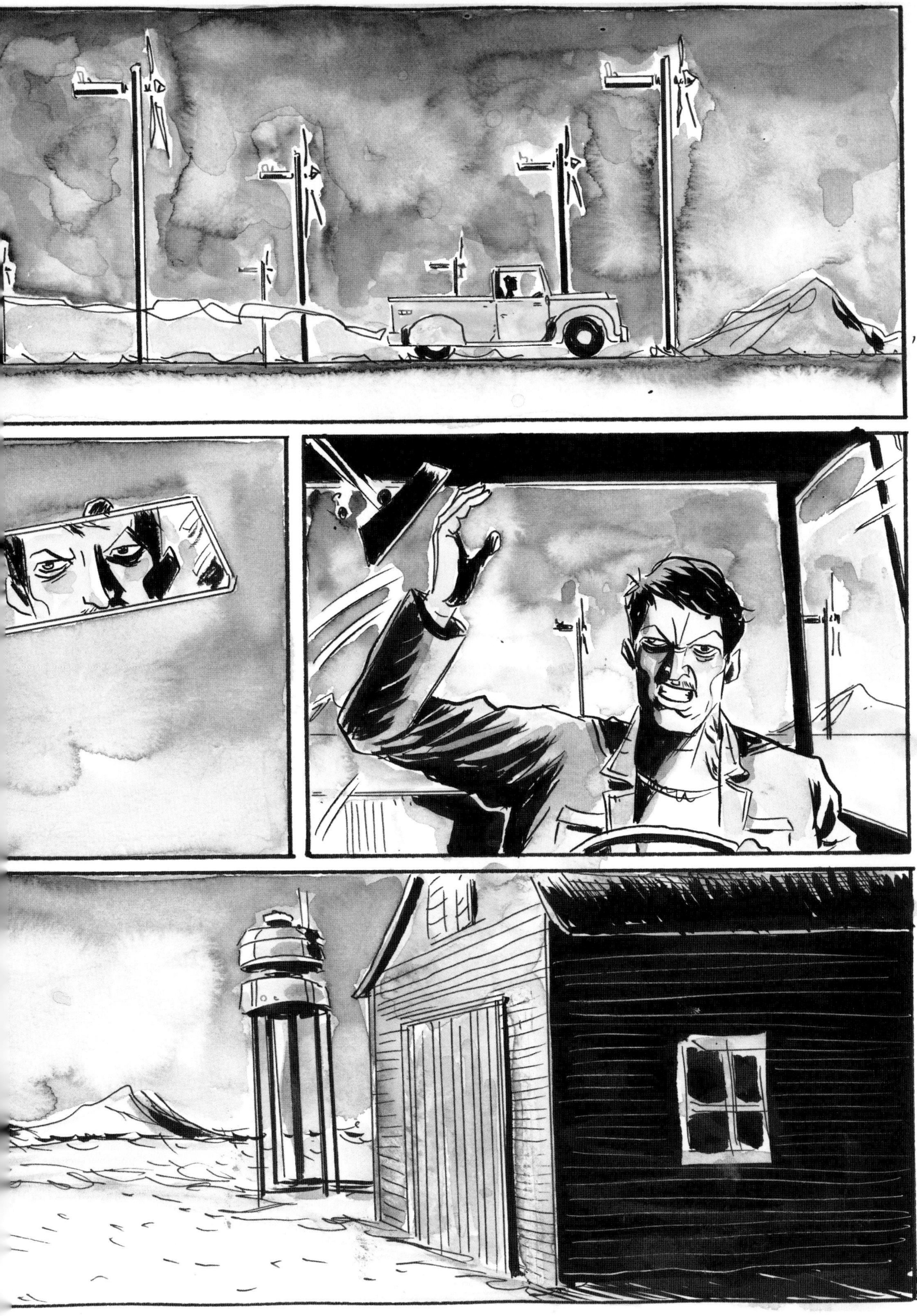

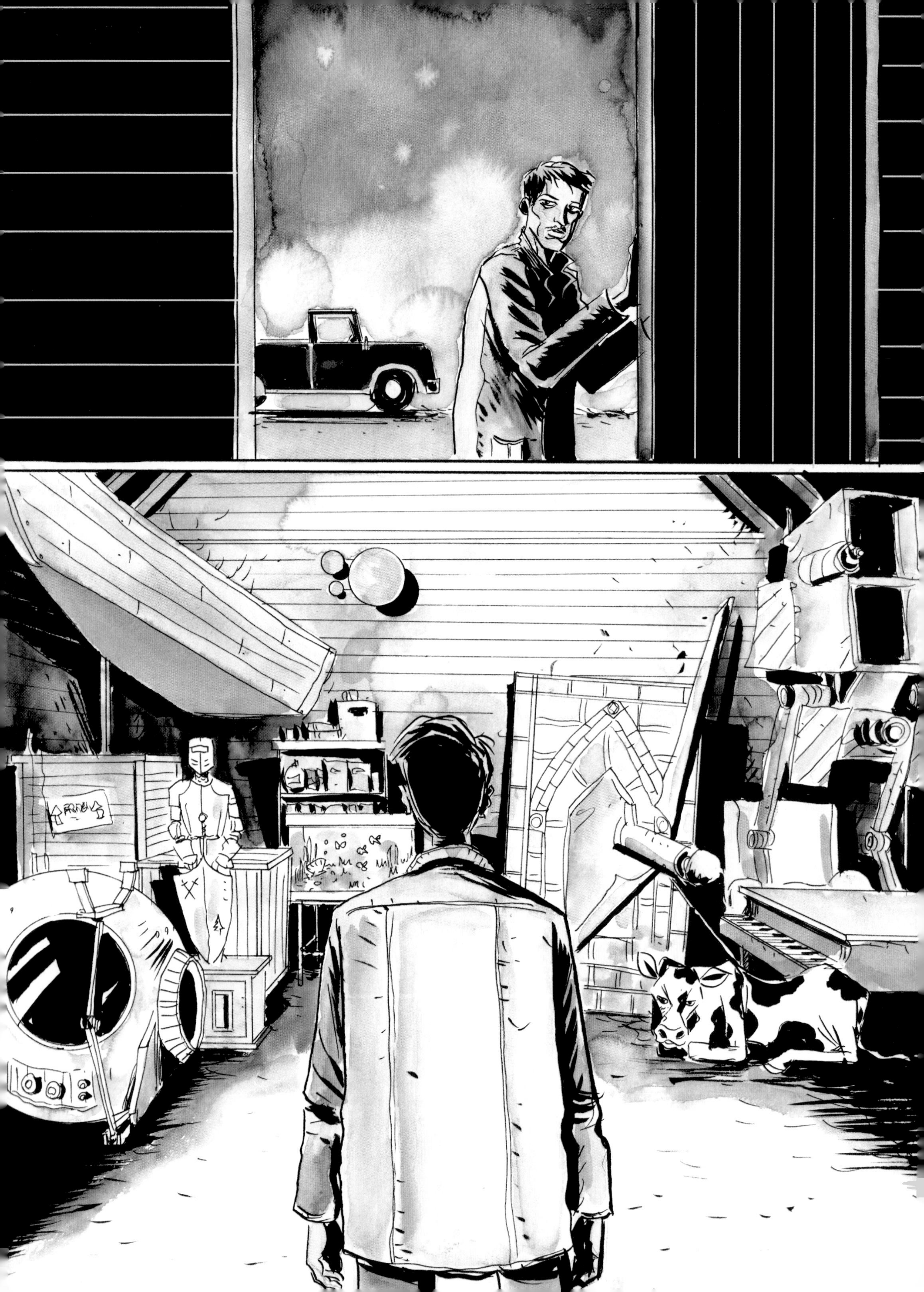

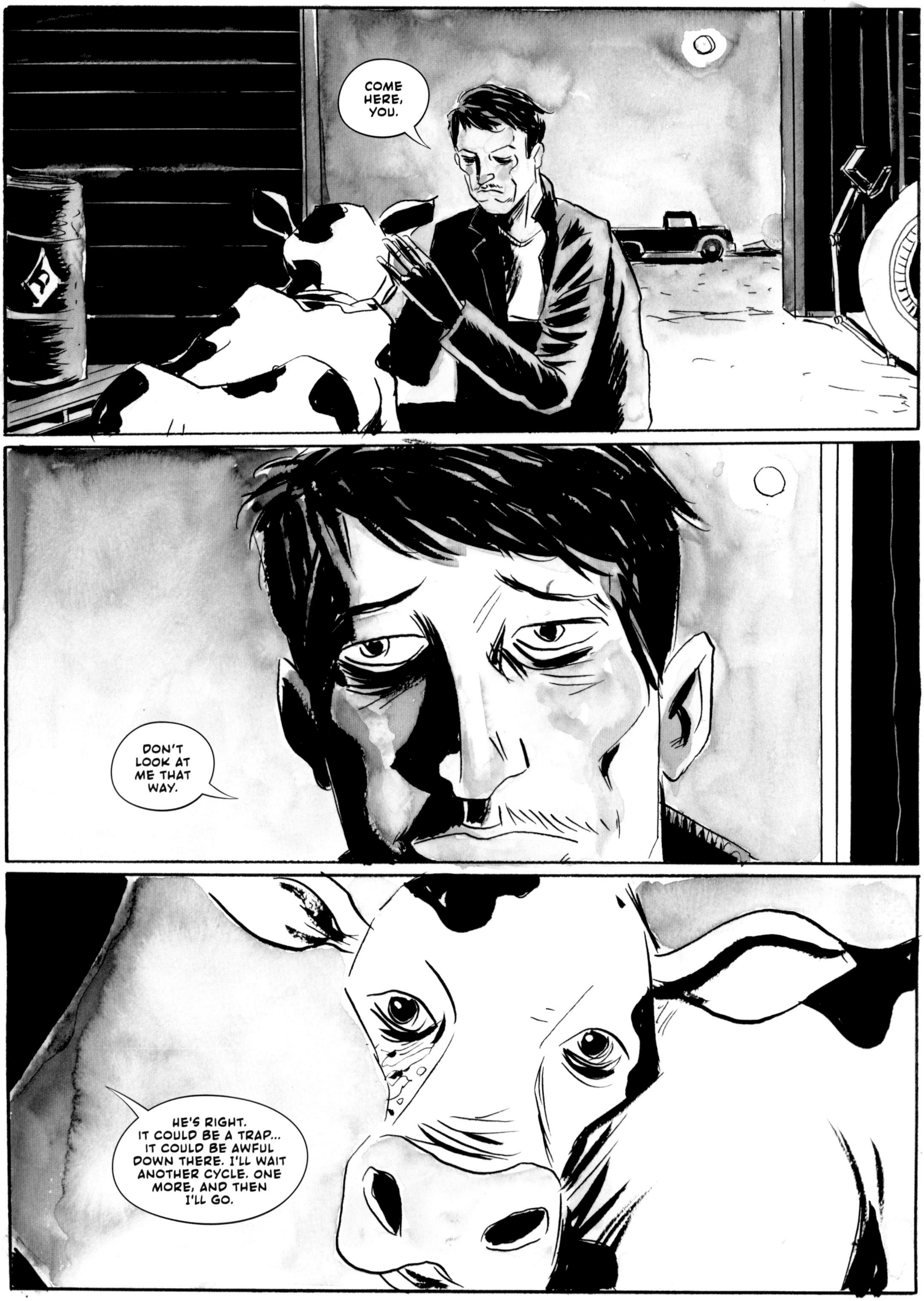
COME HERE, YOU.
DON'T LOOK AT ME THAT WAY.
HE'S RIGHT. IT COULD BE A TRAP... IT COULD BE AWFUL DOWN THERE. I'LL WAIT ANOTHER CYCLE. ONE MORE, AND THEN I'LL GO.

The night after meeting Errant at Modern Home, I can't sleep.

I keep thinking about what he said to me on the deck of the custom. About the possibility of a cure. About the retreat.

I try to push him out of my head, push it away and tell myself it's crazy, tell myself to just get out from under this one, to move, go somewhere else.

There's the girl, too.

Claire.

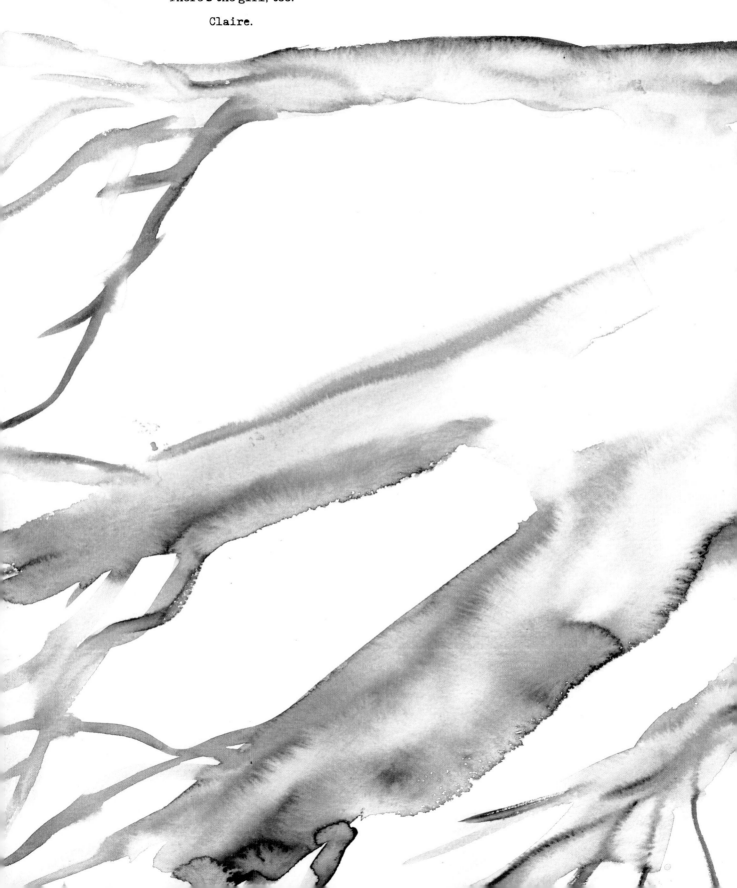

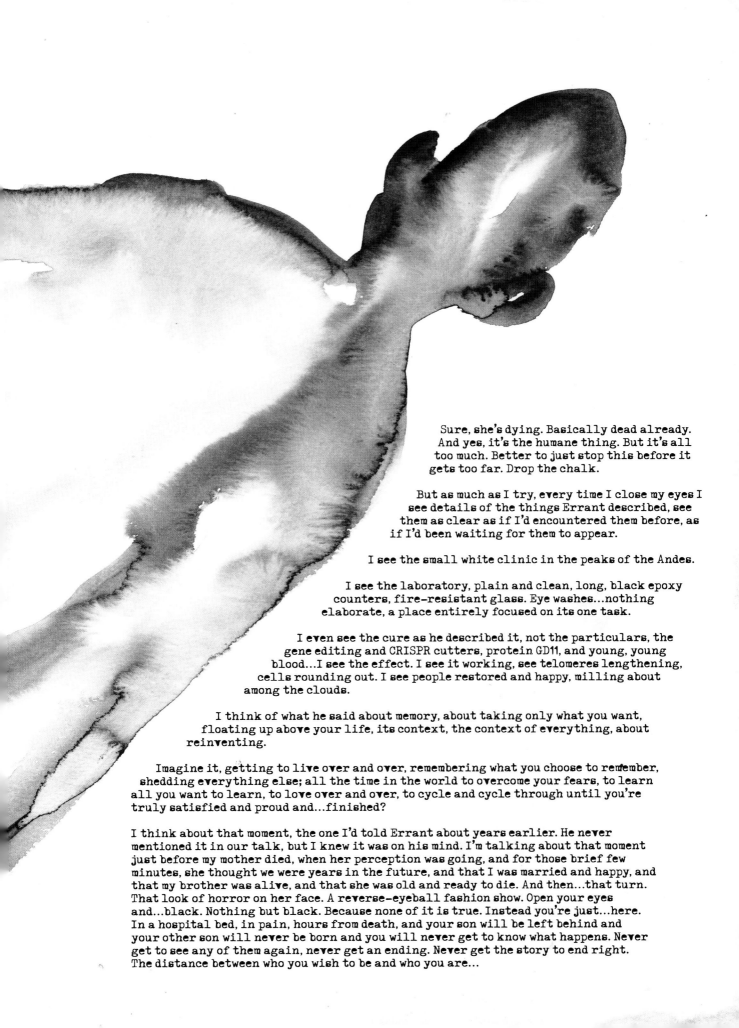

Sure, she's dying. Basically dead already.
And yes, it's the humane thing. But it's all
too much. Better to just stop this before it
gets too far. Drop the chalk.

But as much as I try, every time I close my eyes I
see details of the things Errant described, see
them as clear as if I'd encountered them before, as
if I'd been waiting for them to appear.

I see the small white clinic in the peaks of the Andes.

I see the laboratory, plain and clean, long, black epoxy
counters, fire-resistant glass. Eye washes...nothing
elaborate, a place entirely focused on its one task.

I even see the cure as he described it, not the particulars, the
gene editing and CRISPR cutters, protein GD11, and young, young
blood...I see the effect. I see it working, see telomeres lengthening,
cells rounding out. I see people restored and happy, milling about
among the clouds.

I think of what he said about memory, about taking only what you want,
floating up above your life, its context, the context of everything, about
reinventing.

Imagine it, getting to live over and over, remembering what you choose to remember,
shedding everything else; all the time in the world to overcome your fears, to learn
all you want to learn, to love over and over, to cycle and cycle through until you're
truly satisfied and proud and...finished?

I think about that moment, the one I'd told Errant about years earlier. He never
mentioned it in our talk, but I knew it was on his mind. I'm talking about that moment
just before my mother died, when her perception was going, and for those brief few
minutes, she thought we were years in the future, and that I was married and happy, and
that my brother was alive, and that she was old and ready to die. And then...that turn.
That look of horror on her face. A reverse-eyeball fashion show. Open your eyes
and...black. Nothing but black. Because none of it is true. Instead you're just...here.
In a hospital bed, in pain, hours from death, and your son will be left behind and
your other son will never be born and you will never get to know what happens. Never
get to see any of them again, never get an ending. Never get the story to end right.
The distance between who you wish to be and who you are...

I get up and go to the window. Outside, the snow has melted, the grounds are bare in the moonlight.

I go out on my porch and realize that Bud, Tommy, and Will are out there, too. They're sitting around Bud's small table, asleep. The funny thing is, they all have their astronaut helmets on. They must have taken them from my place while I was out. I can just make out Bud's face through the shield of his helmet. He's sleeping, maybe drunk, and looks peaceful. All three of them look peaceful, slumped in their chairs, fast asleep, waiting for the day to start.

I knew at that moment I would go to this place in the mountains.

I Would go there and come back better.

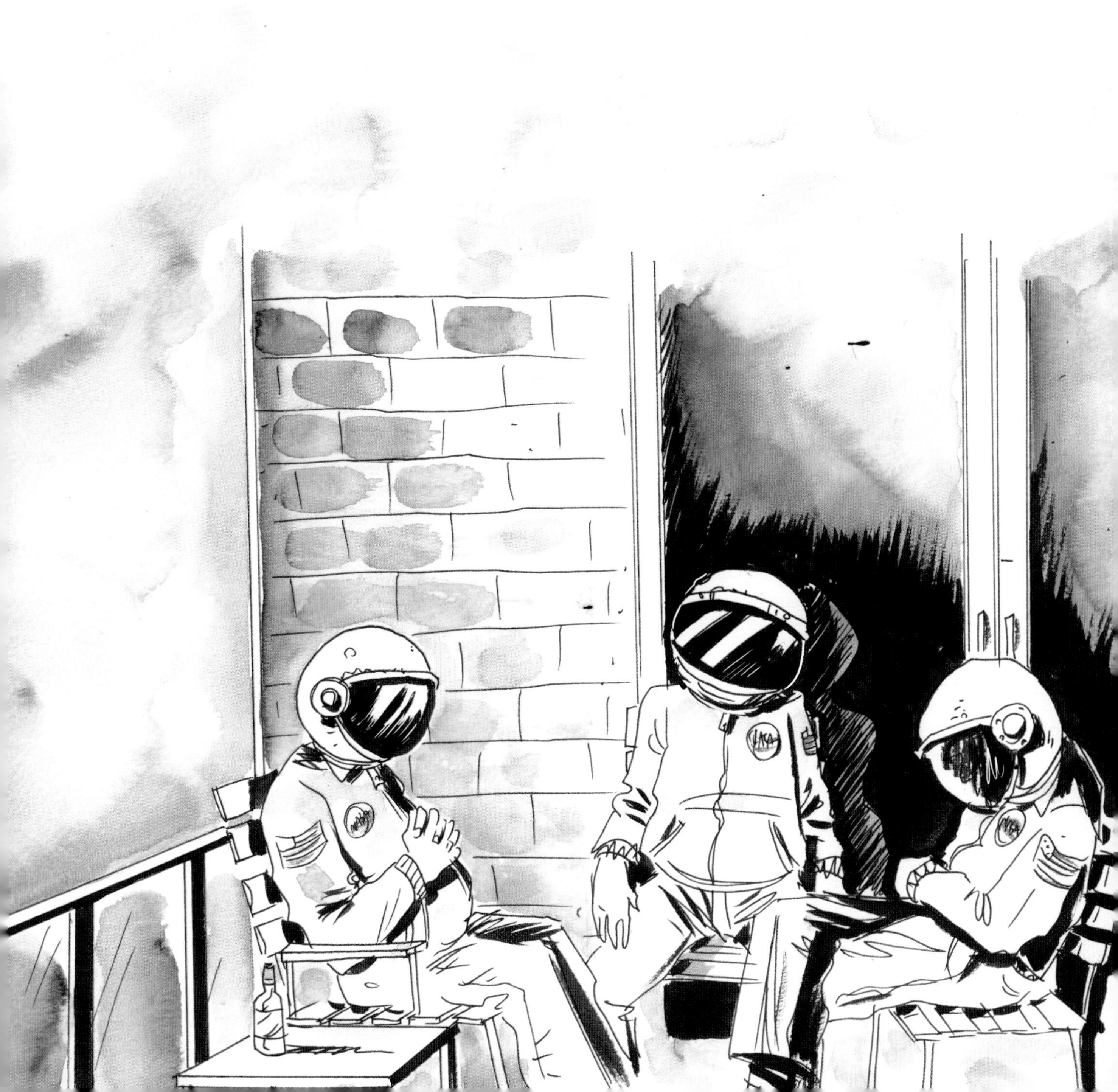

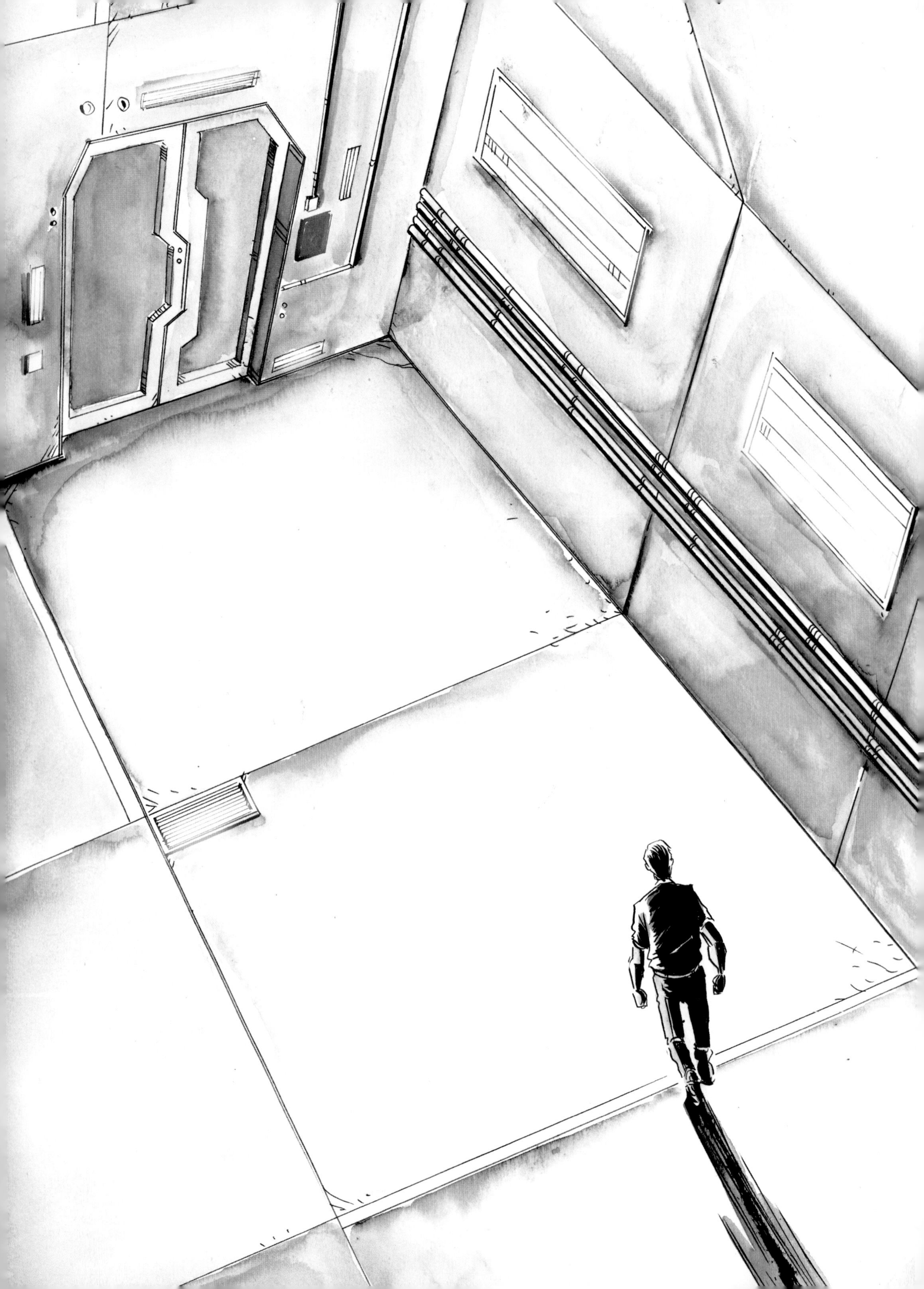

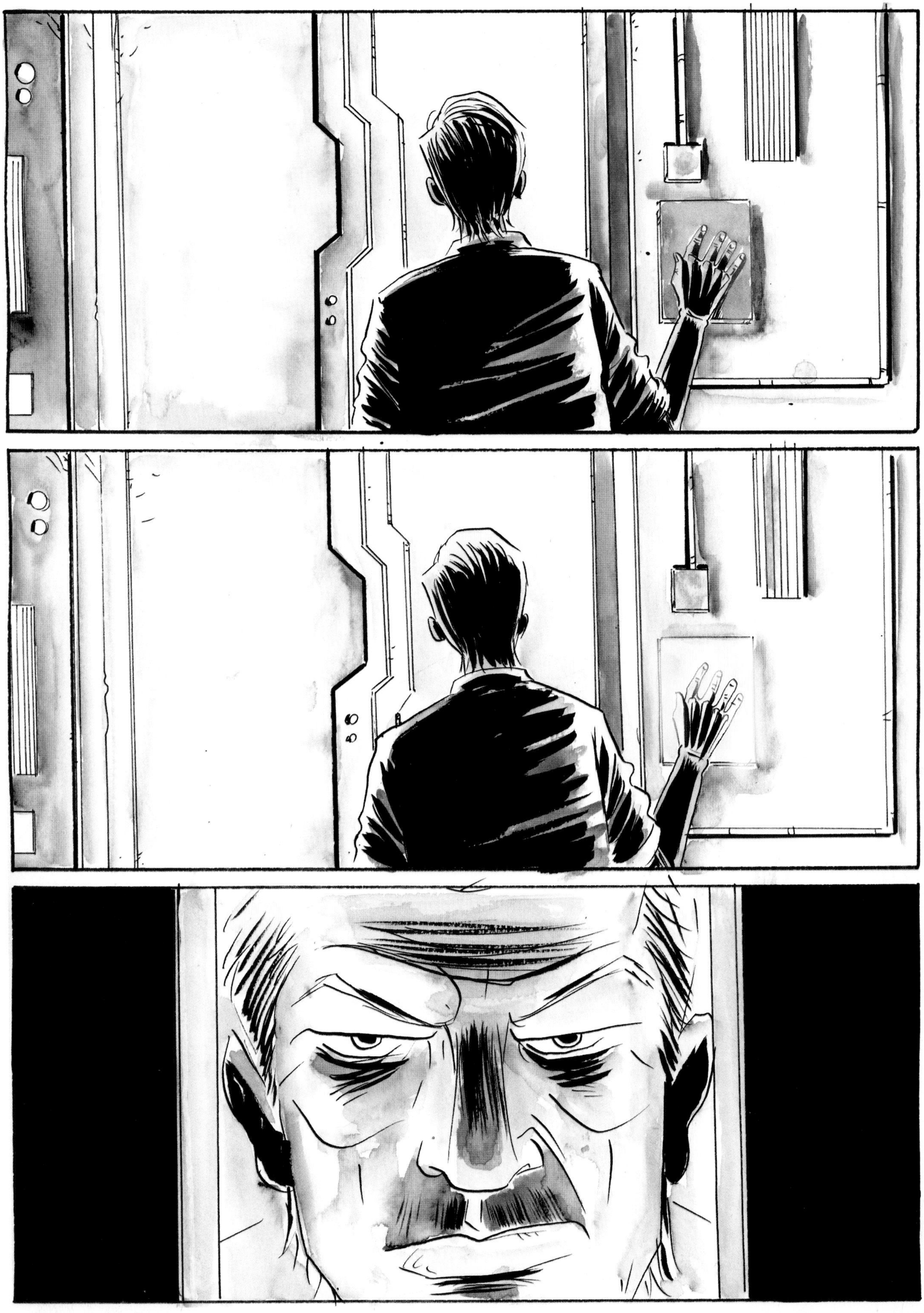

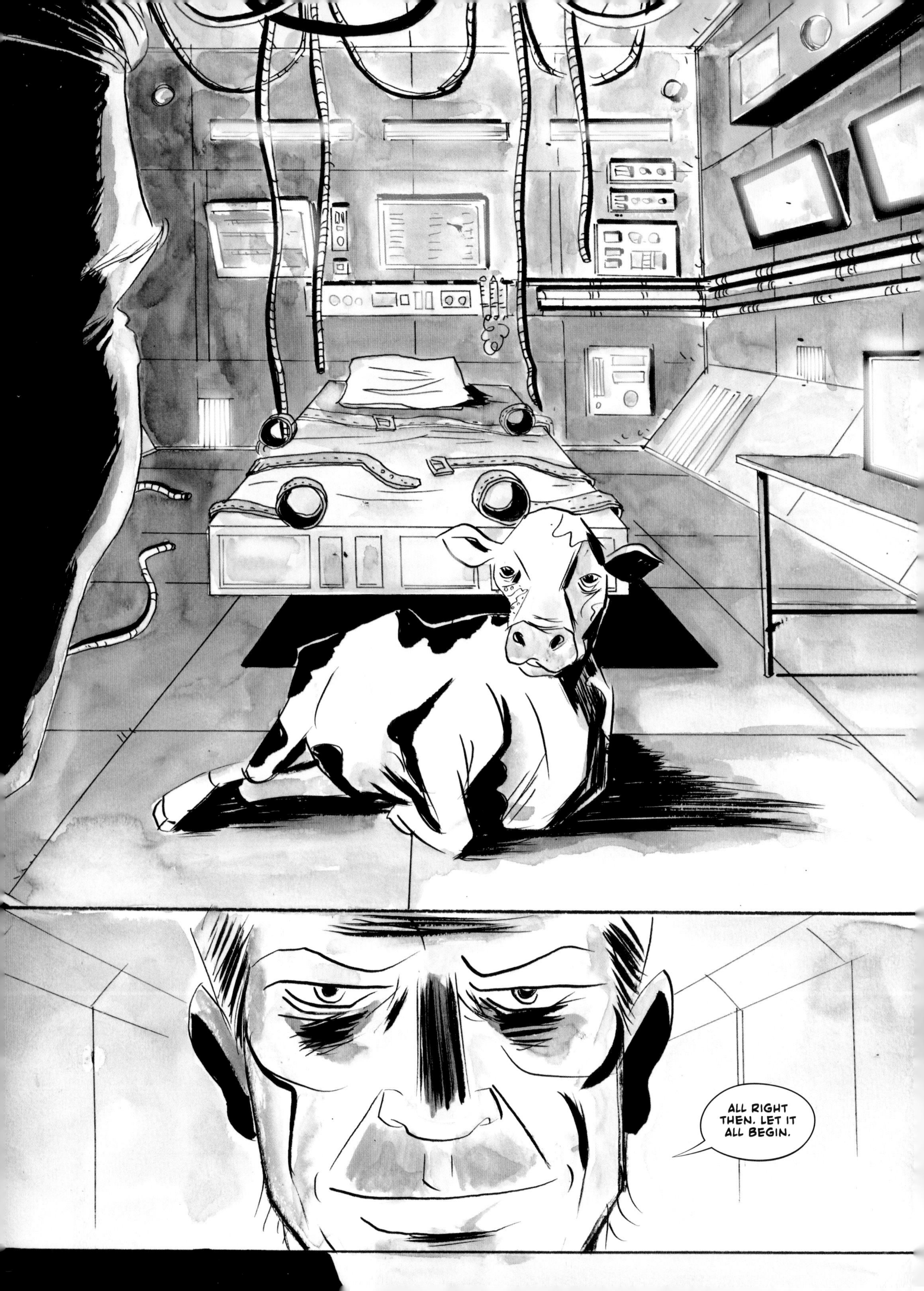
ALL RIGHT THEN. LET IT ALL BEGIN.

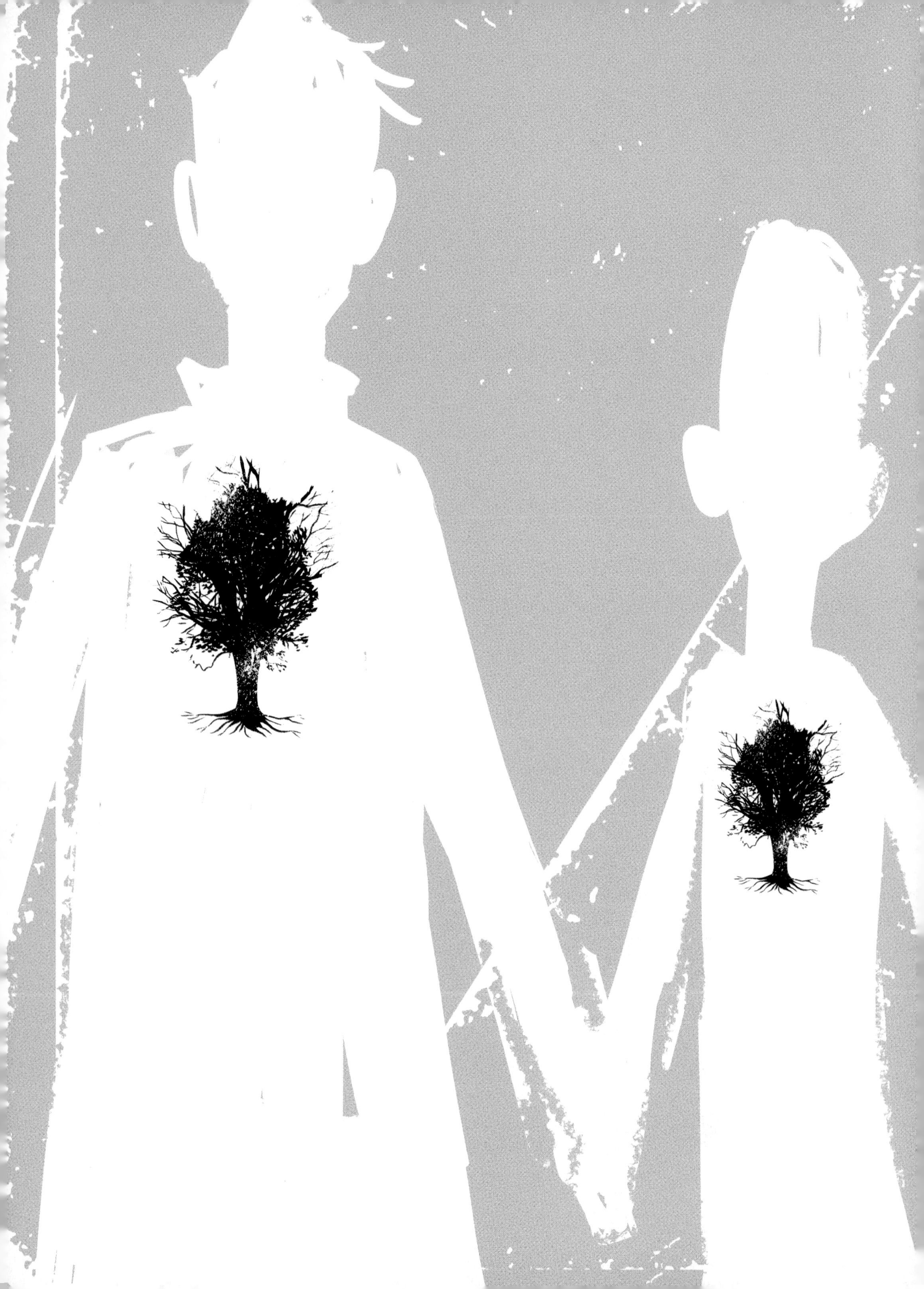

I was once
asked to steal
a forbidden
color.

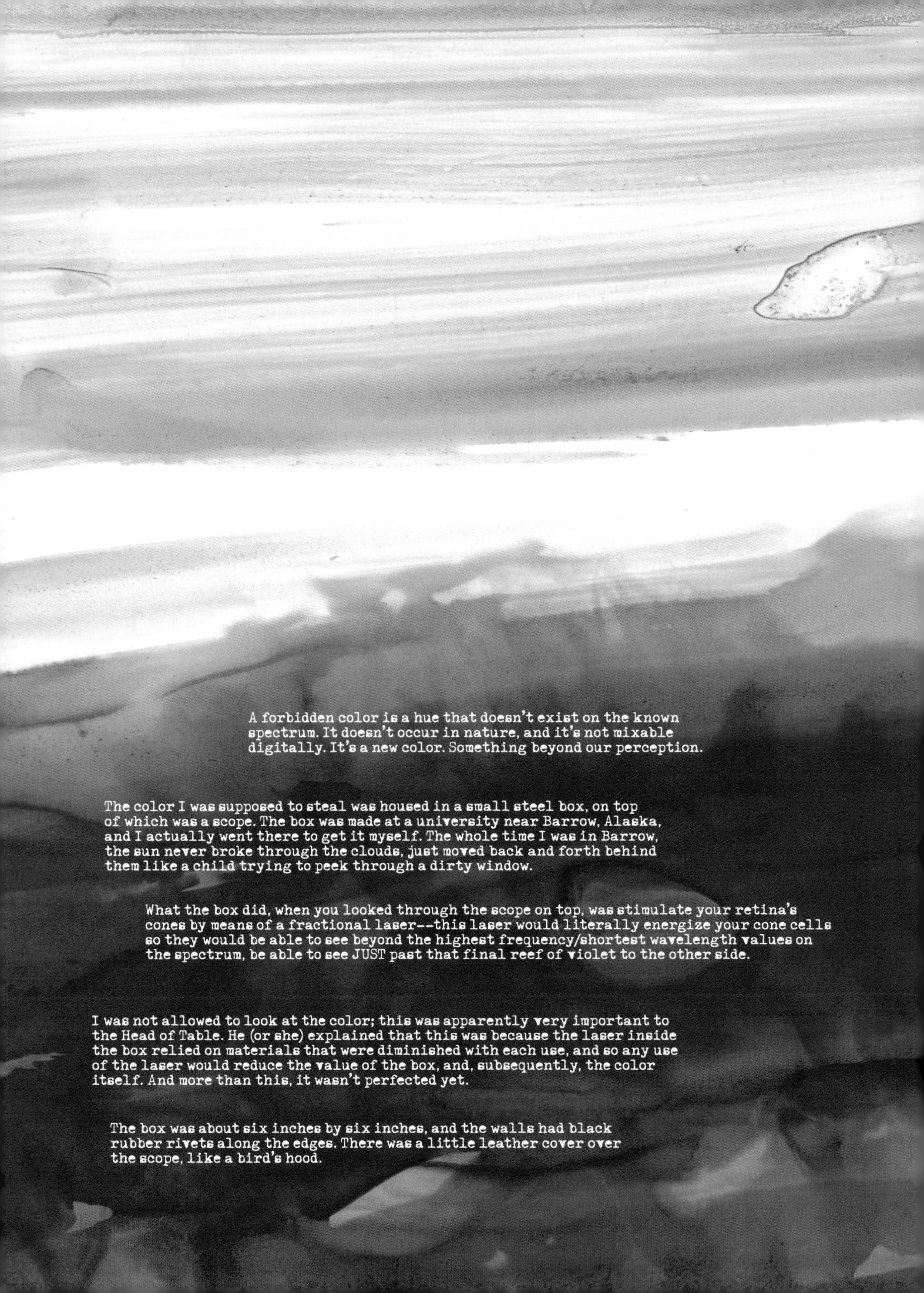

A forbidden color is a hue that doesn't exist on the known spectrum. It doesn't occur in nature, and it's not mixable digitally. It's a new color. Something beyond our perception.

The color I was supposed to steal was housed in a small steel box, on top of which was a scope. The box was made at a university near Barrow, Alaska, and I actually went there to get it myself. The whole time I was in Barrow, the sun never broke through the clouds, just moved back and forth behind them like a child trying to peek through a dirty window.

What the box did, when you looked through the scope on top, was stimulate your retina's cones by means of a fractional laser--this laser would literally energize your cone cells so they would be able to see beyond the highest frequency/shortest wavelength values on the spectrum, be able to see JUST past that final reef of violet to the other side.

I was not allowed to look at the color; this was apparently very important to the Head of Table. He (or she) explained that this was because the laser inside the box relied on materials that were diminished with each use, and so any use of the laser would reduce the value of the box, and, subsequently, the color itself. And more than this, it wasn't perfected yet.

The box was about six inches by six inches, and the walls had black rubber rivets along the edges. There was a little leather cover over the scope, like a bird's hood.

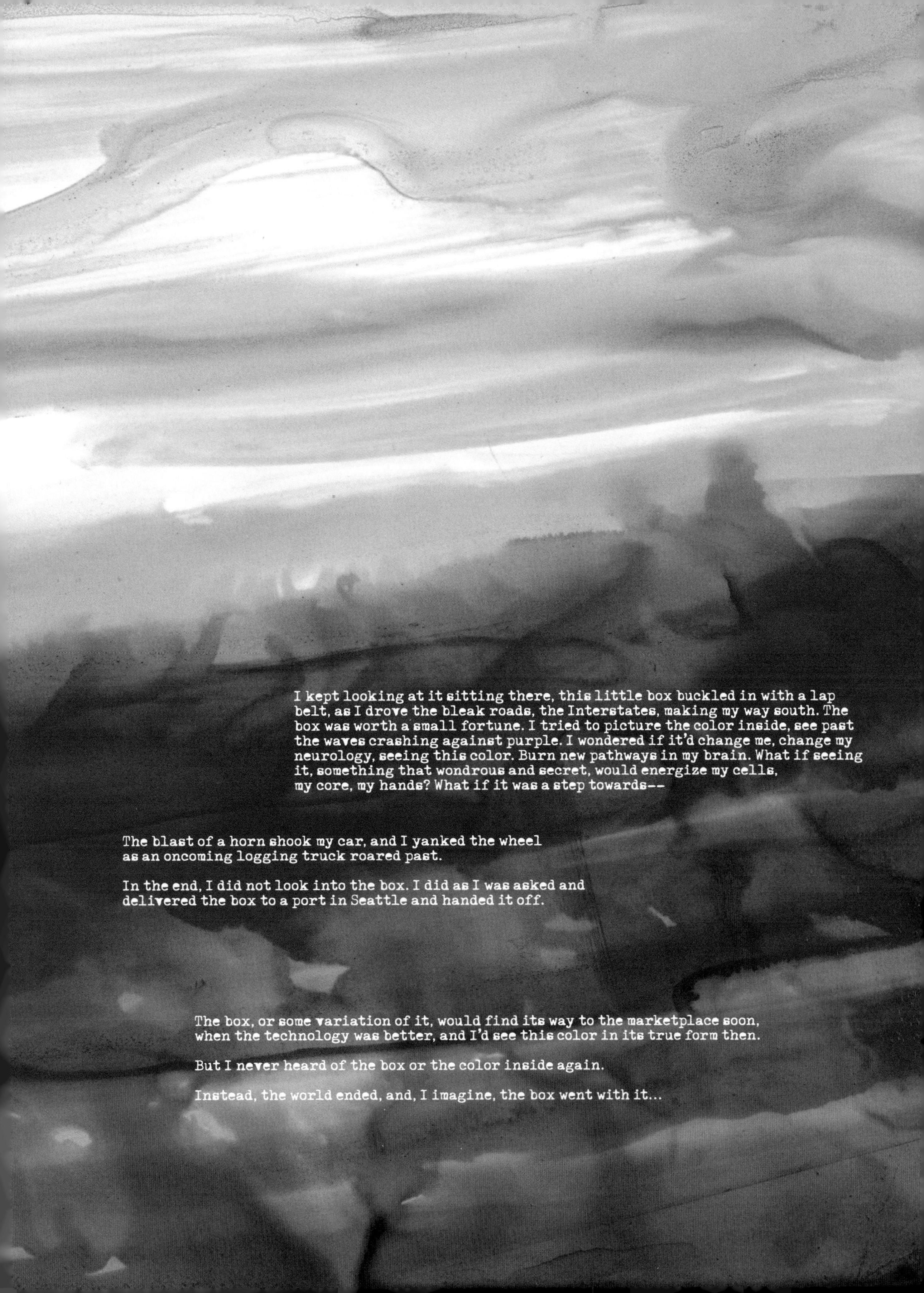
I kept looking at it sitting there, this little box buckled in with a lap belt, as I drove the bleak roads, the Interstates, making my way south. The box was worth a small fortune. I tried to picture the color inside, see past the waves crashing against purple. I wondered if it'd change me, change my neurology, seeing this color. Burn new pathways in my brain. What if seeing it, something that wondrous and secret, would energize my cells, my core, my hands? What if it was a step towards--
The blast of a horn shook my car, and I yanked the wheel as an oncoming logging truck roared past.
In the end, I did not look into the box. I did as I was asked and delivered the box to a port in Seattle and handed it off.
The box, or some variation of it, would find its way to the marketplace soon, when the technology was better, and I'd see this color in its true form then.
But I never heard of the box or the color inside again.
Instead, the world ended, and, I imagine, the box went with it...

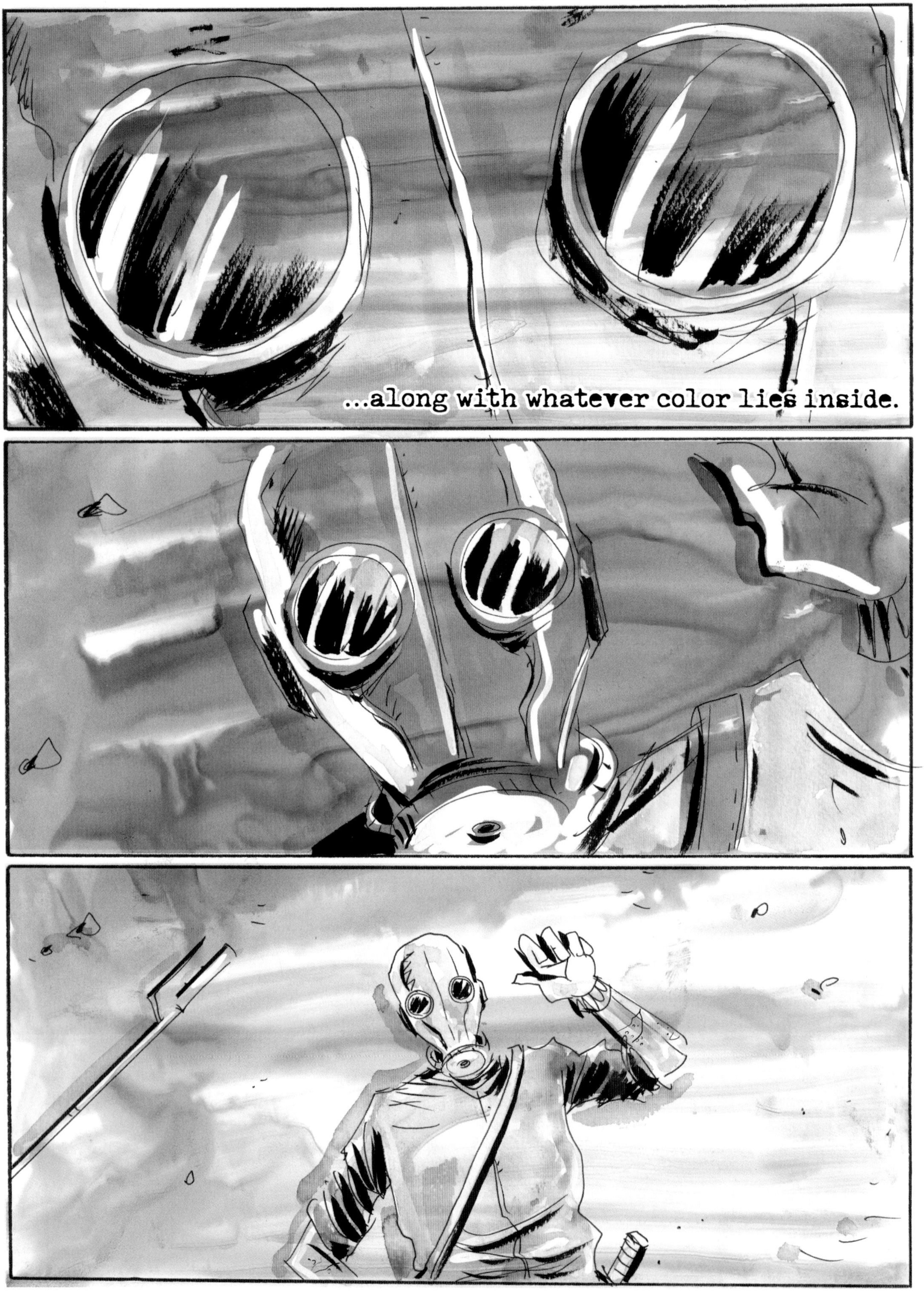
...along with whatever color lies inside.

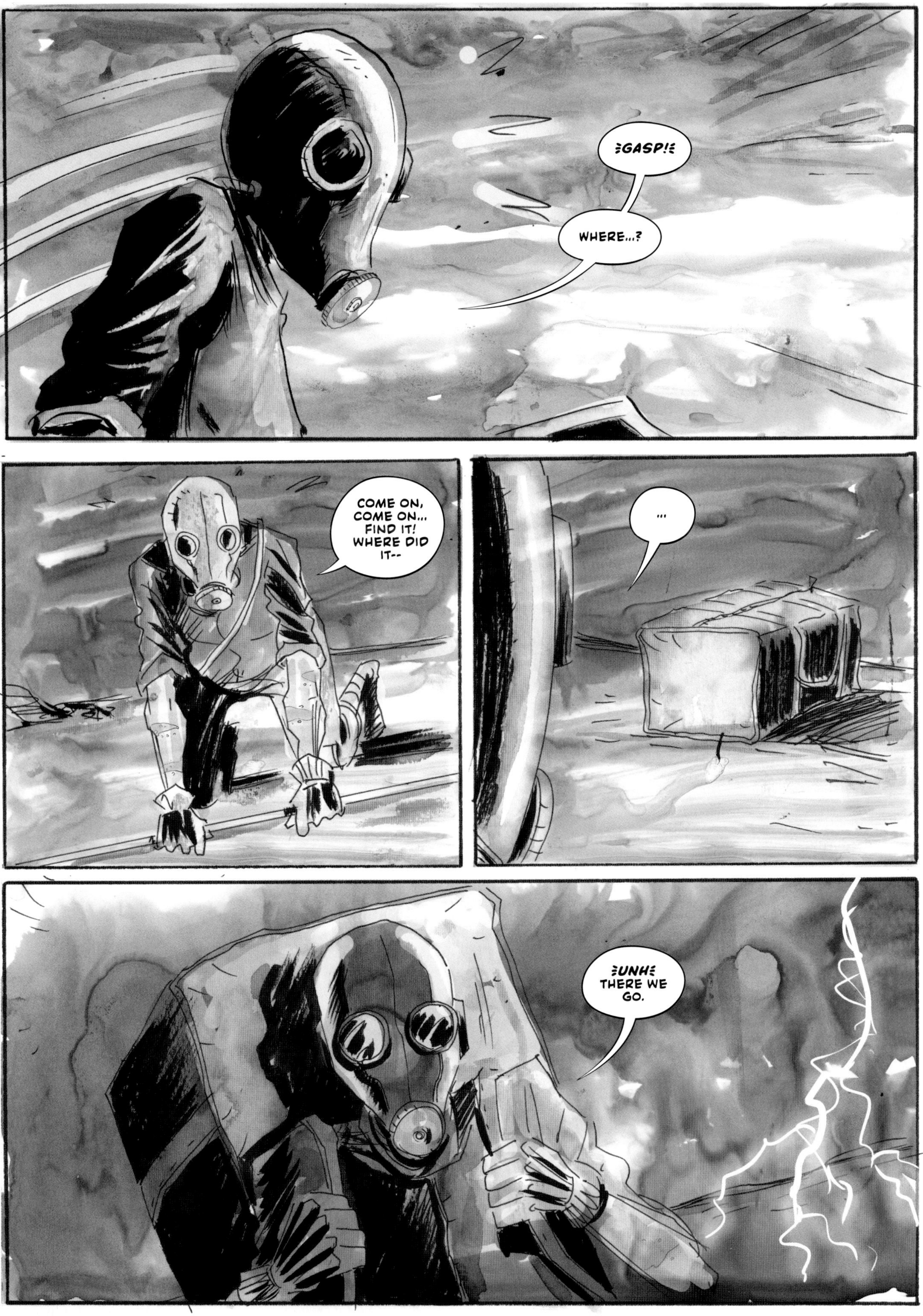
GASP!
WHERE...?
COME ON, COME ON... FIND IT! WHERE DID IT--
...
UNH
THERE WE GO.

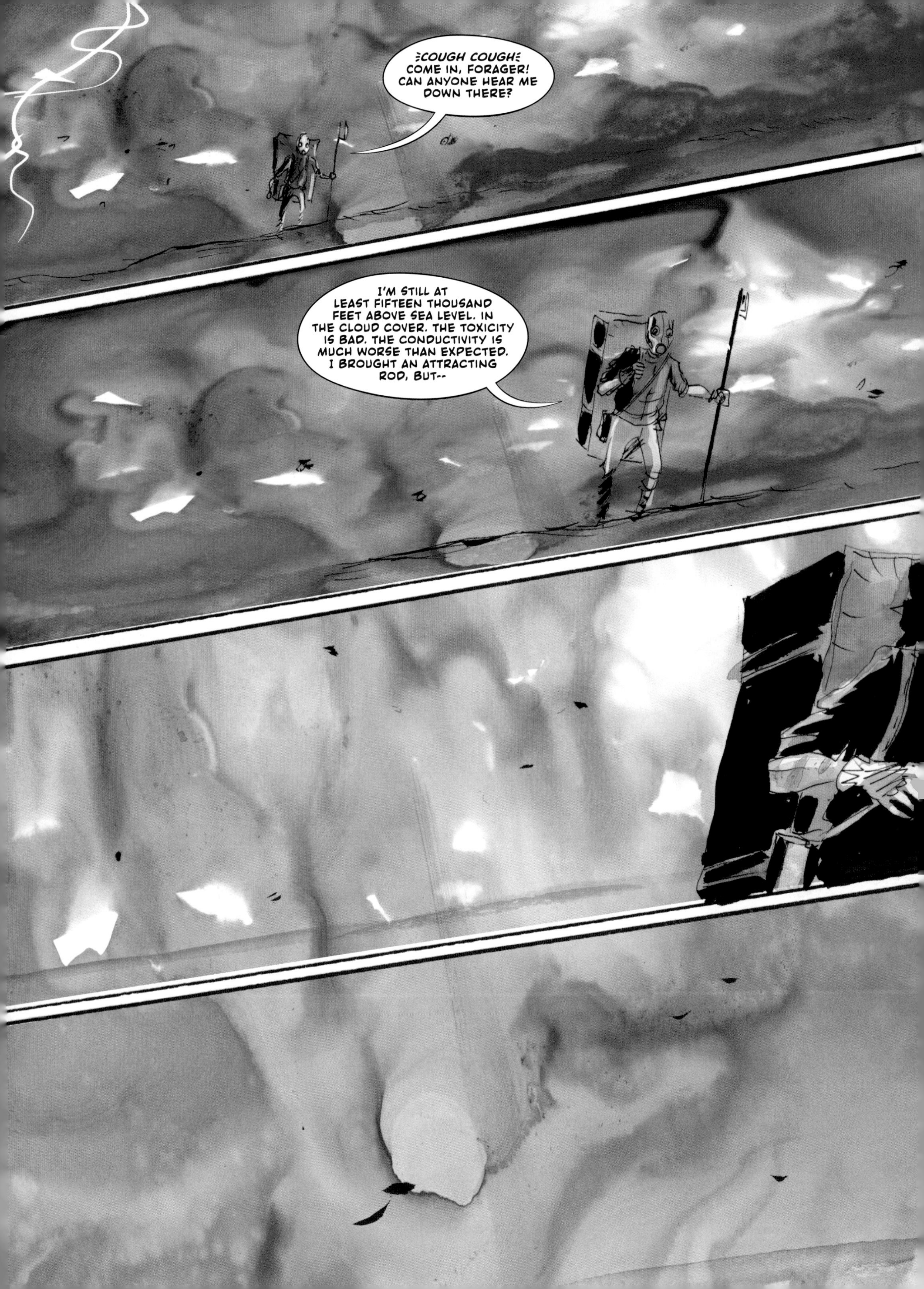

≡COUGH COUGH≡ COME IN, FORAGER! CAN ANYONE HEAR ME DOWN THERE?
I'M STILL AT LEAST FIFTEEN THOUSAND FEET ABOVE SEA LEVEL. IN THE CLOUD COVER. THE TOXICITY IS BAD. THE CONDUCTIVITY IS MUCH WORSE THAN EXPECTED. I BROUGHT AN ATTRACTING ROD, BUT--

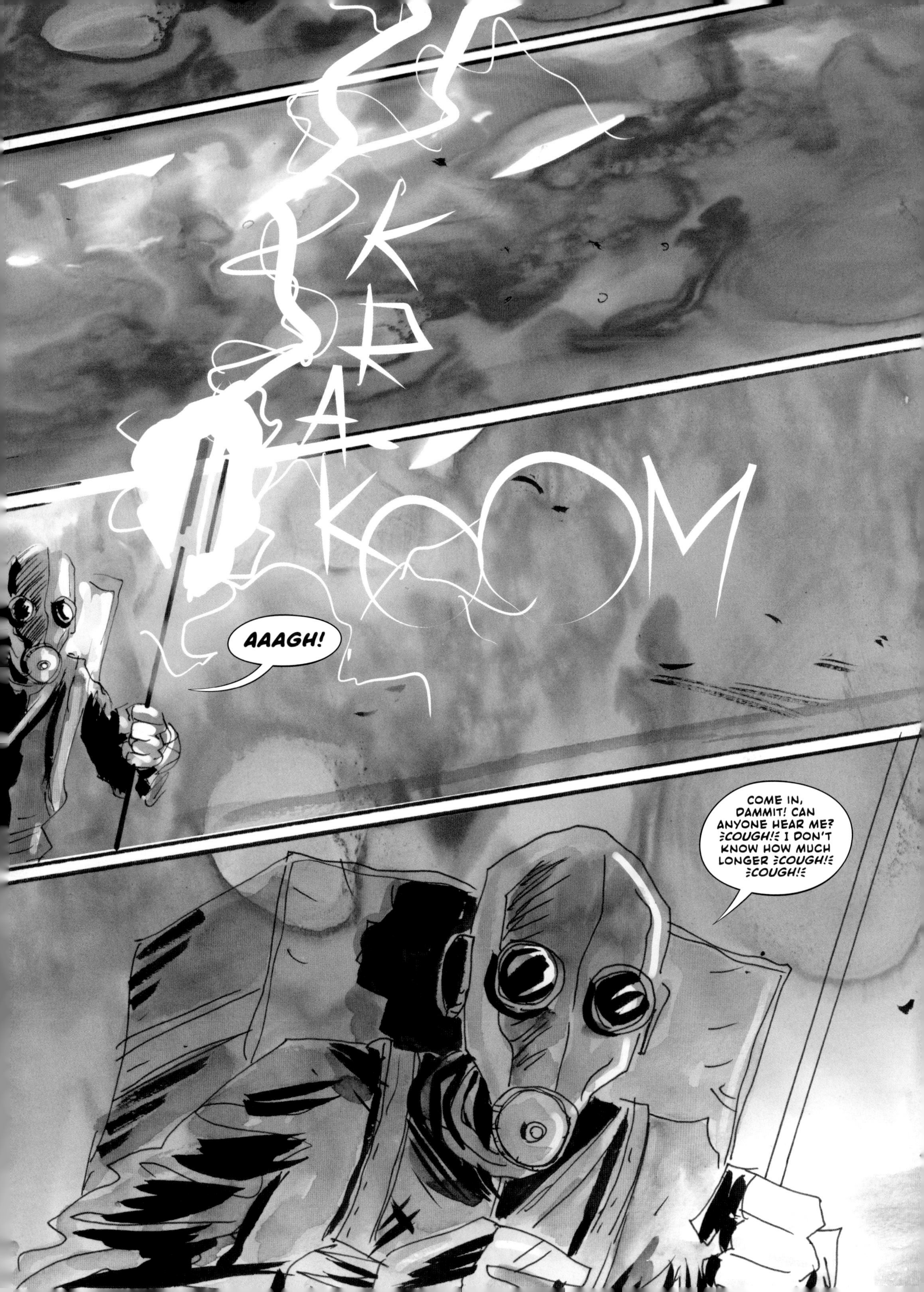
KRAKOOM
AAAGH!
COME IN, DAMMIT! CAN ANYONE HEAR ME? *COUGH!* I DON'T KNOW HOW MUCH LONGER *COUGH!* *COUGH!*

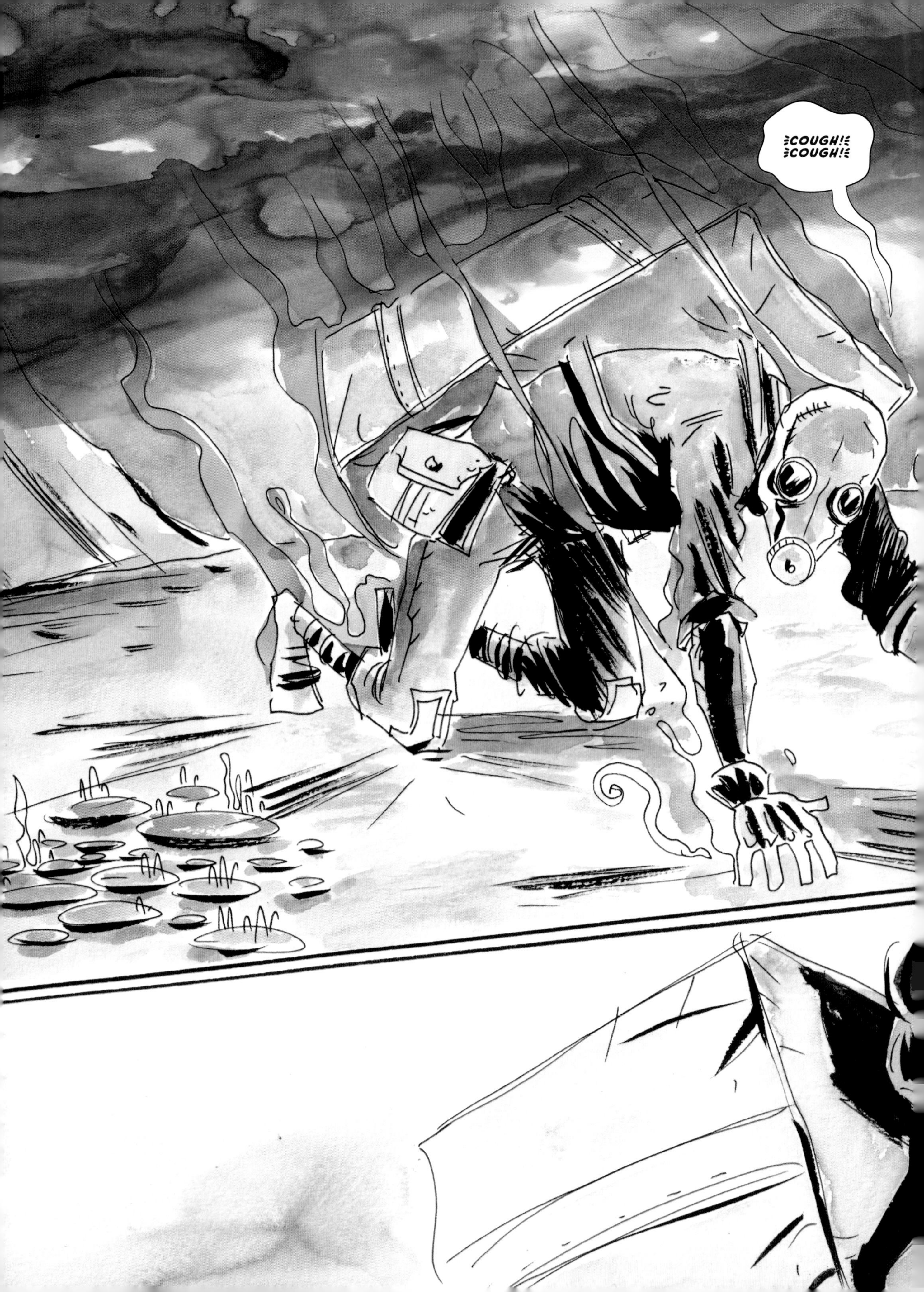
COUGH! COUGH!

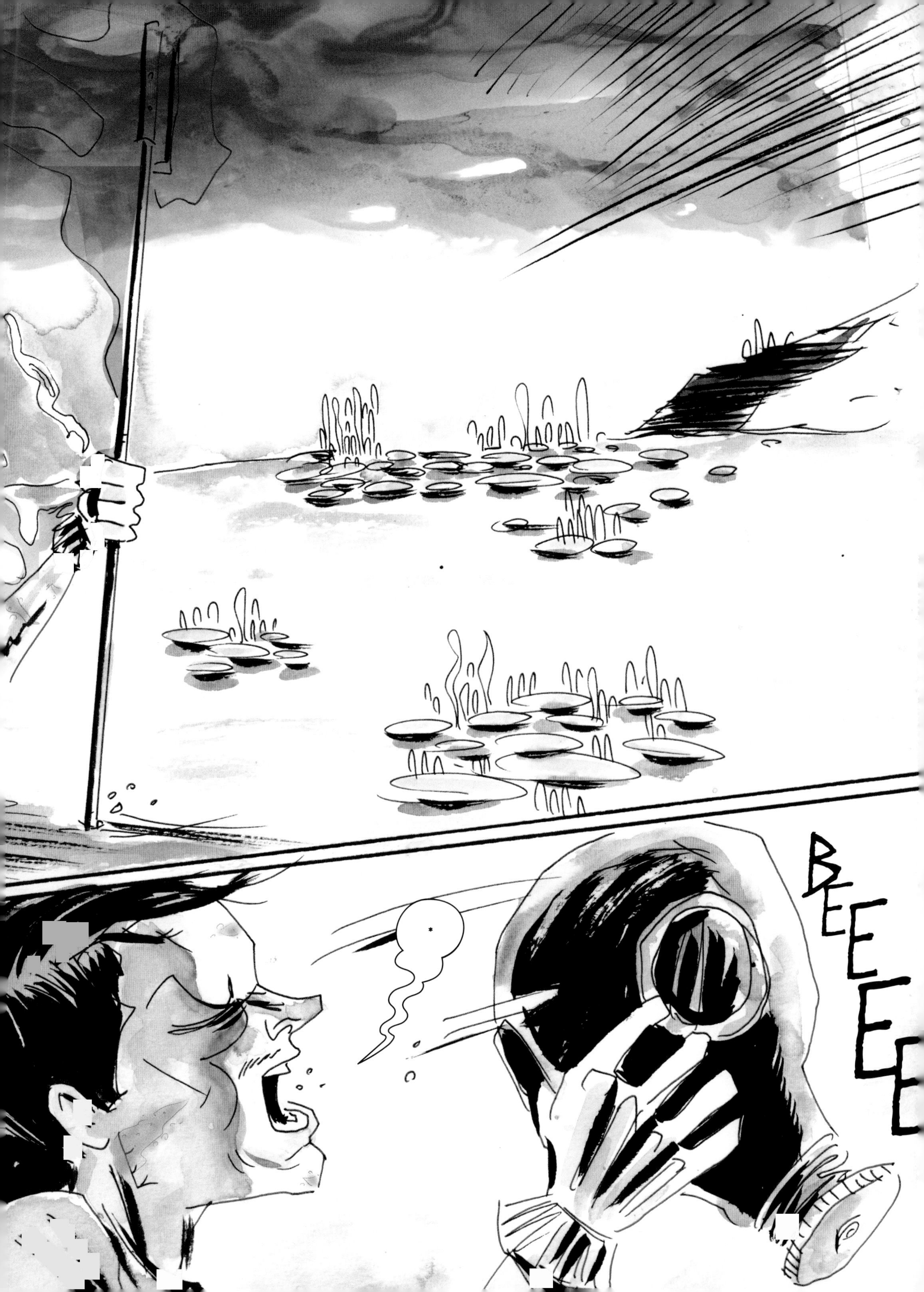
BEEEEE

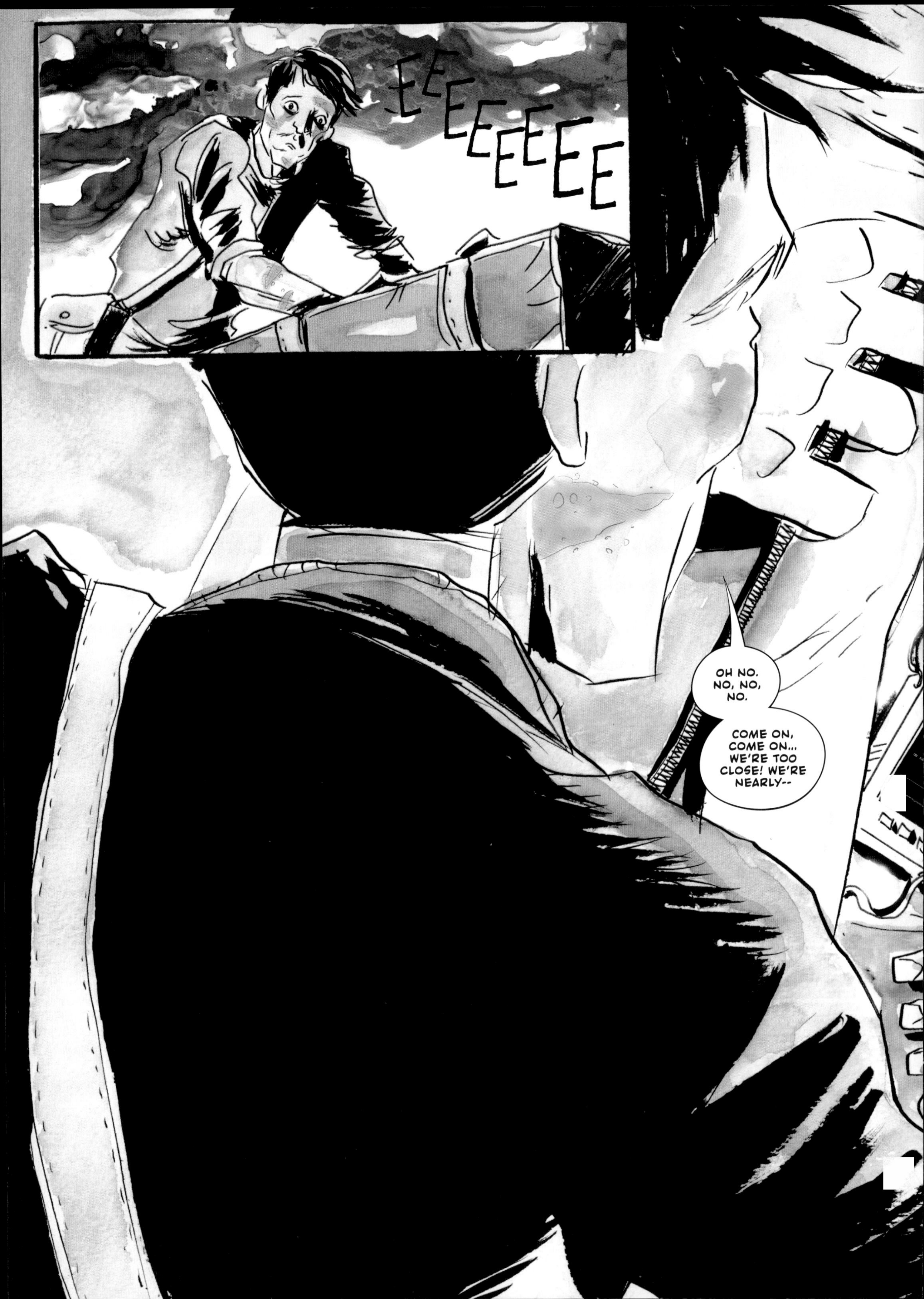
EEEEEEEEEE
OH NO. NO, NO, NO.
COME ON, COME ON... WE'RE TOO CLOSE! WE'RE NEARLY--

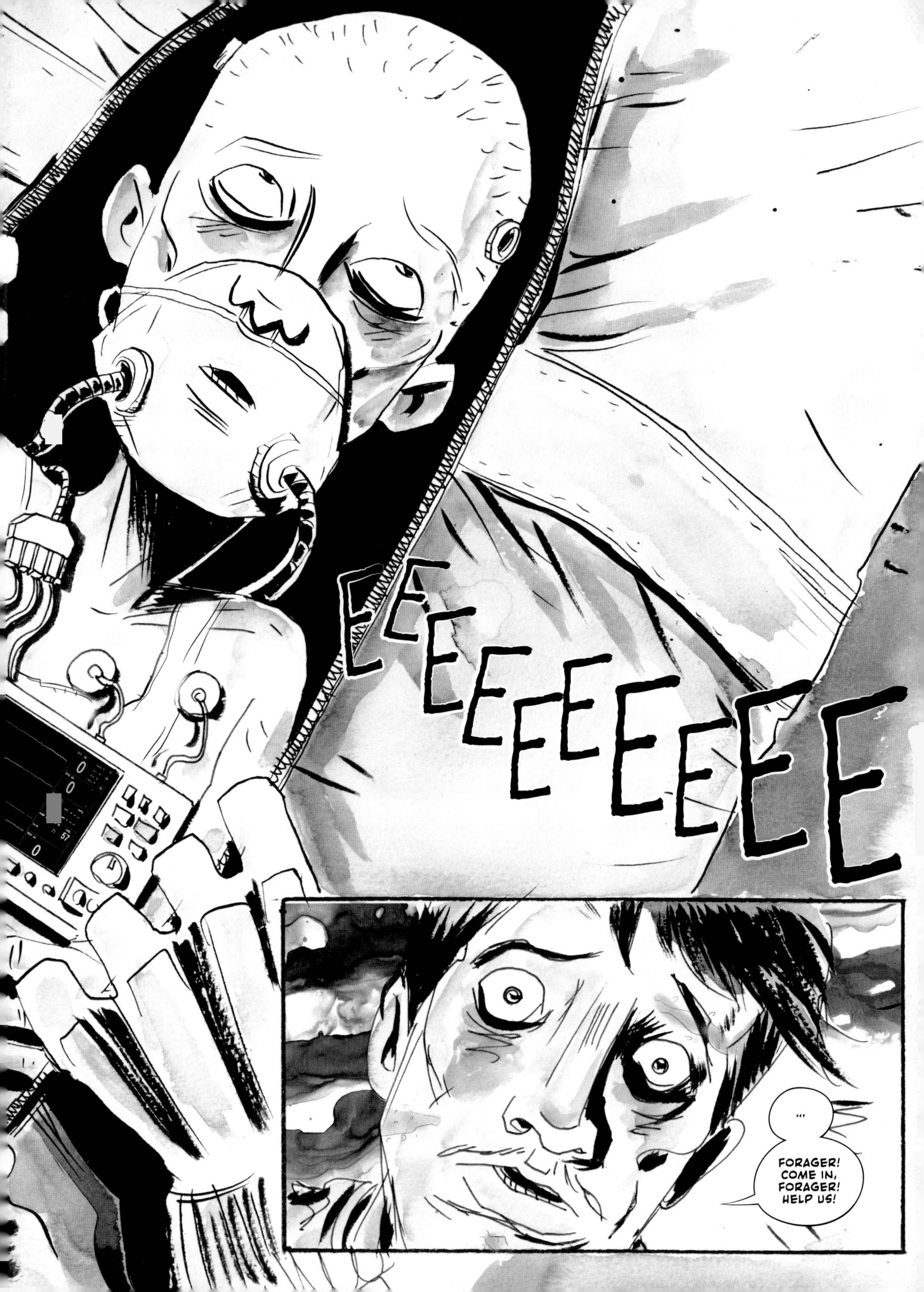
EEEEEEEEEEEE
...
FORAGER! COME IN, FORAGER! HELP US!

PART THREE
FORAGER STATION

This is the part of the story that
I don't like telling.

But it's the most important part.

The part I promised myself
I'd never erase.

The girl's name is CLAIRE.

I first laid eyes on her one month after Errant visited me at Modern Home.

At the time, Claire was living in a children's hospital in Nova Scotia called Heartwell House, a place for kids with debilitating disorders, most of them terminal.

It was affiliated with the nearby university hospital, but was set apart, deep in the woods. A sort of grim outlier station tucked away in the heavy pines of that area. A place no one wanted to ever see or visit.

The realm of children's maladies is ugly, to say the least. The ugliest. And at a facility like Heartwell, you got the sense that nature reserved her worst afflictions just for children. For example, there was a boy at this hospital with something called FOP, Fibrodysplasia Ossificans Progressiva, a syndrome that caused his muscles and ligaments to gradually turn to bone. He was essentially growing a second skeleton over his own, day by day, a slow, creakingly painful and immobilizing process. There was a girl with Epidermolysis bullosa, or "butterfly disorder," a condition that destroyed collagen between skin cells so that the layers of skin rubbed together whenever she moved and tore apart like tissue paper. In short, the place was like a laboratory for cooking up extreme kinds of pain and suffering.

The disorder Claire had was called Neotenic Complex Syndrome, and there were only two other children in the world known to have it. It was a genetic malfunction that actually stopped its host from aging. Not entirely, but for a long while. What happened was that at some point, usually around three or four years old, the complex of genes responsible for senescence--for aging--would seem to shut off, go full dark, so the child would suddenly stop developing and become frozen in time. Siblings younger than them would pass them by, lap them in the race of life. The affected child might be twenty years old, more, but look age four. The secret about the disorder, though, was that the affected child was never fully frozen in time, not really. The aging switch never truly shut off; it remained on, albeit barely, and the terrible thing was that the slowed effect caused different parts of the child's physiology to age at different rates. The brain was usually slowest, never making it past a few years' development. Organs were slow too, with some aging more quickly than others. Your liver might outpace your stomach, which was already outpacing your kidneys...and so on. Some components, like hair and nails, barely slowed at all, so the child could have the hair of an old person, the fingernails of an old person, but the eyes and skin and teeth of a toddler. Over time, the body became "disorganized" in its development. A machine with parts moving at interminably slow, but varying, speeds. And eventually, in the final stage, the machine broke down from this variation.

Claire had reached this final stage when I first saw her. Without intubation, she was likely no more than a few weeks from dying. She was nearly forty years old, almost exactly my age, but she looked like a sickly eight, maybe nine, with spindly limbs and deep, sunken eyes.

Her story was sad. She'd been put up for adoption at birth, become a ward of the state, and lived her life in federally funded facilities. She had neurological issues, cognitive issues, had never developed psychologically...She didn't move much, didn't talk, seemed barely there; it had been a life unlived, now ending. She spent her days in a bed near a window with a crack in it. When it rained, drops of water came through the crack and ran down the glass.

There was one nurse who bought balloons for the children every Monday. He would tie them up at the nurse's station and give them out at night before bed, fastening them to the children's beds. When it rained, this nurse would make sure to fold towels at the base of Claire's window so the water would run down into the cloth and not soak the floor.

Looking at Claire, I felt like I was seeing it square on, confronting it all over again. This was what no one liked to look at, but where it all led. To a room like this, with a crack in the window, a cold, wet towel bunched on the sill, catching dirty rain. I couldn't help thinking of my brother, Nathan, who'd been created with no chance of escaping the dying system that contained him. I thought of my mother, that moment toward the end of her life when she'd thought Nathan had been born, thought that I was married with a family...how happy she'd been...

...then the terror when she'd seen the truth.

I thought of it all--the whole thing, the dumb, mindless cruelty of it, the black water, the way it closes around the ankles of some people, the way it had stopped my mother and my brother and my father, and me and how fear of it seemed to be creeping into the world itself every day, more and more; no stopping it with sunken train cars, no stopping it with metal detectors, or any of it, and I decided I would do this thing.

This was it. This was the door to it all. Not just for me, or for Claire, but for everyone. I could steal us all by stealing her. I would do this.

But how?

How to get her out? That was the issue.

The facility was always busy, and there were cameras, there was security. I knew I could secure a van with the equipment needed to move Claire, but I didn't have a way of getting her out without incident.

There was only one moment all week when she was in a room with an easy access point--a room with a fire door--and this was when she went for dialysis. More often than not, the attendant would leave her alone in there for stretches of time. But the fire door was heavily alarmed and had no unlocking mechanism I could slip from the outside. The only way to open it was to set off the facility's fire alarm system, which would trigger all the fire doors to unlock. Then maybe in the mayhem I could sneak Claire out. But alarms aren't easy to trigger without real fire, real smoke. I could just go in and light a match under one at the right time, but all the alarms were in public view. Recorded too...I'd likely be tackled on the spot, certainly chased down after the fact. I could go home, try to get a bug that could trigger it. But I was worried that Claire might die in the interim.

Every day, she looked worse.

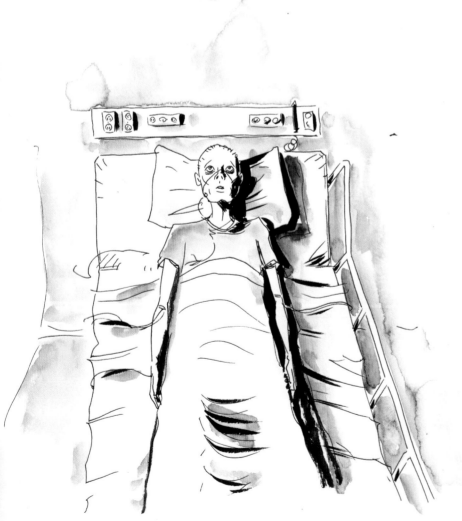

There was a small museum of regional history nearby, and sometimes I'd go there to wander around and think on the problem. The place was dark and winding and full of taxidermy creatures from the surrounding forest, like flying squirrels and porcupines.

Its prize exhibit was a dinosaur skeleton belonging to a species that was assumed to be one of the first to have feathers. The skeleton was small, about the size of a chicken. A plaque overhead showed what the dinosaur may have looked like in life, which was ridiculous, with feathers protruding like long, colored paddles from its head and janky arms. The feathers had only been decorative, not functional, and, in a sad twist of fate, likely led to the creature's demise, having made it slower, more visible, and easier to hunt. Someone had carved the words "me dead" on the thing's skull with a pocketknife.

There were times, wandering around the museum or scoping out Heartwell, that I questioned what I was doing. Questioned whether I should just get out now. But then I'd think of Claire, of Nathan, of my mother, and I'd resign myself to another day of planning.

And then, one morning, out of nowhere, I saw how to do it.

I saw a way that would bring everything full circle.

The perfect answer. Right there in front of my eyes.

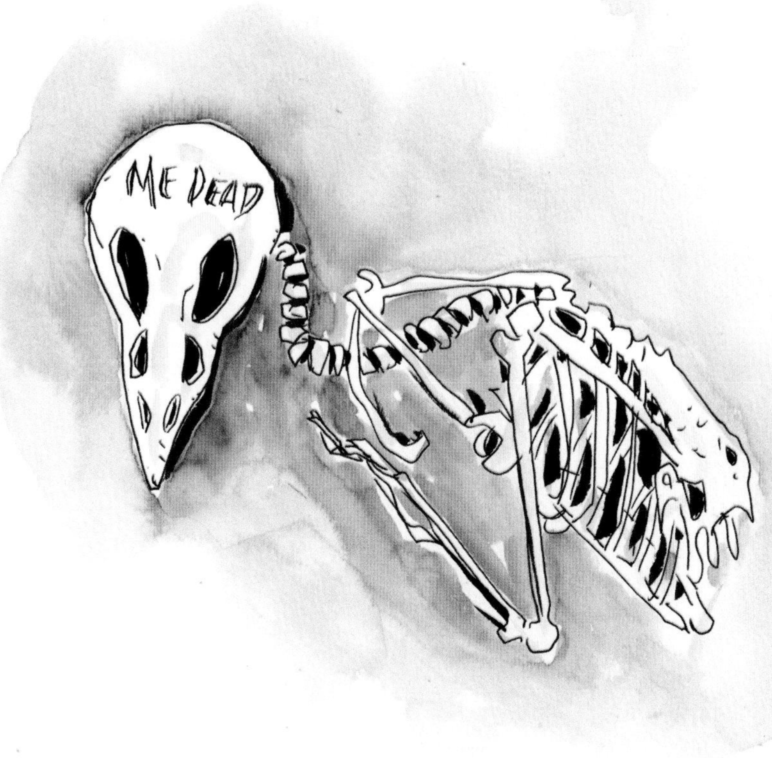
ME DEAD

Four years later, almost to the day, I am on my way to visit the clinic for the first time.

It's in the Andes, not far from the Aconcagua peak.

To get there, I fly into a small airport outside Mendoza, Argentina, and then take a van to the base of the adjacent mountains. At the foot of the range sit three turbine helicopters. When my van arrives, one already has its rotors spinning, blasting wild orbits of wind through the tall grass.

The driver of the van ushers me over, and I get inside, and there, waiting in the passenger area, are two other people.

A man and a woman.

The man is a little older than me, thin, dark-skinned, dressed smartly in tweeds and a bowtie. He has a baseball cap on, made of a fabric I can tell is expensive, with a series of small, metallic stars embroidered across the side. He smiles warmly at me--he has one of those naturally handsome smiles--and raises his hand, hello, and I do the same. As I get in, the pilot reaches back and hands me a headset.

I sit beside the man in the bowtie and across from the other passenger, a woman who looks to be in her mid-thirties. She's wearing a heavy knit shawl with a maze-like pattern that makes me think of ancient pottery, and as I sit she smiles too, albeit thinly, mouth closed. Her face is strong, almost masculine in the set of the brow, the cheekbones, the prominent, slightly witchy chin. I figure her for Greek; her hair is that pure black that looks almost blue in sunlight and she wears it pulled back, but a few rings have fallen around her eyes, which are dark and serious and full of worry.

I immediately wonder how out of place I seem to these two people with my flannel, my jeans, my gym bag rather than a nice duffel or carry-on. The hobo on their helicopter to immortality. But before I can think too much about this, the helicopter takes off.

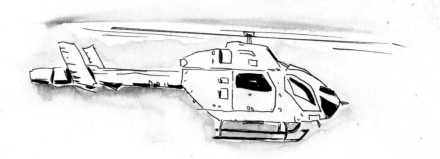

The sudden jolt upward makes the three of us tense and grip our seats. When the shock passes, we all laugh a bit, embarrassed, a little scared. The man in the bow tie fans his heart with his hat.

"And so it begins," he says, the headset bringing his voice so close, right inside my ear. His accent is British mixed with something I can't place.

He flashes that smile again as he puts on sunglasses with the same three-star pattern as his cap.

The helicopter is rising at a startling rate, like an express elevator, and the feeling is disconcerting, like being both weightless and heavy, like there's nothing in you, but you're sinking deeper and deeper into your seat.

The woman is gripping the leather loop above her chair.

"You okay?" I say.

She nods quickly, trying to smile, but just then the helicopter lurches, and she closes her eyes.

The man in the bowtie leans forward and says something in Spanish to the pilot, and the pilot replies.

Then the man in the bow tie turns to us. "He says it's just a little bit more rough air." He makes a small space with his thumb and index finger, then closes the space. Poof, gone.

"So have you been up to it yet?" says the man in the bow tie.

"Been where?" I say.

"To the retreat, of course," he says.

I have not heard it called a retreat before. Errant has always described it as a clinic.

I tell him no.

The woman says no too, still clutching the leather loop.

"I visited last year, before the water was settled," he says. "It was already a sight. Got a batch of it too."

A BATCH?

The woman and I both look at him.

"A batch of what, the cure?" I say.

He nods. "Just the primer, but I already feel it, I tell you. You know how old I am? Guess how bloody old."

The woman and I look at each other-- she is smiling at the idea of this game, though her face is bloodless --then we study the man in the bowtie.

He poses for us, mugging, hands on his hips.

Then, abruptly, he waves us off and says, "Ah, you know what, don't guess. I'll tell you when we get up there. I'll surprise you."

"How does it feel?" I ask.

"The cure?" he says.

He thinks about this a moment, and then he opens a compartment in the door of the helicopter--a compartment I hadn't even realized was there--and he takes out a small pink bottle of champagne.

"Like this," he says, holding up the bottle, "in every cell."

He pops the cork, and the woman screams and we all laugh.

We rise further, and the air evens out. We ascend past sweeps of meadow, and then past thick forests of cypress and spruce, and then the plant life starts to give way.

Above, I can see clouds clinging to the peaks.

The woman pulls her bag on her lap and opens it and rummages around inside for something. She catches me looking and says, "Can't find my gum." Her voice is even closer inside my ear, much closer than the man in the bow tie's sounded--a weird sensation.

I hand her some from my pocket.

"Huh. This is the kind I buy," she says, amused.

"I stole it from your bag."

She rolls her eyes, smiling. "Ah. So what did you do back on Earth?"

"I'm a thief."

"Stop," she says, but her face has become girlish, playful.

"I am," I say. "I didn't steal your gum, but I am."

And I realize just then that I have not ever put it that way before. I told Bud Hunter I stole, sure. Maybe a couple other people, but I'd never qualified myself as a thief, out and out, but here, in this helicopter, it feels right.

She appears to see the truth in this, and just nods and says, "Okay then," seeming to like the absurdity of it. The man in the bow tie has taken off his headset and is talking to the pilot, leaning up between the seats so it's just me and the woman talking through the radio.

"How about you?" I say, as we ascend past a goat with one horn standing on a narrow rock ledge. I can see no viable way to or from the ledge at all. The goat seems to have just appeared there.

The woman tells me she works for Sigil down in Atlanta. She runs a division of their recording studios that spans the Southeast, leasing them out for nonprofit groups.

She asks me how I became a thief, if I really am one, and I tell her I just fell into it, really, and ask her how she became someone who leases recording space?

She laughs. "I fell into it too. My father worked for Sigil before me, and I followed him in, I suppose."

I ask if he's coming to the retreat too, her father.

She tenses a little. "No," she says. "No, he died not long ago."

"I'm sorry," I say, as we pass sharp outcroppings of rock.

"That's all right," she says. "He was visiting Corsica and got caught in a mudslide, if you can believe that." She glances out the window at the rock face scrolling by. By now, there are no plants left, only layer upon layer of timeless black stone, every cubic inch older than the entire human race. "He came to America from Greece alone, no family, no English. He worked for a church, studied elevator repair, and found a job at the Sigil building, married my mother, had me...I'm going on and on. I'm sorry."

"It's okay," I say.

"Thank you. Anyway, in all that time, he'd never gone back home. So finally, last year, he went to visit Corsica, and he was hiking, and there was a flash flood, and he was buried alive."

"Jesus."

"I know. And they never found him," she says, still looking out the window. "They don't know if he was swept out to sea or is still there under the mud. He just vanished."

The man in the bow tie laughs at something the pilot has said to him and pats the pilot's shoulder.

"Want to know the most ridiculous part?" the woman says. "He's missing for weeks, presumed dead, and my mother is dying from it, I'm a mess. And what comes in the mail but this stupid thing."

From the bag on her lap she pulls a floor mat.

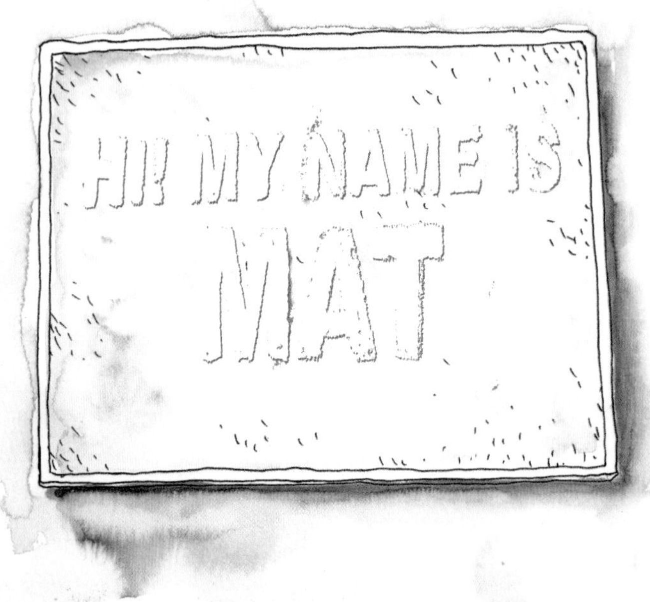
HI! MY NAME IS
MAT

She picks a piece of lint from the fibers.

"His name was Matygus," she says, tossing the lint to the floor. "We were always embarrassed by it growing up, me and my mother. We wanted him to go by Mat. I suppose he sent this home as a joke. He must have mailed it just before he was killed."

I tell her I'm sorry again, and then there's nothing to say for a moment.

The helicopter's turbines are louder, the air thinning out.

The woman tells me her name, Inez, and then turns the talk back to me.

"So why you, why the cure?" she says.

I look down at my hands, as if there'll be an answer there. "I suppose because I'm just... tired of being afraid all the time. Tired of feeling like my life is an egg I'm balancing on a spoon day after day. Because I just live in fear, and this..." and here I look up at her, "this just isn't who I want to be."

She stares at me a moment. "Well, look at that," she says. "I guess you you are a thief. You stole my answer."

"I don't like the forgetting aspect of it, though," she says, abruptly. "That worries me. I don't want to forget. It's ghoulish. That's why I brought the mat, why I brought so much stuff. Too much."

"You hold nearly a hundred years," I say.

"I know, I know. But still, I don't like it. I don't want to forget myself, even the ugly stuff. I know some people are doing this to escape, to start over altogether, but I just want a little relief from the panic, you know? So I can live braver. Be me, but, I don't know...better."

I hold up a pen.

"Ha! Right? I bought new journals, and we're like ninety years away from it," she says.

The helicopter lurches a bit, and I make a joke about wanting to forget that last bump, and she laughs.

"You know," she says, "I'm glad I met you. I'm glad we're riding together."

"Me too," I say, and it occurs to me then how much I like her, how attracted to her I am. I want to take this cure and be free of my fear and go with her down the mountain and start over. I want to engage and be tied to things, part of things with her. Just take the cure once, roll back the clock a little, not forever, just a bit, and barrel into it all head first with Inez. Hell, maybe we don't even need the cure, I think, maybe we just go for it.

"Here we are," says the man in the bow tie...

Then, suddenly, we are passing through clouds...thick, white clouds...

...And next we are through. I see it.

The retreat.

Immediately, what strikes me about the place is the ambition of it. I pictured a small hospital, a laboratory, something utilitarian, but instead it looks like a whole town. It's situated on a lake, and all around are strips of greenery, thin bands of grass being rolled out.

"See, the water is finally settled," says the man in the bowtie, pointing to the lake, to a series of pipes running from it straight into the dirt.

"They're getting heat coils up the back for the mountain peaks, solar thermal," he says.

I look at the far end of the retreat, and I can see there are small roads leading down the mountain on that side. Construction vehicles under tarps, behind low, corrugated warehouses.

It occurs to me that the place isn't being set up as a temporary site while any final tests are run, or a preliminary retreat. The cure, as it stands now, takes a month to administer, and will need to be readministered every few years, at least, to remain vibrant, so it makes sense that the retreat would have lodging, but what is being built here looks more expansive and more permanent than anything I'd expected.

"How many people are up here now?" asks the woman; apparently we are thinking similar thoughts.

"Around five hundred," says the man in the bow tie. "About two hundred that stay year-round."

Year-round. I see Inez recoil at the thought. She turns and catches me looking at her, but I don't look away. I look into her eyes, straight on, wanting her to see in mine the same conviction I know she feels.

"You'll go back down," I say, apropos of nothing. The words seem to affect her; her shoulders relax a little, her grip. It's what she needed to hear, and I mean it with everything inside me.

We will teach each other to be better. We will go down, no matter how bad things have gotten.

Admittedly, in the four years since my Heartwell theft, Errant's prognosis of events has felt more prescient. Nothing horrific has happened, no massive attacks, no total breakdown; it's the little things...the ways in which people seem to be pulling away from each other, into stories of their own making. A cyber-bug in a certain kind of pipe elbow causes a nationwide water shortage for a month. A nuclear plant in China overheats, and the event is thought to be retaliatory. You can almost feel it, the low scrape of seats backing away from the table by an inch here, an inch there. Like Errant had said...the paranoia and protectionism of old age. And the simple failures of age too. Services breaking down. Money printed wrong. A bank losing funds digitally, then regaining them twenty-four hours later. No military state, no civil war in the streets. Just the erosion of any kind of certainty. Everyone unsure. Making up his own explanations.

Modern Home cut back business, did only custom homes now.

Bud Hunter died, and no one collected him for over twenty-four hours.

But all this will change, I tell myself, as the shadow of our helicopter passes over the nearest buildings. This is the start of something new.

The man in the bow tie suddenly remembers the bottle of champagne in his hand and takes flutes from another compartment in the door and pours us each one.

We clink glasses and take a sip.

As the helicopter descends, I close my eyes, and I can almost feel it, every cell in my body fresh and pink and tingling with energy.

How I stole Claire
was the balloons.
The balloons the
nurse brought in
every Monday and
gave to the children
at night before
bed.

During the afternoons, he tied them up at the nurse's station.
They hung there, right below a central fire alarm, for hours.
The man he bought the balloons from sold them from a grocer's
just down the road. The grocer kept the helium tanks he used to
fill the balloons beneath a souvenir and kitsch counter just
outside the store. A roadside kiosk. The tanks were locked at
night, but only by a small bicycle padlock. And the tanks were
standard in every way, aluminum, three feet tall--the same
size as hydrogen tanks used for car fuel cells, among other
things. But hydrogen is flammable, all the way down to a 75%
mixture with helium. You switch out helium for hydrogen, the
balloons get filled, the latex thins...the balloon ignites.
Nothing dangerous, but a flash of light and heat, enough to set
off a fire alarm, easy.

When I took Claire from the
room, she was asleep. I put her
in the van and covered her with
blankets to keep her warm.

For a brief moment, she opened her
eyes and cried out...

... a terrible shriek...

...but I couldn't tell if it was for
shock, or joy, or nothing at all.

As we drove, I thought about
my first memory. How it had,
in fact, spoken to the last
moments of my life.

The balloon with the light
in it, blinking in my
father's fist above my
dying mother.

The balloon from a
faraway place that
would give us the great
prize we'd all been
waiting for.

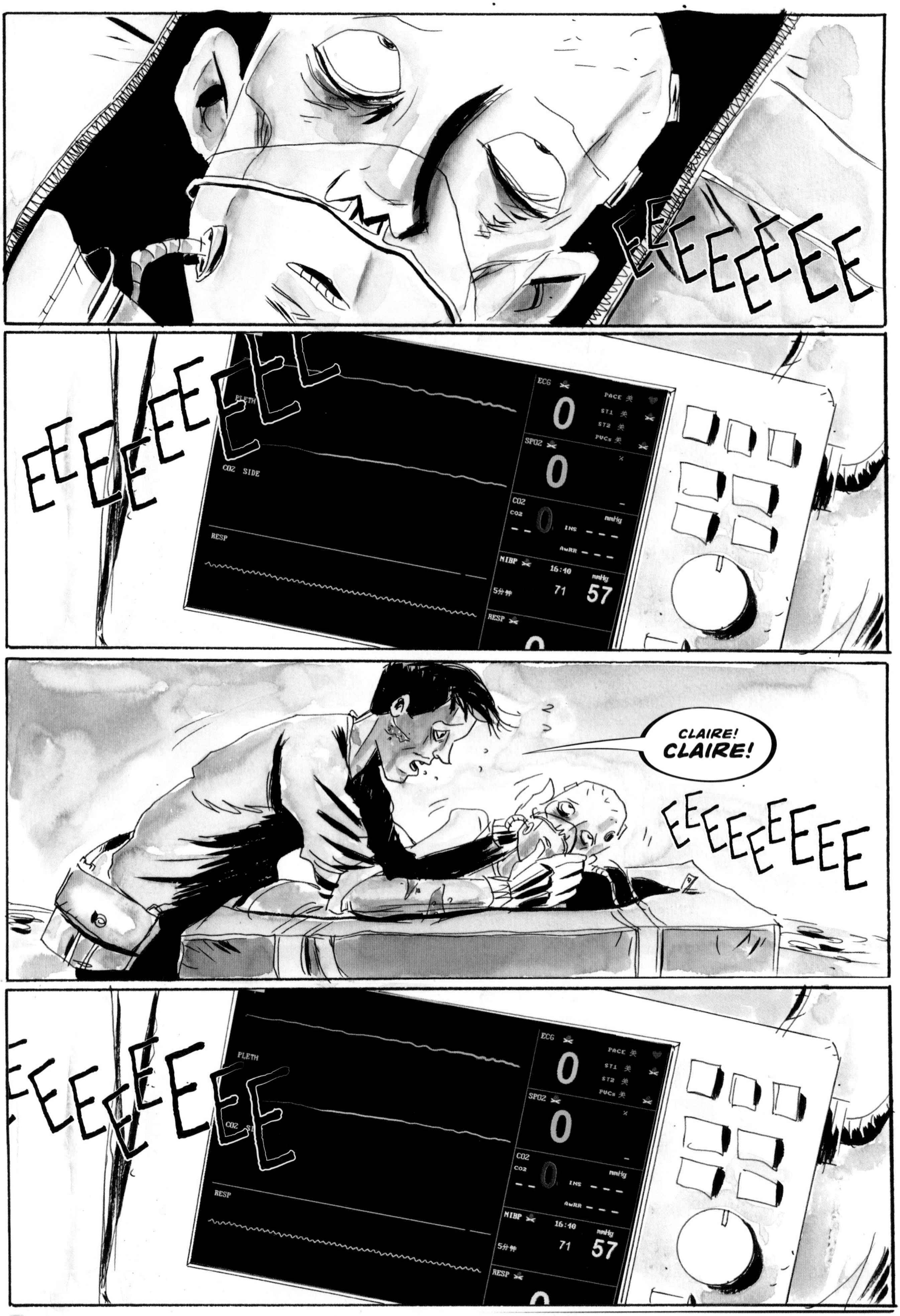
EEEEEEEEE
EEEEEEEEE
PLETH
CO2 SIDE
RESP
ECG
PACE
ST1
ST2
PVCs
SPO2
CO2
mmHg
INS
AwRR
NIBP
16:40
5分钟
71
57
CLAIRE! CLAIRE!
EEEEEEEEEE
EEEEEEEEE

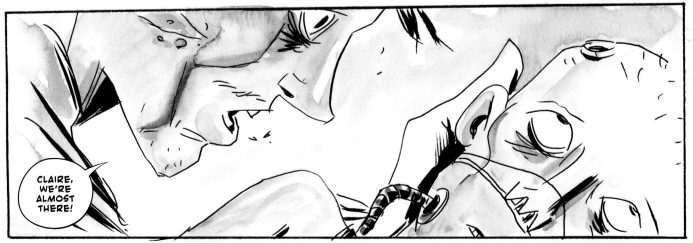

CLAIRE, WE'RE ALMOST THERE!

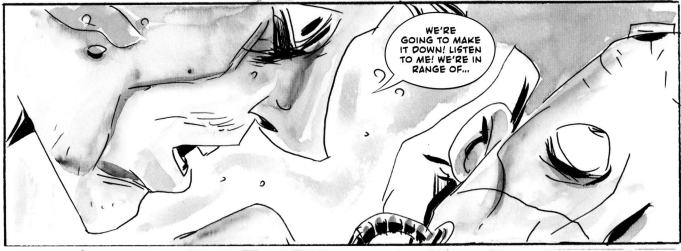

WE'RE GOING TO MAKE IT DOWN! LISTEN TO ME! WE'RE IN RANGE OF...

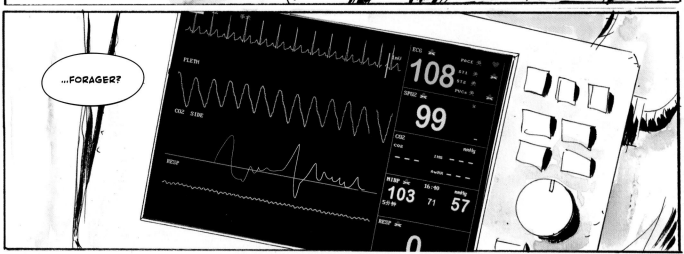

...FORAGER?

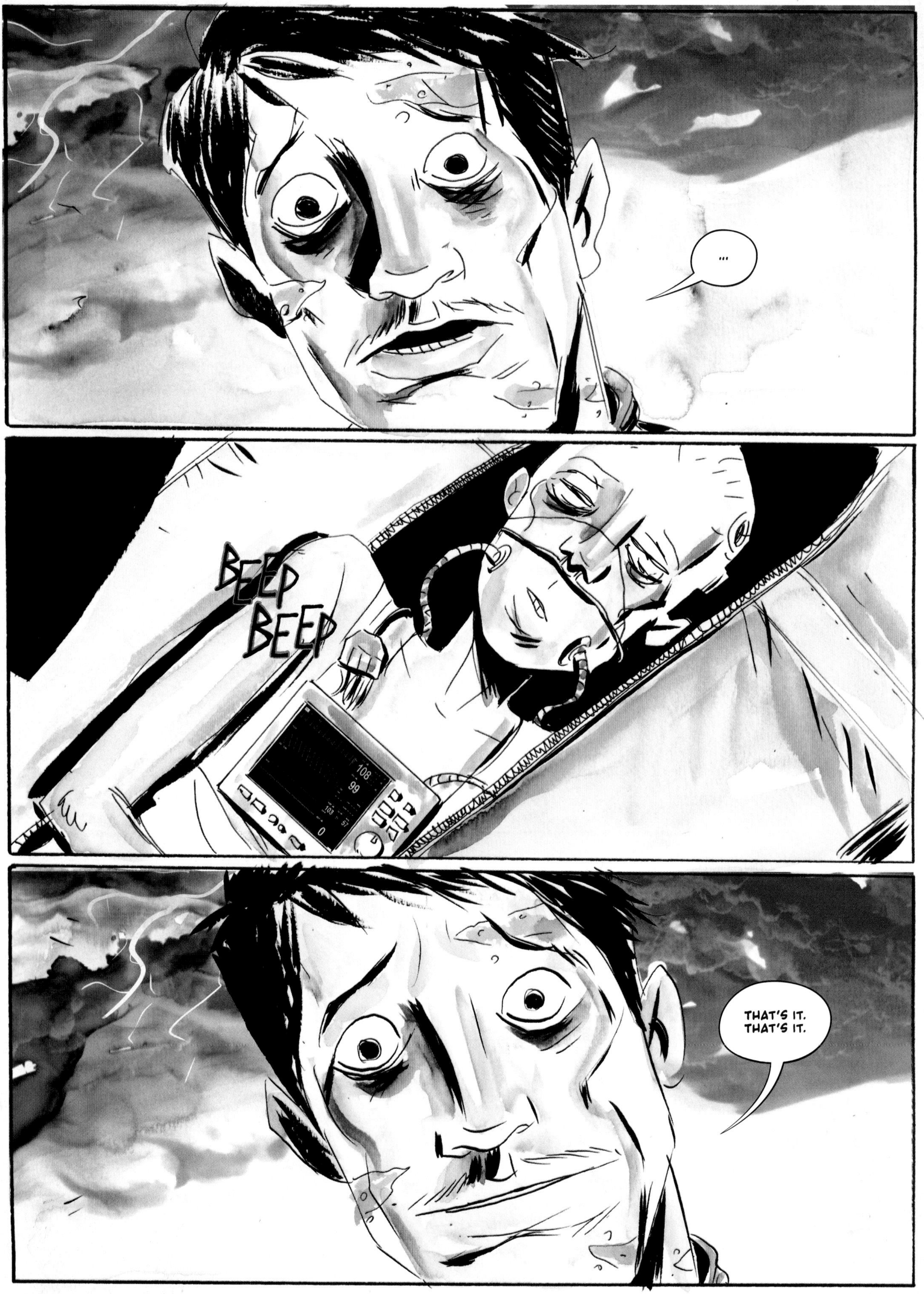
...
BEEP BEEP
108
99
103
57
0
THAT'S IT. THAT'S IT.

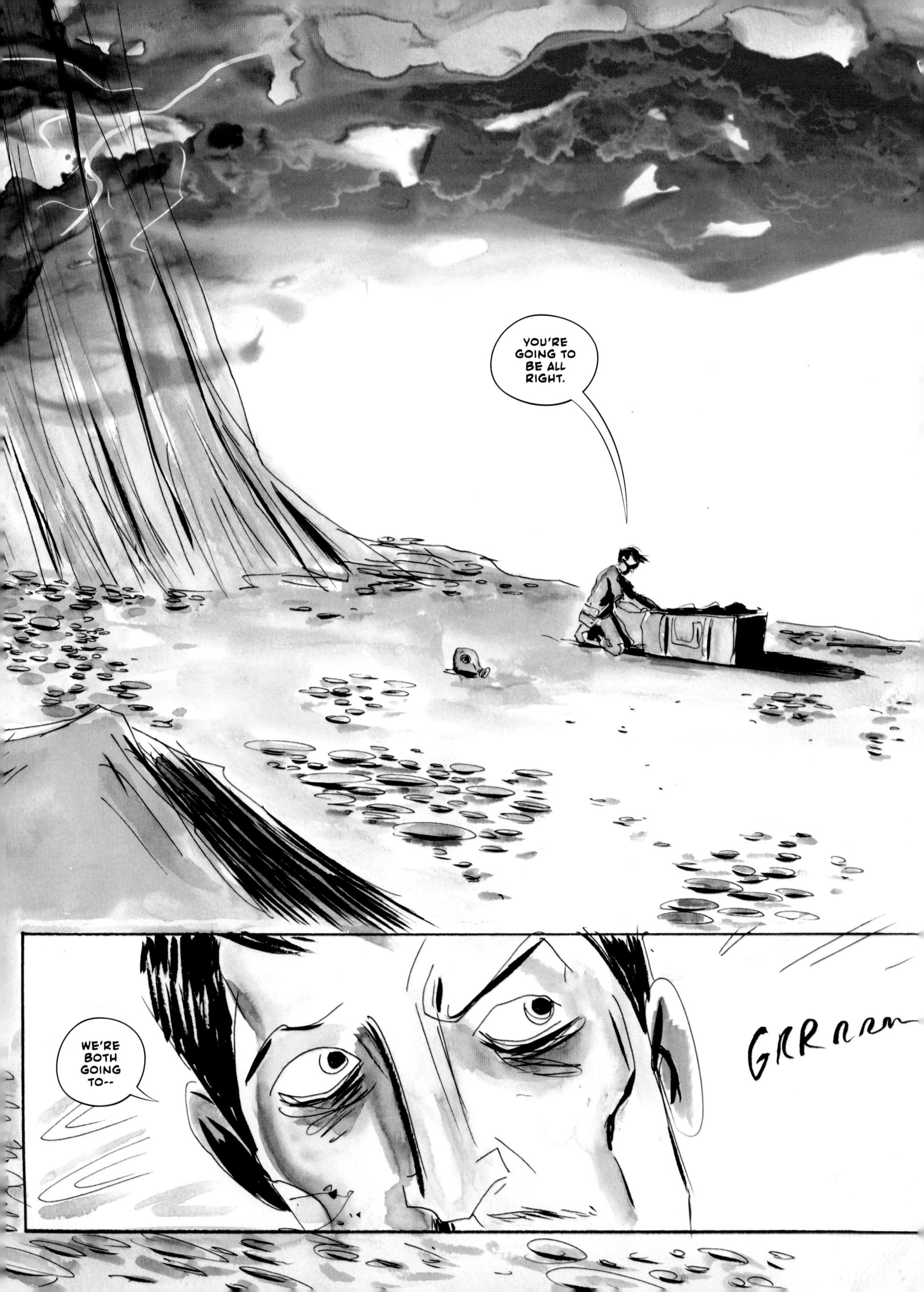
YOU'RE GOING TO BE ALL RIGHT.
WE'RE BOTH GOING TO--
GRRRRM

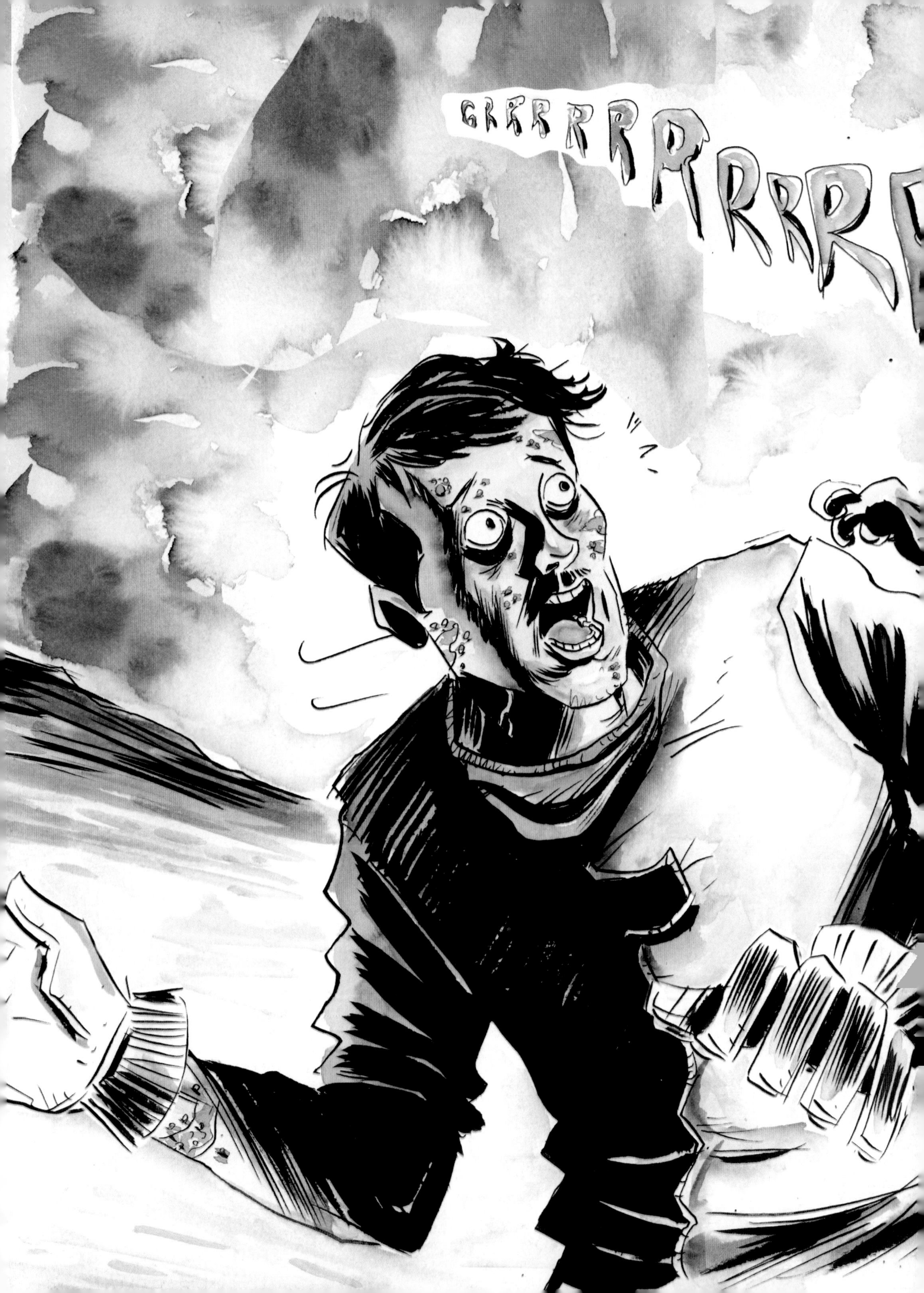
GRRRRRRRRRRR

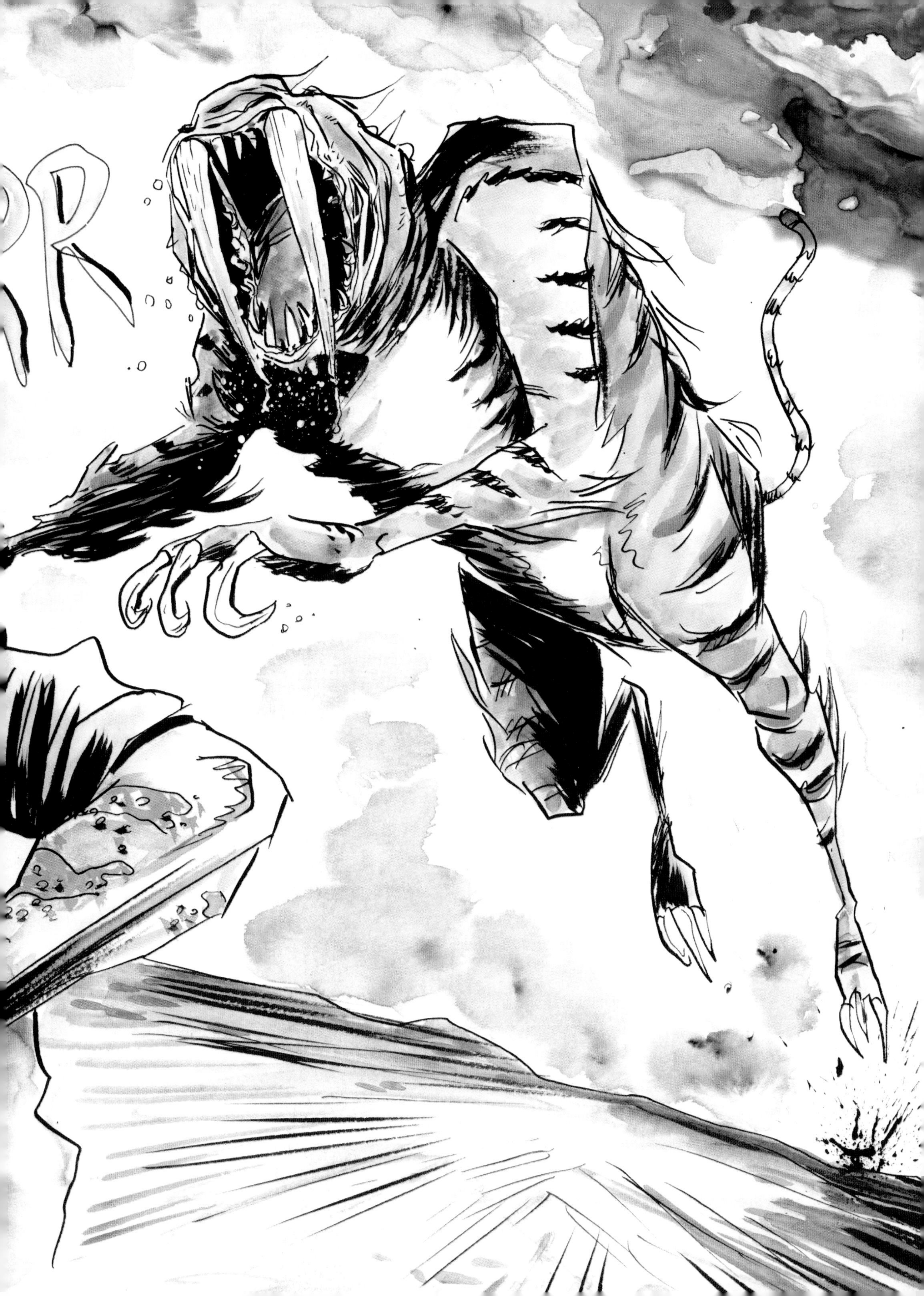

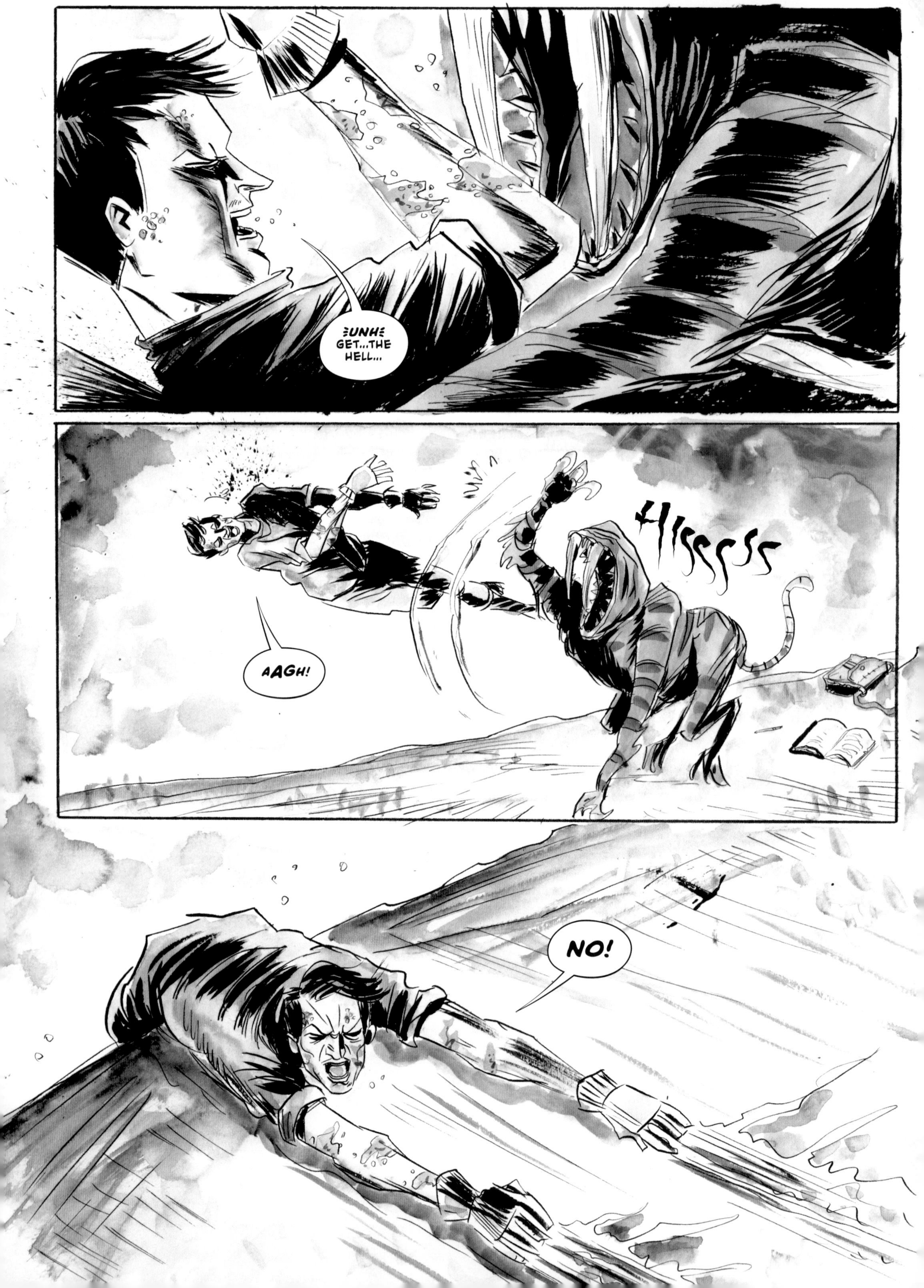
UNH GET...THE HELL...
AAGH!
HISSSSS
NO!

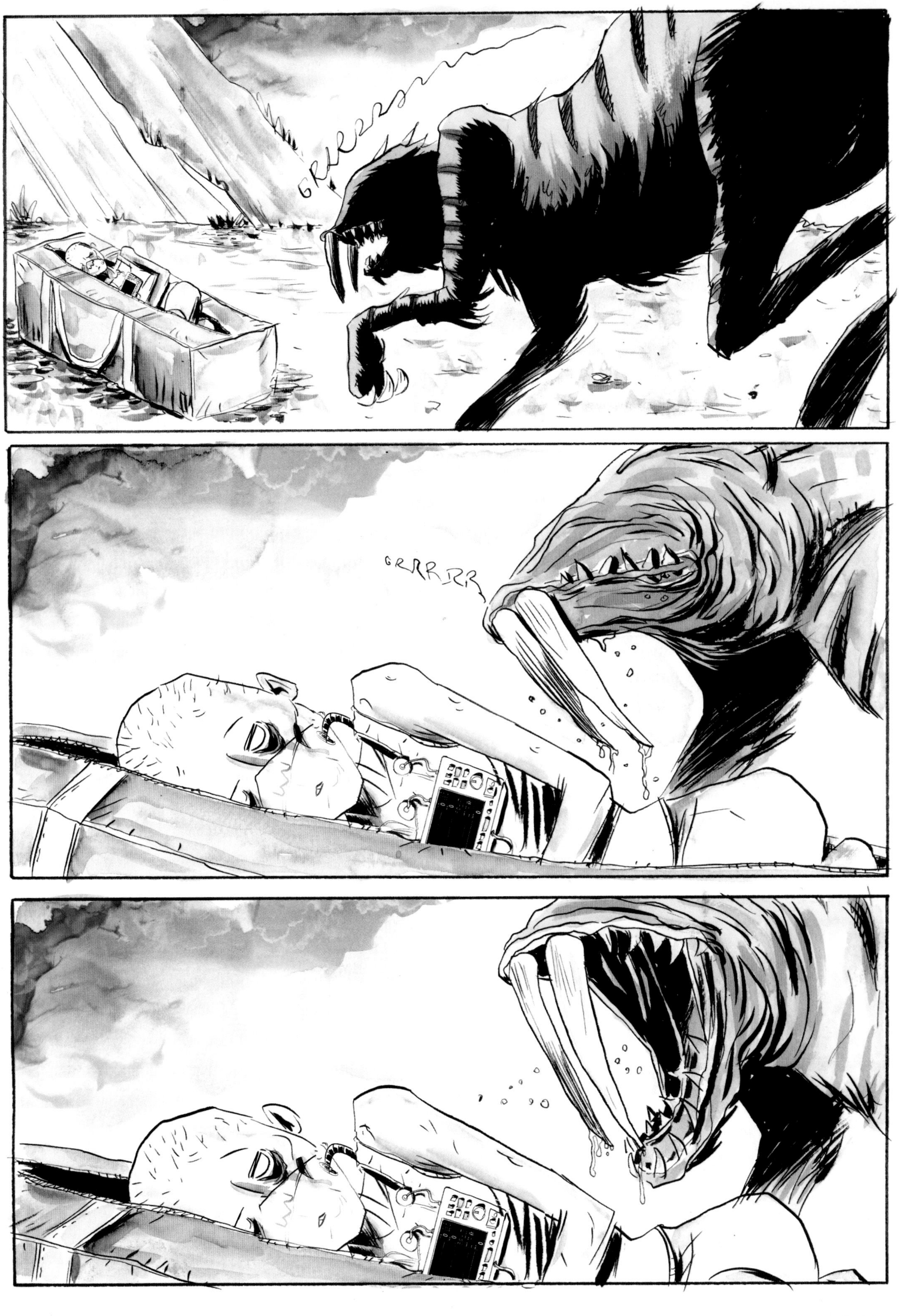

GRRRRR
GRRRRR

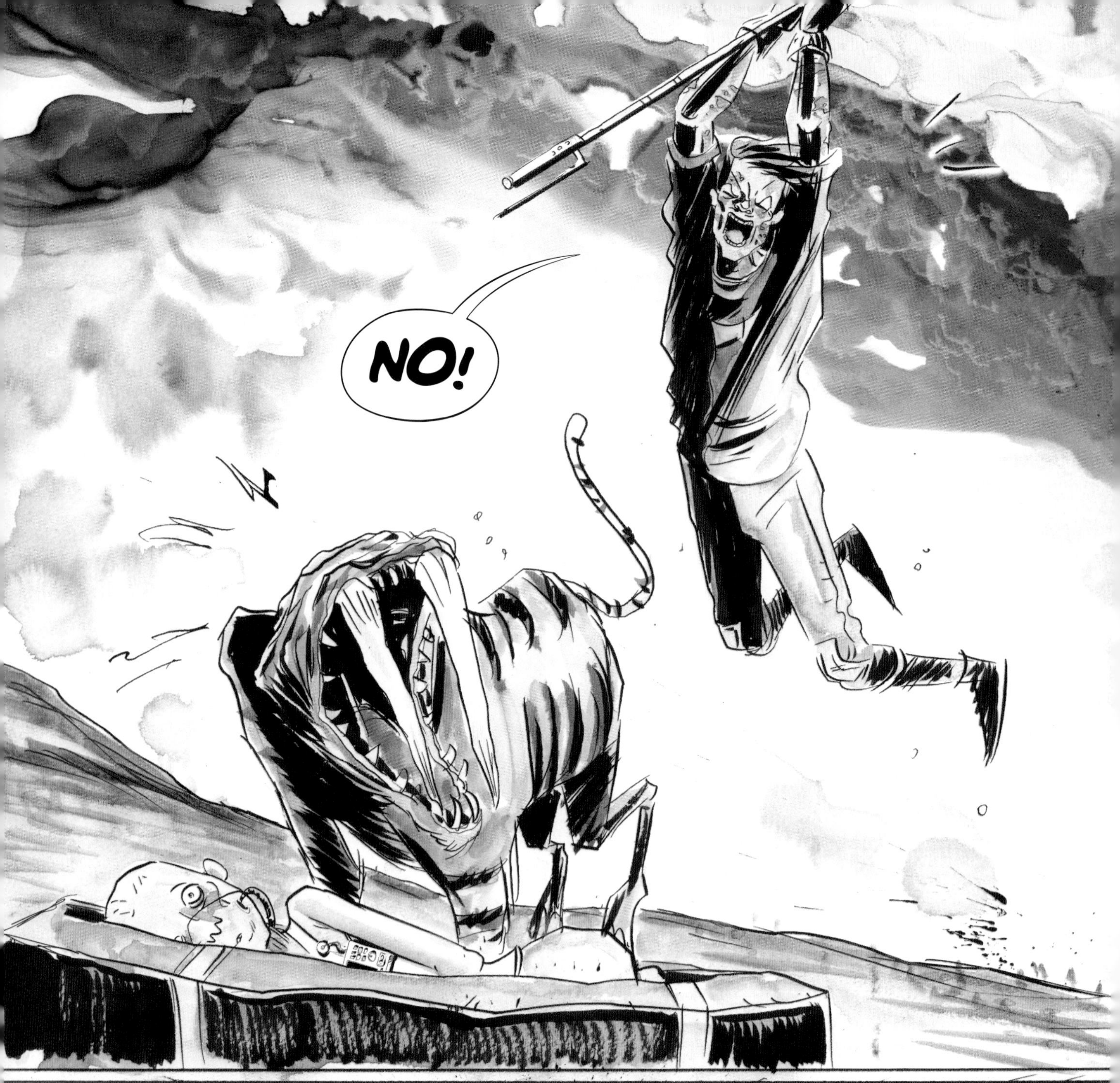
NO!

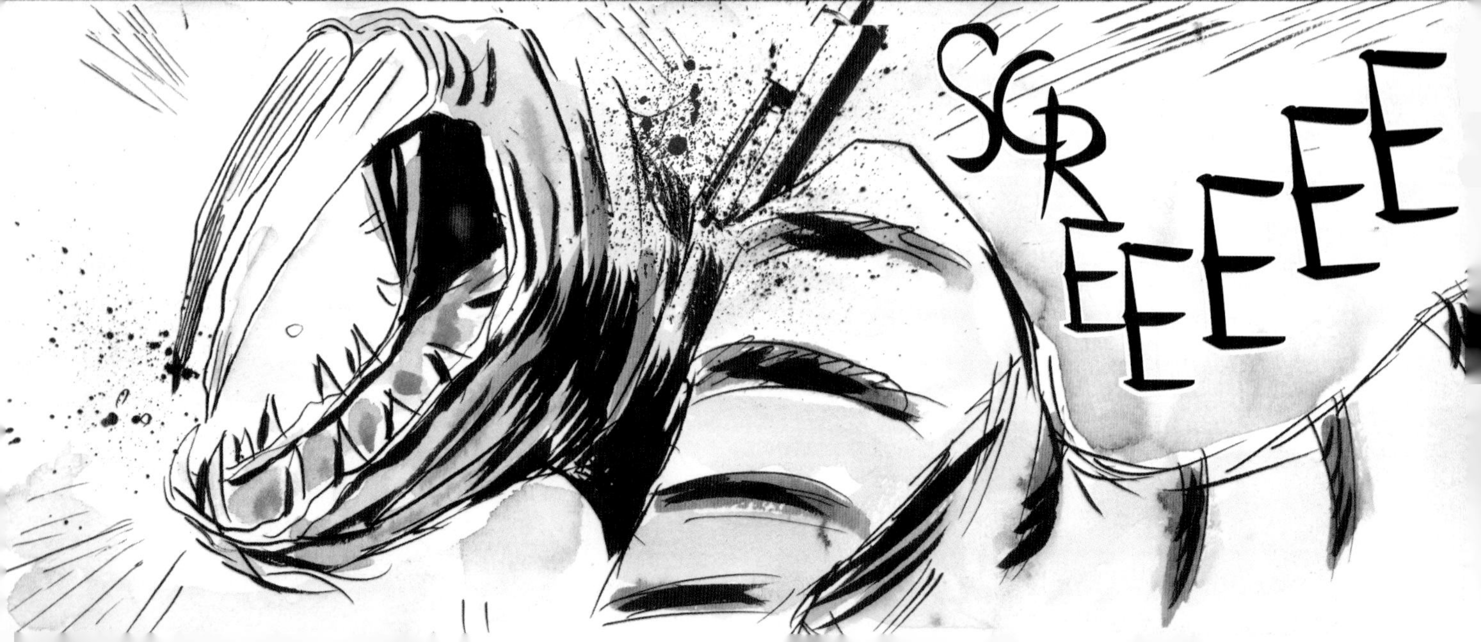
SCREEEEEE

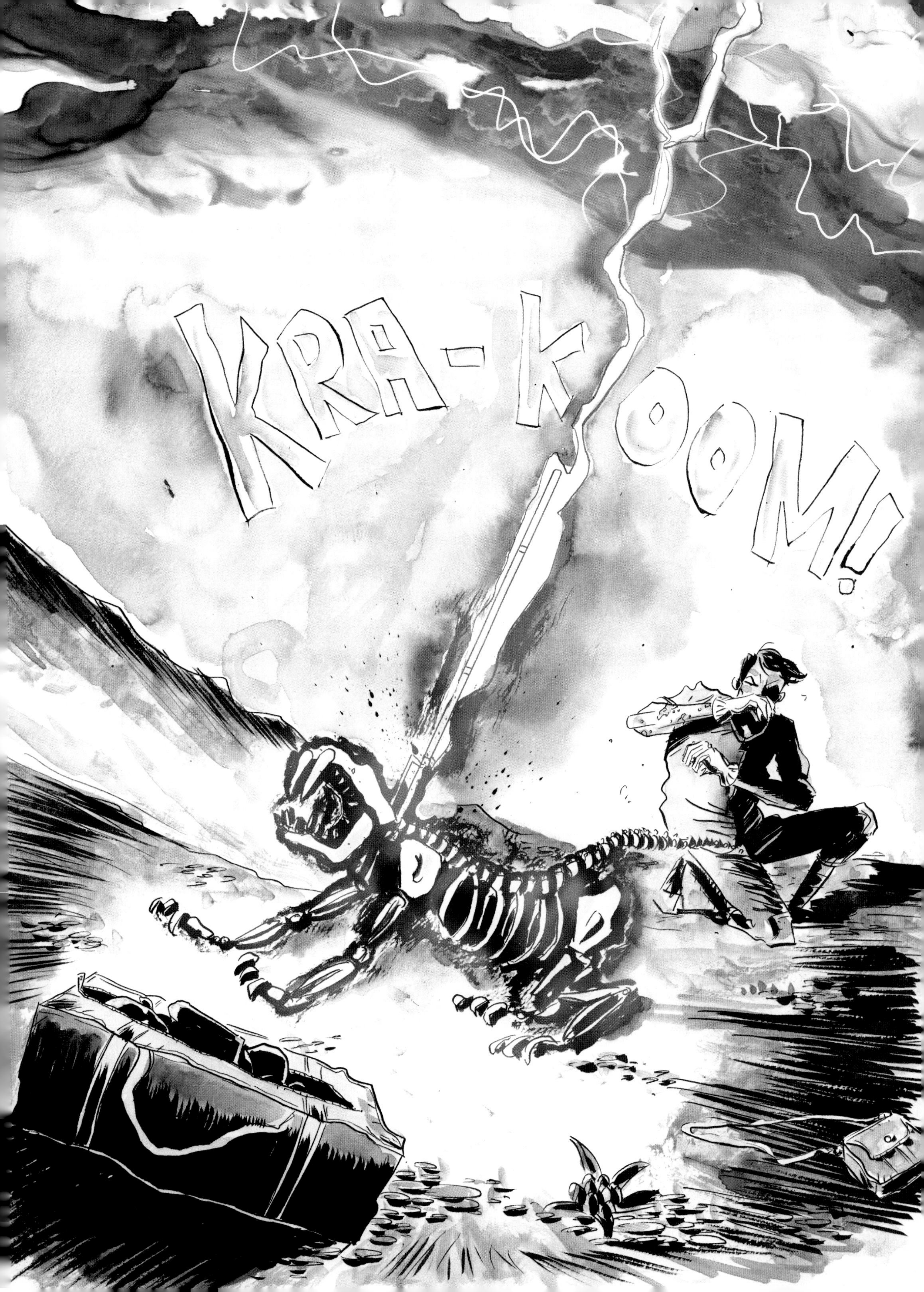
KRA-KOOM!

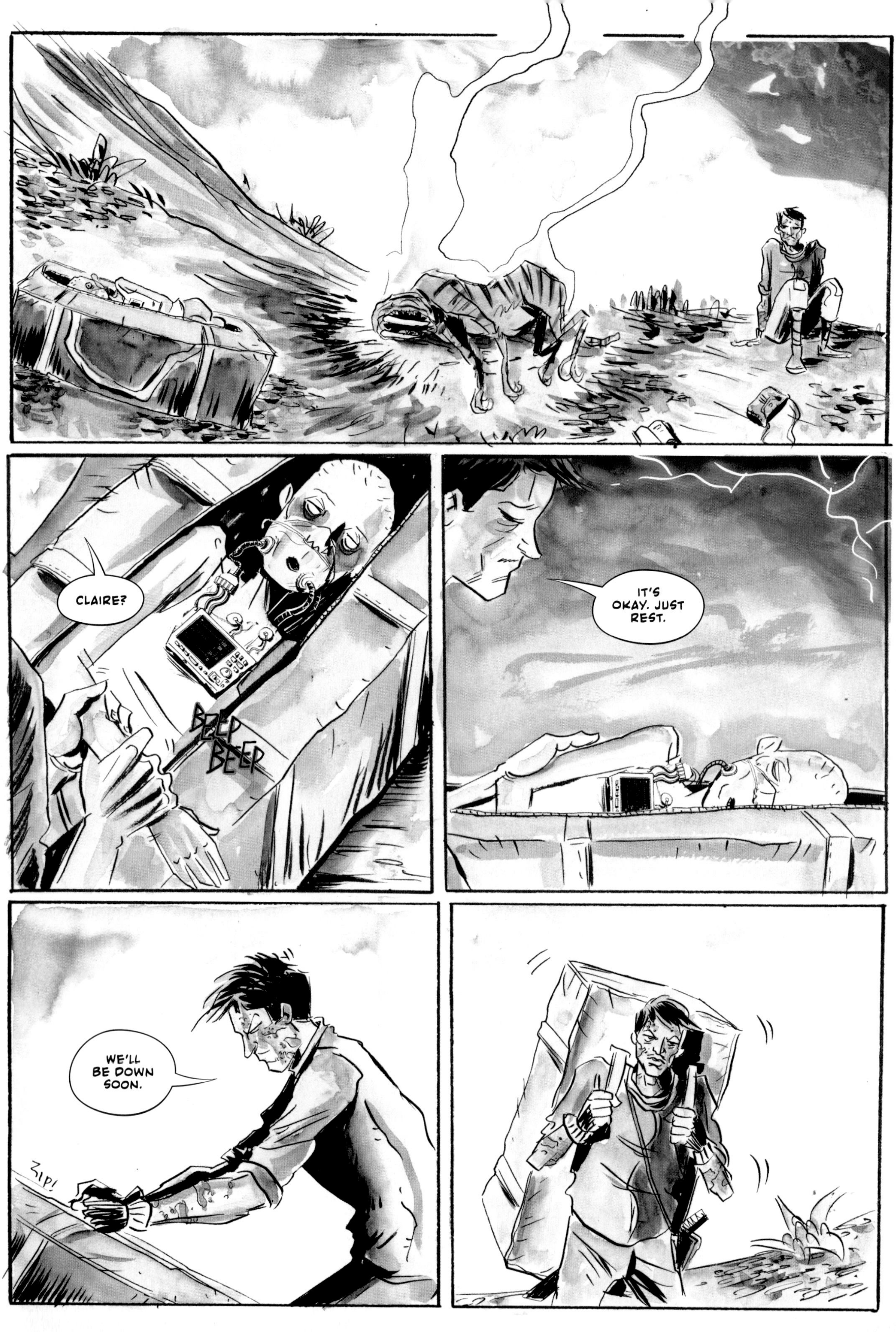
CLAIRE?
BEEP BEEP
IT'S OKAY. JUST REST.
WE'LL BE DOWN SOON.
ZIP!

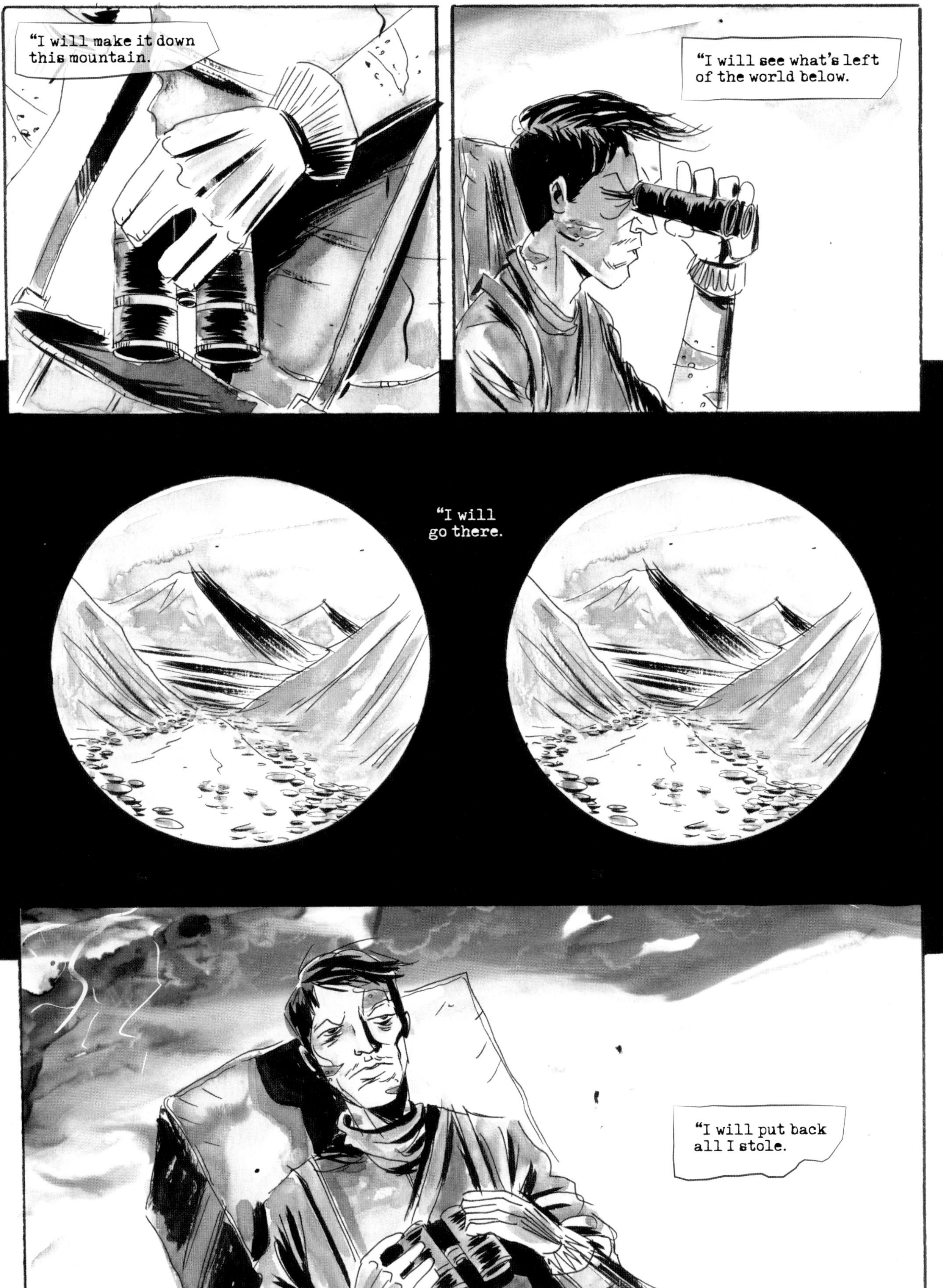
"I will make it down this mountain.
"I will see what's left of the world below.
"I will go there.
"I will put back all I stole.

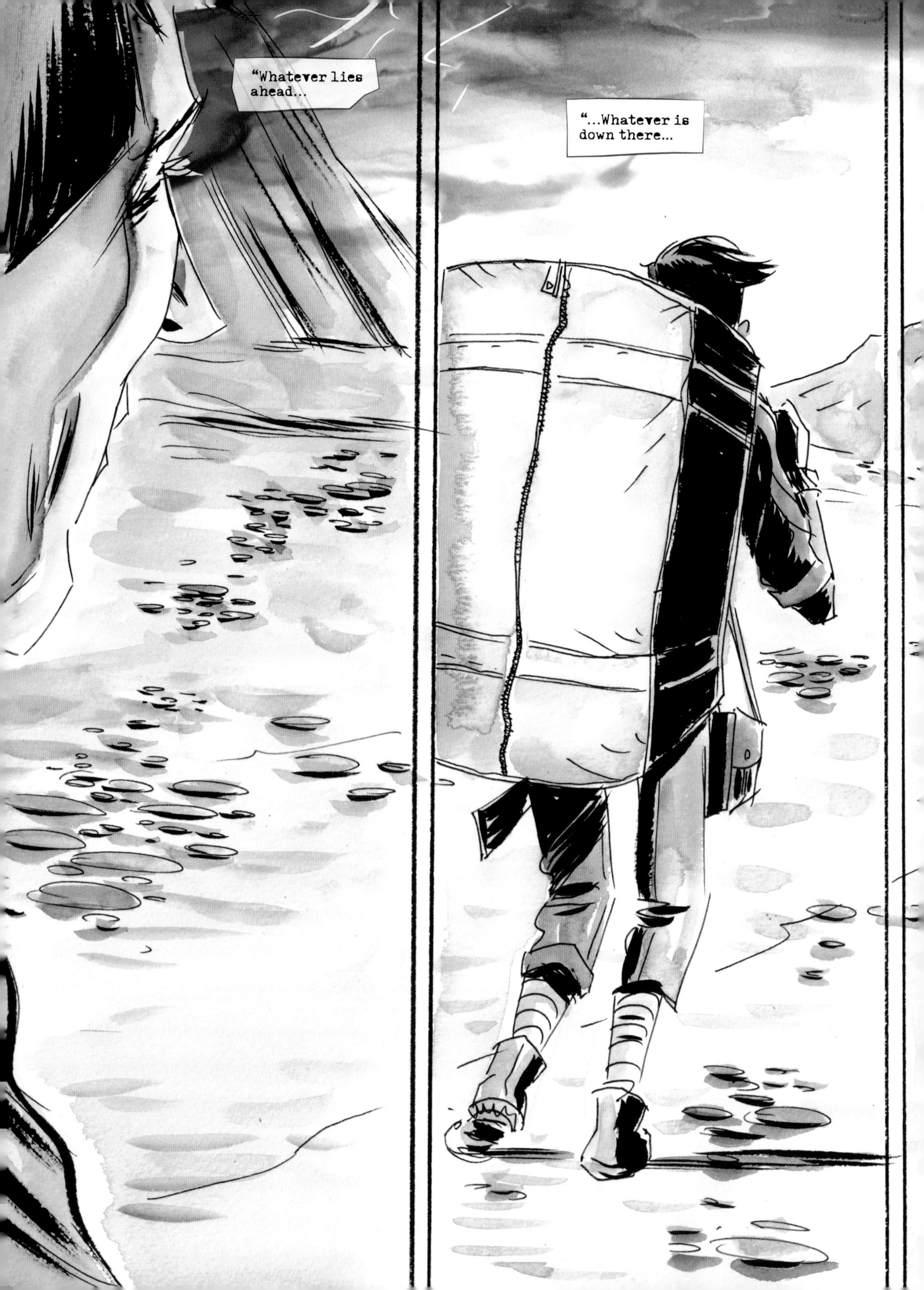
"Whatever lies ahead...
"...Whatever is down there...

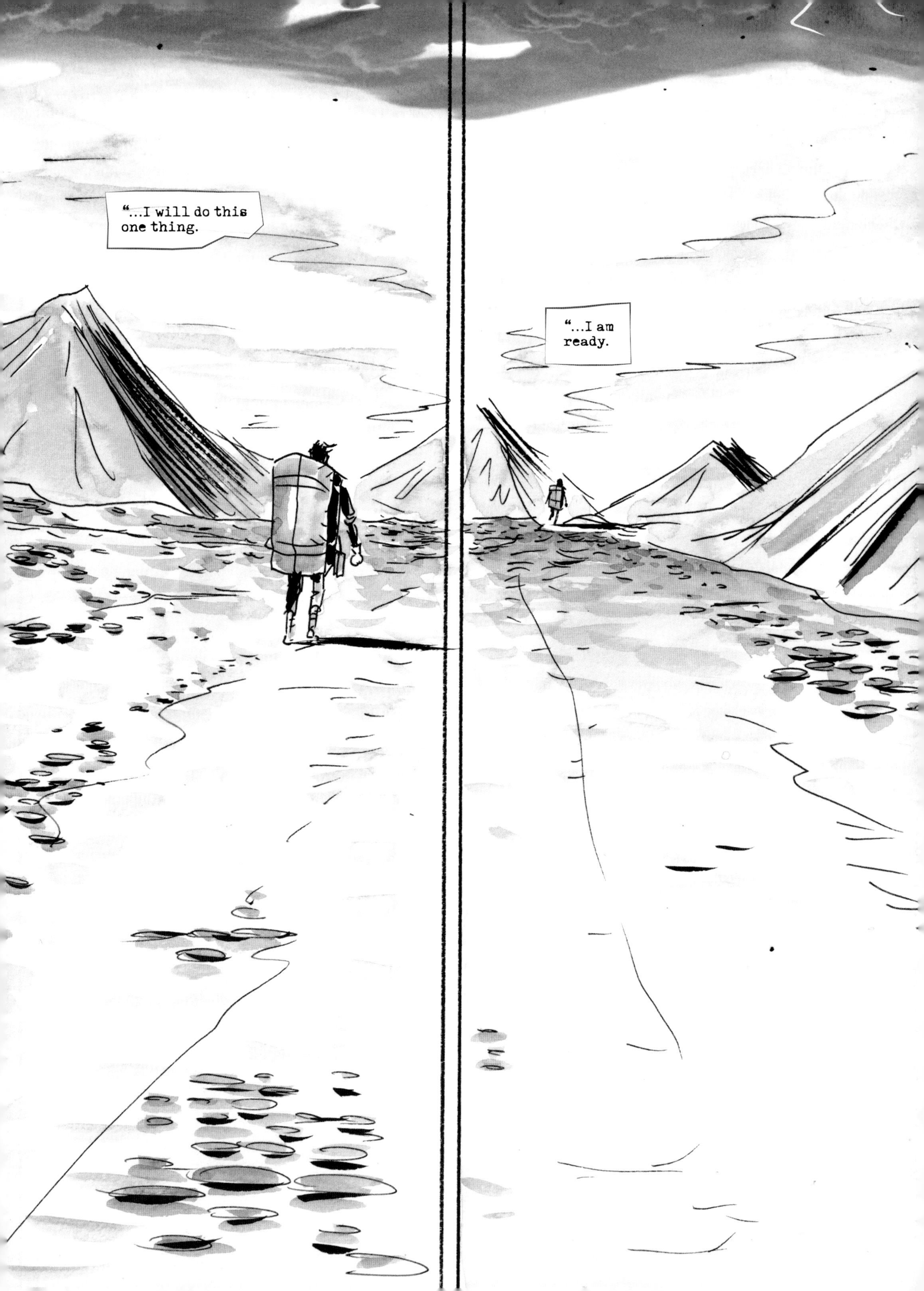
“…I will do this one thing.
“…I am ready.

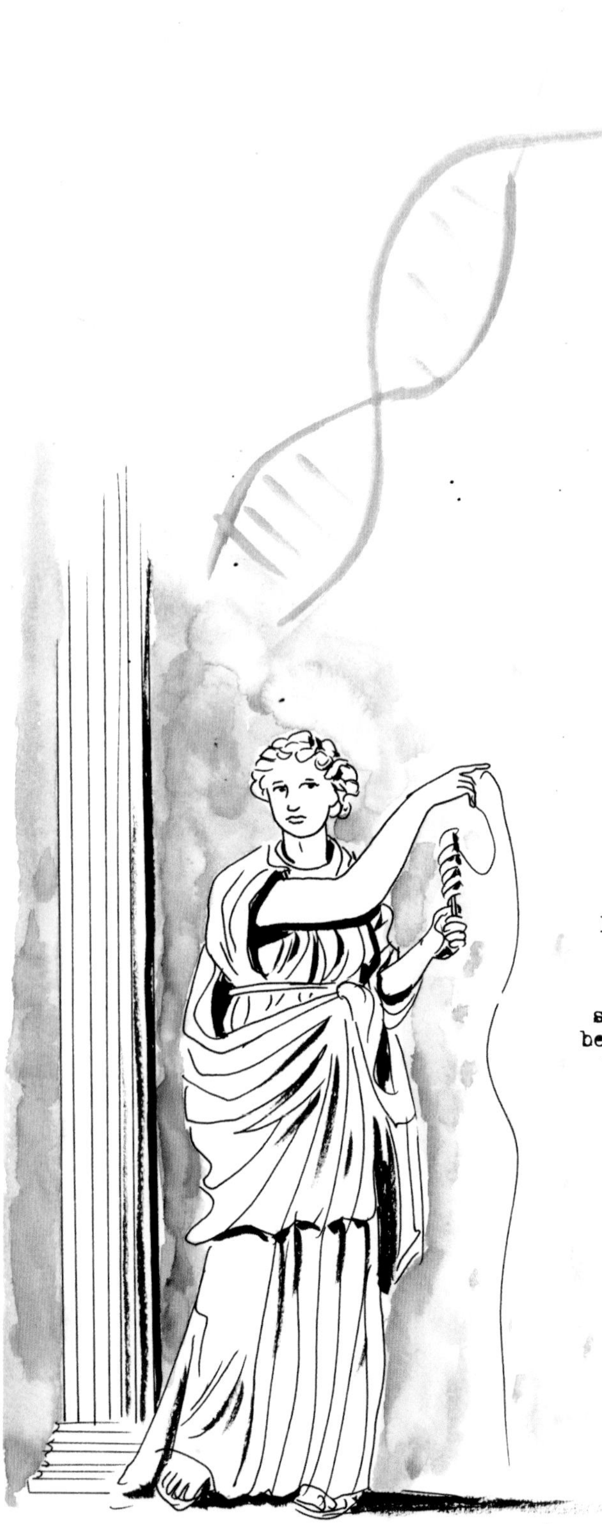

"...I am ready."

How many times did I write those lines in my notes?

How many times did I erase them?

How many years have I let slip by?

It wasn't supposed to be this way.

I look back at my notes, at my descriptions of the cure itself, and they're imbued with hope. The lexicon I used to explain the reaction, bubbles bursting in the body.

The way the cure for death worked was relatively simple.

The path to its discovery began in late 2011, when a research team at Sigil stumbled onto the gene resposnible for aging.

They hadn't been looking for it at first.

They were working on cataloguing CREB and zif268 genes at the time--genes linked to memory and retention. Along the way, though, a new gene caught their attention, one of the peripheral genes caught up in the cluster they'd been studying.

What the team noticed was that, when one particular gene was damaged in young mice, the mice began to age prematurely; injury to the gene basically caused the mice to go into a kind of immediate and rapid old age. The mice developed arthritis, arterial and neural plaques; their bones turned thin and brittle, their skin deteriorated. Even at barely a year old, the mice became suddenly and irrevocably old. Team Sigil named this newly discovered "aging gene" Klotho, after the Greek Goddess who spun the thread of life.

In January 2012, an expanded Sigil team began working doggedly to explore and better understand the Klotho gene, and by the following year, the team was making significant discoveries.

First, in February, using designer plasmids, the researchers actually managed to breed a batch of mice with overactive Klotho genes. And what the researchers found was that these new Klotho-mice ended up living about a full year longer than normal mice--a 35% increase in lifespan. The team was elated, and orders were given to divert more funding, more resources, to exploration of Klotho. It was thought that if the researchers could make a bigger breakthrough, say, get a batch of Klotho mice to live 100% longer, the doors would open for expanded trials.

For the next two years, the Sigil team's research boomed, but little progress was made. The team tried all manner of chemical and bacterial aggravators, but nothing seemed to stimulate a mature Klotho gene into hyperactivity beyond that 35% mark. Then, finally, in December 2013, the team made a break-through; they discovered an enzyme that appeared to be responsible for the restriction and modula-tion of the Klotho gene--an enzyme that kept the Klotho gene from overproducing peptides.

So in early 2014, team Sigil changed tacks. No, they hadn't been able to stimulate mature Klotho genes into hyperactivity, but maybe, by inhibiting a Klotho restrictor, they might unleash the gene to produce more peptides. The idea was: what if, instead of trying to soup up your car to outrun the cops, you simply took the cops off the road?

By the end of the year, team Sigil had developed an inhibitor that looked promising, and on December 31st, the team tested this inhibitor on a group of mature lab mice. One week passed. Two weeks. Three weeks went by, with no substantive reaction in the mice.

The team grew skeptical; word began to spread through the research community that the treatment was a failure.

Three of the team's assistant leads actually began searching for openings at other laboratories.

But then, suddenly, to everyone's surprise, in January 2015, the mice began to show signs of cellular rejuvenation. Their coats thickened; their bones grew denser, stronger, and more pliable. Cataracts disappeared, leaving their little eyes glassy and pink; muscle tissue became more elastic--the mice could scamper again, could reach on hind legs. They could no longer reproduce, and the span of memory did not seem to increase with the span of life, but overall, upon taking Klothovan, the mice grew young. And they stayed young, showing no signs of cellular decay, until treatment was stopped, at which point the mice resumed aging at a natural and recognized pace.

All that remained was to prove the Klotho gene
worked the same way in humans. In children with
progeria, the fast aging disease, the link was
inconclusive. But if they could get their hands
on a patient with an inverted variation of the
syndrome, a patient in whom aging had been
prohibited...

And so Claire.

And me.

And Klothovan.

Here is what I wrote about how Klothovan felt
for me, the first time I was dosed. My notes,
copied verbatim:

"Beman, the man in the bow tie, was right. It's like
champagne.

"There's no pain, no keeling over and writhing.
Just this low, warm tingling all over. Like a wave
sizzling on the beach, like you're a sand moat
filling with surf. This feeling in every cell
that you're being...refilled? Plumped up.

"It's like you suddenly realize how depleted your
body was. The wrinkled sacks of your knees. The
tired weaving in your shoulders. They become new
and strong and, all at once, you realize how worn
down you were. You were a glass half empty, even if
you saw yourself as half full.

"And now all I can think about is the biological
capital of youth. That essence, that thing that you
have as a kid, a physical element, but a psychologi-
cal, even spiritual element--a deep, cellular
knowledge that you are rich in life. You have the
stuff that matters most. You are buoyant with it.
Buoyant. You see it in that way teenagers look at
you...that sly, slow-blinking way. Like they're
looking down even when they're looking up at you,
like: I might have acne, I might not be having sex
yet, I might not have money or freedom or anything,
but I'm richer than you, because I am FULL.

"I am full.

"I will go down the mountain and be a better person now.

"They will help Claire up here, and I will take her down.

"The next time I write, I will be proud of myself."

These were my words. I am nearly twenty-five cycles
in, centuries, and I no longer remember my child-
hood. Have only notes on the years after my first
time taking the cure.

And yet, looking back over them, there is nothing
optimistic about my descriptions of the retreat
and its relation to the world below.

My notes are like this:

"The lodging is being expanded. We're taking in
another three hundred, maybe four hundred people
within the year.

"Looking for ways to put Klothovan in the water,
which will make it easier.

"No news on Claire.

"Errant says patience, hopefully a version will
help her...he is working on a song that he says..."

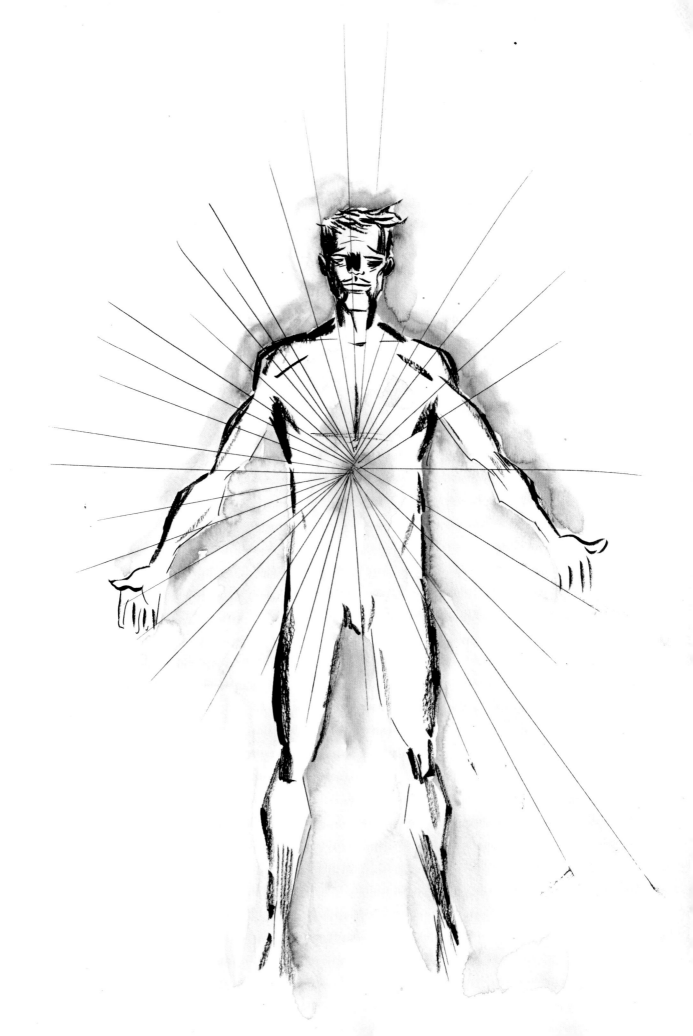

My notes on the world below make it clear
I did go down the mountain a few times in
that first decade.

Some are erased. Some are still here.

What's clear is that things below worsened very
quickly, in a matter of years, not even decades.
Worsened in the ways you'd expect, yes--in power
failures and dwindling resources--but even more
so through a kind of continued, frantic retreat
from one another...countries backing away. People
backing away within those countries. A kind of
entropic double spiraling...the collection of
units breaking apart, spinning outward and
farther from the center, while every single unit
spun tighter into itself. It wasn't just that the
center no longer held; it was the sense that the
center was the problem, the enemy, the thing to
escape. The center was a distraction from the
real conflicts, happening in YOUR life,
happening here at the edges, farther out.
The heart, it pumped out bad blood, bad
cells of information, was itself
made of bad stuff...

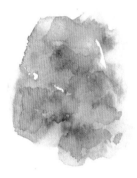

And then, one day,
it just happened...

Imagine, as I asked you to
earlier, pages ago, years ago, that
you are a member of the pygmy
tribe in the Congo.

You are small and dark-
skinned, and I am too.

Together, led by the goat,
that happy goat, we come across
that spot on the ground. The dry,
gray spot, charred and crackling.
The small frog dead inside.
The smell like
burnt hair.

Imagine what you feel, seeing it there. You back away as it advances, advances so fast, faster than you thought possible. It's like at sunset, all day the sun has just been there, not REALLY moving, but now, sinking against the trees, all you can see is how quickly the day is dying, how quickly it all goes...the shadow is at your feet.
Reaching. Spilling forward.

You feel all this, looking at the ashy spot. Watching the growth accelerate, watching the grass wilt at the edges, turn gray and crinkle up, bend and curl toward the earth.

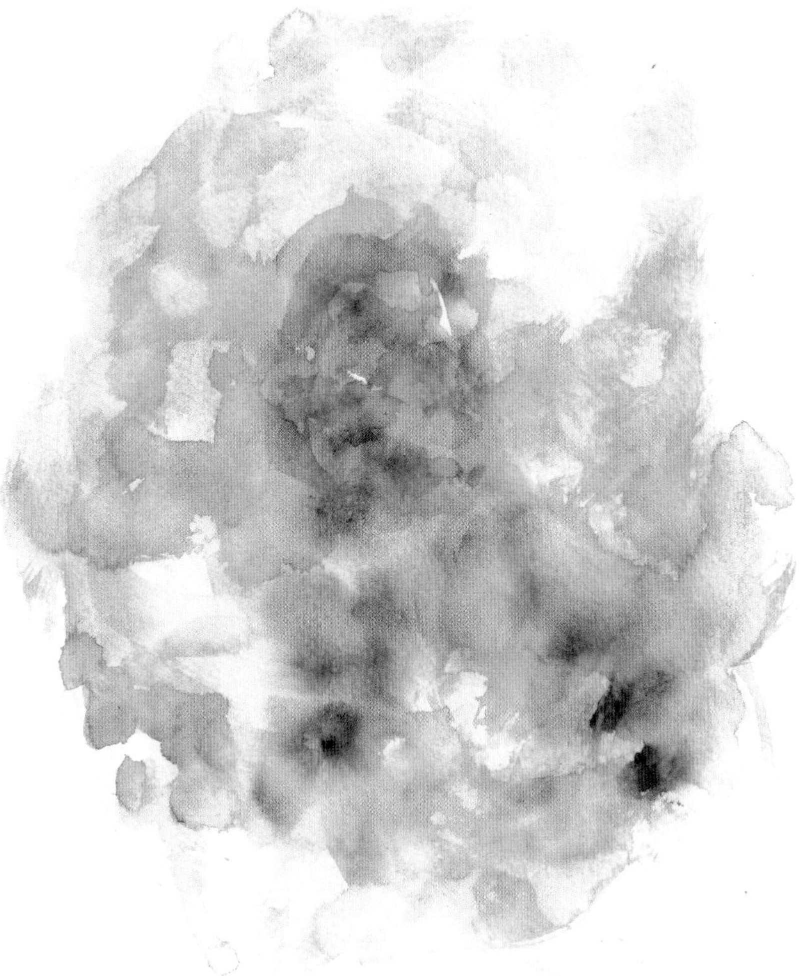

What you don't know is that it's a kind of blight, engineered in a laboratory, a combination of brown moss blight and botulism. It has been made by your country, or maybe another--there's no telling anymore--and it has been made to draw people back to the center. It has been made to frighten them back from the edges. But something has gone wrong...a bug in one of the components has made the bacteria more resilient than expected. Who put the bug there?
Did we? Did they? Again, no one knows.

But the spot grows at an
exponential rate, every day.

Anything that crosses its path dies.

Will it cross water? Cross oceans?

It will.

It lives in seaborne algae and in
fish and in birds...

And now everyone is moving from the
cradle to the edges. The very edges,
to escape the Dying.

The retreat takes in more people, and
more, nearly four thousand, before
closing itself off. It is still a
secret place, thank God. No one knows
about the cure. And there is no sense
of it being a real refuge,
though it is.

ut the spot grows a
onential rate, ev

And for a while, months, there is
still word from below to listen to. Up
on the ridge, we listen. There is word
of masses of people trying to cross
the ocean, find some place to escape
the Dying. People digging bunkers.
People climbing mountains. People
running into the spot itself.

But, eventually, around 2050,
things below go black.

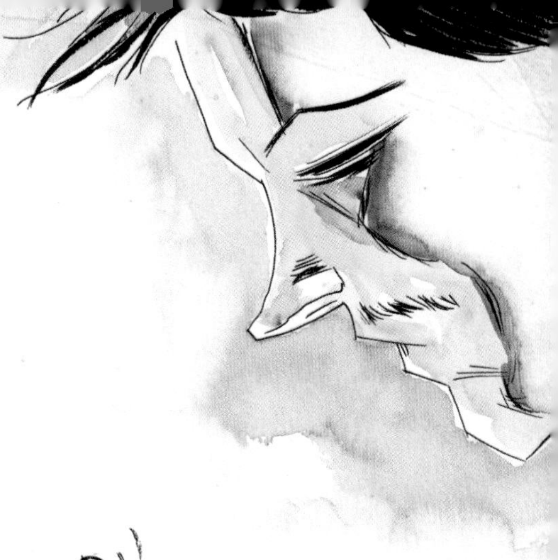

My notes in the years after this are scribbles and erasures that I have copied here.

My last entry comes around 2186:

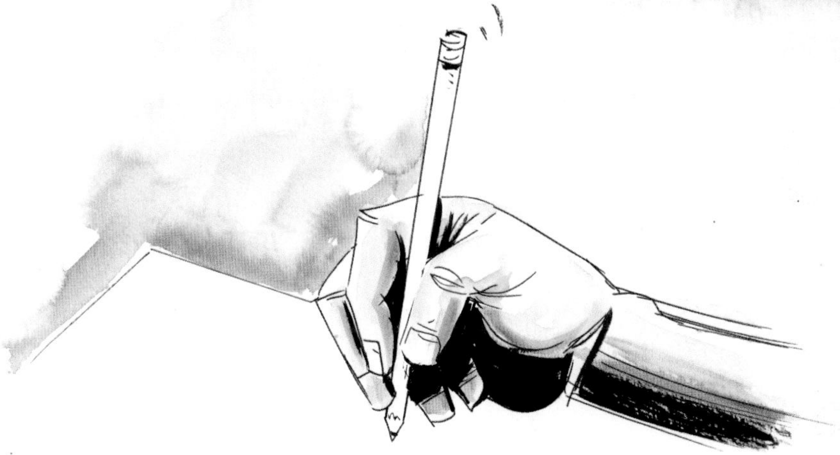

"After two cycles more I am back with Inez and, still, all we want to do is go down. But there is no way. Without the cure, the Dying would kill us. And whatever's down there...

"The sky has changed, the clouds. They move at high speed, furiously torn apart and spun back together. What did they do to the sky? Was it a bomb? Was it chemical? Was it us?

"There are rumors that people below tried to climb the mountain, but that there are defenses now. Did we put them there in the early years? I have no notes on this. I can't remember. My neighbor Max says we did. Inez is not sure. Are they plants, the weapons? I heard they're plants. Maybe there are no defenses...Maybe the natural world has just...changed? Maybe the plants were changed by the Dying?

"We'll wait a while and listen, Inez and I. But we will make it down. At the FIRST SIGN things are okay, we will.

"We'll remind each other.

"An expedition called Forager is being planned. They will go down soon and send word back. They are bringing a boat with them to travel up the coast.

"We will wait for word from them. But we will be brave, we will."

And it's sometime around here that my notes stop altogether.

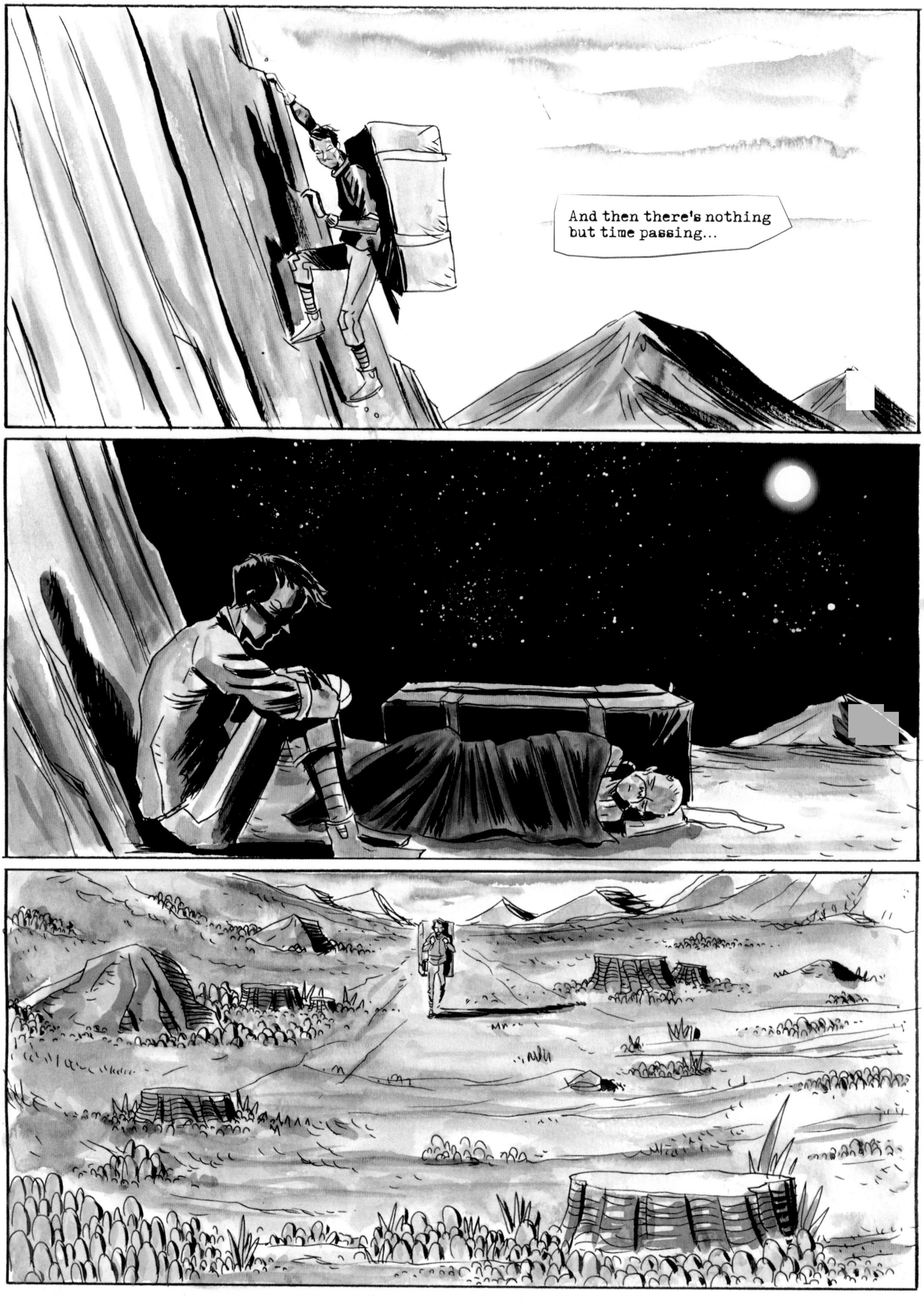
And then there's nothing but time passing...

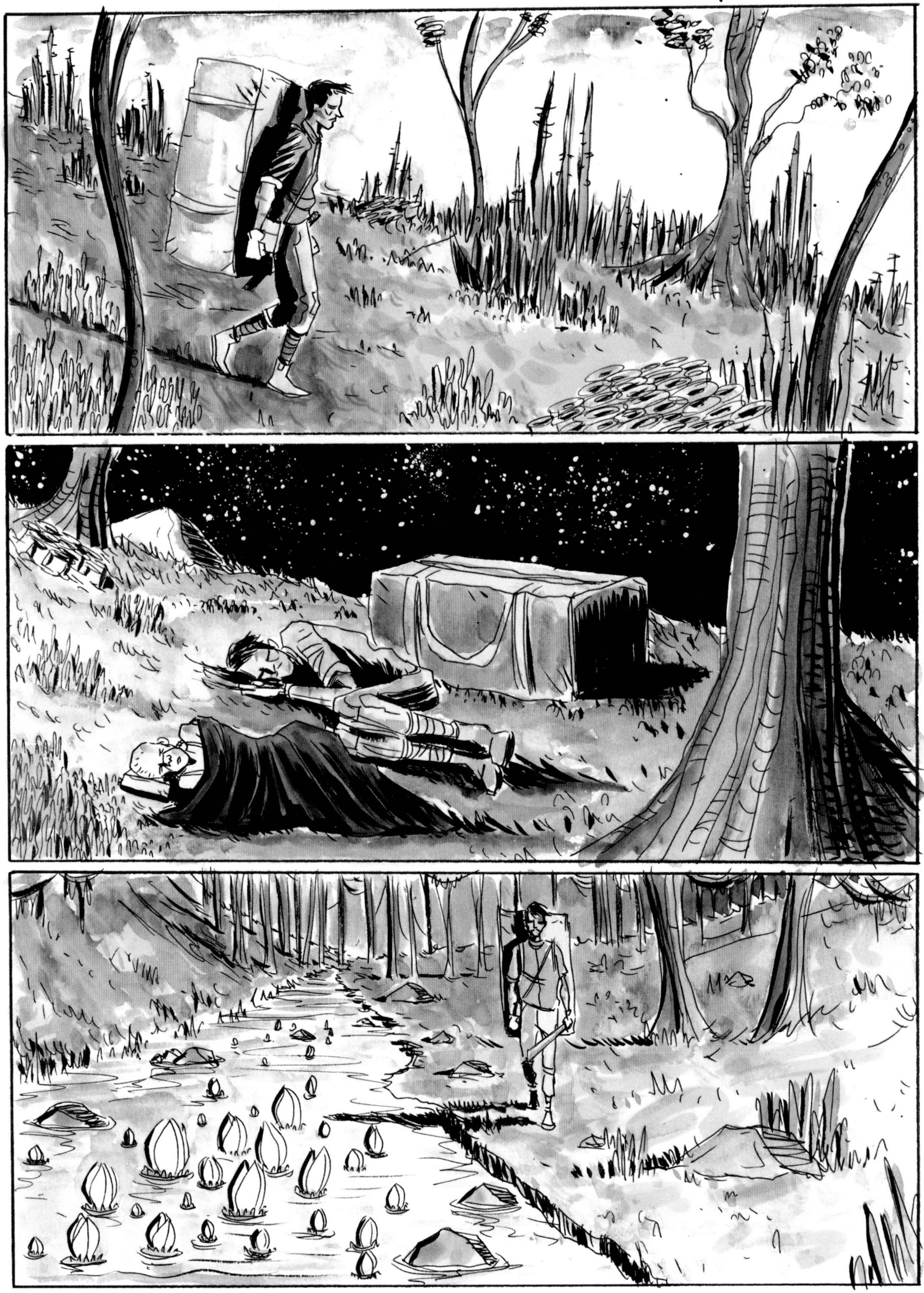

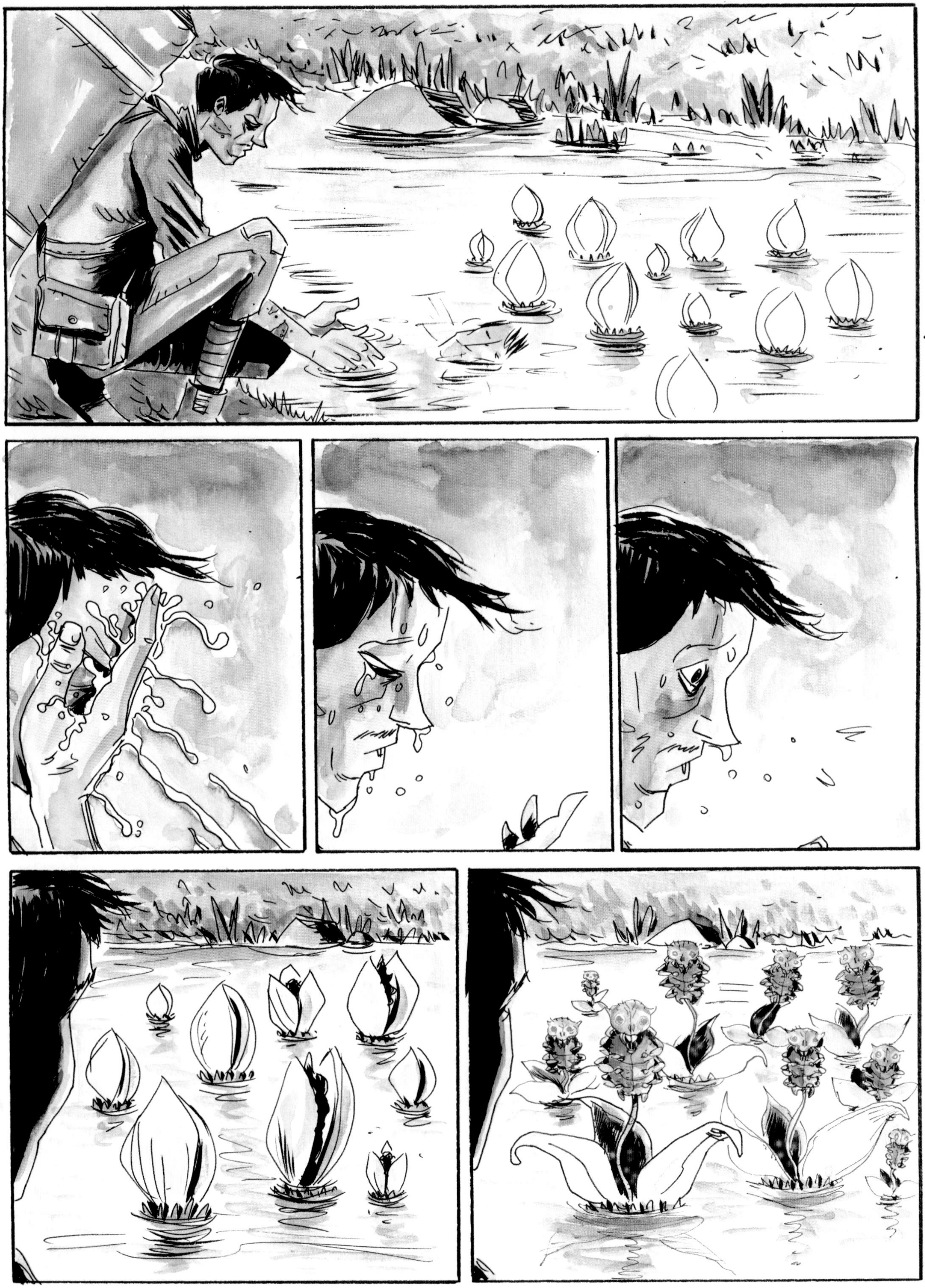

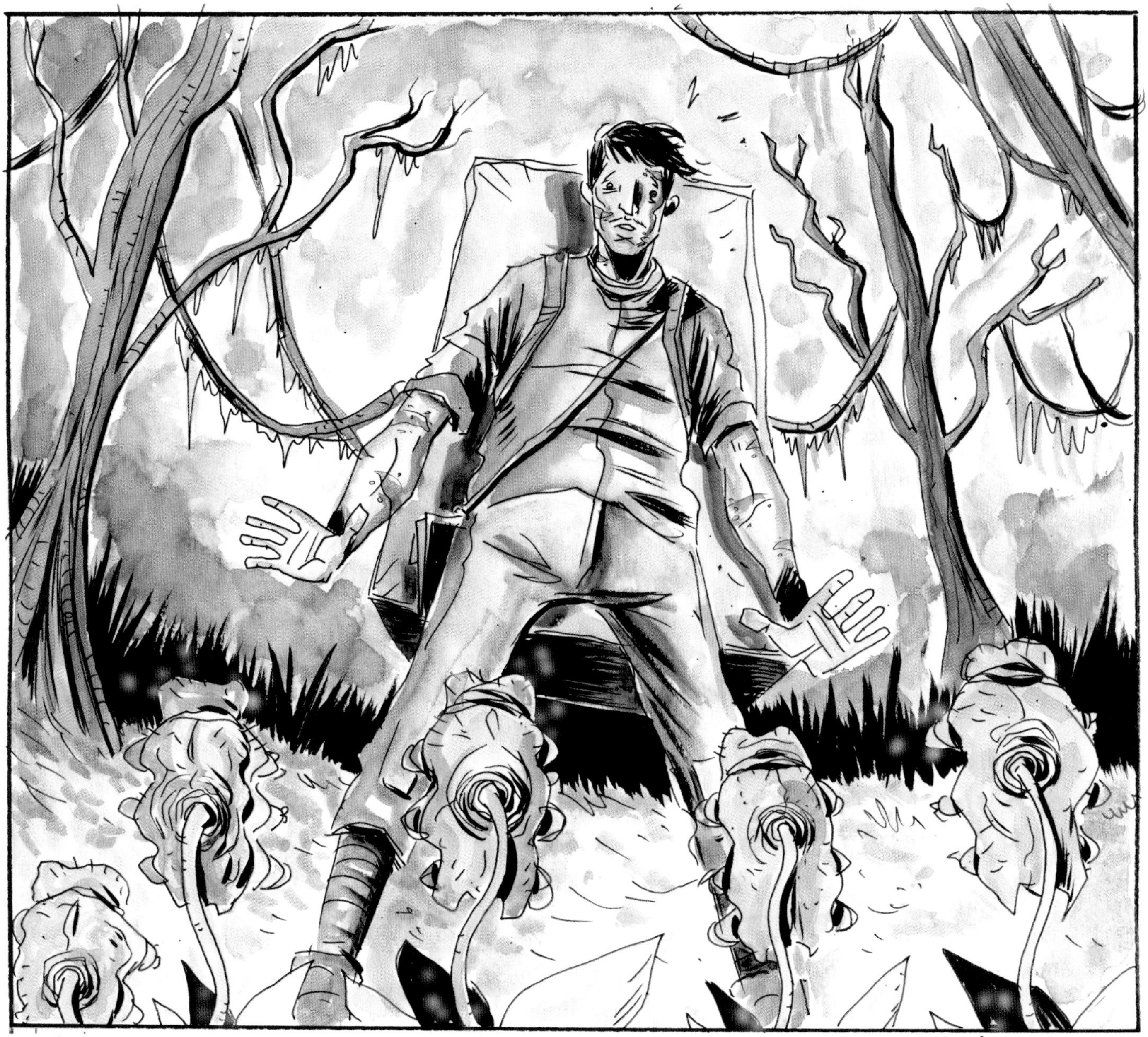

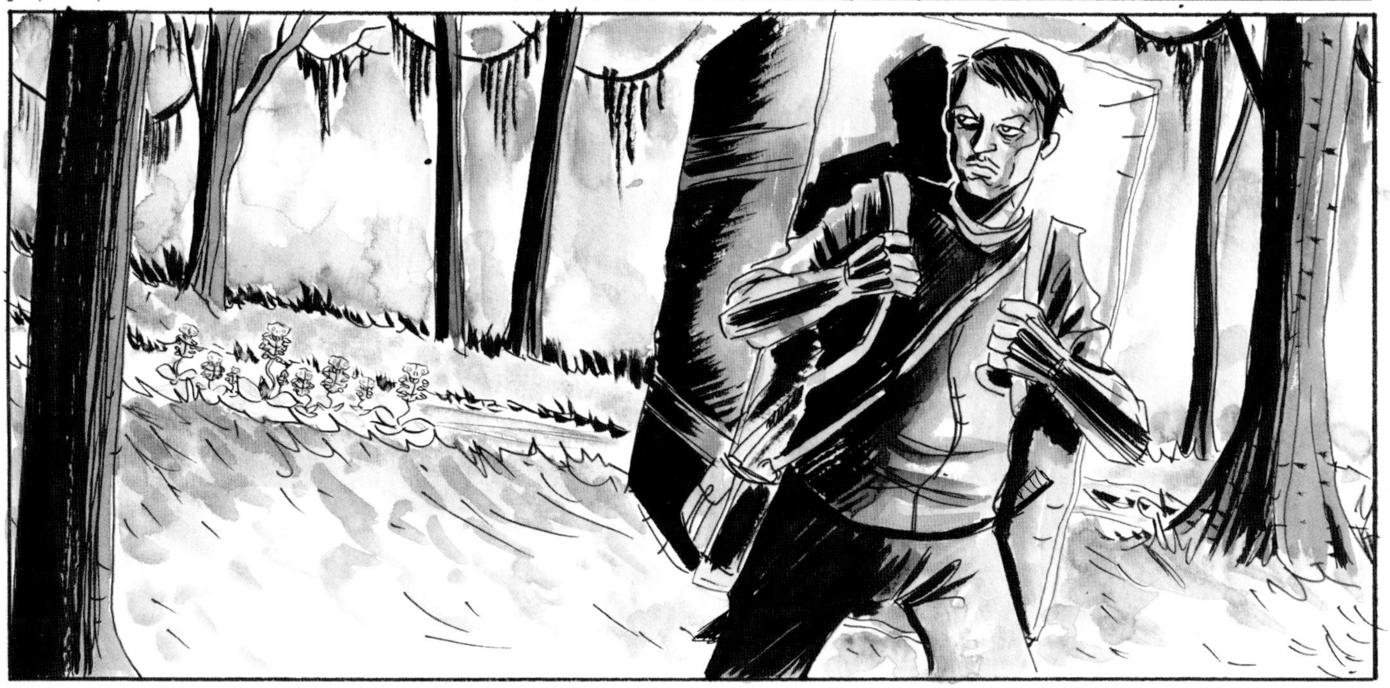

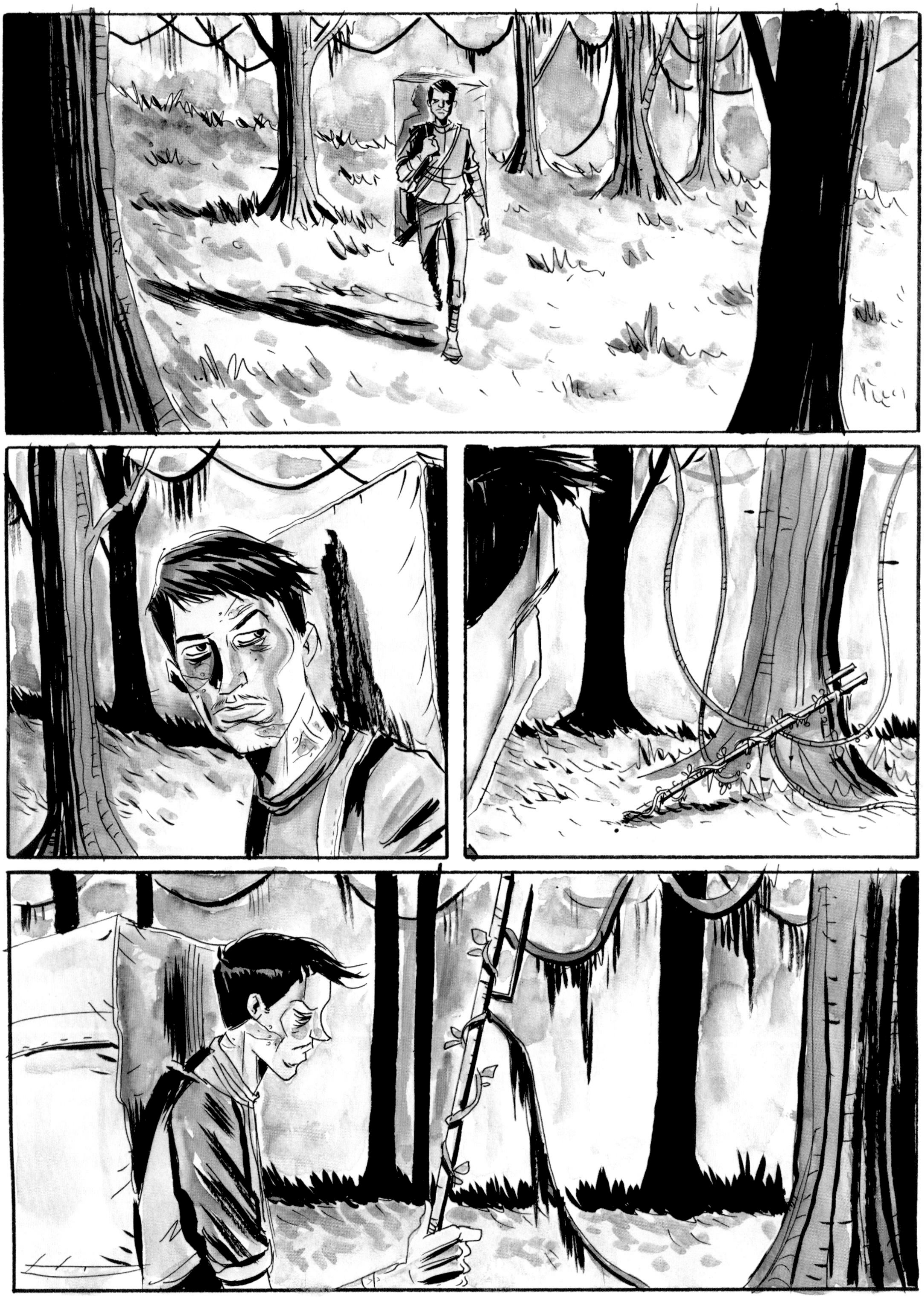

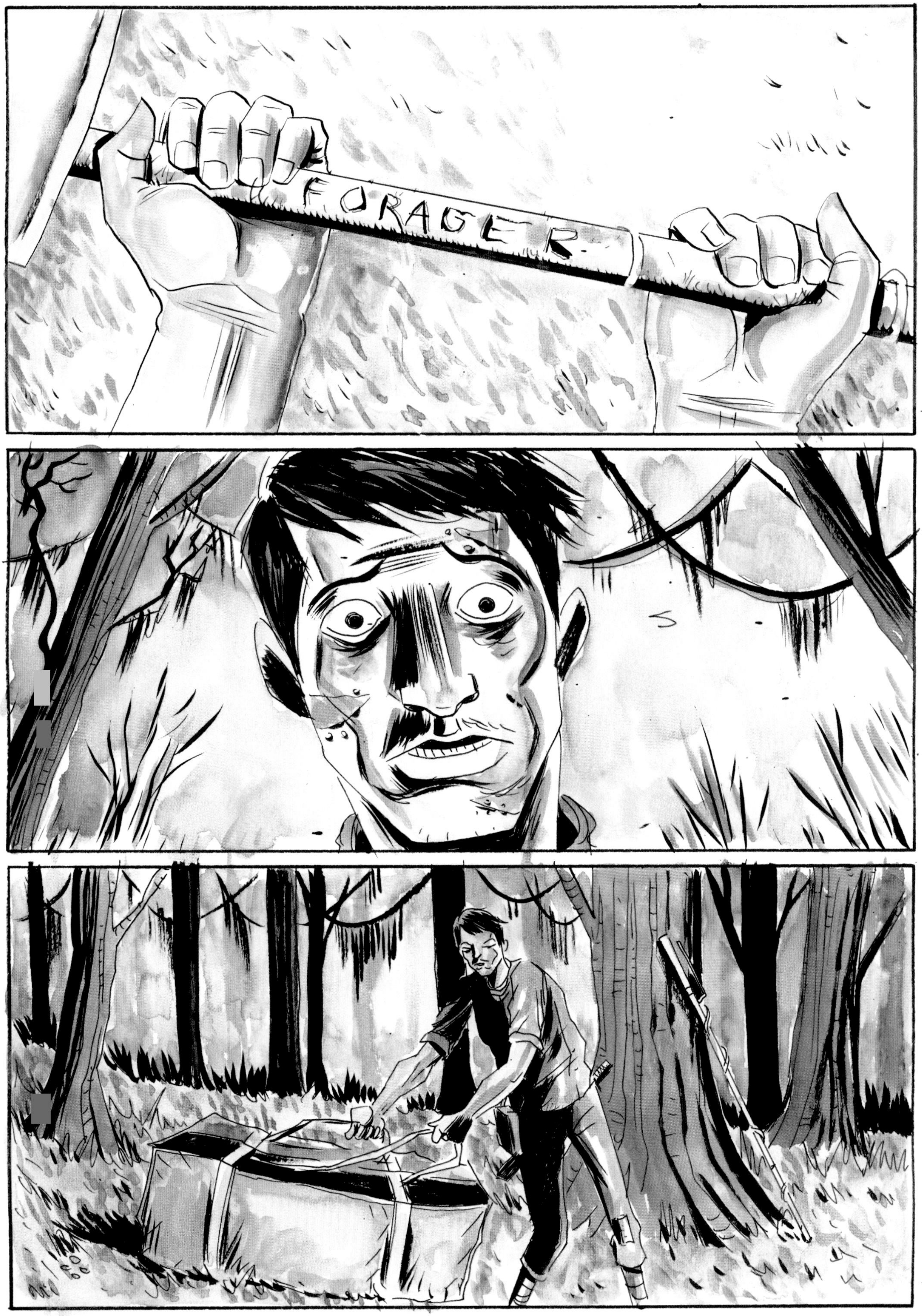
FORAGER

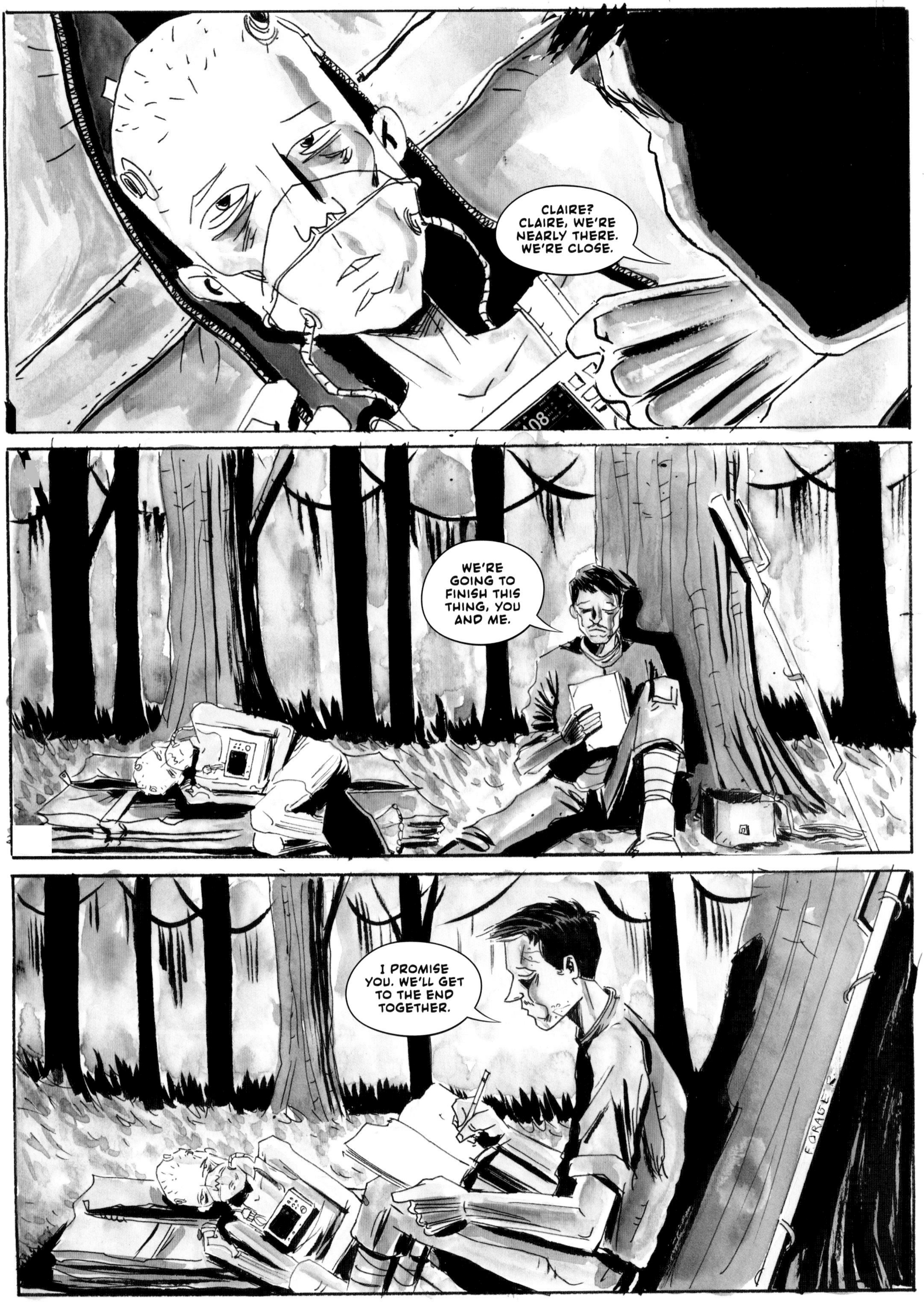
CLAIRE? CLAIRE, WE'RE NEARLY THERE. WE'RE CLOSE.
WE'RE GOING TO FINISH THIS THING, YOU AND ME.
I PROMISE YOU. WE'LL GET TO THE END TOGETHER.
FORAGER

It always happens on a plain day, doesn't it?

Something that blows your life apart.

A boring morning. Clear, blue sky.

When you're concerned with details and distractions, lost in that context of busywork that makes a real event feel like a bomb.

I am nearly twenty cycles in when I find the journals.

An ocean of time since I stopped writing.

I have just come back from the night shift at Water when it happens.

I parted with someone not long before, a woman named Elena, and I am cleaning out the shed behind my home and I just...stumble on them. I'm not cleaning things out of anger, or sadness; it's just a small, lazy gesture of renewal.

I've become used to these gestures. I've grown comfortable, is the truth. My memory is fluid, but the memories of activities learned...the body wisdom remains.

Ghost skills...I know how to the play the violin, the piano, the guitar...I know how to paint as well as some of the masters whose work I longed to steal so many years earlier, though I don't remember acquiring these talents.

There have always been new people to be with--have I been with them before? Maybe. But they will be new to me again. Everything will be, over and over. I have become my own island, in a way, this small, enclosed landscape I explore at my leisure, round and round, cycle after cycle, following a skill, a relationship, a desire toward small, harmless discoveries.

Do I know how to carve and build a table? I do.

Will I be happy with this woman for a while? Maybe.

I make findings, then let the ever-shifting sands cover them. Follow a river to the next hill.

The day I am cleaning the shed, I am doing just this: looking for some small discovery about myself to push me forward, something amusing or curious.

The books are on a shelf at the back of the shed. They
sit in a row of unused journals and look no different
from the empty ones. In truth, I nearly miss them
altogether. The journals are simple and uninterest-
ing. No cloth covers or fancy binding, just paper.

Each has a green silhouette of a tree on the front,
nothing more.

I open one up and find blank pages inside.

I open another...the same. Blank.

I take the row off the shelf, planning to throw them
out, when I notice two books that seem slightly darker
than the rest. A little worn, a little smudged.

I open the first and see it's half full of writing.
Notes.

I figure it belongs to Elena. She had a habit of
writing down what she wanted to explore next, what
cycle, what talent. Maybe this was hers. I sit down in
the shed and read it.

"My first memory..." are the words.

Hours later, I am still sitting on the floor of the shed.

How to describe that feeling? Like you've somehow run aground while
crossing the middle of the ocean. Like the ship of your life has become
impaled on a hidden spike of rock.

My back ached, my jaw throbbed from clenching my teeth... Sitting there, I
felt as I imagined it must have felt for me watching my mother fall that
first time. Her body descending, cutting life into two halves, before and
after.

Now this moment would be that for me--I knew it--the words on the page
cleaving my life. I could not remember the life described, not exactly,
but I could feel it there, beneath the surface. And this person, this man
telling me about my life, the one written into the pages of this book...he
was me. I could feel it. All the pain and fear...and who was I now? Who was
the person who'd come into the shed? That was the horror of it.

I thought of the last few cycles, the endless chain of days, of jobs, of people, Inez as a repeating link. Really it was a chain of nothing but me, though, wasn't it? A life curling around itself in an endless spiral.

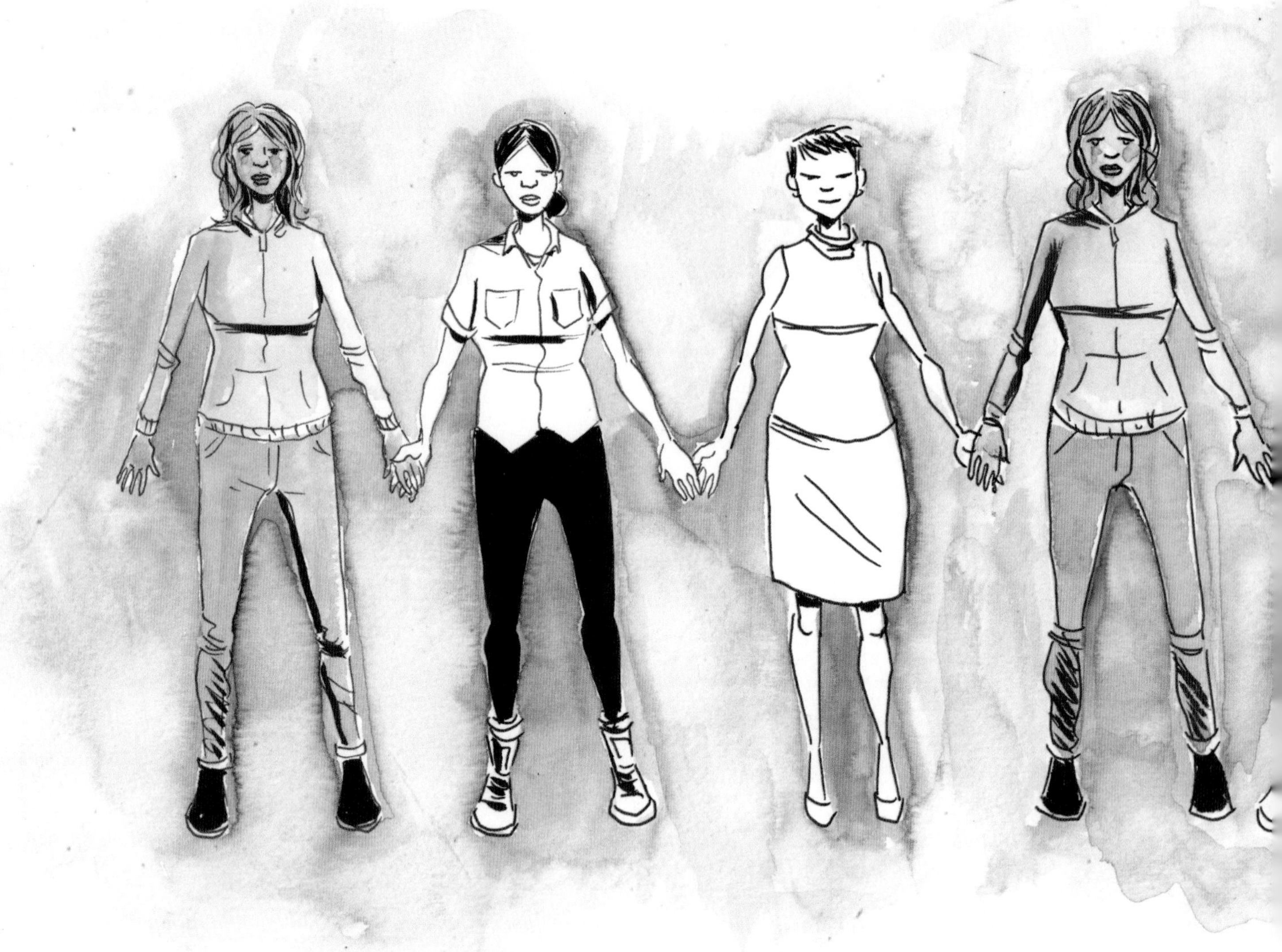

I looked away from books at the ring of mountains in the distance. They looked too close all of a sudden, encroaching... the ring of jagged points like a heartbeat, going round and round and round...

The thing was, I had been happy.

That was the worst part. I'd been okay with it all, hadn't I?

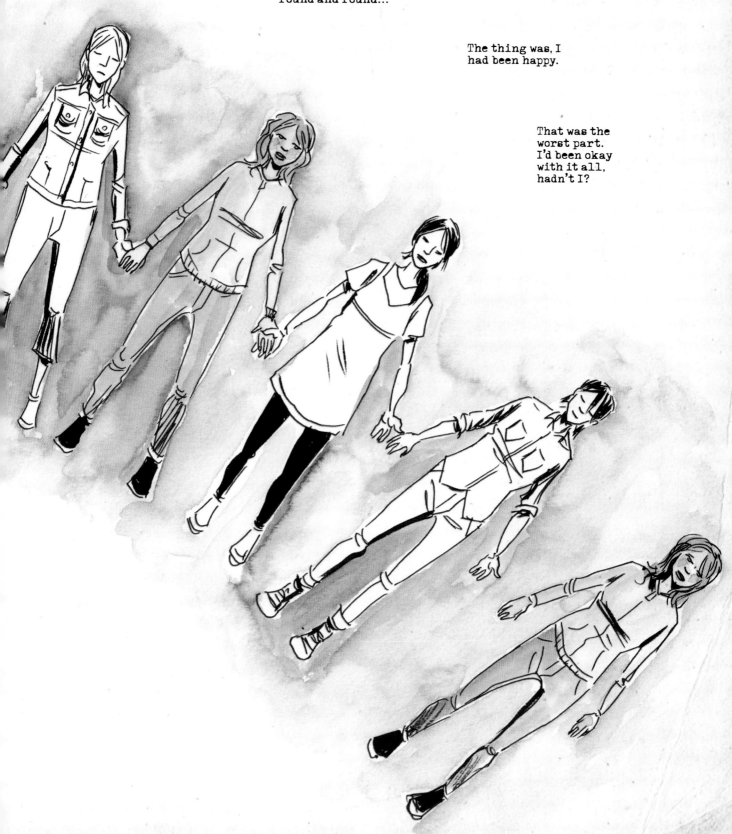

My stomach seized, and I nearly threw up right there.

And something occurred to me then, a truth that just slammed into me with a nearly physical force. What I knew at that moment, sitting in my shed, was that I had been wrong. Wrong about everything, yes, but the moment that flashed through my mind was singular and specific. It was the same moment I'd told Errant about, the one that recurred and recurred. The instance at the end of my mother's life just before she'd died, when she was lying in her hospital bed, lost in the fantasy that my brother Nathan was alive and grown and that I was content too. I had no memory of her face but I could see it in my mind then, the warm, sleepy joy. I could picture it. Happy and relaxed. Everything was all right. She was in a good place. How she'd gotten here, she didn't know, but here she was.

And then it had come back to her.

The truth.

Nathan had died. She was dying. The distance between the person she wanted to be, and who she was, all suddenly apparent.

And the terror in her eyes...the horror at knowing the truth.

But that's where I was most wrong. I saw that now. All this time I'd thought her horror was at remembering--at seeing herself as she was, rather than how she'd hoped to be at the end.

But I knew now that wasn't the case at all; she hadn't been horrified at remembering.

She'd been horrified that she forgot in the first place.

That she'd lost her place in her own story.

I knew this to be true, because I felt that way now, felt it with every cell in my body.

And just as I knew this, I also knew who I was.

I was a thief. I was a liar, to others and to myself.

And above all, I was a coward.

A coward in every aspect of my life.

I said this to myself out loud, there in the shed. "I am a coward."

I had two books in my hand, both filled with notes about my life before this place, filled with longing and fear, and at my feet were all the empty books I was supposed to fill.

I said it again.

"I am a coward."

And then I got up.

I would not be a coward any longer. I would use the notes in the first two journals to write a new book, a third book, this one. A book that had a beginning, a middle, and above all, an end.

I would cycle through only to steal what I needed to get Claire. I would work Ridge and listen for some sign that there was anything but death below, and at the first signal, anything, I would go.

And as I decided this, I was flooded with relief. I was happy to know--that was the strange truth of it. I was glad to see myself as I was.

I would take Claire and finish my story.

I hurried to my car.

I had been with Inez not long before. She had
begun to fade from memory, but just barely. We'd
been together a long time, this much I knew. We'd
had a good run. But now, as I thought back, I
couldn't remember anything urgent about our
relationship. I remembered walking by the wind
turbines and making dinners my hands knew how
to make... I remembered being fine, and this
brought on another wave of nausea.

I shook off the feeling and looked through the
queue for her address. She was living just across
the retreat, on the other side of the reservoir,
by Agro.

I drove over that afternoon, the journals with
me. As I drove past the reservoir, I thought
about what I'd say to her. She'd forgotten what
she'd wanted to do, who she'd been, as I had too.
But she would come back to herself when I showed
her. She would look at the books, and at me...we
would find our way out of this place together.
Make each other brave.

I reached her house. It was a small, white cape
nestled in a line of other homes. A nice street,
with moon-lawns of deep blue-green grass.
Again, I had the strange feeling that I was
looking at something stolen as I approached the
door...the lane like something lifted from the
world below and set down here, thousands of feet
in the sky. Everything out of context. She liked
being around other people. I remembered this
about her now. She liked being in town.

I parked and walked up to her door. On the lawn
beside hers, a greener crawled about, clicking
like a bug.

I knocked on the door and waited.

I took a deep breath. This would work, I thought. This was going to work. And just then I saw the mat I was standing on.

Her father's mat, the one from her story.

I quickly stepped off of it, knowing now what it had meant to her.

I actually went to brush it off, but as did I saw how deeply worn the thing was. The fibers all torn, the words faded. Little continents of mold at the corners.

I heard footsteps from inside.

As they neared, a terrible thought occurred to me: maybe she'd wanted to forget? Maybe she wasn't who I thought she was.

The door lock clicked open.

No, I thought. She'd forgotten what the mat had meant to her, and now I would tell her. I would tell her everything and she would be grateful to me. We would go down together.

We would go back to where we left off...

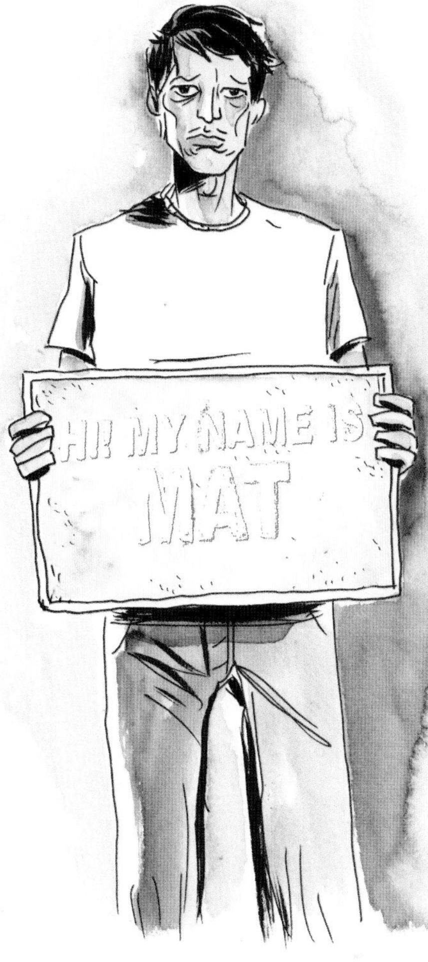
HI! MY NAME IS
MAT

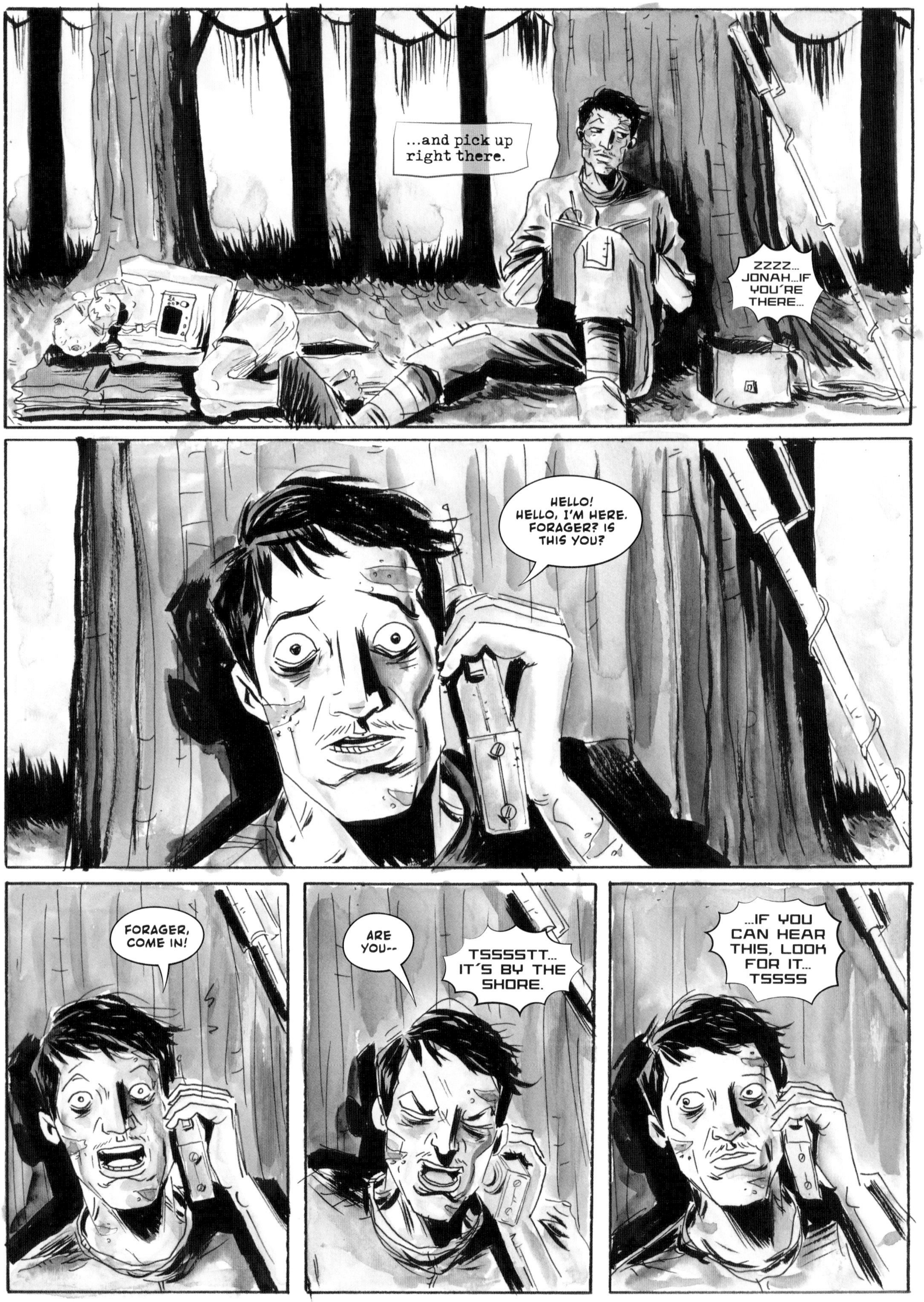
...and pick up right there.
ZZZZ... JONAH...IF YOU´RE THERE...
HELLO! HELLO, I'M HERE. FORAGER? IS THIS YOU?
FORAGER, COME IN!
ARE YOU--
TSSSSTT... IT´S BY THE SHORE.
...IF YOU CAN HEAR THIS, LOOK FOR IT... TSSSS

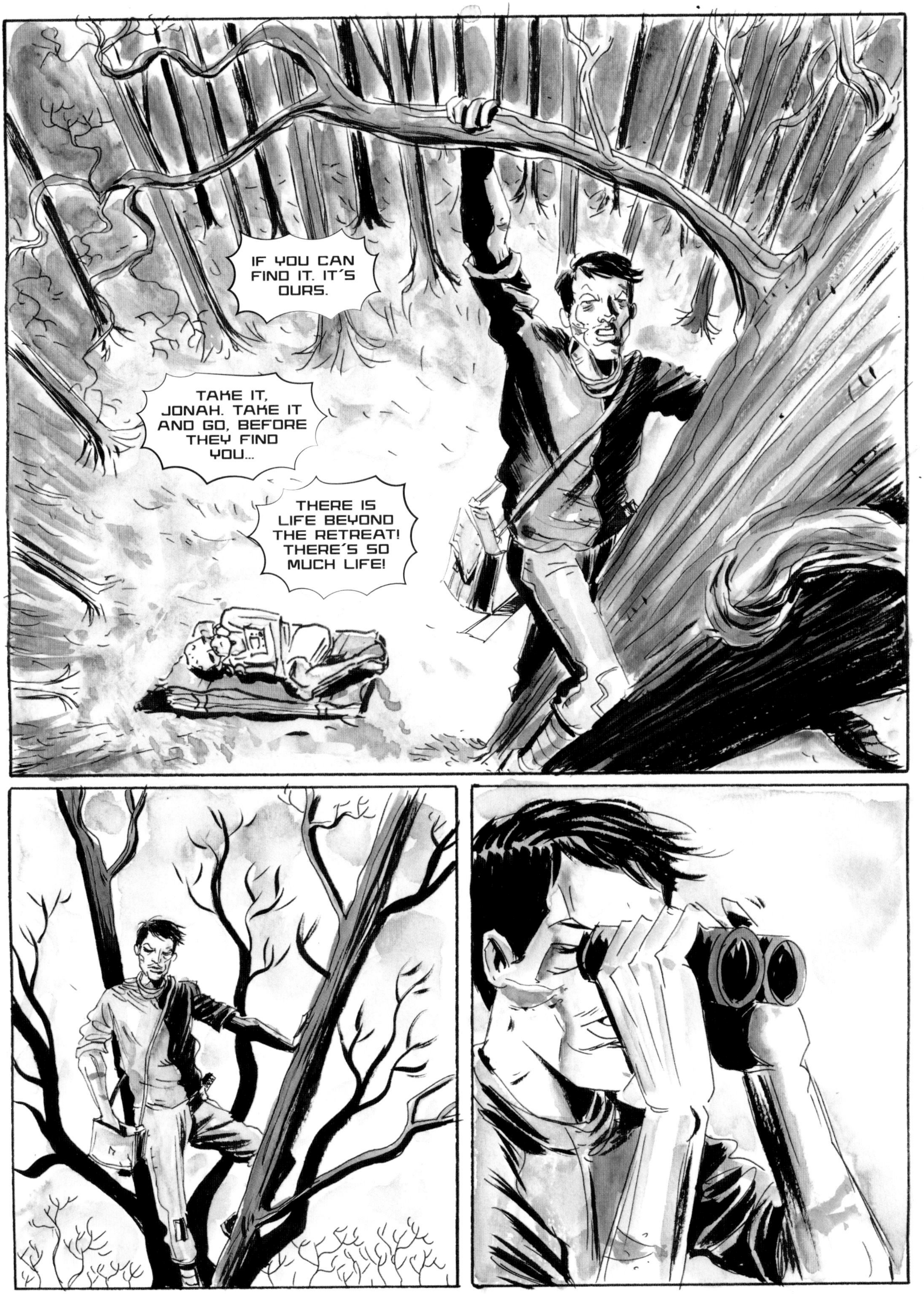
IF YOU CAN FIND IT. IT´S OURS.
TAKE IT, JONAH. TAKE IT AND GO, BEFORE THEY FIND YOU...
THERE IS LIFE BEYOND THE RETREAT! THERE´S SO MUCH LIFE!

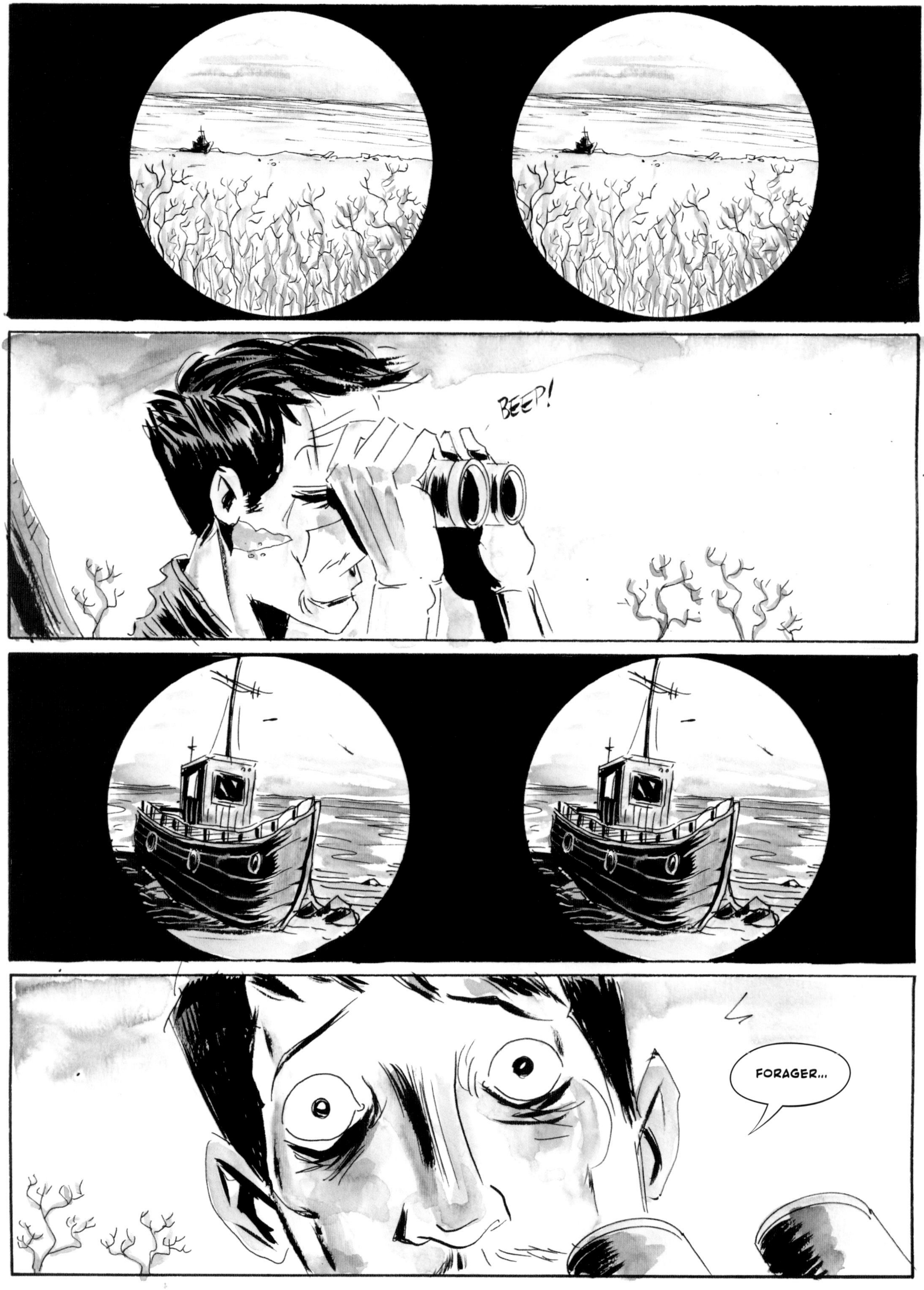
BEEP!
FORAGER...

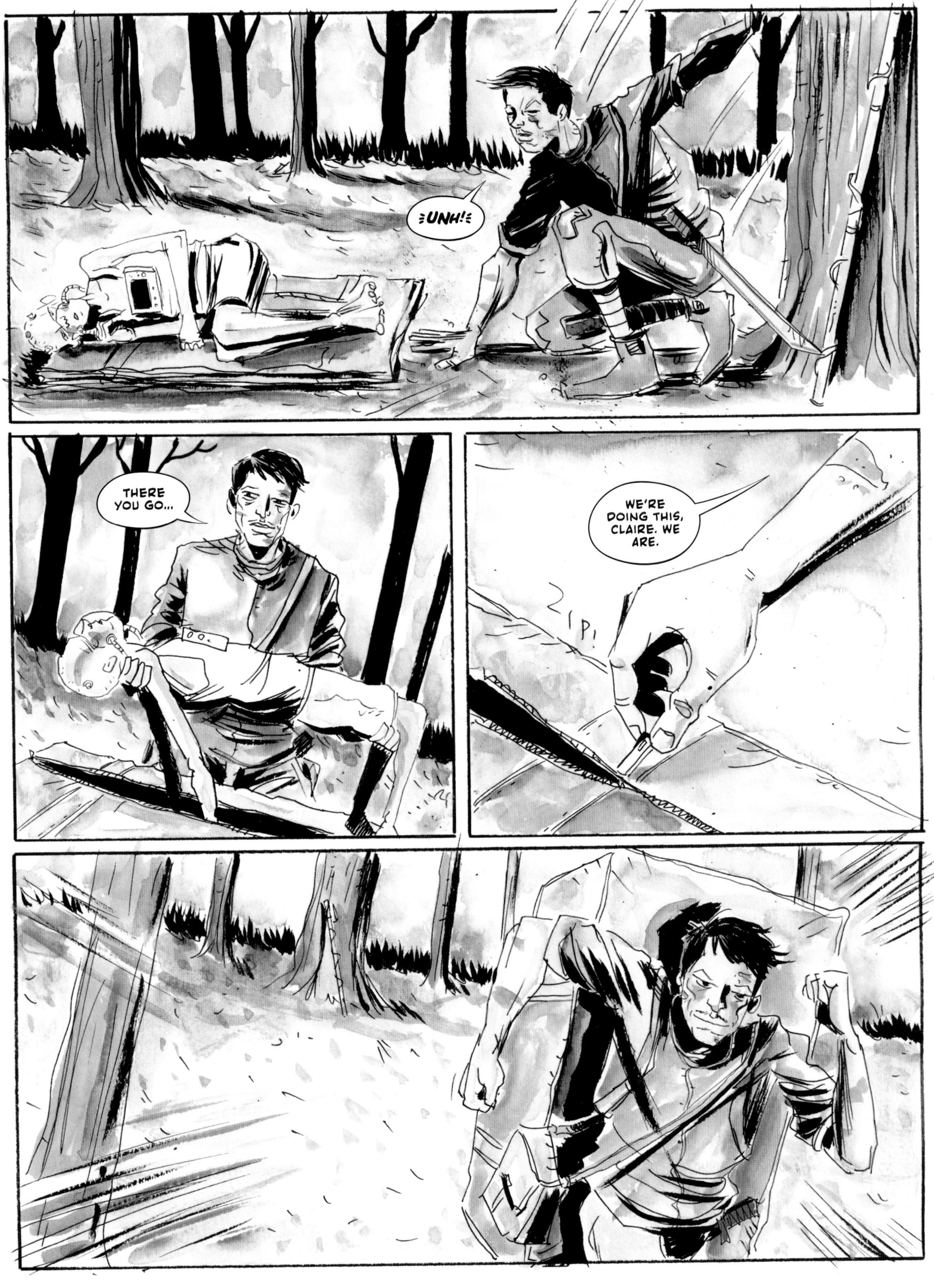
UNH!
THERE YOU GO...
WE'RE DOING THIS, CLAIRE. WE ARE.
ZIP!

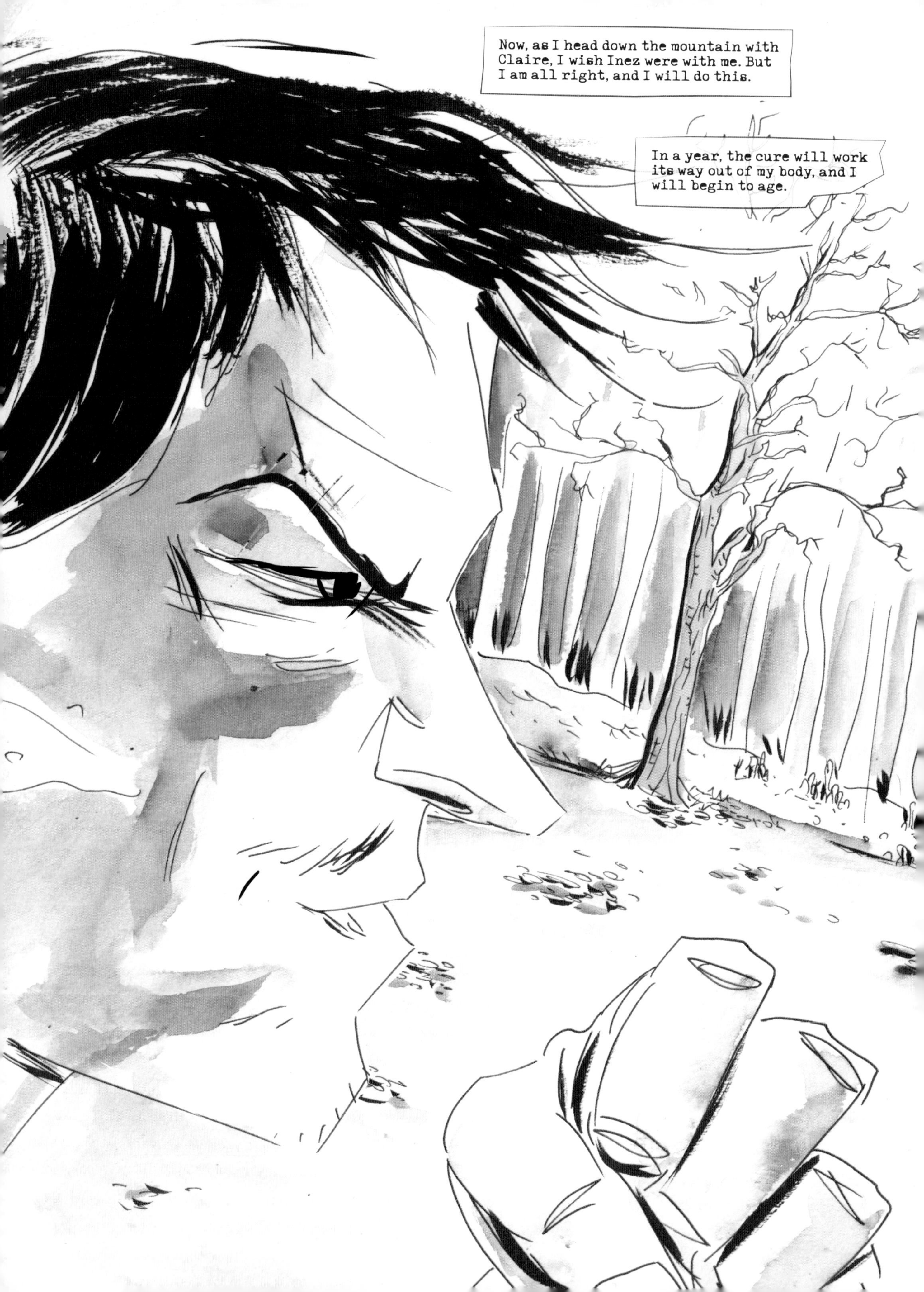
Now, as I head down the mountain with Claire, I wish Inez were with me. But I am all right, and I will do this.
In a year, the cure will work its way out of my body, and I will begin to age.

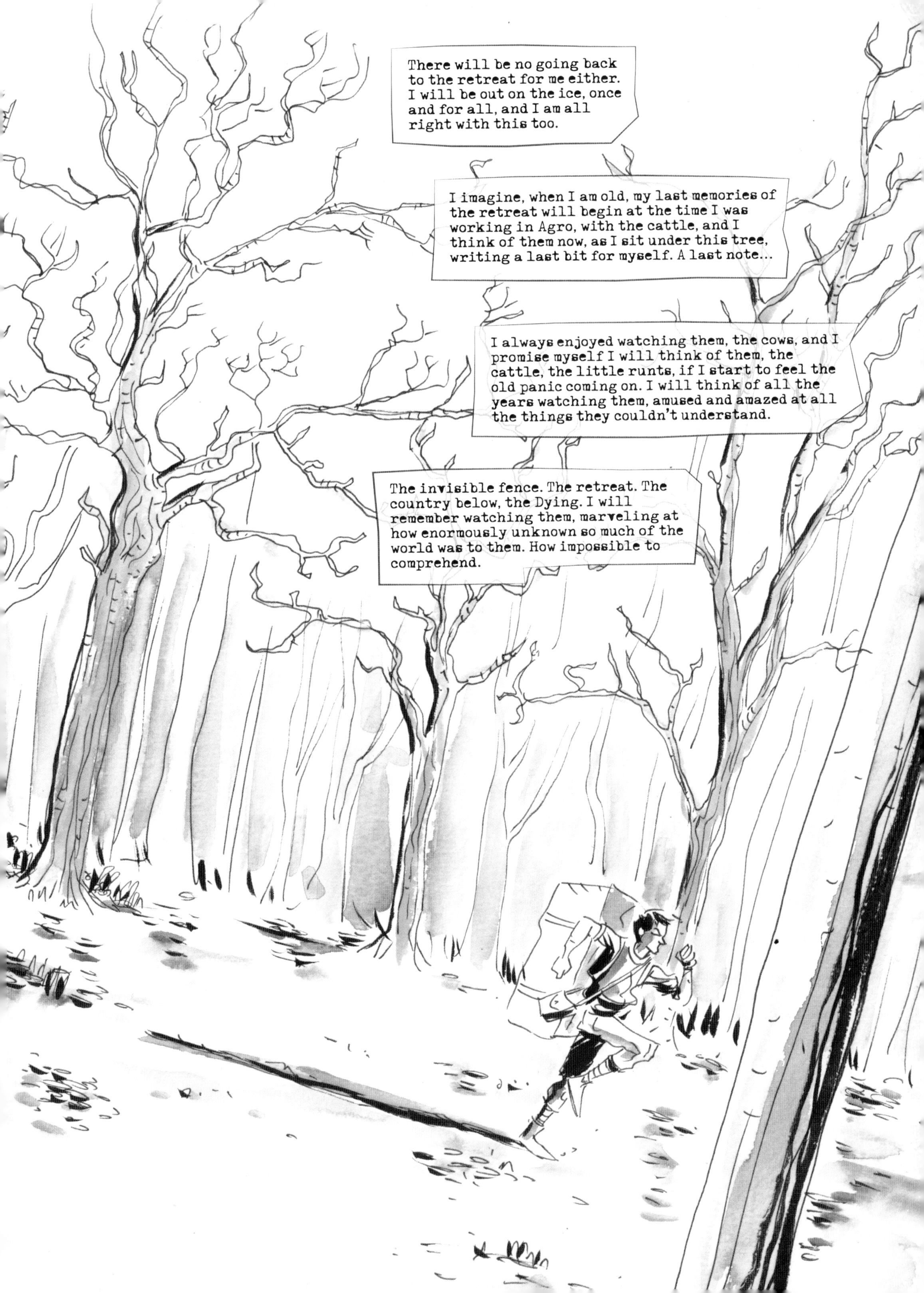
There will be no going back to the retreat for me either. I will be out on the ice, once and for all, and I am all right with this too.
I imagine, when I am old, my last memories of the retreat will begin at the time I was working in Agro, with the cattle, and I think of them now, as I sit under this tree, writing a last bit for myself. A last note...
I always enjoyed watching them, the cows, and I promise myself I will think of them, the cattle, the little runts, if I start to feel the old panic coming on. I will think of all the years watching them, amused and amazed at all the things they couldn't understand.
The invisible fence. The retreat. The country below, the Dying. I will remember watching them, marveling at how enormously unknown so much of the world was to them. How impossible to comprehend.

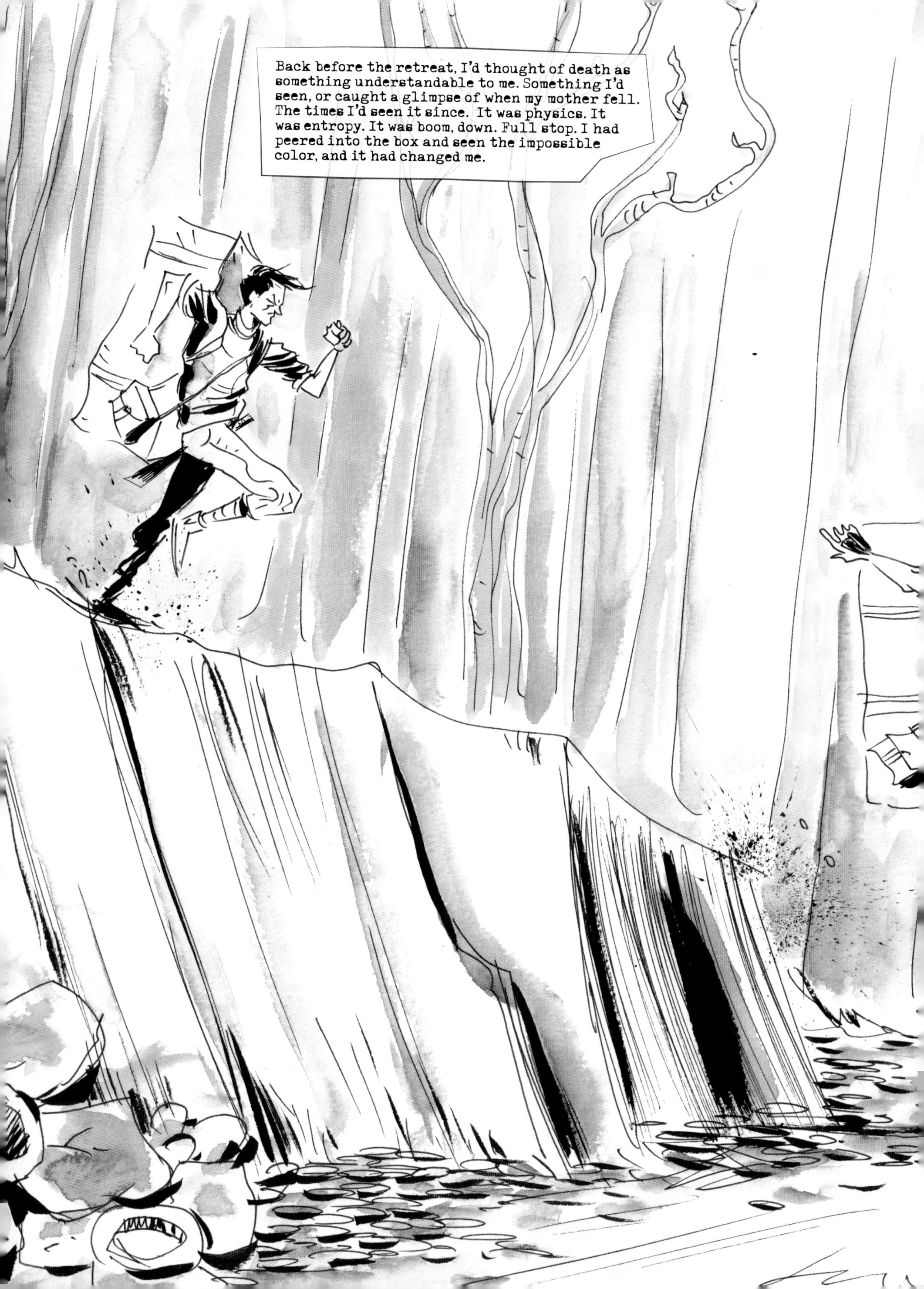
Back before the retreat, I'd thought of death as something understandable to me. Something I'd seen, or caught a glimpse of when my mother fell. The times I'd seen it since. It was physics. It was entropy. It was boom, down. Full stop. I had peered into the box and seen the impossible color, and it had changed me.

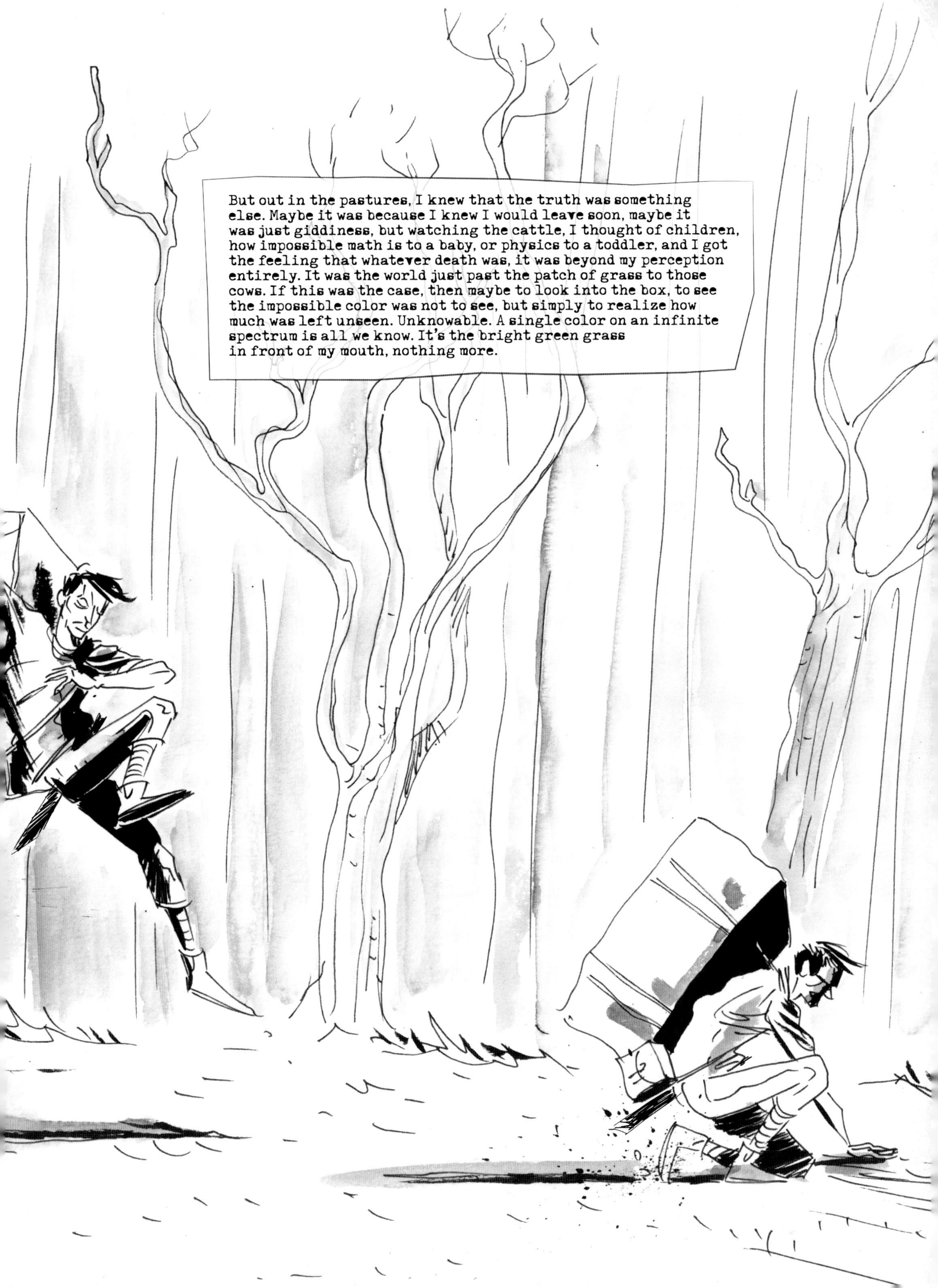
But out in the pastures, I knew that the truth was something else. Maybe it was because I knew I would leave soon, maybe it was just giddiness, but watching the cattle, I thought of children, how impossible math is to a baby, or physics to a toddler, and I got the feeling that whatever death was, it was beyond my perception entirely. It was the world just past the patch of grass to those cows. If this was the case, then maybe to look into the box, to see the impossible color was not to see, but simply to realize how much was left unseen. Unknowable. A single color on an infinite spectrum is all we know. It's the bright green grass in front of my mouth, nothing more.

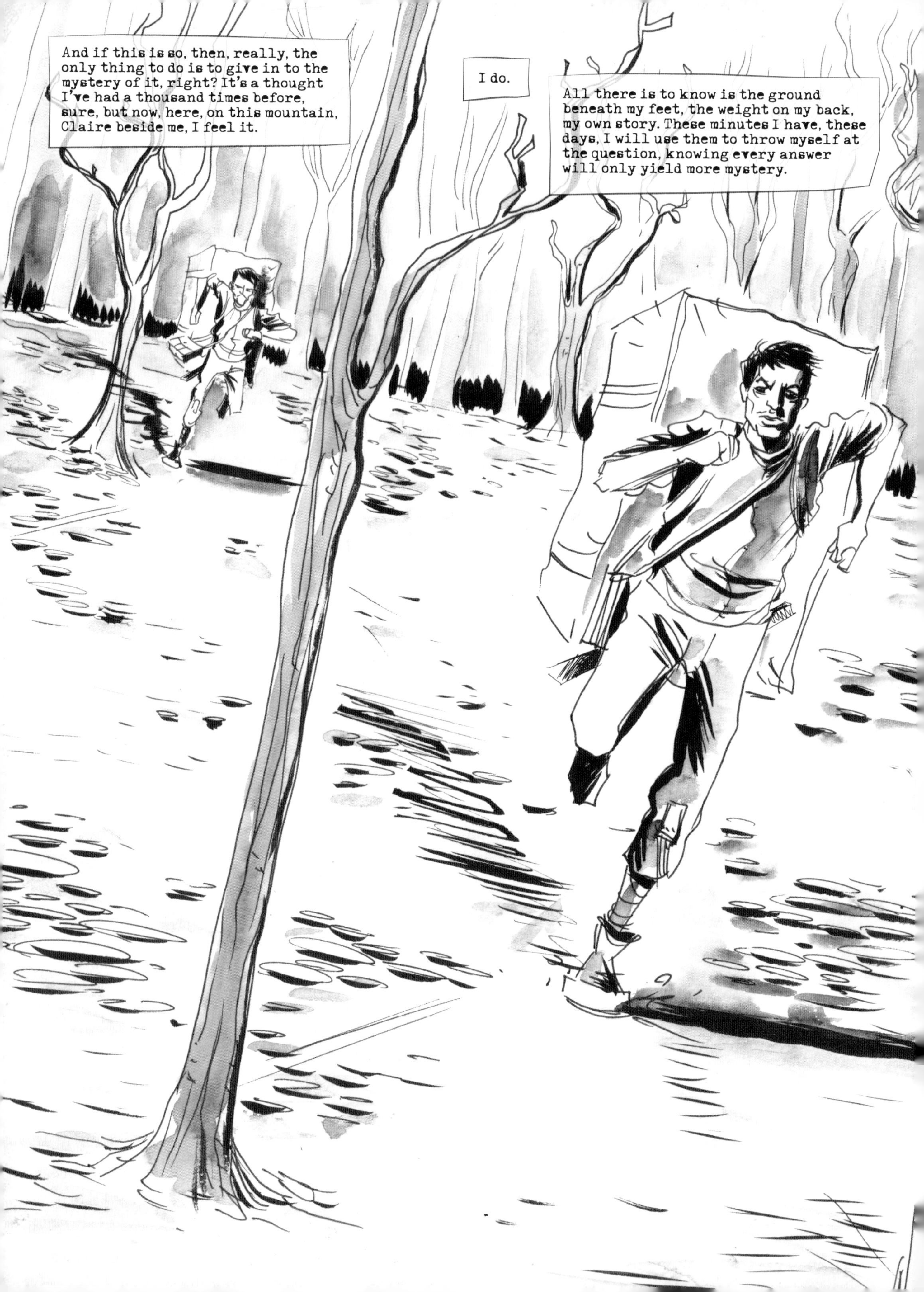
And if this is so, then, really, the only thing to do is to give in to the mystery of it, right? It's a thought I've had a thousand times before, sure, but now, here, on this mountain, Claire beside me, I feel it.
I do.
All there is to know is the ground beneath my feet, the weight on my back, my own story. These minutes I have, these days, I will use them to throw myself at the question, knowing every answer will only yield more mystery.

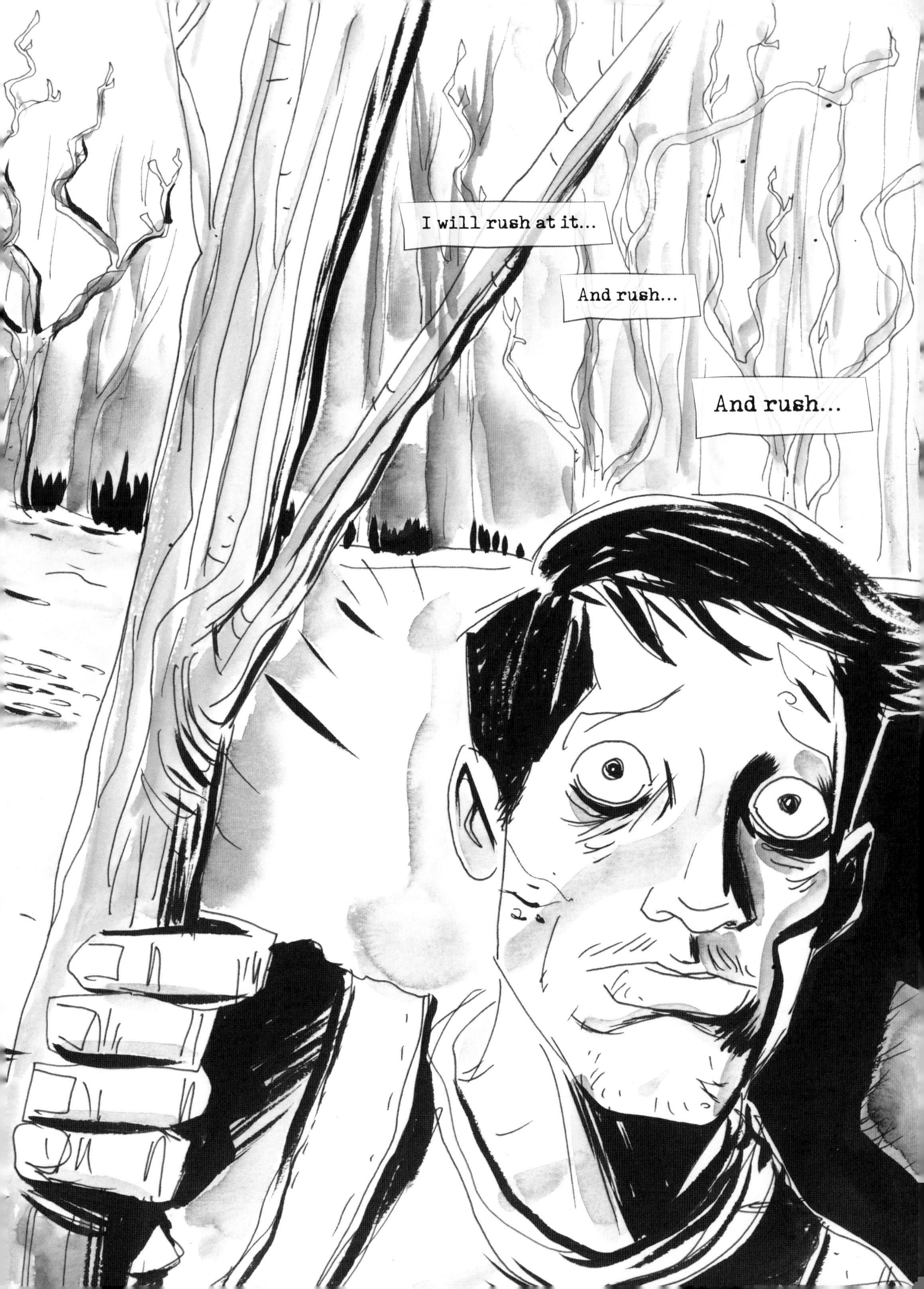
I will rush at it...
And rush...
And rush...

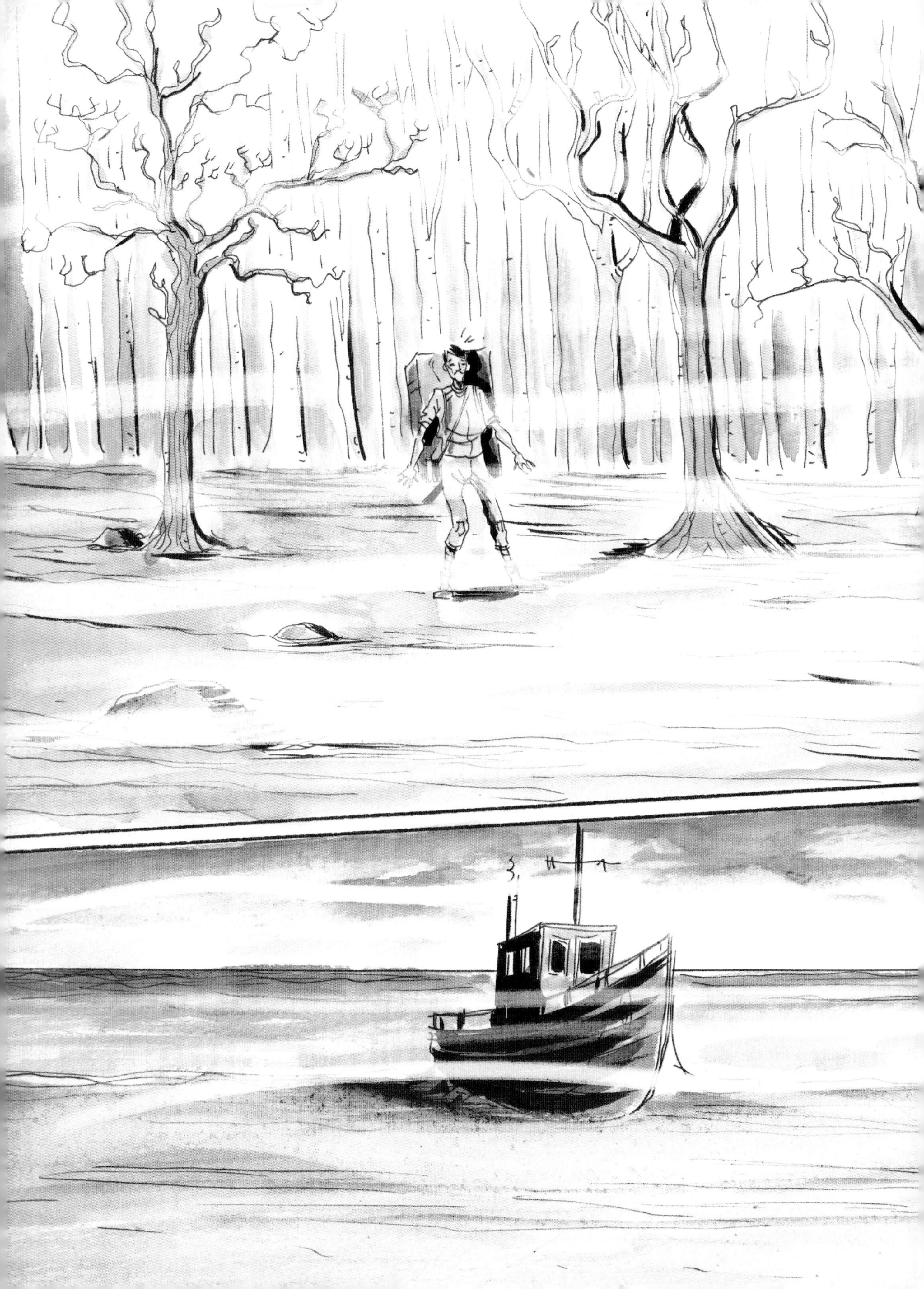

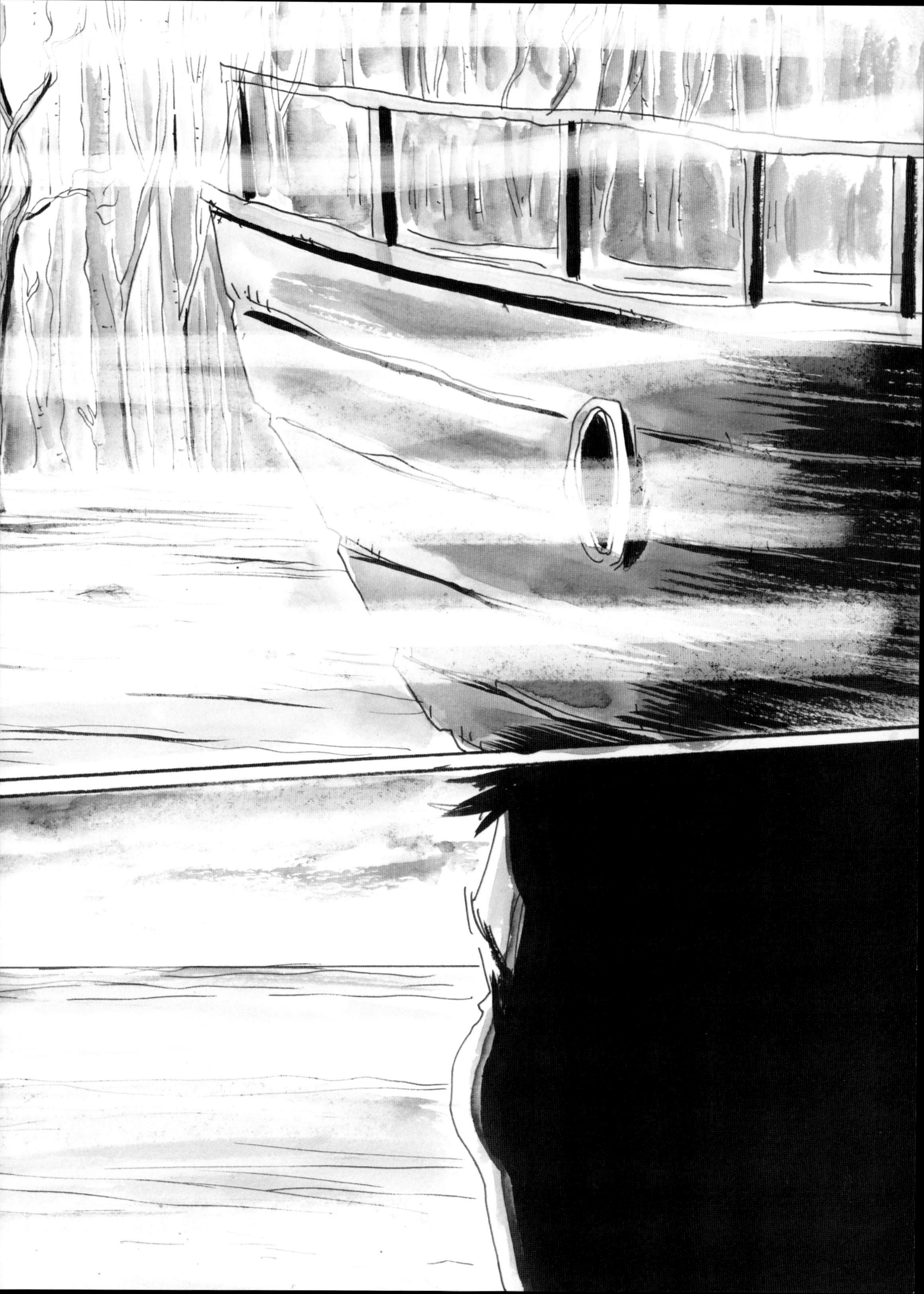

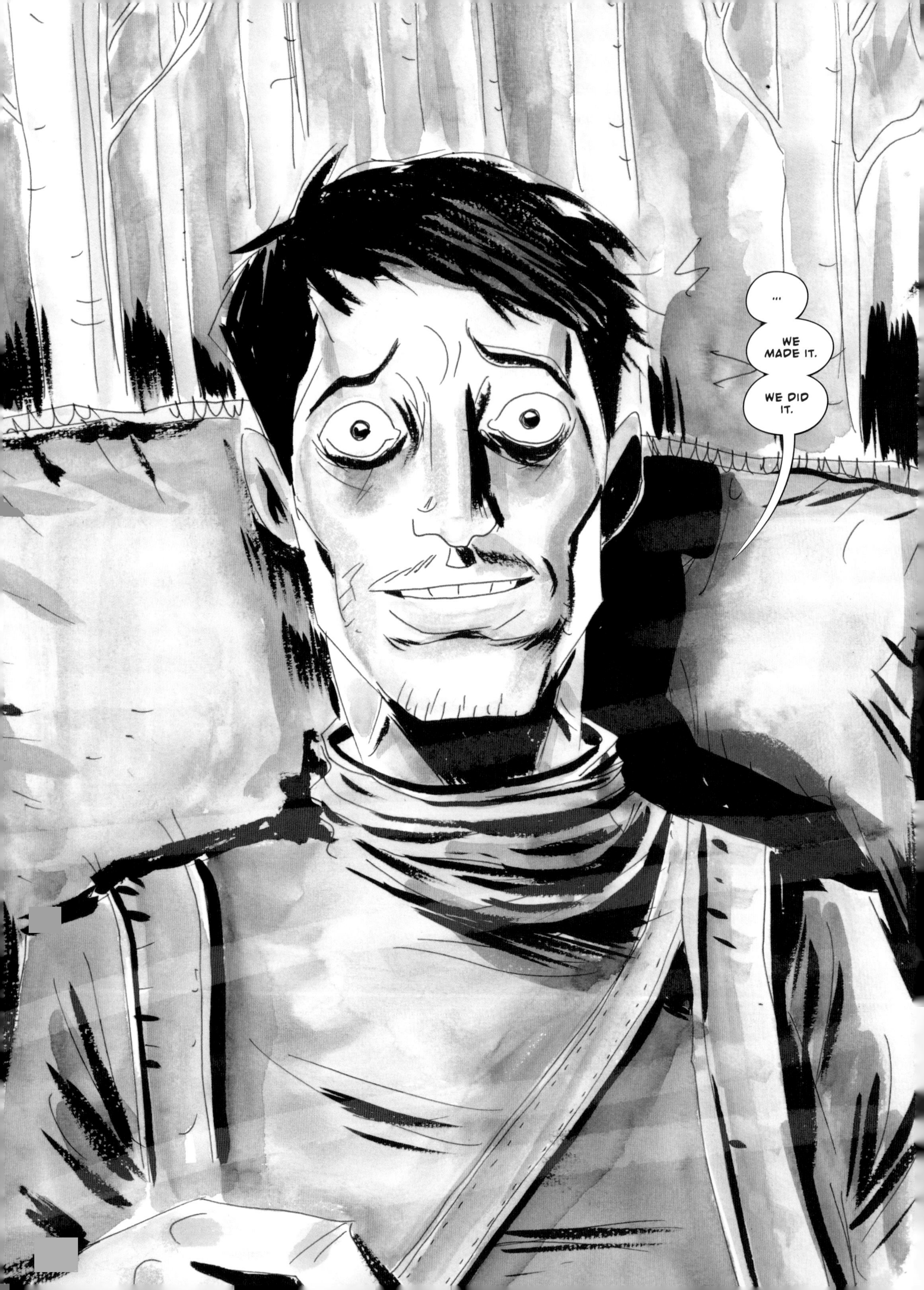
...
WE MADE IT.
WE DID IT.

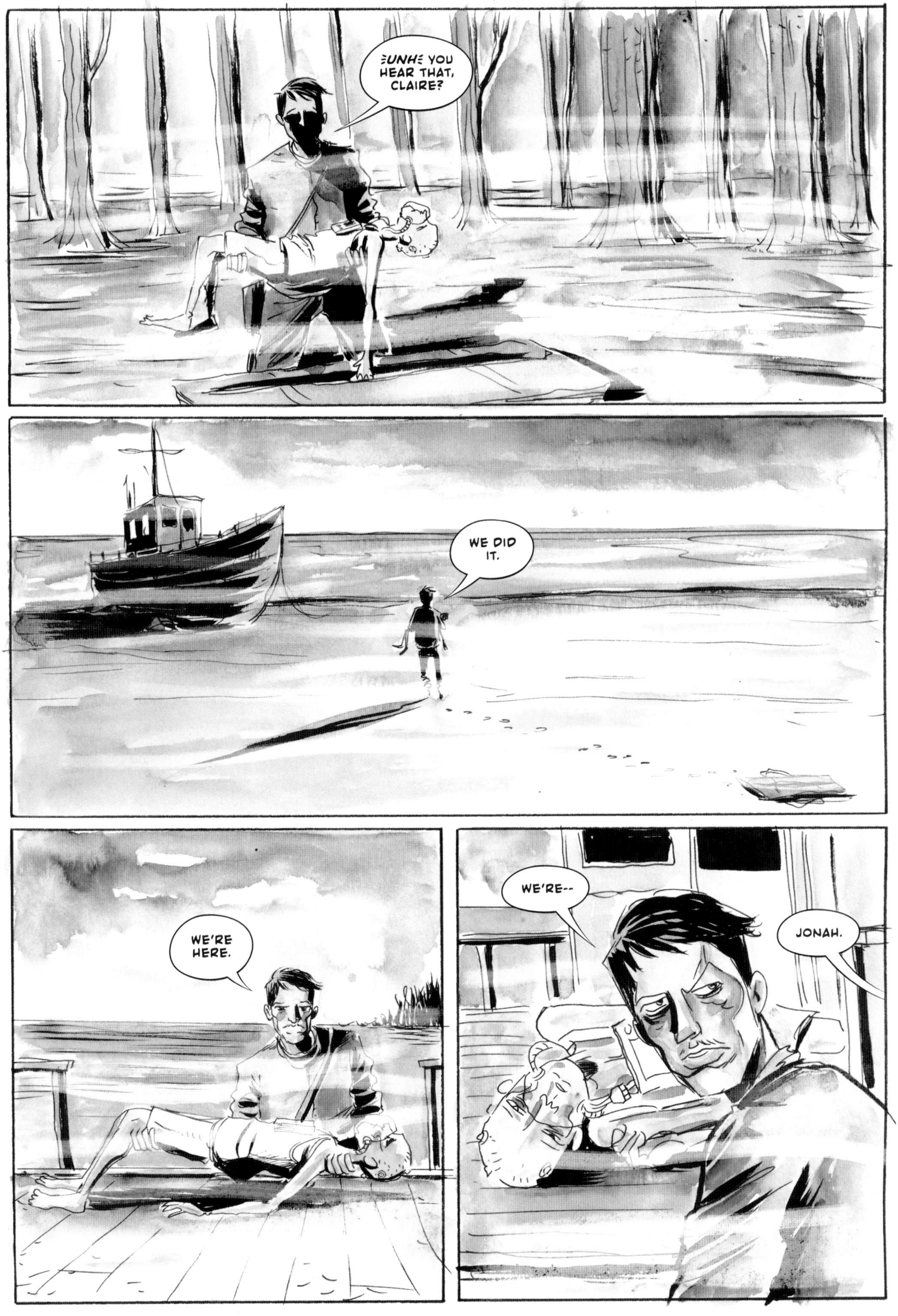

=UNH= YOU HEAR THAT, CLAIRE?
WE DID IT.
WE'RE HERE.
WE'RE--
JONAH.

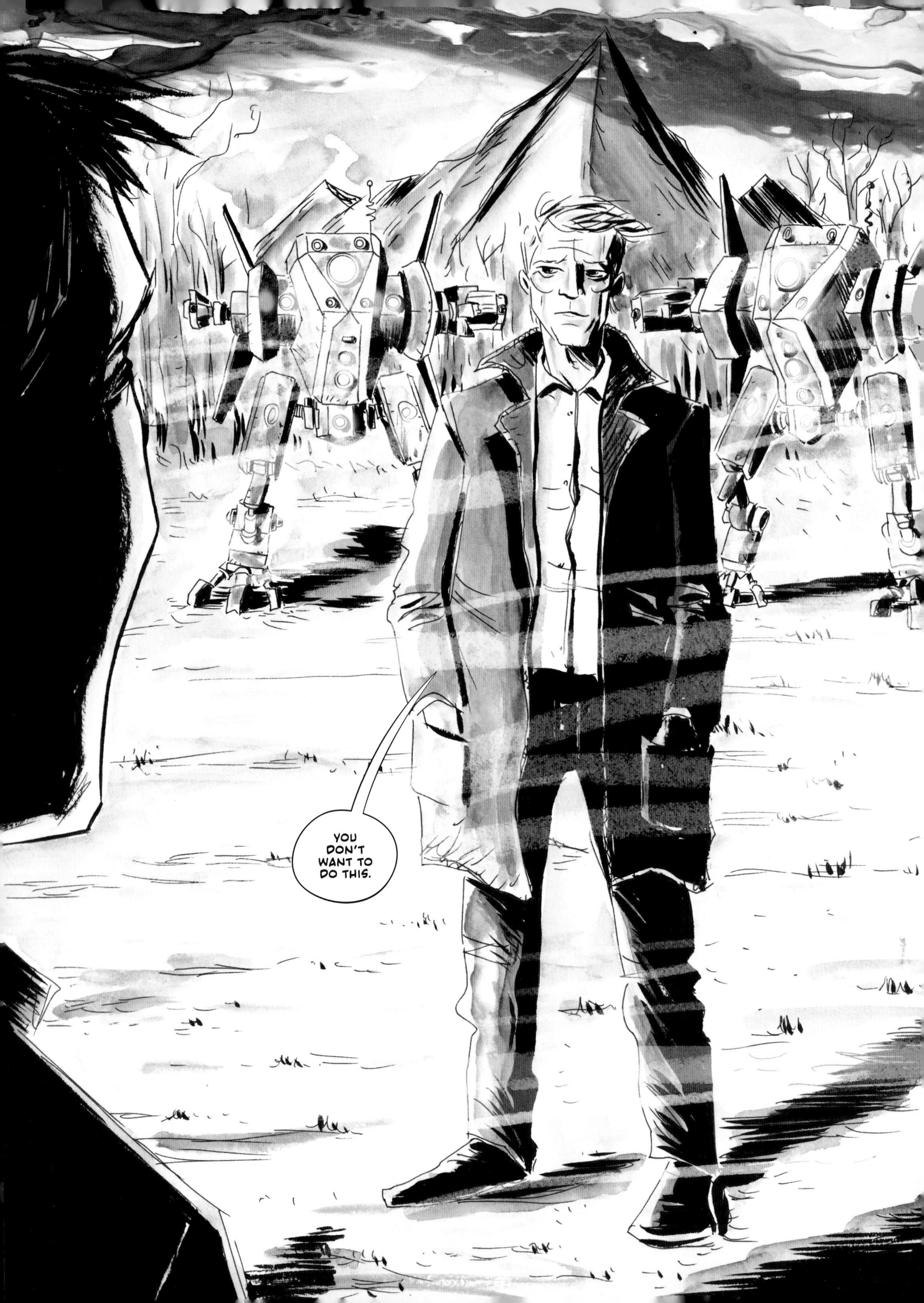
YOU DON'T WANT TO DO THIS.

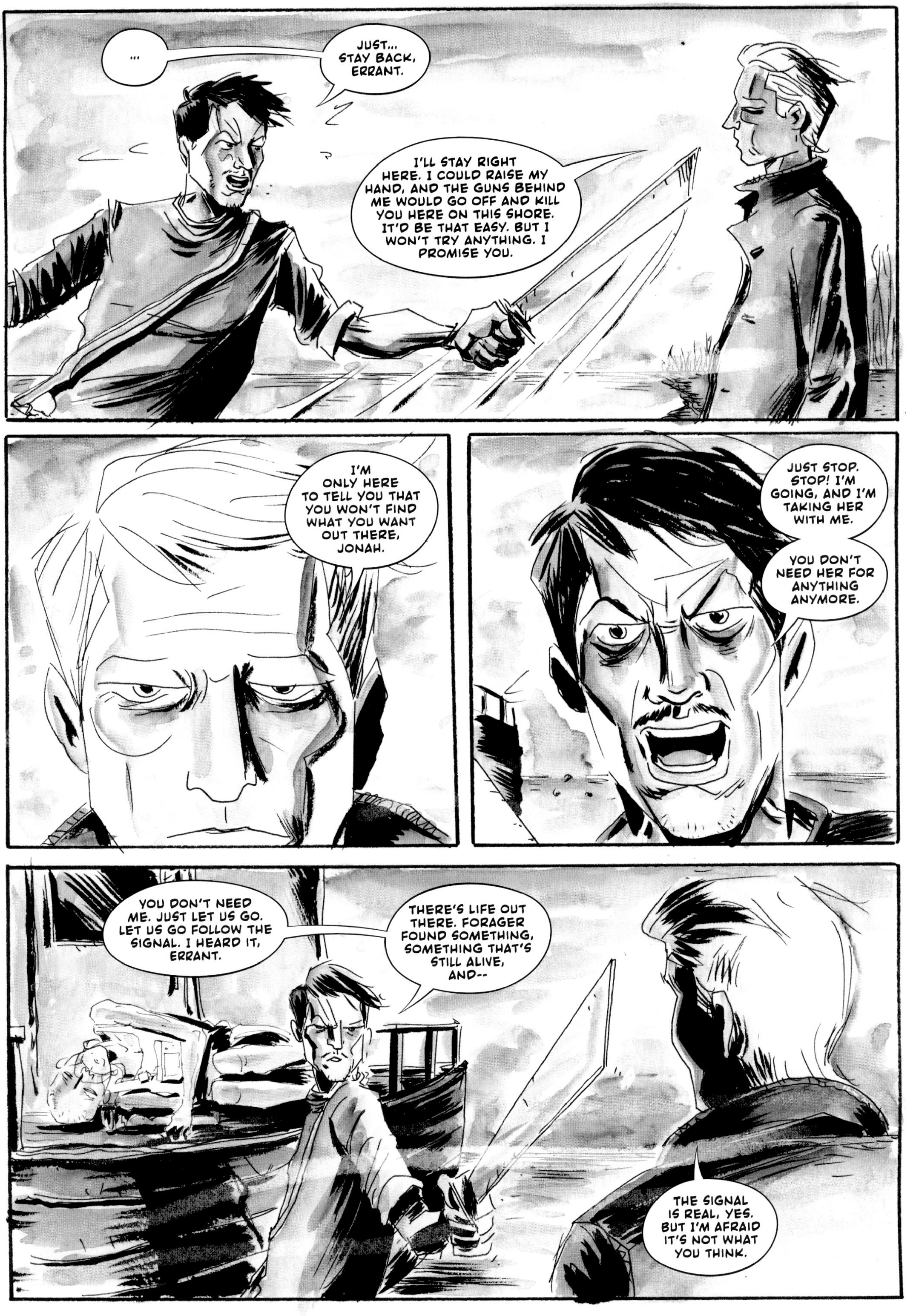
...
JUST... STAY BACK, ERRANT.
I'LL STAY RIGHT HERE. I COULD RAISE MY HAND, AND THE GUNS BEHIND ME WOULD GO OFF AND KILL YOU HERE ON THIS SHORE. IT'D BE THAT EASY. BUT I WON'T TRY ANYTHING. I PROMISE YOU.
I'M ONLY HERE TO TELL YOU THAT YOU WON'T FIND WHAT YOU WANT OUT THERE, JONAH.
JUST STOP. STOP! I'M GOING, AND I'M TAKING HER WITH ME.
YOU DON'T NEED HER FOR ANYTHING ANYMORE.
YOU DON'T NEED ME. JUST LET US GO. LET US GO FOLLOW THE SIGNAL. I HEARD IT, ERRANT.
THERE'S LIFE OUT THERE. FORAGER FOUND SOMETHING, SOMETHING THAT'S STILL ALIVE, AND--
THE SIGNAL IS REAL, YES. BUT I'M AFRAID IT'S NOT WHAT YOU THINK.

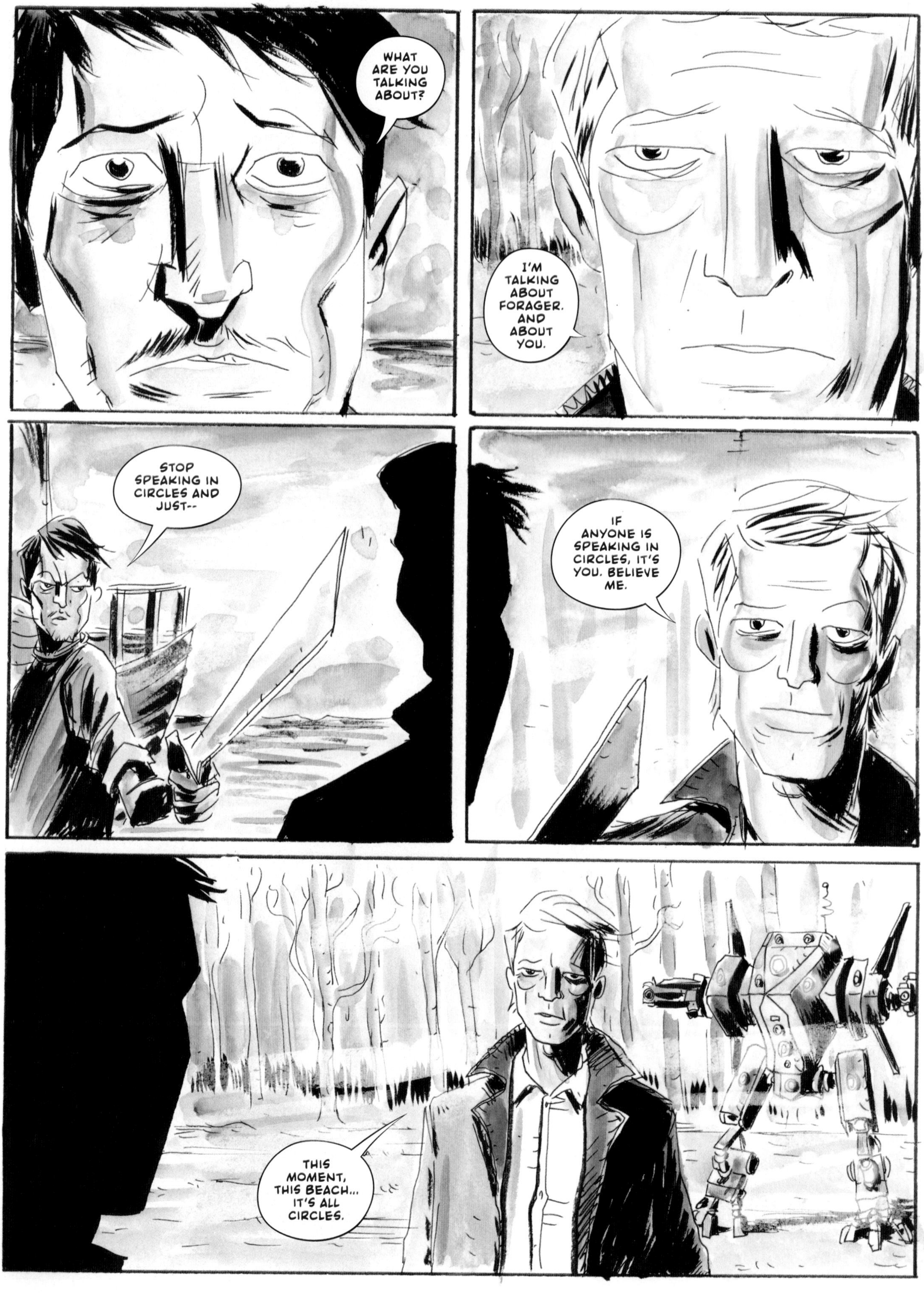
WHAT ARE YOU TALKING ABOUT?
I'M TALKING ABOUT FORAGER. AND ABOUT YOU.
STOP SPEAKING IN CIRCLES AND JUST--
IF ANYONE IS SPEAKING IN CIRCLES, IT'S YOU. BELIEVE ME.
THIS MOMENT, THIS BEACH... IT'S ALL CIRCLES.

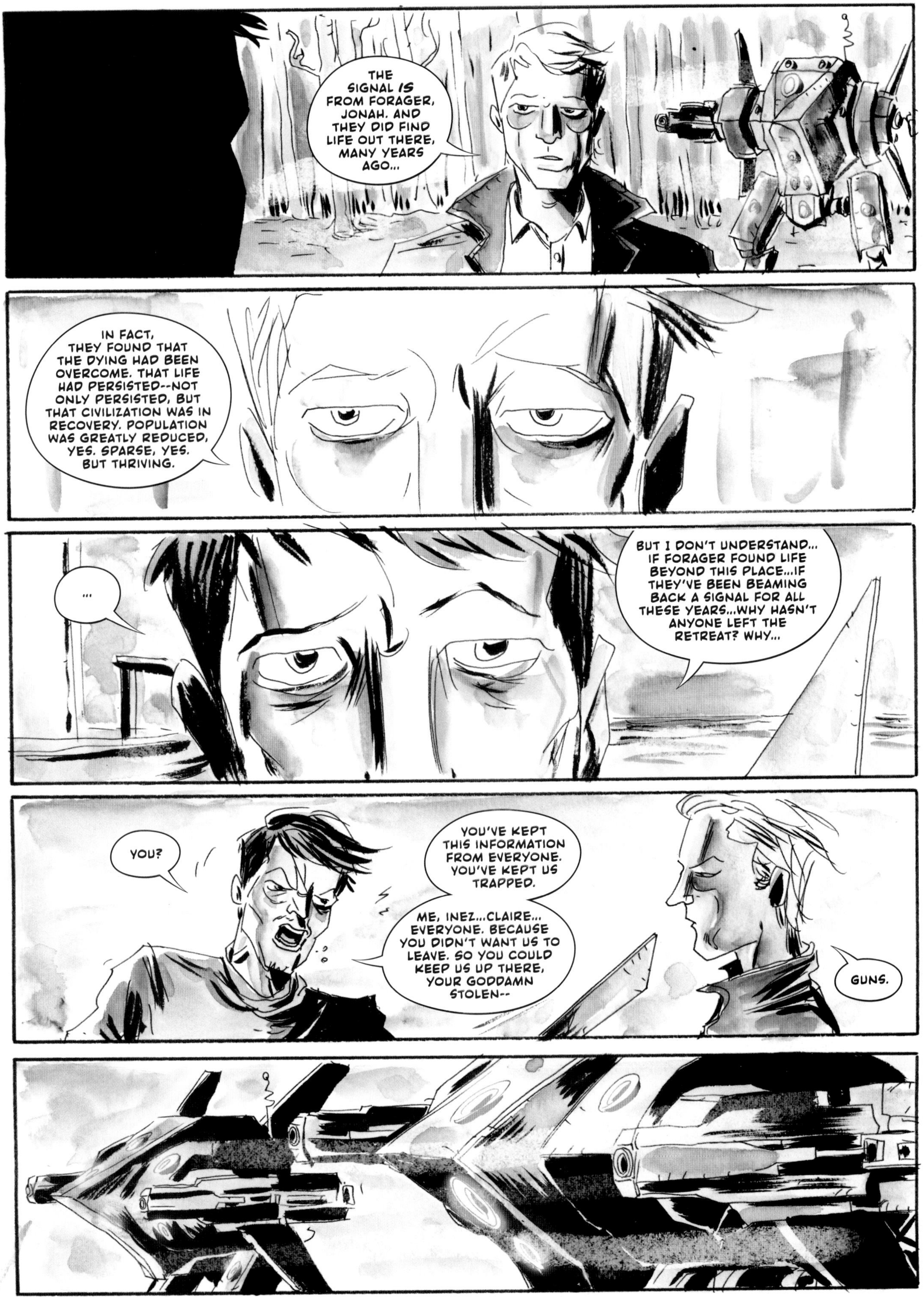
THE SIGNAL IS FROM FORAGER, JONAH. AND THEY DID FIND LIFE OUT THERE, MANY YEARS AGO...
IN FACT, THEY FOUND THAT THE DYING HAD BEEN OVERCOME. THAT LIFE HAD PERSISTED--NOT ONLY PERSISTED, BUT THAT CIVILIZATION WAS IN RECOVERY. POPULATION WAS GREATLY REDUCED, YES. SPARSE, YES. BUT THRIVING.
...
BUT I DON'T UNDERSTAND... IF FORAGER FOUND LIFE BEYOND THIS PLACE...IF THEY'VE BEEN BEAMING BACK A SIGNAL FOR ALL THESE YEARS...WHY HASN'T ANYONE LEFT THE RETREAT? WHY...
YOU?
YOU'VE KEPT THIS INFORMATION FROM EVERYONE. YOU'VE KEPT US TRAPPED.
ME, INEZ...CLAIRE... EVERYONE. BECAUSE YOU DIDN'T WANT US TO LEAVE. SO YOU COULD KEEP US UP THERE, YOUR GODDAMN STOLEN--
GUNS.

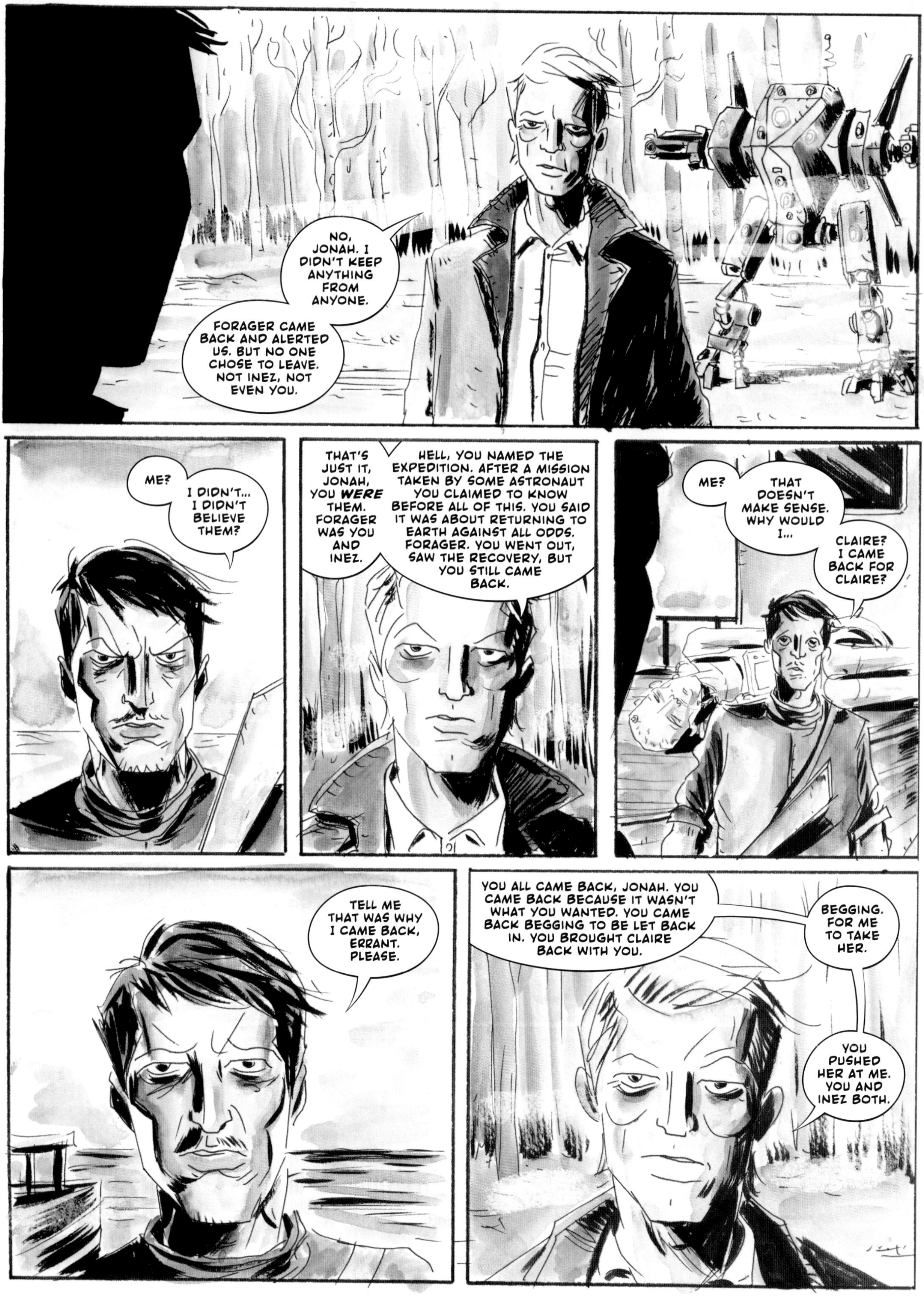
NO, JONAH. I DIDN'T KEEP ANYTHING FROM ANYONE.
FORAGER CAME BACK AND ALERTED US. BUT NO ONE CHOSE TO LEAVE. NOT INEZ, NOT EVEN YOU.
ME?
I DIDN'T... I DIDN'T BELIEVE THEM?
THAT'S JUST IT, JONAH, YOU **WERE** THEM. FORAGER WAS YOU AND INEZ.
HELL, YOU NAMED THE EXPEDITION. AFTER A MISSION TAKEN BY SOME ASTRONAUT YOU CLAIMED TO KNOW BEFORE ALL OF THIS. YOU SAID IT WAS ABOUT RETURNING TO EARTH AGAINST ALL ODDS. FORAGER. YOU WENT OUT, SAW THE RECOVERY, BUT YOU STILL CAME BACK.
ME?
THAT DOESN'T MAKE SENSE. WHY WOULD I...
CLAIRE? I CAME BACK FOR CLAIRE?
TELL ME THAT WAS WHY I CAME BACK, ERRANT. PLEASE.
YOU ALL CAME BACK, JONAH. YOU CAME BACK BECAUSE IT WASN'T WHAT YOU WANTED. YOU CAME BACK BEGGING TO BE LET BACK IN. YOU BROUGHT CLAIRE BACK WITH YOU.
BEGGING. FOR ME TO TAKE HER.
YOU PUSHED HER AT ME. YOU AND INEZ BOTH.

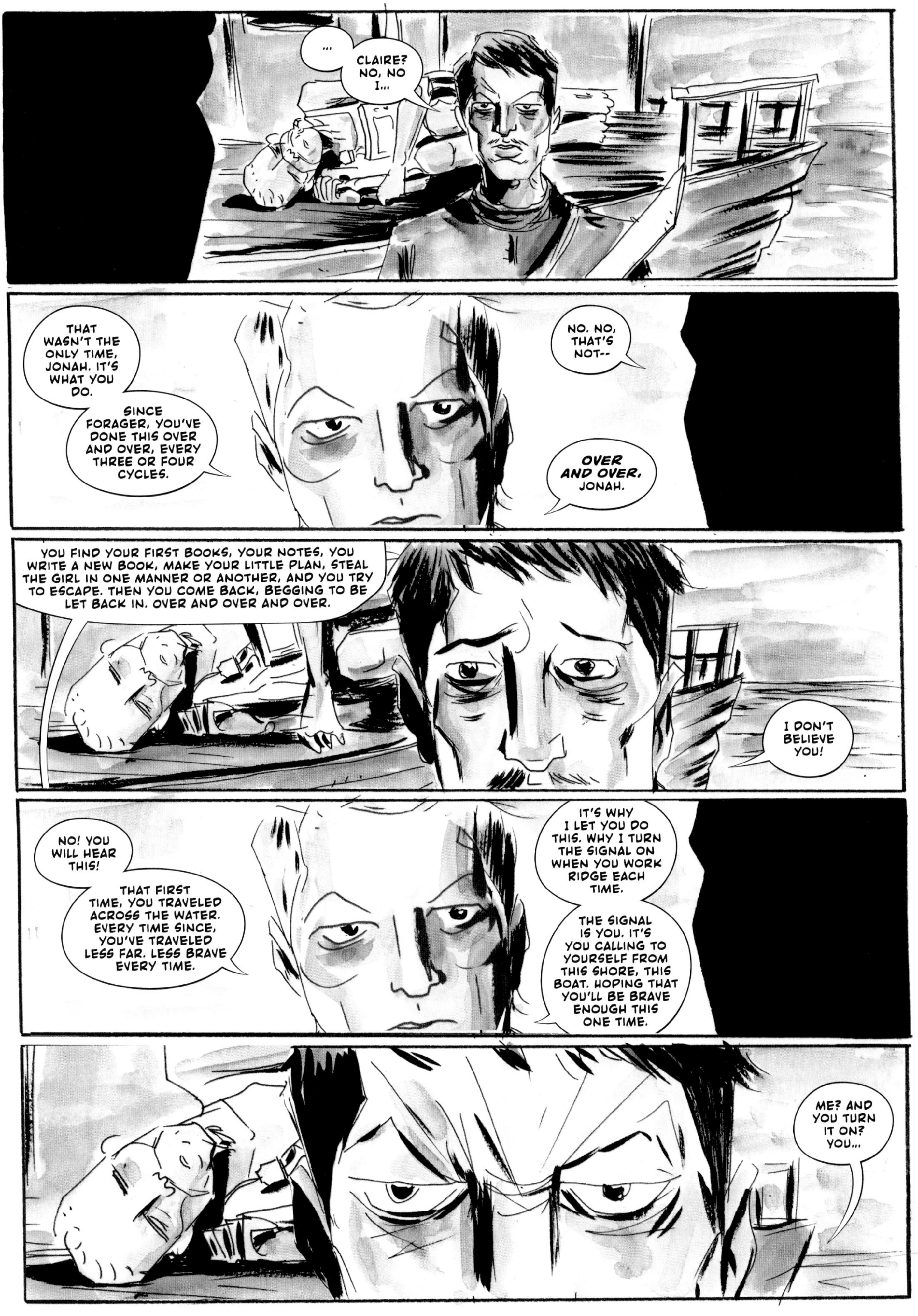
...
CLAIRE? NO, NO I...
THAT WASN'T THE ONLY TIME, JONAH. IT'S WHAT YOU DO.
SINCE FORAGER, YOU'VE DONE THIS OVER AND OVER, EVERY THREE OR FOUR CYCLES.
NO. NO, THAT'S NOT--
OVER AND OVER, JONAH.
YOU FIND YOUR FIRST BOOKS, YOUR NOTES, YOU WRITE A NEW BOOK, MAKE YOUR LITTLE PLAN, STEAL THE GIRL IN ONE MANNER OR ANOTHER, AND YOU TRY TO ESCAPE. THEN YOU COME BACK, BEGGING TO BE LET BACK IN. OVER AND OVER AND OVER.
I DON'T BELIEVE YOU!
NO! YOU WILL HEAR THIS!
THAT FIRST TIME, YOU TRAVELED ACROSS THE WATER. EVERY TIME SINCE, YOU'VE TRAVELED LESS FAR. LESS BRAVE EVERY TIME.
IT'S WHY I LET YOU DO THIS. WHY I TURN THE SIGNAL ON WHEN YOU WORK RIDGE EACH TIME.
THE SIGNAL IS YOU. IT'S YOU CALLING TO YOURSELF FROM THIS SHORE, THIS BOAT. HOPING THAT YOU'LL BE BRAVE ENOUGH THIS ONE TIME.
ME? AND YOU TURN IT ON? YOU...

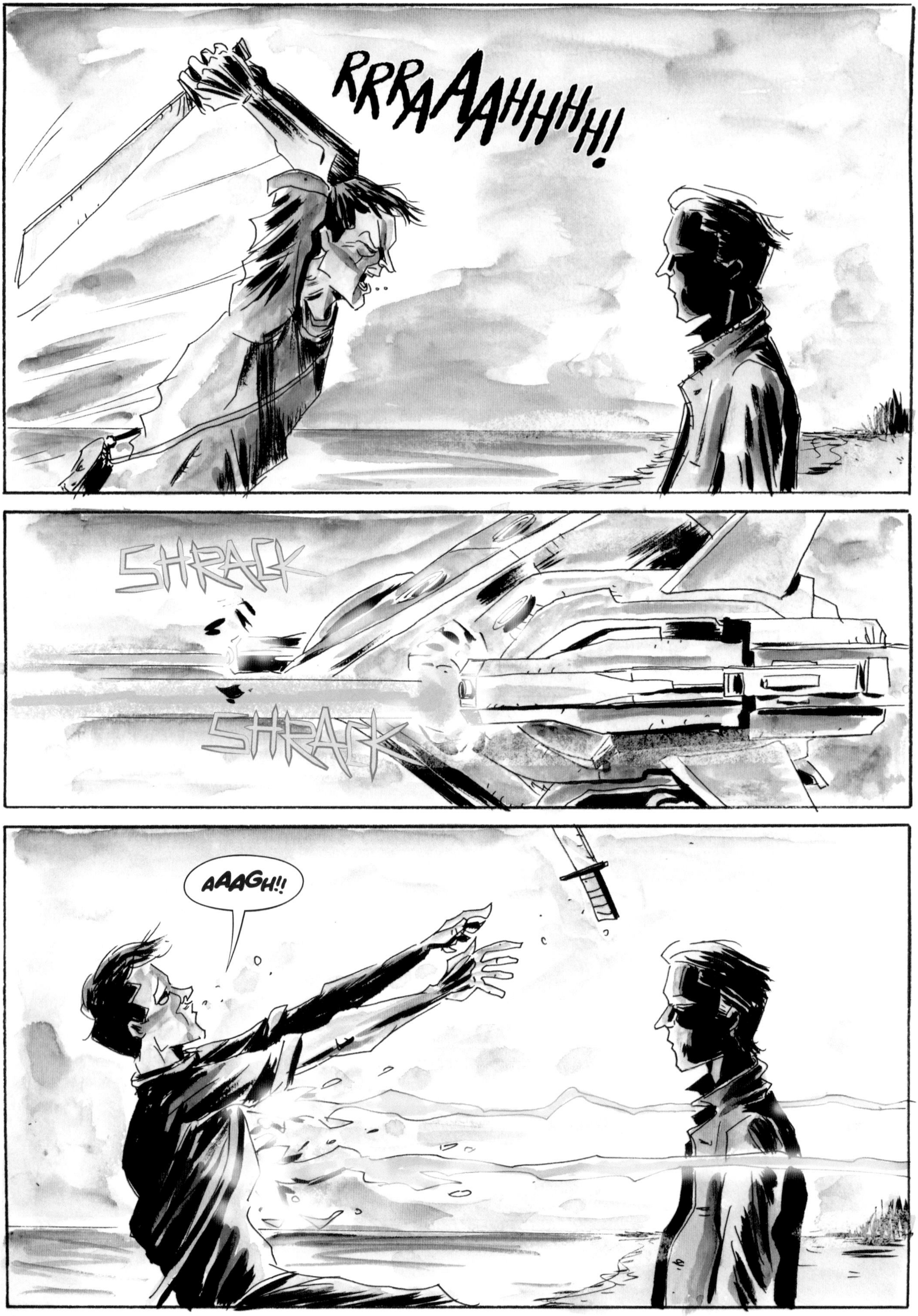
RRRAAAHHHH!
SHRACK
SHRACK
AAAGH!!

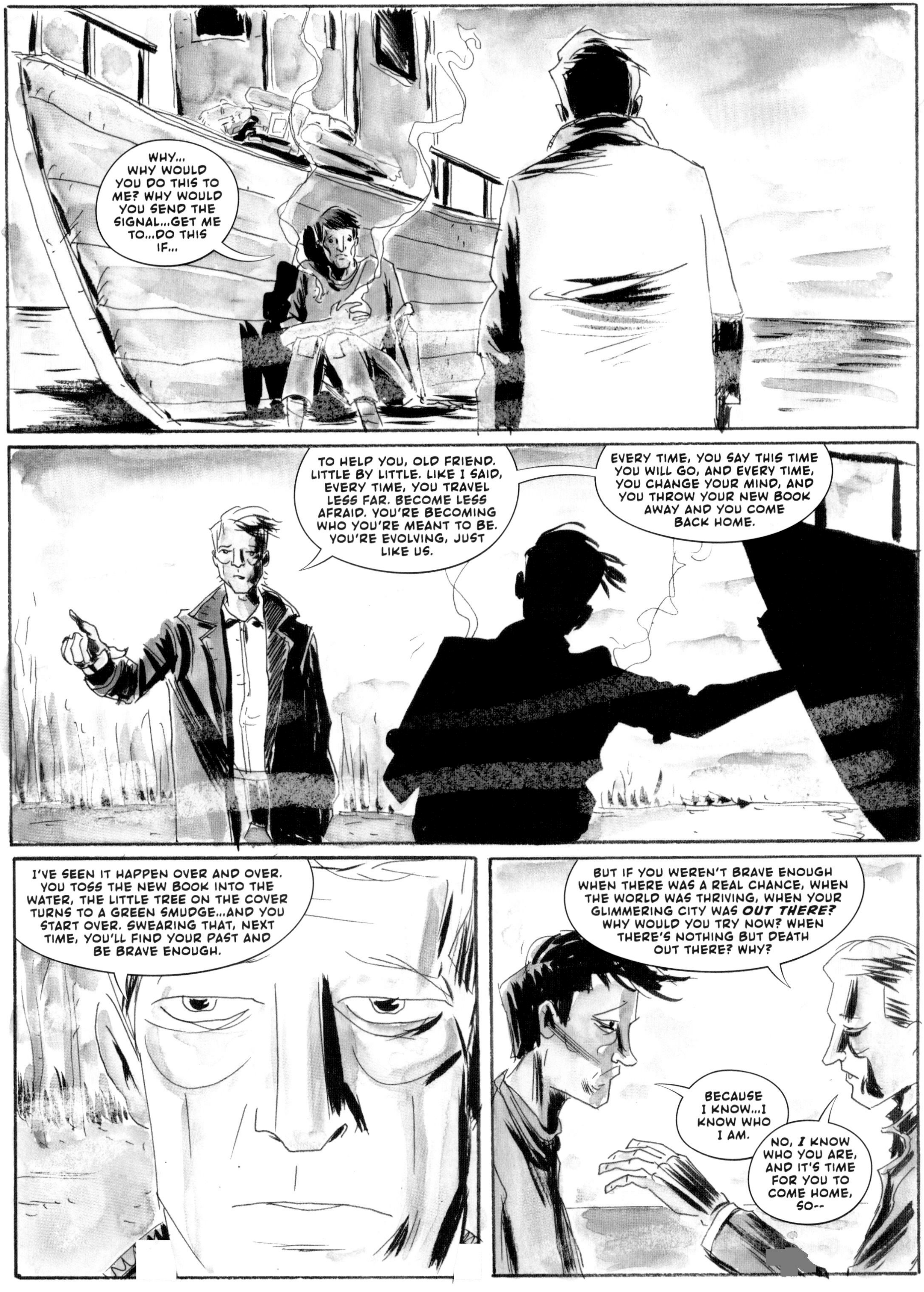
WHY... WHY WOULD YOU DO THIS TO ME? WHY WOULD YOU SEND THE SIGNAL...GET ME TO...DO THIS IF...
TO HELP YOU, OLD FRIEND. LITTLE BY LITTLE. LIKE I SAID, EVERY TIME, YOU TRAVEL LESS FAR. BECOME LESS AFRAID. YOU'RE BECOMING WHO YOU'RE MEANT TO BE. YOU'RE EVOLVING, JUST LIKE US.
EVERY TIME, YOU SAY THIS TIME YOU WILL GO, AND EVERY TIME, YOU CHANGE YOUR MIND, AND YOU THROW YOUR NEW BOOK AWAY AND YOU COME BACK HOME.
I'VE SEEN IT HAPPEN OVER AND OVER. YOU TOSS THE NEW BOOK INTO THE WATER, THE LITTLE TREE ON THE COVER TURNS TO A GREEN SMUDGE...AND YOU START OVER. SWEARING THAT, NEXT TIME, YOU'LL FIND YOUR PAST AND BE BRAVE ENOUGH.
BUT IF YOU WEREN'T BRAVE ENOUGH WHEN THERE WAS A REAL CHANCE, WHEN THE WORLD WAS THRIVING, WHEN YOUR GLIMMERING CITY WAS *OUT THERE?* WHY WOULD YOU TRY NOW? WHEN THERE'S NOTHING BUT DEATH OUT THERE? WHY?
BECAUSE I KNOW...I KNOW WHO I AM.
NO, *I* KNOW WHO YOU ARE, AND IT'S TIME FOR YOU TO COME HOME, SO--

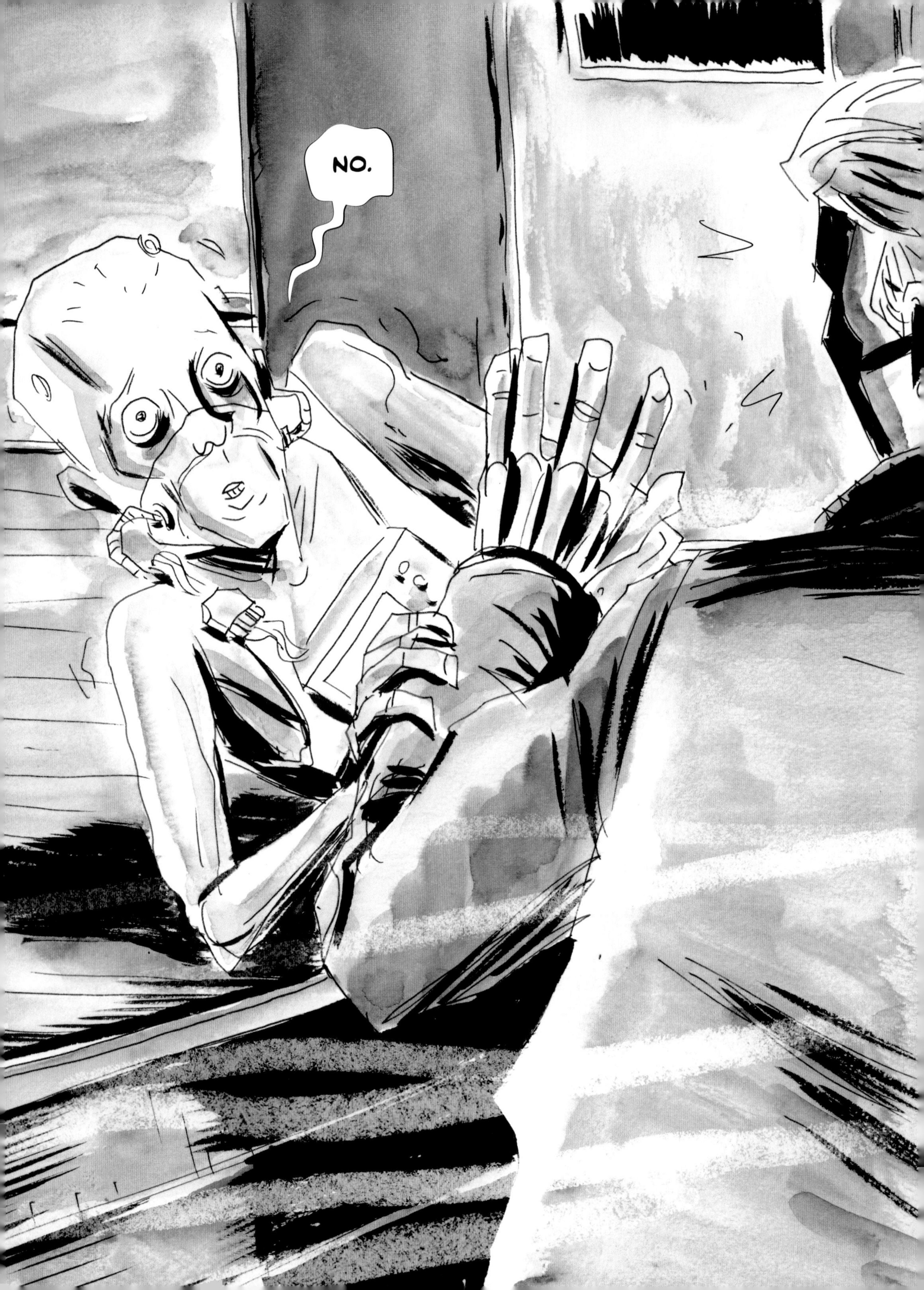
NO.

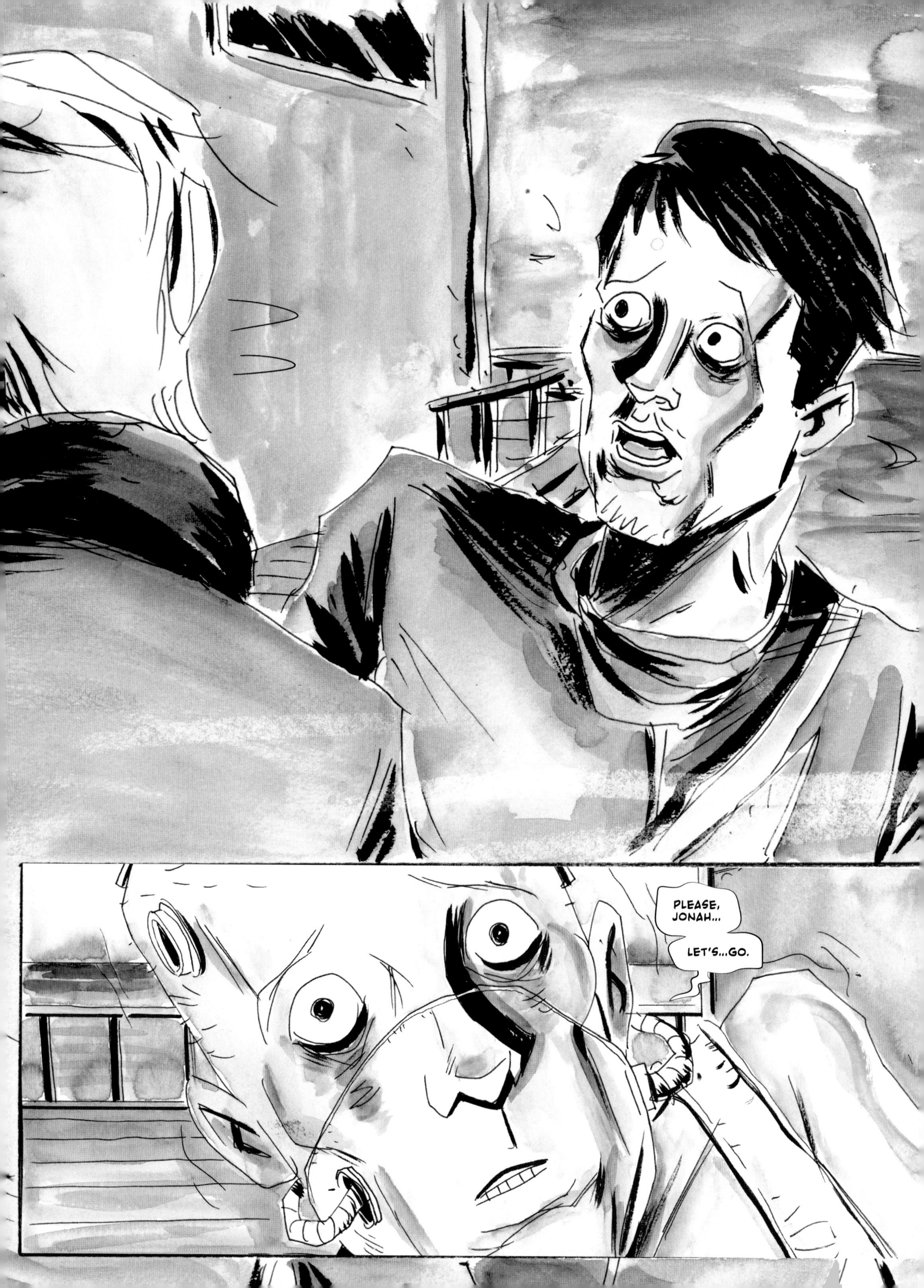
PLEASE, JONAH...
LET'S...GO.

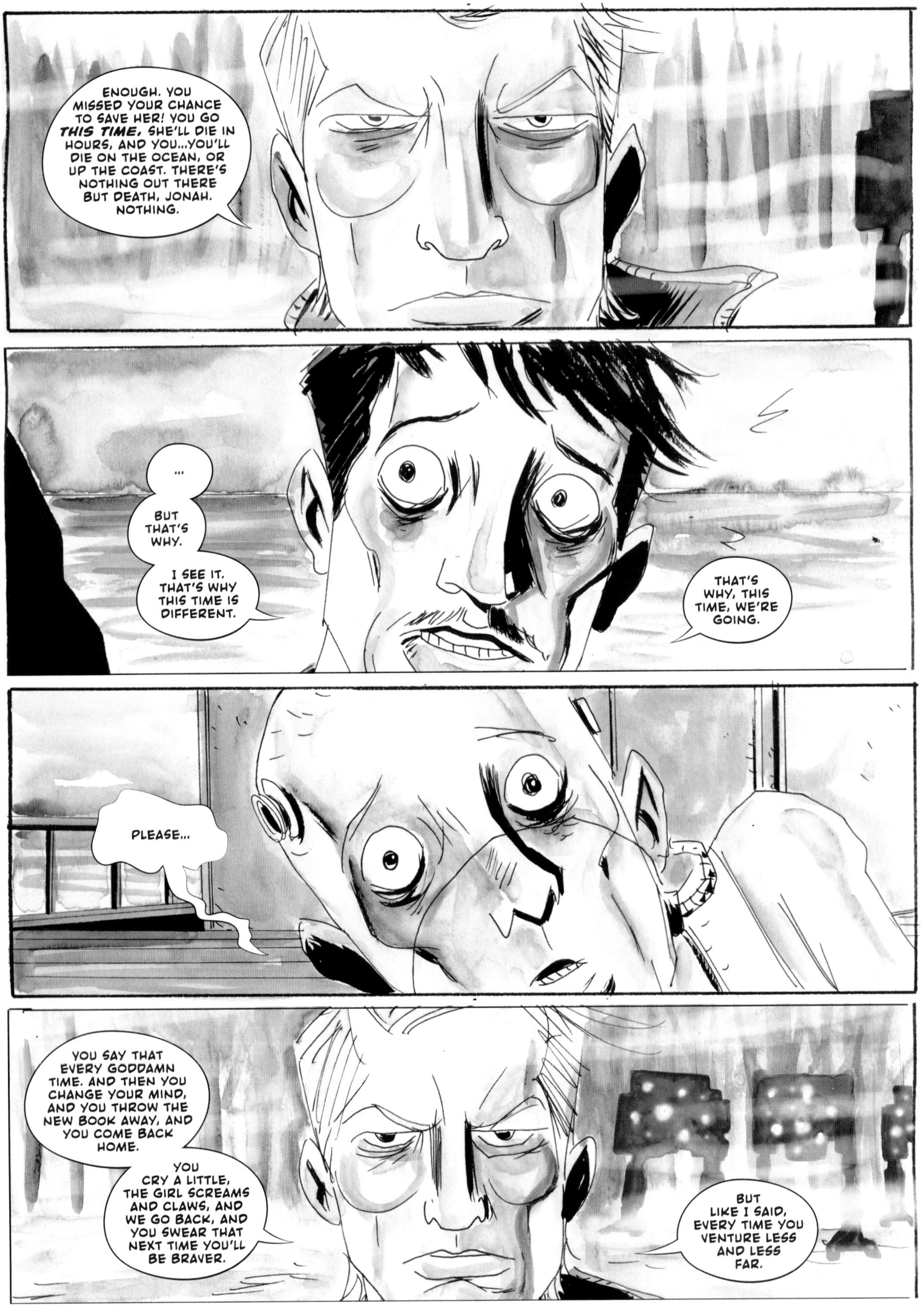

ENOUGH. YOU MISSED YOUR CHANCE TO SAVE HER! YOU GO THIS TIME, SHE'LL DIE IN HOURS, AND YOU...YOU'LL DIE ON THE OCEAN, OR UP THE COAST. THERE'S NOTHING OUT THERE BUT DEATH, JONAH. NOTHING.
...
BUT THAT'S WHY.
I SEE IT. THAT'S WHY THIS TIME IS DIFFERENT.
THAT'S WHY, THIS TIME, WE'RE GOING.
PLEASE...
YOU SAY THAT EVERY GODDAMN TIME. AND THEN YOU CHANGE YOUR MIND, AND YOU THROW THE NEW BOOK AWAY, AND YOU COME BACK HOME.
YOU CRY A LITTLE, THE GIRL SCREAMS AND CLAWS, AND WE GO BACK, AND YOU SWEAR THAT NEXT TIME YOU'LL BE BRAVER.
BUT LIKE I SAID, EVERY TIME YOU VENTURE LESS AND LESS FAR.

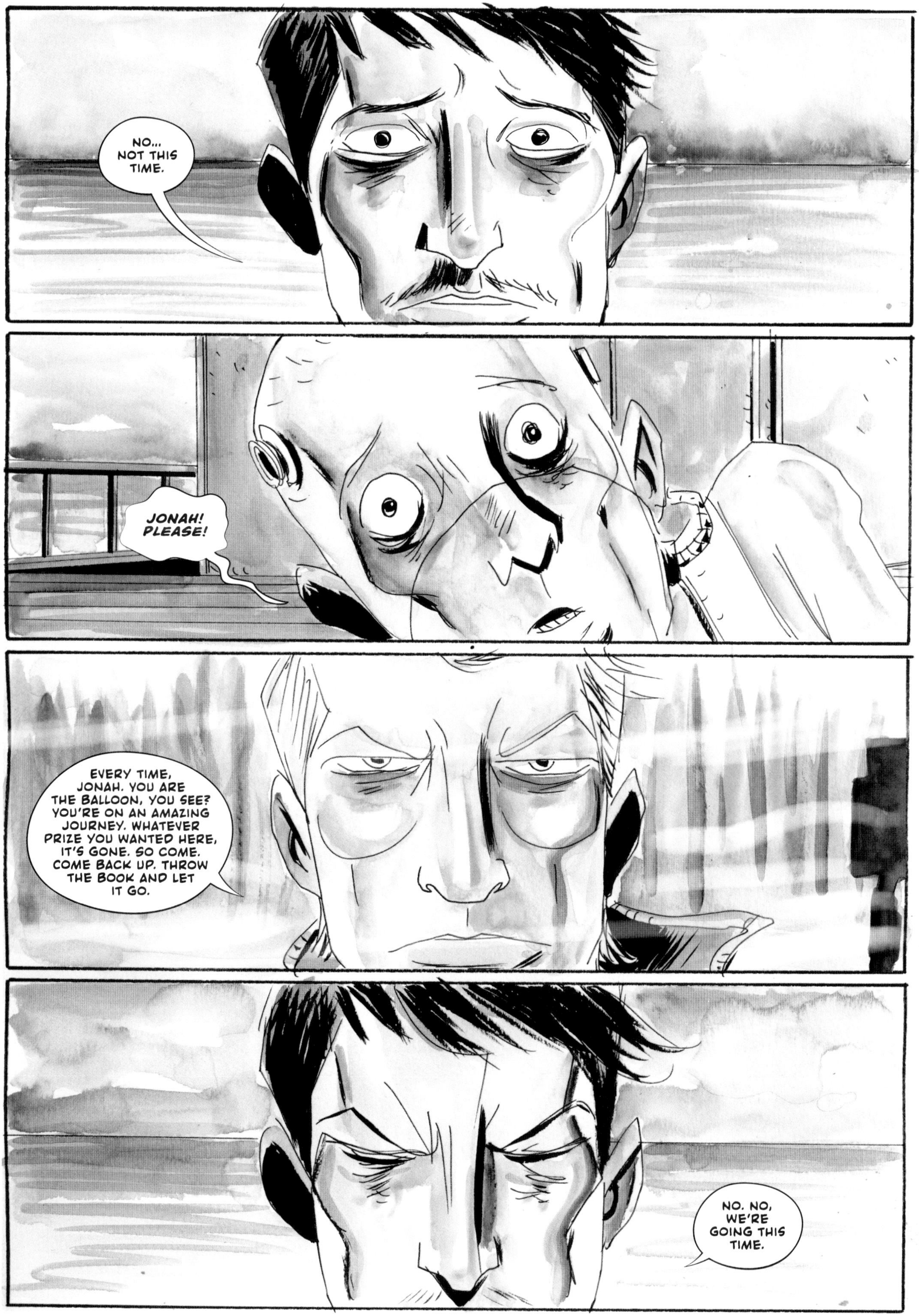
NO... NOT THIS TIME.
JONAH! PLEASE!
EVERY TIME, JONAH. YOU ARE THE BALLOON, YOU SEE? YOU'RE ON AN AMAZING JOURNEY. WHATEVER PRIZE YOU WANTED HERE, IT'S GONE. SO COME. COME BACK UP. THROW THE BOOK AND LET IT GO.
NO. NO, WE'RE GOING THIS TIME.

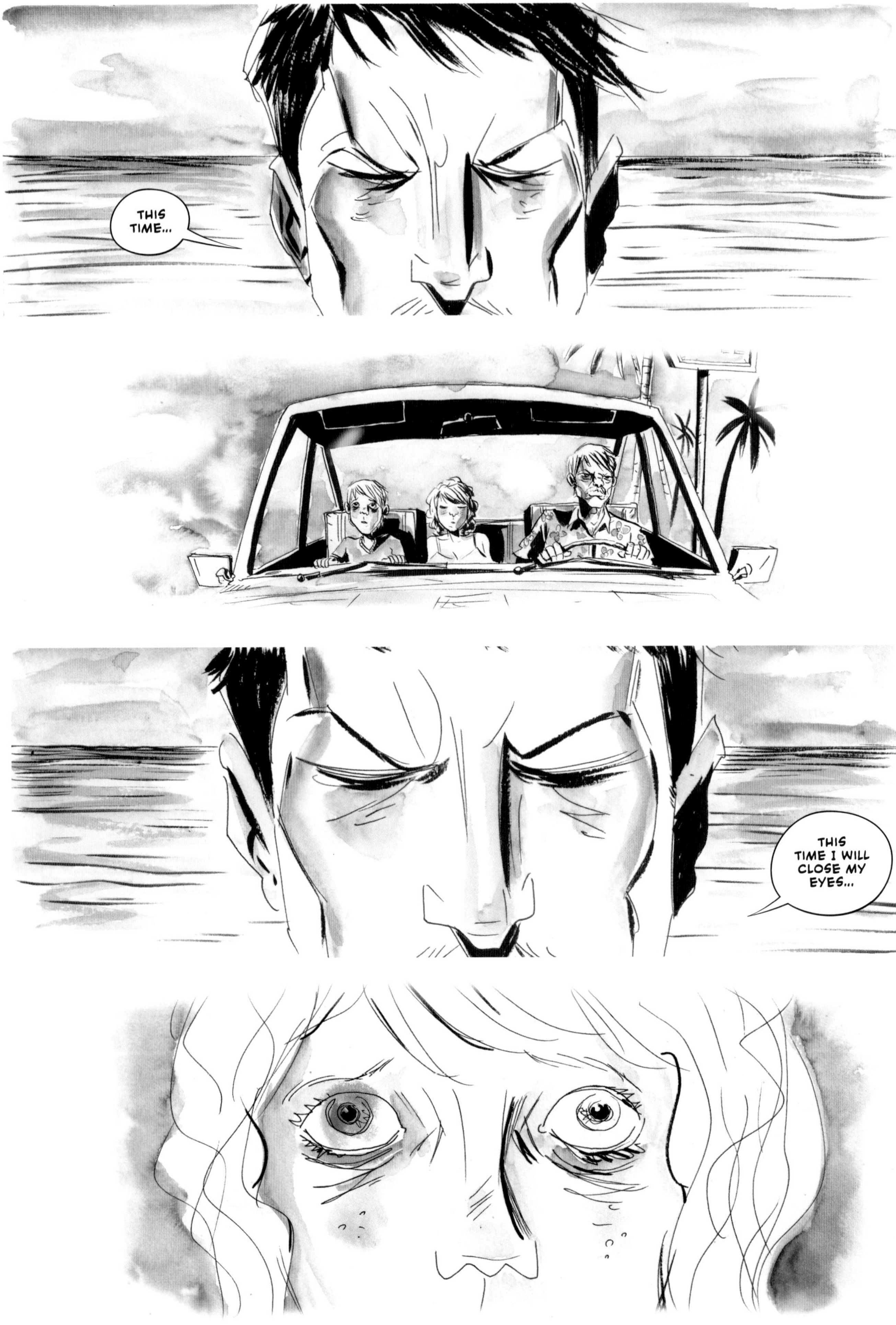
THIS TIME...
THIS TIME I WILL CLOSE MY EYES...

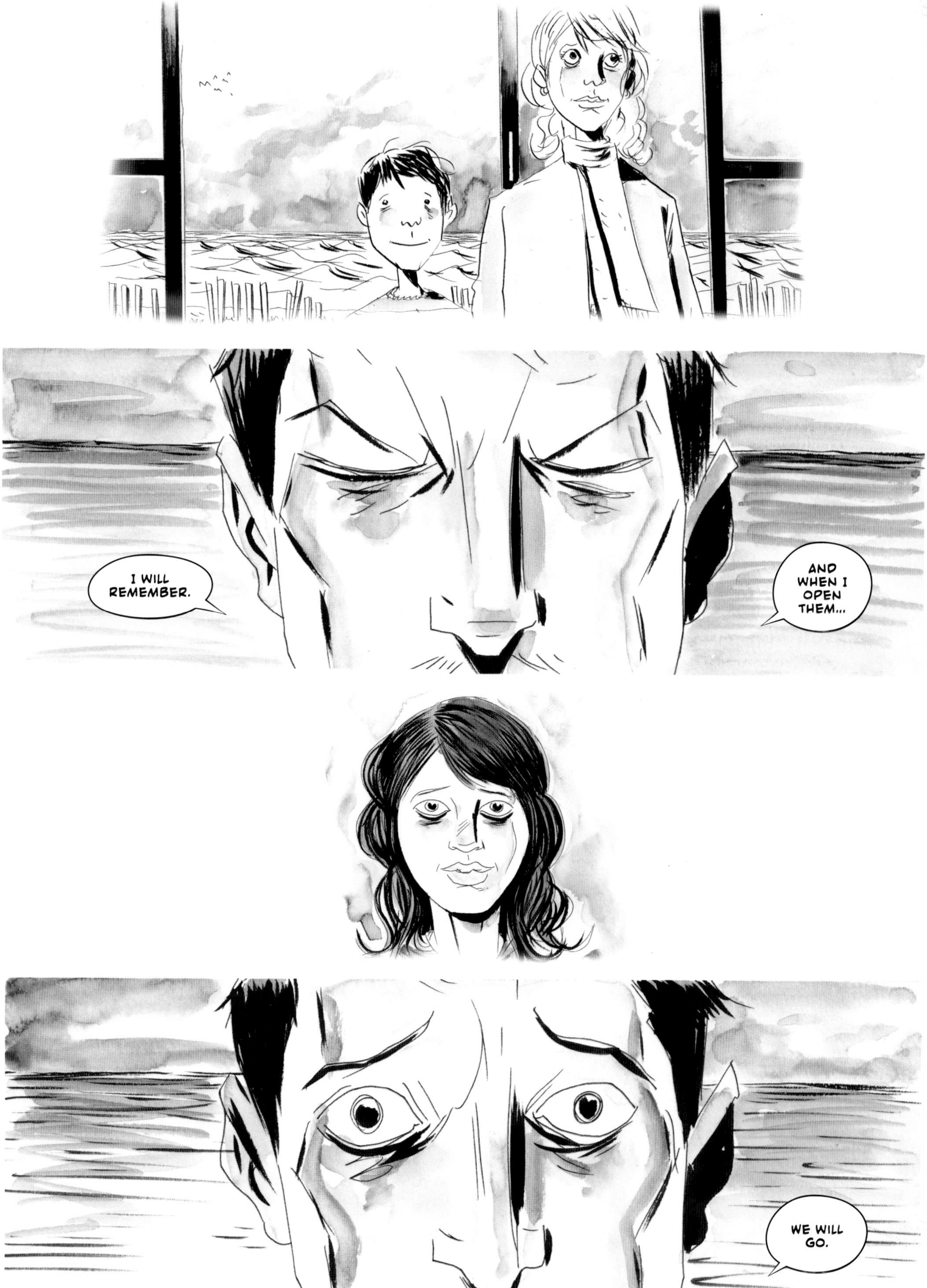
I WILL REMEMBER.
AND WHEN I OPEN THEM...
WE WILL GO.

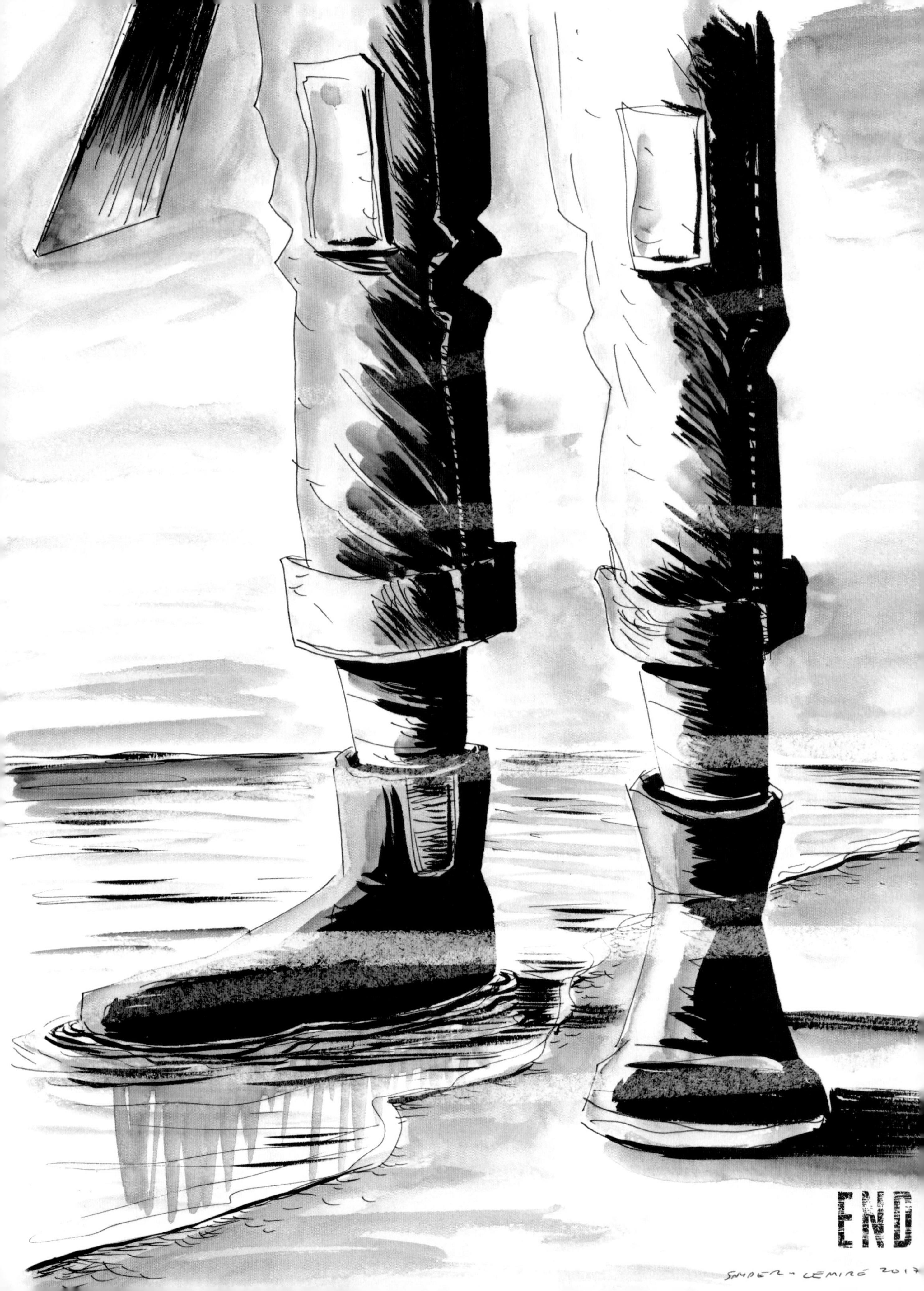
END

about the authors

Scott Snyder

Snyder is the writer of *Wytches, Severed, American Vampire, The Wake, Batman,* and *All-Star Batman* among other comics. His story collection, *Voodoo Heart,* was published by the Dial Press. He has taught fiction and comic book writing at Sarah Lawrence College, Columbia University, and NYU.

Jeff Lemire

New York Times bestselling author Jeff Lemire is the writer and artist of acclaimed literary graphic novels such as *Essex County, The Underwater Welder, Sweet Tooth,* and *Trillium.* He is co-creator and writer of the bestselling sci-fi series *Descender* with Dustin Nguyen, and of *Plutona* with Emi Lenox.

Lemire's list of accolades includes nominations for eight Eisner awards, seven Harvey Awards, eight Shuster Awards with many of his properties currently in development at major studios for film and TV.

His forthcoming novel *Roughneck* will be published by Simon and Schuster in early 2017.